W9-BBS-893
DISTRICT LIBRARY
MICHIGAN 49045

GRIPPING TALES OF ADVENTURE AND DANGER IN A LAND WITHOUT LAW

* * *

Sequoia Scout

Tracker Will Reed has been seeking his fortune in the High Sierras for ten years, until one horrific night catapults him onto a new path—toward Spanish California. Few have dared to travel through this harsh land, especially now, with Indians on the warpath. **But Will has never shied away from danger.**

The Year of the Grizzly

Trouble brews between the American military and Mexican banditos. Both are determined to grab the wealth of central California's cattle ranches for themselves . . . and the Reed family rancho lies directly in their path. **Three rugged men of honor must join forces to battle against greed and power.**

Shooting Star

Andrew Jackson Sinnickson locked horns with Jack Powers, the first and worst of the California bad men, in the Bear Flag Rebellion. Now hordes of treasure seekers flock to the gold fields . . . straight into the hands of the ruthless Powers and his gunslingers, whose only "justice" is a harsh exploitation. **Andrew is determined not to let Powers win.**

LEGENDS OF THE WEST

VOLUME ONE

Sequoia Scout

The Year of the Grizzly

Shooting Star

BROCK & BODIE THOENE

TYNDALE HOUSE PUBLISHERS, INC., CAROL STREAM, ILLINOIS

Visit Tyndale's exciting Web site at www.tyndale.com

For further information on Thoene titles, visit www.thoenebooks.com and www.familyaudiolibrary.com

TYNDALE and Tyndale's quill logo are registered trademarks of Tyndale House Publishers, Inc.

Legends of the West Volume One first printing by Tyndale House Publishers, Inc., in 2007.

Designed by Stephen Vosloo

Edited by Ramona Cramer Tucker

Scripture quotations are taken from the *Holy Bible,* King James Version.

This novel is a work of fiction. Names, characters, places, and incidents either are the product of the authors' imaginations or are used fictitiously. Any resemblance to actual events, locales, organizations, or persons living or dead is entirely coincidental and beyond the intent of either the authors or publisher.

Library of Congress Cataloging-in-Publication Data
Thoene, Brock, date.
Legends of the West / Brock & Bodie Thoene.
p. cm.
ISBN-13: 978-1-4143-0116-7 (hc)
ISBN-10: 1-4143-0116-2 (hc)
I. Thoene, Bodie, date. II. Title
PS3570.H463L44 2007
813′.54—dc22 2006039065

Printed in the United States of America

13 12 11 10 09 08 07
7 6 5 4 3 2 1

JOHN WAYNE, LEGEND OF THE WEST*

Brock and I grew up three blocks from one another north of the river in Bakersfield, California.

Saturday mornings, along with most of the kids in our neighborhood, we made our way to The River Theater on North Chester. It was a seedy, ancient little building that dated back to the silent movies of the 1920s. Folding wooden theater seats groaned and squawked when lowered to sitting position, which meant everyone got popcorn before the movie started, lest he or she disrupt the program.

I always sat with my girlfriends on the right side of the aisle, eight rows from the front. Carved into the arm of my favorite seat were graffiti initials and a date in the early 1930s that commemorated my father's and his younger brothers' visits to the theater. After they had arrived in California, they had gone to see their first all-talking John Wayne Western in a five-cent Saturday matinee. Papa later told me that when they saw the cattle stampede and heard the thundering hooves, they were sure the cows were going to break through the screen and trample them all! His youngest brother dove under the seat for cover!

** For more "John Wayne, Legend of the West" stories, see Legends of the West series introductions for Volumes Two, Three, and Four, by Brock and Bodie Thoene. For further information visit: www.thoenebooks.com and www.familyaudiolibrary.com.*

In our growing-up years, Brock and I and the gang were still flocking to see the John Wayne Westerns. In spite of Vincent Price and his spooky films like *House on Haunted Hill,* which made us shiver, Duke was always our favorite star. We can still remember seeing now-classic Westerns like *Red River, She Wore a Yellow Ribbon, The Searchers,* and *The Alamo* . . . sitting in the same theater seats our parents had occupied as kids. Of course, by our day, admission to a double feature at The River Theater had gone up to twenty-five cents from the five-cent bargain of our fathers' day. For another quarter we could buy popcorn, a Coke, and one of those gooey, all-day Sugar Daddy suckers that pulled your fillings out.

Life was a lot simpler when we could gaze at the screen and step into John Wayne's Old West. The good guys were good. Duke was a good guy. The bad guys, who came in a variety of shapes and sizes, were bad because they made wrong choices.

Though the good guys were confronted with terrible odds and life-threatening opposition, they always clobbered evil by the end of the last reel.

In REEL-life Westerns we learned that this was the way REAL life was supposed to be played out. A man's word was his bond. A handshake was better than a contract. Though we lived in an imperfect world, we grew up seeing movies that helped us believe that there really was Right and Wrong. Happy endings depended on making right moral choices; choices that were based on the Ten Commandments. Keeping your word was the path to honor, no matter what it cost you along the way. If a fella made a mistake, he could admit it, make amends, and turn his life around to do what was RIGHT!

John Wayne's legends of the West taught us kids basic truths. We have not forgotten those lessons.

Fast-forward twenty years. Brock and I were married, and through a series of amazing events (which I'll write about in later introductions for books in our Legends of the West series), we worked as writers and researchers for John Wayne at Batjac Productions.

Yes, we knew Duke personally. Yes, he was every bit as big and wonderful and honorable in REAL life as he was in REEL life. When he said something to you, you listened. When he made a promise, he remained true to it. When he stuck out his big hand to seal a bargain, it was better than a contract.

At the time, I was a brand-new Christian seeking how I could best serve the Lord through storytelling. I remember the day Brock and I spoke with Duke about our hearts' desire for our writing to be used to teach eternal truth about living for Jesus Christ in a very complicated world.

Duke gave us that funny, amused smile that let us know he knew the answer. "Always remember this when you write," he said. "You can teach folks what they need to know as long as it's in a good story. You can have your character preach it, but nobody's gonna listen and believe the message unless your character lives out the truth in the story. That's why a great Western legend is timeless."

Duke sipped coffee from a Batjac mug. "The stories of men and women who tamed the West are God's American parables," he insisted. "They teach our hearts to recognize and follow the truth. Conflict. Good and Evil. Life was simpler in those days, but it wasn't better or easier. In a great Western, the choice between heaven and hell is presented to a man in a time and a place in American history before there were the restraints of society and law. In the legends of the American West, a man's heart is laid bare. In the American West, a man had to choose whether to serve 'the Man Upstairs' or the devil."

Deep blue eyes searched our faces with a steady gaze. "So you two tell folks the Truth. Write great stories about men searching for God in a wild, untamed land . . . and I guarantee lives will be changed. I think that's why you're here. To learn how to do that before I'm gone. You've got to carry the torch for the next generation. I want your word you're going to do it!"

We promised we would do our best always.

Then we shook hands on it. That handshake meant something to Duke and to us. It was a solid commitment. The kind of commitment that would last a lifetime.

Pretty good advice from a great man, right? Duke taught Brock and me the most important principles of writing a good story. So when folks read our books and are touched or changed or find the Lord in the pages, we always remember the big man whose film career spanned from 1928 to 1979. Duke taught us how to tell the truth of God's love for us in a good Western yarn before we wrote anything else. He taught generations of moviegoers that a great story is one that teaches eternal truths through telling parables. The stories in our Legends of the West series are truly American parables for our generation.

With gratitude and the knowledge that we will meet Duke and many of our friends from Batjac Productions in heaven, we dedicate our Legends of the West series to our mentor, John Wayne.

Near the end of his life Duke said, "A man can count all his true friends on one hand."

And we answered, "Count us in."

A lot of years have passed since 1979. It's a different world. But the truth never changes. So we're still here. Still writing. Our handshake with Duke is still all the contract we need.

Bodie Thoene, 2007

Sequoia Scout

For ten years, Will Reed has been seeking his fortune through tracking in the High Sierras. Then one horrific night catapults him onto a new path—toward Spanish California. Few Americans have attempted to travel through this harsh land, especially now with Indian tribes on the warpath. Will has never shied away from danger, but this time he'll find more than he ever dreamed. . . .

For Penny and Woody Watson,
with blessings and thanks

CHAPTER 1

When Will Reed came to his senses, he looked up into the low ceiling of the tiny brush shelter and knew immediately where he was. But when he tried to leap to his feet, he discovered that his hands and legs were bound with rawhide thongs. His lunge upward accomplished only a clumsy lurch, and he fell face forward on another man.

"Get off me," screamed Aubrey. "My leg's broke!"

Outside the hut, the rhythmic chanting of the Mojave Indians was accompanied by the eerie dry clicking of gourds and punctuated by increasingly wild yells.

Will rolled off Aubrey as gently as he could and came to rest faceup beside Forchet, who was still unconscious. The Frenchman's breathing was ragged, and a raspy gurgle brought to memory the arrow that had penetrated Forchet's chest just before a club had crashed into the back of Will's head and everything went black.

Aubrey, nearly hysterical, was sobbing. "I don't want to die . . . don't kill me . . . I don't want to die. . . ."

No help there, Will decided. He forced himself to think rationally about the spot they were in—what he knew about the terrain and the possibilities for escape. His heart pounded faster as the rhythm of the gourd-accompanied chants gained in tempo.

Aubrey changed his moan to "They skin folks alive. They're gonna peel us. . . . Why can't they just kill us and be done with it? Why'd I ever come on this trip?"

Outside, another yell went up from the dancers. Will heard more brush being thrown on the fire and then the thunderous roar as the flames blazed higher. Did the Mojaves intend to set fire to the brush shelter that served as their prison cell? Aubrey could be wasting his breath fretting about being flayed. Roasted alive might be their sudden fate.

Forchet stirred, rolled half over on his side, and fell silent again. The light from the brush fire outside illuminated the open flap of his buckskin shirt. Under the shirt, tucked in a leather strap that Forchet wore over one shoulder, was the concealed sheath of a skinning knife. Had the Indians searched the French trapper and found the knife?

Will's glance flew toward the uprooted creosote bush that served as the doorway. No movement there yet. He heaved himself up to a sitting position, frightening Aubrey.

"What—what are you doing?"

"Shh!" Will hissed. He scooted over toward the unconscious Frenchman by bunching his heels up under him and thrusting himself across the small rocky space. Two pushes, and he was sitting upright beside Forchet's chest.

"What is it?" inquired Aubrey loudly.

Will shook his head angrily from side to side, silencing Aubrey, then gesturing with a jerk of his chin toward the now barely visible knife handle.

Aubrey raised up on one elbow, and his bushy eyebrows rose almost to the level of his hair. Like a fool, he made as if to stand. His face contorted with pain, and he shrank back with a groan. He waved his bound hands toward his injured leg.

Will nodded grimly and attempted to lean sideways to reach the knife handle with his fingertips. Halfway down he overbalanced and fell onto Forchet. The Frenchman didn't even groan.

There! Will's fingers brushed the wooden handle of the skinning knife. The rawhide straps cut deeply into his skin as he tried to spread his tightly wrapped wrists. He could barely force his fingers far enough apart to grasp the handle. Only the last joint of two fingers had any purchase on the rounded wooden end.

From outside came a sudden glare, another crackling roar as

more brush was thrown on the fire, and a chorus of shrill howls. Will's attention was torn away from his goal. The end of the knife squirted from between his numb fingers.

Doggedly he set to work again, fixing all his concentration on the task of grasping the knife. He drew it slowly toward Forchet's chin, afraid that a jerk would loosen his grip. Beads of sweat stood out on his forehead, gathering into large drops that rolled into his eyes.

Forchet stirred and heaved a deep sigh, rustling his coal black beard. To Will's horror, the wounded trapper began to roll back again, carrying the precious tool away from his reach.

Every muscle in Will's body tensed, and his toes curled inside the leather moccasins he wore. He dared not yank or twist. He could only hang on desperately with his fingertips as Forchet completed a slow turn away, the motion of his body drawing the weapon from its sheath.

Will stared in stunned disbelief at the initials *GR* engraved on the blade. Flickers from the fire glinted on the steel. He pivoted slowly back upright, clutching the Green River skinning knife. The heavy blade came to rest on the topmost strap that bound his hands. Before attempting to saw at the rawhide strands, he threw a triumphant look at the terrified Aubrey.

"You've got it!" Aubrey's words exploded with a rush.

At the same instant there was an emphatic clap of hands to gourd drums and a resounding stamp of Mojave feet. The dance ended abruptly.

Aubrey stared, wide-eyed, at Will.

Had the Indians heard Aubrey's exclamation? Will wondered. Or did the halt in the dancing and chanting mean they were coming for the white men? Was it too late?

Then, just as suddenly as the ceremony had ended, another one began. The pounding and shaking of the rattles resumed and so did the chanting.

Both trappers sighed their relief. Will grimly set to work sawing the leather thongs. Now the tightness of the bindings helped because he could steady the blade downward against them. Will blessed Forchet's attention to his equipment as the recently sharpened edge began to bite into the rawhide. But Will could only work it a fraction of an inch at a time with his fingertips.

Scarcely two minutes went by, but their passage seemed like hours. Finally the rawhide strip snapped apart. He was left with a loop still tied around each wrist and a length hanging down. But his hands were free. With one slash of the knife, his feet were loose as well.

He could see the pleading in Aubrey's eyes.

"Don't worry," he whispered into Aubrey's ear. "I won't leave you behind or Forchet either. If the raft is still on the bank where they jumped us, we'll ride the river out of here."

Will cut through the thongs on Aubrey's arms even before he finished speaking, but he was afraid to meet Aubrey's eyes. Will knew the chance of eluding recapture while trying to move an unconscious man and a cripple past fifty Indians was almost nonexistent. But he couldn't risk Aubrey starting into his moaning despair again. At least this way they could go down fighting.

Aubrey's bound hands sprang apart with an audible twang. Looking for a place to break out, Will turned his attention to the heap of brush that formed the back wall of their cell. He needed a spot that he could drag the other two men through without signaling their escape by too much rustling and shaking of the hut.

He spotted an arch in the yucca-palm branches that afforded an opening near the ground. The space was plugged with a clump of mesquite, which could be easily pushed out. Holding the knife at the ready, Will plunged headfirst into the brush, breaking out of the makeshift prison. With the hut shielding him from the fire, the deeper darkness beyond called him to save himself. Instead he cleared the mesquite from the hole and prepared to rescue his compatriots.

Back into the hut he went, mentally urging Aubrey to be ready. Every second was precious.

He saw Aubrey's arms reaching out toward him, eager to be pulled to safety. Will stretched out his free hand, his fingertips finding Aubrey's trembling grasp. Aubrey had just locked his grip on Will's wrists when the brush doorway in front of the hut was pulled aside. A shaft of light from the Indian bonfire blinded both men.

Will sprang forward in a rush. His right hand pushed the knife-point toward the intruder in a savage thrust, but he was off balance with his lunge and his vision was dazzled by the light. Instead of striking home, the blow was knocked aside.

A forearm as lean and hard as a dried mesquite limb crashed into the side of Will's head, staggering him. Two dark hands as strong as steel traps closed over his wrists and shook the knife from his grip.

Will was on his knees, expecting the next instant to be his last. But the knife slash did not follow.

Instead his assailant turned back to the doorway of the cell and rapidly pulled the brush shut. Will waited in the darkness to see what would happen next. He could not make out the features of the strong intruder, but he knew the man was an Indian.

Will's eyes adjusted to the darkness again, and he could see the attacker kneeling and facing him only a couple of feet away. The Indian spoke in a low but audible tone, and his words were in English. "You must keep still. My name is Mangas. I am Apache. I tried to tell the Mojaves that you were not Spanish and to not attack you, but they would not listen. I have convinced two of the old chiefs to let you go, but the young warrior men will not listen. I cannot save you all, but if one of you will lead the war party away, I will put the other two safely on the river."

Even though the chanting and dancing outside continued unabated, the stillness inside the prison was suddenly absolute.

In a moment Will spoke. "It was up to me before, and I guess it still is now. How much time have I got, Mangas?"

"A few minutes only. You must hurry. I will try to put them on the wrong trail—this is all I can do."

"All right then. I'm ready." Will grasped Aubrey's hand. "Good luck. Take care of Frenchy as best you're able."

Mangas handed Will the skinning knife.

Will accepted the weapon, then shook the Indian's hand and stared into his eyes. "Someday maybe I'll get to hear why you're doing this, but for now, thanks."

"Go with God," replied the Apache.

Will turned and dived through the opening into the inky night of the Mojave Desert. He crawled swiftly over the brush at the back of the Indian camp. He had heard that these Mojaves drank a fermented brew made from cactus. He fervently hoped that they had been soaking in it this night.

Plunging through a screen of creosote bushes, he rolled down an embankment into a ravine and came up desperately clutching the knife. Shaking sand from his ears, he strained to hear a change in the sounds of the camp. Still no cry of pursuit.

Which way to run? he wondered. *The sand either direction along the river will leave too good a trail, so it's cross-country for me.*

He scrambled up the other side of the draw, then glanced over his shoulder at the glare of the fire. *Straight away from that is as good as any.*

Will climbed a sandstone bluff and stood just below its crest so as to not be skylined against the night. He was on the opposite side of the river from the trail he and the other trappers had been following when they were captured. The Indians had taken everything but the Frenchman's knife. Now Will was alone in the desert without map, compass, or food and headed away from the only certain source of water.

A sudden clamor from the camp behind him replaced the chanting with cries of anger and outrage. From the bluff Will could see sparks rush outward from the glow of the fire as warriors grabbed flaming branches and began a hurried search of the camp.

Will watched just long enough to see the sparks gather together again in a body and race upstream along the riverbank. *Good,* he thought. *This Mangas fellow knows his business. He's sent them away from me and away from the direction of the raft at the same time.*

Will remembered hearing Beckwith describe the land west of the river as flat plains, brushy and dry, rising slowly to meet the eastern slope of the Sierras.

He frowned as he remembered that tonight Beckwith was floating facedown in the river with his body full of arrows.

Unless I find some way to get off this plain by daybreak, that's what I'll look like. Come first light I'll stand out like a black cat on a snowbank.

For the next three hours he loped over the brush plain with the silent, ground-covering trot of a coyote. Fixing his sight on the North

Star, Will kept it on his right shoulder as he ran. He heard the angry buzz of a rattlesnake's warning but never saw the reptile as he raced on into the night.

Pressing his elbows tightly into his aching sides, he forced himself to keep going. The Mojaves would be on his trail by now, and within an hour it would be daylight.

Ahead lay his only hope. He believed a line of the Sierras, though yet unseen, reared themselves not too far to the west. Will's long legs had tramped many miles from his uncle's Vicksburg home, but they had never been called on for such an effort as this. Travel at night made it difficult to judge distances, but Will figured he had covered fifteen miles or so when the sky behind him began to noticeably lighten.

He threw nervous glances back the way he had come. Whenever he could, Will directed his path over rocky surfaces that would leave less trace of his passing, but finding a place to hide before full daylight was his main concern. Fortunately, a rising east wind was blowing dust over his tracks almost as soon as he made them.

There were precious few spots that offered any chance of concealment. The scrubby creosote brush was not over three feet high. In the thickest places it formed clumps big enough for a man to lie down in, but if he let himself get surrounded, the Mojaves would search an ever-decreasing circle till he was again their prisoner.

✳ ✳ ✳

From the high mountain plateau, the old Indian's gaze lingered on the distant horizon. At the extreme edge of his vision flickered an orange star that pulsed and flared in time to an unheard rhythm.

He hunched his shoulders deeper into the rabbit-skin cloak. An involuntary shiver reminded him of a nearby responsibility, and the old man bent over the sleeping form of a child.

The deeply etched lines on the Indian's weathered cheeks softened for an instant as he tugged another blanket of rabbit fur around the boy.

A drowsy, eight-year-old voice murmured, "Is it morning already, Grandfather?"

"No," replied the elder. "It is still some time yet before dawn. Sleep," he instructed.

The mounded heap of rabbit skin and child stirred and sat up. "But why are you awake, Grandfather?"

"I keep watch, boy," replied the old man. "But now, since you are awake, look there."

The orange glow the ancient eyes turned toward was no longer alone in the dark line that separated desert sand from sky. Both the young and the old saw the flare multiply into many, as if the low star were dripping a cascade of sparks.

A deep, guttural sound came from the man.

"What did you say, Grandfather? What are those lights?"

For a time of silence that the child respected there was no reply. Then Grandfather spoke in measured tones, "There is evil about tonight, and you see its dance."

"But the bright lights are pretty," protested the boy. "They fly around like sparks from our campfires. Where is our campfire, Grandfather?"

"Hush now," urged the ancient voice with a hint of impatience. "These flickers hide wickedness behind their bright show. We have no fire because we do not want to attract such moths to our flame. Lights such as those are always ready to snuff—" The old man broke off his answer because his listener had gone back to sleep as abruptly as he had awakened.

Crouched on a rocky ledge high above the desert sweep, the elder Indian studied the glints of flame rushing about. The pinpoints were slowly drawing closer to the mountains on which he and the child rested, and he dreaded to see them come. The east wind seemed to propel them along.

He watched until the finest thread of pale blue touched the easternmost rim of the bowl of night. As the dawn spread its gray hand, it pushed back the dark so that the sparks dimmed and faded. But in each place, just as he had warned, Grandfather watched each light be replaced by a form of blackness, scurrying over the land.

Suddenly he found what he had been seeking. At the near rim of the desert floor, appearing almost beneath his feet and near a Joshua tree, was a lone dark insect creature. It moved in a purposeful rush, seeming to look for a place to hide before the fast-approaching light of day.

Grandfather stood once more. The surging wind was in his face, just as the rays of the sun glinted into his narrowed eyes. "Hurry," he whispered urgently, without saying to whom he spoke.

The wind acted as if it had heard him and obligingly raised his tempo. From the east flowed an airborne river of dust. Wispy at first, like smoke, the blowing sand soon formed a dagger-strike of black that competed with the sun for possession of the land.

The dust cloud knifed across the desert, blotting out the farther horizon. It next overshadowed some of the black figures that had fallen behind the others. The partition of swirling dirt extended itself upward from the ground like a curtain that concealed by being raised instead of lowered.

The cloud of sand passed between pursued and pursuers. As Grandfather watched from his perch high above the scene, an enormous convulsion of the dust storm enveloped even the lone figure at the very base of the mountain.

"Good." Grandfather nodded in approval. Then, "Come, boy," he urged the sleeping child. "Day is here."

* * *

The change in elevation had grown more acute. From the flat plain nearer the river, the land now had a noticeable rake to it. The increased pressure on Will's legs took a toll on his lungs and strength, slowing his pace. More than once he was thankful for the breeze that pushed him from behind. He passed more Joshua trees, their contorted shapes in the early light resembling men frozen in moments of great torment.

His guiding star was gone, but in its place the elongated shadows of the trees pointed him on toward the west. Ahead, the glimmering rays of the sun touched the highest peaks of the southern Sierra Nevadas. But Will did not see the arriving day as friendly. The spreading glow that already sharpened the images of trees and rocks threatened to pin his dark form against the dusty gray landscape.

Should he halt his march, Will knew a Mojave spear would complete the work the sun's rays had begun.

He set his course toward the tallest tree on the horizon. The rise in the desert floor broke sharply against a line of cliffs. No relief in that change of elevation, for the cliffs were sheer. Slick rock faces of sandstone offered no handholds. He was running into a horseshoe-shaped rim of rock, but no direction in view offered any more hope of escape than another.

Panting, he stumbled over the uneven ground, aimed toward the shadow cast by the tallest Joshua tree as it flowed up and into the cliffs.

This remnant of night shadow appeared unnaturally elongated, even though produced by a tall tree. The shadow stood out against the pale sandstone wall as if made of some darker, coarser material.

As Will passed the tree, he threw another glance over his shoulder. Far behind him on a distant ridge he could make out dark moving dots, the pinpoints of torchlight flickering out against the morning glare of the sun. Racing on, he pushed his burning legs for more speed. Gasping the dry desert air in great gulps, his throat felt like a parched cornstalk planted in the middle of his chest.

When he reached the sandstone wall, there was nowhere left to run. An unbroken wall of rock stretched both ways from Will's perch in the shadow of the Joshua tree's limbs. His pursuers moved relentlessly nearer.

There was a crack in the rock face behind Will, but nowhere was it wider than a handbreadth. As the sun climbed above the desert, the protecting shadow of the tree began to shrink. Will leaned against the rock. For the first time all night, he faced the wind and gravel as it pelted his cheeks. In between breaths he prayed for a way out, prayed that all his efforts had not been wasted, that somehow there was a way of escape. Or was his time on earth truly over? Had all of his hopes come to this?

Then, as if in answer to his desperate prayer, the veil of dust and sand descended, howling into a blinding storm that drew a thick dark curtain between Will and his pursuers.

Ten years of trapping had brought him to this moment. Ten years in search of a fortune. Ten years since the mountain men had come east to the trading post of his uncle with their stories of the high lonesome—stories that had caused the young Will Reed to lie awake at night and dream.

When he'd left Vicksburg, he had been a young colt—lean, gawky, but full of promise. The years had added bone, muscle strength, and the sinew of endurance. Two dozen trips west with men like Jedediah Smith and Jim Bridger had given him wisdom in the ways of the harsh and beautiful land. Two years among the Cherokees had made him more Indian than some Indians.

Will had never returned to Vicksburg, though he had never made his fortune or found his promised land. The restless spirit his uncle had cursed had brought Will to this moment when all that separated him from death was a shifting curtain of sand.

He covered his face with his red kerchief and pulled his buckskin coat close around him. Turning his back to the wind, he let the hide clothing bear the brunt of the stinging grit. Like a lean brush wolf, he curled his body into a crease of the rock face and hoped that the storm that had saved him would not suck the breath from his burning lungs.

✶CHAPTER 2✶

The east wind swirled dust around the feet of Don José Dominguez as he stood in the hall of his hacienda. He stared at it morosely, then stomped his boots as if he could scare the dust away like he would a mouse.

He had forgotten that his new boots were too small even on his rather small feet. Stomping sent a wave of pain through already pinched toes. Characteristically, Dominguez swore at the boot maker but would not stoop to remove the offending articles. He also swore at his Indian housekeeper, although the dirt now dancing in the air around his head had come into the hallway when he had pitched his filthy chaps onto the tile floor.

The picture of Dominguez's overstuffed body perched atop his tiny feet mirrored the relationship between his ambition and the quality of his soul: one was far too ponderously inflated to be supported well by the small stature of the other.

Dominguez, a bad soldier and a worse officer, was quick to take credit and unable to stand blame. But he had somehow managed to live to retirement. A threat to expose the misdeeds of a relative of higher rank had obtained him a pension in the form of a land grant. The relative, acutely aware of what an embarrassment Don José was likely to be, made sure that the rancho being offered was far away, near the dusty presidio of Santa Barbara.

Dominguez proceeded to make life as miserable for his ranch hands as he had for his troops. When the Indians he hired from the mission ran away, he insisted it was because they were "shiftless renegades," not because he disciplined them harshly for the smallest infraction. And if they refused to work the hours he demanded, it was because they were lazy, not because he fed them only two scanty helpings of beans and barley a day.

His cattle did not thrive because his land was not the best and there was certainly not enough of it. He whipped a vaquero until the man could not stand for suggesting that he might be overgrazing. It was the subject of land and how much he did not have that drove Don José Dominguez into his most frequent diatribe.

"It is the law!" stormed Dominguez. "It was supposed to happen ten years ago and more. Governor Figueroa is a weakling and a fool."

"Calm yourself, my son," soothed the short priest, Father Quintana. "Figueroa is a good Catholic and respects the church—"

"Figueroa is supposed to uphold the law. And the law says the missions are to be secularized and the land turned over to the Indians."

"But the heads of my order do not believe that the neophytes are ready to manage their own land," argued the priest.

This last comment brought a snort of derision from the bull-like nostrils of Dominguez. His barrel chest swung around with such momentum that the little father flinched in fear of being knocked over.

"Of course they cannot manage their affairs. The mission lands should belong to us, the soldiers who fought for them. So should the mission Indians. We need them to work the land." Dominguez's eyes narrowed, and he peered down at the priest with suspicion. "Whose side are you on, Father?"

"Yours, of course, I assure you," pledged Quintana, his open hands raised to placate the don's anger. "There is a time coming when the church's lands will be forfeited to the state and redistributed, and I . . ." His voice died away.

The burly ranchero was without mercy and completed the sentence for the priest. "And you want to make certain that you are in line to receive some. Isn't that right, Quintana?"

"My order is headed by fine men. But they would actually *insist* on giving all the land to the Indians. Can you imagine? I would become a parish priest, living on the donations of dirty farmers."

"Instead of being a ranchero with a fine home and hundreds of Indios working for you." The thickset Dominguez turned on his thin legs toward the window overlooking his front pasture. "And I will be the leader I should be. Instead of six thousand acres I should own ten, no twenty . . . even a hundred times as much," Dominguez said. "And in the meantime, we will continue to supplement our income, eh, Quintana?" The ranchero swiveled back toward the priest.

The little priest stiffened.

Dominguez knew his point was well taken. The priest had buried much of his conscience, but he hated the reminder of how far he had fallen from his supposed role as pastor and shepherd to the flock of the mission Indians.

"We only ship off to the Sonoran mines those neophytes who prove to be renegades—the ones without remorse for their backsliding or chronic running away," the priest protested.

"And if we encourage their rebellious ways or 'accidentally' capture a few wild Indios along with the runaways," Dominguez needled, "well, it is just 'God's will.' Isn't that right, Quintana?"

"I have seen no laws being broken," said the gray-robed friar primly.

"Bah! You are blind at very convenient times! A hypocrite of the first water!"

* * *

For three days the warm Santa Ana wind had blown from the east and swept across the foothills of Santa Barbara.

Francesca Rivera y Cruz blamed her restlessness on that wind. "It will wither the wildflowers before they have a chance to grow," she had complained to her father over breakfast this morning.

Her brother, Ricardo, accused her of not caring for the health of the flowers at all. "You only care that the schooner of that pirate Billy Easton won't be able to come into the harbor in such a wind. Admit it, Francesca. Bolts of cloth and lace handkerchiefs are the reason for your impatience with the Santa Ana."

Perhaps Ricardo is right, she mused when the winds had finally shifted and a cool ocean breeze wafted in from the west.

Throwing open the louvered shutters, she stepped onto her balcony and breathed deeply of the sweet cool air. The schooner of trader Easton had been spotted off the coast and would no doubt be making anchor in this gentle breeze. But this assurance did not drive away the restlessness of her heart.

Francesca pulled the comb from her shining black hair and let it tumble down over her shoulders. The fingers of the sea breeze touched her face softly, and she closed her eyes. What was it, this restlessness? Not the desire for a new dress or a few yards of fabric! What did that matter when there was no man she cared to impress?

White clouds scudded across the bright California sky. In the distance she could see the seabirds playing on the currents of wind. Those familiar sights did not give her peace. She felt the presence of *something* very near. *Nameless and frightening!* Like nothing she'd felt before. Yet she longed to learn the name of this fear and know its face.

A whisper of things to come had blown in on the Santa Ana wind and stirred her heart with the warning that nothing would ever be the same.

* * *

Captain Alfredo Zuniga believed in his natural superiority. He was born to command, to be recognized as a leader of men. He had been a junior officer in Santa Fe, New Mexico, when Manuel Armijo was the governor of that province.

Zuniga emulated Armijo, who was fond of remarking that "God rules the heavens and Armijo rules the earth." The young officer rapidly gained a reputation as a brave and ruthless Indian fighter.

If Zuniga was admired by his subordinates, he was also feared by them. He had the eyes of a shark—lifeless and deadly. With a small man's resentment of larger statures, he lost no opportunity to prove his superiority by the code *duelo.*

Zuniga killed men for slight or imagined offenses. He thought nothing of manufacturing offenses to eliminate rivals. One saber duel that ended another man's life was over a bad debt that Zuniga did not intend to pay. On another occasion he had skewered a man in order to possess his woman.

Most soldiers considered California to be a backwater, a dead-end posting, but Zuniga had requested the assignment to Presidio Santa Barbara. Civilized society did not tolerate the likes of Captain Zuniga, and he knew it. He found his heart's desire: a location where he was the only law, accountable to no one but himself.

He had no regard for anything except superior force. It was his way with enemies and women alike. And if he could project a cool detachment, it was only while gauging the opponent's strength, probing for the weakness that was always present somewhere. Once found, he would take full control.

Zuniga never offered to compromise unless at the bottom of the agreement the benefits were all his. It made him very suspicious of compliments.

"Captain Zuniga, you are a fine military man," observed Don Dominguez over a glass of brandy. "You are new here, but you have kept order exceptionally well. Why, I imagine that it is only petty jealousy on the part of your superiors that keeps you from rising to the position you deserve."

Captain Zuniga put down his glass with an audible clink, as if his every action required military precision. He leaned over the mahogany table. His piercing eyes above the saber scar on his cheek bored into the ranchero's. "Don José, you did not bring me here to compliment me or discuss my career. What is the purpose of this meeting?"

"You are very direct. I like that also." Dominguez offered the crystal decanter to the captain, who shook his head. The ranchero refilled his own glass and sipped it before continuing. "I intend to own a much larger rancho than I do at present when the mission lands are secularized."

"So," said Zuniga abruptly, "what has this to do with me? Figueroa decides when—if ever—it will take place, and his appointee will be in charge of the distribution."

"Just so," agreed Don José, "exactly my point. Don't you see that timing is everything? We must be ready to present claims for the newly available land and help the governor make up Figueroa's mind."

"Why do you say 'we'? I am neither a ranchero nor a confidant of Figueroa."

"But you are ambitious, are you not, my good captain? You would rise in rank and prestige?"

"And salary," added Zuniga. "I wish to own a fine house and be wealthy. I will not retire with a thank-you and a few hectares of land on which to grub out an existence."

"Of course not," Don José said cajolingly. "Let me pose a question to you: What would Figueroa do if there was a revolt among the neophytes?"

"He would order me to crush it, as was done here in '24."

"And if he were convinced that the padres' mismanagement had caused the revolt, what then?"

Zuniga studied the question for a minute, then smiled. "He would be convinced that it was time to complete the secularization of the missions but not transfer the property to the Indios."

"Again, just so. And what better person to advise him on the proper distribution of the lands than the military hero who crushed the revolt?"

Captain Zuniga sat back in the finely carved chair, contemplated his glass, and then raised it in salute. "You may count on me."

Don José lifted his glass and touched it to the rim of the captain's. "To your very good health, Captain. I was certain we would see eye to eye on this matter."

CHAPTER 3

The old Indian did not expect to find the man alive. What the desert covered with a mantle of sandstorm, it most often claimed for its own. Still, there was always a chance that a member of his own tribe, stolen by the Mojaves, had escaped. It had happened before that a woman or a child managed to avoid recapture and find their way back to the valley.

For this reason Falcon had descended farther into the barren landscape than his herb gathering normally took him.

His grandson Blackbird, riding easily on his grandfather's back, scanned the stony face of the cliffs with his sharp, young eyes. "See, Grandfather, sitting against that rock."

Falcon's eyes followed the line of his grandson's thin brown arm and pointing finger. A figure in scuffed and dirty buckskins was resting against the shady side of a boulder. The knees were drawn up, and a head could be seen lolling back on the curved surface of the stone.

"Stay here, Blackbird," said Falcon, setting the boy down. He added sternly, "Don't follow me unless I tell you to come."

Falcon approached the reclining form cautiously. He studied the man from a dozen feet away. What he saw was a powerfully built man with dark red hair and beard. The man's eyes, though closed, appeared sunken into his head, and the skin over his cheekbones was stretched tight.

It was several minutes before Falcon detected the flutter of breath in the man's chest. Falcon unslung his doeskin water bag from around his neck and untied the rawhide thong that closed its neck.

Cupping his palm beneath the man's mouth, Falcon carefully poured a small amount of the precious fluid into his hand. At first the unconscious man seemed insensible to the moisture presented to his lips. In another moment the lips began to work, sucking the drips from Falcon's palm.

Falcon added another small amount of water to his hand, and the man drank it greedily. Strong throat muscles worked as if his gullet were trying to reach out and grasp the source of the moisture.

Falcon poured another handful of water, watching the opening of the container carefully as he did so. When he looked back at the man's face, Falcon was startled to find green eyes staring into his.

Falcon controlled himself with difficulty, fighting the instinct to jump back. "*Ojos verdes,*" he murmured, giving the Spanish for "green eyes."

Falcon's own language had no reference to eye color, since none of his people had any other shade than brown.

* * *

Will awoke from his troubled dreams in a daze. He had felt moisture on his lips, and now he stared into the clear brown eyes of an old Indian. Concern and some confusion appeared in the Indian's eyes but no animosity. Will gestured toward the water sack as a plea for another drink.

The Indian presented it without hesitation, letting Will drink his fill.

"Thank you," gasped Will when he had finished swallowing half the bag's contents. "Thank you," he repeated, nodding and handing the water sack back.

"Español?" the Indian asked.

"No, not Spanish," answered Will. "American."

"A-mare-can. Smit. A-mare-can."

Will shook his head to indicate that his fuddled brain did not comprehend. When the Indian extended the drinking sack again, Will gladly accepted and took another long swallow.

"Smit," the Indian intoned again.

Something clicked in Will's memory then, something he had carried since the trappers' rendezvous when Jedediah Smith had shared his tales of California. "Smith? You mean Jedediah Smith?"

The Indian nodded, smiling, his prominent nose bobbing up and down. "Smit, yes. Trap-per."

"A trapper. Yes, that's what I am," agreed Will, pointing to his chest.

Both men sat in silent appreciation of their first clear communication. Then the old Indian seemed to decide something. He turned his head and made a short, birdlike sound.

A moment later a round-eyed boy wearing only a breechclout stood beside the old man. He gazed at Will with grand curiosity, and Will appraised them both with the same interest.

The child appeared to be eight or nine years old. His shoulder-length hair was parted in the middle, and a headband of woven reeds braided with blackbird feathers encircled his head. He wore two strings of tiny round seashells around his neck. His frame was small and his skin color much darker than that of the desert Indians from whom Will had fled.

Will's eyes lingered on the shell necklace. Smith had spoken of Indians beyond the great Sierra Mountains who used shells as money. These two must be far from home if that was the case.

The old man was unsmiling. Also dark and of small stature, he too wore a choker of larger shells around his withered neck. Falcon-feather ear ornaments hung to his shoulders. His headband was made from the down of an eagle. He had a deep scar on his upper left arm. *Probably the wound of an arrow,* Will thought. A longer scar across his left ribs looked like it had been made by a knife.

The Indian lifted his chin and put a hand proudly on the shoulder of the young one. "Chock," he said and touched the blackbird feathers of the boy's headband.

Chock sounded like the call of a blackbird. There was no mistaking the fact that the Indian boy's name was Blackbird.

Will pointed skyward and then back to the child. "Blackbird." He said the word in his own tongue. Then, "Chock."

The mouth of the old man twitched slightly as if this immediate understanding of the Indian word on the part of the white trapper pleased him. Now he touched the falcon feather at his ear, then his own chest. "Limik," he intoned.

So the old one is called Falcon, a name of honor. Will raised his hand in the air and brought it down with the swiftness of a falcon falling upon its prey. "Falcon," he said and repeated the Indian word as well: *"Limik."*

Will was pleased that the language of these Indians would be easy to master. Words seemed to take on the sound of the objects they labeled. The cry of a falcon did in fact sound very close to limik.

Now it was Will's turn. "Will Reed." He reached out to lay his finger against the child's reed headband. "Reed," he repeated as little Blackbird ducked away from his touch.

Falcon grabbed the child by the arm and scowled at him. He pulled off the headband. "Reed," he repeated. *"Español, Tule."*

Tule was indeed the Spanish word for "Reed"! So the old man understood some Spanish!

"Sí!" Will cried with relief.

At least simple communication would not be a problem. Were they mission Indians far from the California padres? Will had only heard about such folk from the handful of trappers who had actually been there. These people with their shell necklaces and dark skin—were they from the ocean called Pacific?

Will was not alone in his relief. Both Blackbird and Falcon grinned as Will continued in Spanish, "Are you from California? Mission Indians?"

"No." Falcon put an arm protectively around Blackbird. "In Español we are known as Tulereños."

"People of the Reeds?"

"Sí." Falcon nodded. "We are a free people. The Reed People. Not mission Indians."

Will had heard from the staunch Methodist Jedediah Smith of the proud tribes of California who refused the protection of the mission fathers. For over fifty years the Spanish missions had clung tenaciously to the coastline of the fabled western land, but seldom did anyone of white blood venture into the vast interior valley with its great waterways and thick reeds. Those Indians who ran from the Catholic missions fled to the tules. Fifty years of runaways had been enough time for the Spanish language to come in bits and pieces even to Indians like these, Will knew.

"What do you call yourselves? In your own language?"

Falcon's chest puffed out, and he shook back his long graying hair. "We are Yokuts."

"Yokuts," Will repeated the word once and then again. He knew that acknowledging the difference between the name the Spanish had given Falcon's people and the one they had always carried was a sign of respect.

Falcon gave a nod. It was a good thing, his expression seemed to say, that he and the boy had come in search of the one who ran from the dreaded Mojaves.

The headman of the Reed People gestured for Blackbird to produce a buckskin stuff sack from around his neck. Reaching in, he withdrew three pieces of jerked venison, which the three companions gnawed on in thoughtful silence.

His strength returning, Will was able to get to his feet. He picked up the knife. The American saw both Yokuts glance at the weapon. "Mojaves attacked my—" he groped for a word—"my group, my tribe."

Falcon let out a long hiss that the boy mimicked an instant later. "Mojaves fight Yokuts, too."

The three formed a line and set off toward the west. At six foot three, Will towered over Falcon's five foot six. Blackbird kept sneaking glances over his shoulder at Will.

Their path wound up through a rocky ravine. The creosote brush, boulders, and Joshua trees looked no different to Will than countless other dry washes he had explored without result. The ground was parched and dusty.

When they turned into a canyon almost hidden from the desert floor by a low range of hills, Will realized they were following a dry creek bed. Its meandering course led them to ever-higher elevations, where an occasional yucca palm bloomed on the rubble-strewn slopes. The composition of the hillside changed to more rock and less dust, its uniform brown color giving way to streaks of red and orange.

The Indians showed no signs of weariness, but Falcon's consideration of Will was such that they paused every mile to let him lean heavily on a walking stick.

Presently, they filed into a cliff-sided arroyo where the climbing was even steeper. This passage soon gave way to a narrow grassy valley dotted with oak trees. At the head of the valley the group paused, and Falcon offered its name. "Te-ha-cha-pi."

Was this the place Jedediah Smith had told Will about as they shared the warmth of a campfire?

Clouds had piled against the line of mountain peaks surrounding the little valley. As they made another descent, again their path beside a trickling brook and the oak-tree-covered hillsides gave proof of how much moisture was trapped by the encircling summits.

Denser growths of oak trees appeared, and Will began to spot larger numbers of animals. A lumbering bear retreated over a ridge, and a herd of pronghorns flung up their heads in uniform alarm. A corkscrew motion of their tails and fifty white rumps disappeared into a side canyon. The land was thick with game. Will remembered the awe in Smith's voice when he had spoken of it.

The little procession stopped again on a rounded grassy knoll. Will made his way from the end of the line to stand beside Falcon and Blackbird. He expected to see a winding descent to another brushy canyon.

Just as Will lifted his eyes to the west, a shaft of sunlight broke through the cloud cover.

"*Trawlawwin,*" said Falcon, swinging his arm in an arc that took in all the view from south to north. "In Español, San Joaquin."

Before Will lay the broadest expanse of green valley he had ever seen. From its southern terminus at the Tehachapis, Will looked west across to the distant range of coastal mountains. To the northwest as far as he could see was the unbroken sweep of a vast plain stretching onward until grayish white clouds and rolling emerald vistas merged.

"The Promised Land," Jed Smith had called it. "Or maybe a glimpse of what heaven looks like!"

Beams of light performed a show for Will, dazzling his vision with scene upon scene of startling beauty. Here a patch of orange flowers painted a broad splash of color on a verdant hillside. The next ray of sun roved over fields of wild oats. Just-forming heads swayed with the rush of breeze like vibrant waves breaking against the rust-colored rocks. Beyond a chorus of nodding purple blossoms and past marching ranks of yellow blooms, the winding silver ribbon of a great river flashed a momentarily brilliant reflection. Following the river's course backward, red-helmeted flowers drew Will's eyes to the mountains on his left hand. There the sunlight revealed that part of what he had taken for clouds was really a fringing mantle of snow lingering on the highest peaks.

"It's beautiful," he exclaimed. "A crazy quilt of color made by God Almighty." He quoted the phrase Smith had used when he described this place. Indeed, there were no adequate words for it.

The Yokuts may not have understood all his words, but they had no trouble deciphering his feelings. In a tone of awe undiminished by ears of repeating the experience, Falcon murmured, "We say *tish-um-yu* . . . ah, flower-blooming time."

It was beautiful, yes. The kind of vision that made a man's heart ache, and yet . . .

There were other things about this land that Will had heard. Tales of tragedy and brutality. When Jedediah had described it, he had pulled out his well-worn Bible and issued this warning to the men who sat enraptured by his tale of the land beyond the Sierras: "Beyond what a man can imagine, the place is. I cried out to God that I had found Eden once again in that great valley."

And then his eyes had locked on Will's, as though he saw something in Will's future. "Remember, son, this warning. . . . Even Eden had the serpent. It was in a place of perfect beauty that man brought Death to us all."

CHAPTER 4

"You are most welcome, señoritas." Billy Easton swept off his straw hat. Bending over his white pantaloons and bare feet, he made a "leg" that was worthy of a French courtier.

The ladies coming on board the schooner-rigged vessel *Paratus* twittered behind their fans. All about the deck were spread the trade goods with which the *Paratus* was loaded: silks and laces from China, otter pelts from the Russians of northern California, exotic spices from Pacific islands with unpronounceable names.

Across one-quarter mile of placid water from the schooner lay the presidio of Santa Barbara. The whitewashed adobe walls and red-tile roofs stood out clearly against the dark green hillsides. Farther inland, but just as prominently in view, was the mission. The settlement bustled with activity on this fine spring afternoon. It was clear that all was well in the Mexican province of California.

Like a conjuror opening his program, Easton produced a silk handkerchief from out of nowhere and presented it to Francesca Rivera y Cruz. "A gift so that we may bargain as friends, sweet lady."

Easton's courtesy earned him a blushing smile from Francesca but a swat on the arm with a folded fan from her chaperone, Doña Eulalia.

"Aunt, you must apologize to Señor Easton," demanded Francesca, a slender young woman with black eyes and creamy pale skin. "He was only being polite."

"He should not be so forward," announced Doña Eulalia loudly, to the amusement of Easton's crew. "And you should not be so brash as to accept a gift from this, this . . ." Words failed the good aunt, but the word *pirate* came to everyone's mind, including Easton's.

It was an image he cultivated. Easton had long before discovered that while men bargained for hides and tallow with dour faces and closely watched ledgers, women preferred romance with their trade goods. From the gold ring in his earlobe to the long hair pulled straight back from his face and gathered in another gold ring at the nape of his neck, Easton looked the part of a privateer.

The truth was almost as fanciful. The son of a Yankee whaling skipper and his Hawaiian wahine wife, Easton had inherited his father's love of the sea and his mother's rich brown skin and easy smile. He had shipped with his father at the age of eight as a cabin boy and been first mate of a trading schooner at eighteen.

Now a muscular and solid five-foot-ten-inch man of thirty-five, Billy Easton sold his wares—whether "pirated" or bargained fair and square—up and down the coast of Spanish California, charming ladies of all ages.

He produced another silk handkerchief with a flourish. "A thousand pardons, most excellent Doña Eulalia. I meant no offense. Naturally I wished to offer a sample of my humble goods, poor and unworthy though they are, in comparison to such noble beauty as you yourself possess."

Now it was the aunt's turn to blush, which she tried to hide behind the ever-present fan. With a coyness not exactly suited to her age, she simpered, "You are quite forgiven, señor. I am most protective of my niece and sometimes speak abruptly."

"Understandable and commendable," replied Easton, the barest hint of a smile escaping below his drooping mustache. Extending his arm in its billowing silk sleeve, he offered, "Will you honor me by allowing me to escort you on a tour of my wares?"

Completely taken in by Easton's charm, Doña Eulalia quite graciously accepted the invitation.

✵CHAPTER 5✵

That first night Will and the Yokuts made a cold camp high above the San Joaquin Valley. The valley floor grew dusky purple in the twilight, and fingers of smoke rose skyward, marking widely scattered Indian villages below.

Falcon pointed to a distant plume. "Our village."

The boy chirped, "They thought we would return tonight. They will think the West has taken us." At this remark, the old man whirled as if to strike the child. But Blackbird was far too fast, dodging and scrambling across the boulder out of reach.

He had broken some taboo, Will guessed. The Mojave Indian raiders were east of the valley. What in the West was more terrifying to the People of the Reeds?

Will did not ask the meaning of this comment. He understood the ways of the Indian. Some things were only spoken of in hushed and reverent tones in the shadowy steam of the village sweathouse. Two years of living among the Cherokee nation had taught Will not to ask questions but to simply live and wait. The answers inevitably came in their own time.

Tonight he did not question the wisdom of the fireless camp. They were still on the fringe of territory where the Mojave raiders might track them. It would be foolish to offer the enemy proof that they remained within reach of attack. Yet it was the distant western mountains that the old man scanned now. He stood for a long time on the flat table of a boulder that jutted out from the side of the mountain. Only when the last purple silhouettes were lost in darkness did he finally turn away.

Falcon tossed a rabbit-skin cloak to Will and gently took the remorseful boy under his arm. The three ate jerked meat in silence before Blackbird and Falcon curled up together beneath the old man's cloak to ward off the chill of the Sierra night.

Will's back was against the rough hide of the boulder that had been warmed through the night by his body heat. It now returned the warmth to him. The predawn air was sharp beyond the rabbit-skin cloak.

Will opened his eyes, surprised to see that the old Indian had resumed his post on the rugged granite table. He had left his cloak spread over the sleeping child, and now, dressed only in his breechclout, he searched the western horizon for a sign of the talking smoke. He seemed undaunted by the chill, yet his senses must have been keen. For as soon as Will opened his eyes, Falcon seemed to know. Turning away from the west, he strode quickly back the two dozen paces to where Blackbird slept.

Without a word, he yanked the warm cloak from the boy, who sat up and jumped to his feet in one movement.

Will stood as well and rolled up his covering, tossing it to the old man.

"We have far to go," said Falcon. "We will eat as we journey."

The light of the sun touched the distant western mountain peaks before it seeped into the valley floor. The two Indians moved down the rugged trail like deer. Quick and agile, the old one moved with the same untiring endurance as the boy. It was plain to Will that the slow pace of yesterday's hike had indeed been in consideration of the white man they traveled with. After a night of rest, it was expected that Will would keep pace. His long stride and sure step did not slow them down.

The swiftness with which they covered the ground did not conceal the details of the country Jedediah had told him about. Men had doubted the tales of wonder as they listened, but now Will knew his trapper friend had reported truthfully.

The rest of the trek to the Yokut encampment was one of vision upon vision and wonder upon wonder. Coveys of quail scurried at the walkers' approach, and no fewer than two hundred quail top-knots bobbed into the gooseberry thickets with every flock they scattered.

Ground-squirrel mounds extended for acres . . . a sign of vast underground rodent cities. Overhead, red-tailed hawks dived and soared.

"Swoop, swoop," pointed out Blackbird, indicating the redtails.

"Yes, they are swooping," responded Will.

"No, no. No swoo-ping. Swoop, swoop," insisted Blackbird.

Will gathered that what he had taken for an English expression describing the hawk's hunting motion was actually the Yokut name for the bird.

A muted bugling echoed up from the swampy area just ahead of their path. Two dozen thick-bodied elk moved from their grazing with an unhurried, deliberate motion. When the herd had put the marsh between themselves and the humans, they stood gazing back at the intruders.

It seemed impossible to Will that Jedediah's serpent could have found this Eden.

In the moist soil of the valley floor, the height of the grasses increased. The wild-grain stalks waved over the flowers, hiding the brilliant colors from view. A vagrant wind parted the stalks, allowing a flash of crimson to come to Will's eyes, then concealing it again. A moment later another stray breeze uncovered an expanse of orange, and so on, until it seemed that the swirling puffs of air were playing a guessing game with Will. What color would be revealed next?

It was late afternoon when they came to the banks of a swiftly flowing stream and turned to follow its course northeastward toward the mountains. For the first time since descending the pass, they followed a recognizably human trail.

The breeze carried a faint smoke to Will's nostrils, and with it he caught the welcome aroma of roasting meat. Blackbird broke from his place in the middle of the march, running ahead to announce their return.

Before the village came into view, Will could hear Blackbird's excited chatter. The scout guessed that a proclamation of the white man's arrival was something the small boy wanted particular credit for.

One more bend of the river and they entered the encampment. A semicircle of reed huts surrounded a clearing with a cooking fire in its center. Two small children squealed and ran to hide behind a young woman who was working near the water's edge.

An older woman was tending the meat Will had smelled. Green willow poles were fixed in the ground around the cooking fire. To each stick was tied a rabbit carcass, and the weight of the meat pulled the stick down to the perfect roasting height above the fire.

In front of one of the huts, a ponderously heavy man was chipping arrow points on a buckskin ground cloth. He rose slowly, leaving his tools and obsidian rocks on the ground.

When the squealing children had been shushed, Will could tell that he was being introduced. He heard Falcon repeat his name and the designation "A-mare-can." The rest of the speech was not understandable but must have related the circumstances of his rescue.

The introduction was short-lived. A shout from across the stream drew everyone's attention. A Yokut man, a hunter about Will's age, came out of the screen of willows directly opposite the camp and forded the creek.

He called Falcon's name. The warrior sounded excited about something, waving his arms and pointing back the way he had come.

Falcon left Will's side to join the newcomer. The heavy man who left his toolmaking entered the discussion also. Falcon was quiet and questioning, the other two loud and angry.

Will wondered if the Mojaves had raided the valley ahead of his arrival. Maybe that was what this unsettling report was about.

The women and children were silent and staring. No one paid any attention to Will at all. He stood awkwardly at the edge of the encampment, waiting for the noisy tirade to subside.

The toolmaker seemed to remember Will first. He stretched out a thick, muscled arm and leveled a calloused finger at Will's face. The tone of his words was accusing, and he was obviously blaming Will for whatever evil had just happened. The toolmaker repeated the gesture and accompanied it with a demanding slam of his fist into his hardened palm.

Falcon's reply was an emphatic cutting motion of his hand. In any language it meant "Enough!" He pivoted sharply on his heel and returned to the American. It seemed that now the entire camp was drawn into a line confronting Will.

The old Indian explained, "Two hunters left our camp on the same day that I went east. They have not returned. That man, Coyote, says he followed their trail to the River of Swift Water but no farther. He returned to bring word."

"Meho, the toolmaker, thinks you are the cause," Falcon added, "but he feels hate deep in his heart since his wife was taken by the West."

"I will help track the missing men," offered Will. He shook off Falcon's refusal. "I owe your people a debt, and Meho must be shown how I will repay."

An hour later, Will was back at his profession—tracking. Falcon accompanied him, and the other two men went also, but they were not happy about Will's presence. Meho was openly angry, scowling at the scout whenever their eyes met. The other man was stoic but clearly suspicious. Each time Will looked in Coyote's direction, he found the warrior already watching him.

The tracks of the two missing hunters were not obvious but clear enough to those who knew what to look for. A moccasined footprint showed occasionally in the dust. One of the two men was considerably larger than the other, as Will could tell from the greater length of his stride. The shorter man walked with a limp. His right foot made an indistinct track, as if he could not press the heel all the way down.

The trail ended at the bank of a river that was indeed swift flowing. Grass growing along the edges of the watercourse was stretched flat against the bank by its force. When Will spotted a twig in the current, he got only a glimpse before it completely disappeared.

The two warriors tied their bows and fox-skin pouches of arrow points into compact bundles, which they slung over their backs. Both men plunged into the water, pushing hard for the opposite shore.

Falcon turned to the scout. "Do you swim, Will Reed?"

When Will responded that he did, the old man replied, "Good. Then we will not need to carry you."

The water was bitterly cold, and the current so powerful that Will could make no headway against it. He wasted no time fighting it but took a long angle toward a bend of the river downstream and let the water carry him there.

Will was the last to cross. The others had already restrung their bows and were prepared to continue the search. The big man, Meho, sneered at Will and said something contemptuous to Coyote.

A brief search of the shore located the spot where the two missing hunters had emerged from the river. Several tracks in the mud of the bank were evident. Will spotted a flint arrow point under a bush, where it must have fallen from a hunter's pouch.

The three Yokuts became noticeably tense. The river seemed to mark a boundary between known and unknown, between safety and danger. There was no obvious sign of a greater hazard nor any indication that enemies had been near the missing men. Still, Will scanned the rolling hills that marched along beside them. He kept a close eye on the treetops ahead for any unusual flights of birds that might betray the presence of others.

The trail was proving harder to follow now. It was obvious that both men had been hunting. They had separated and were traveling about one hundred yards apart. Will and Falcon were following the one with the limp. In about a mile, the tracks showed that the man had turned aside to stand on a rocky outcropping and survey the landscape.

When he did the same, Will noted a swampy area of thick grass just beyond a screen of elderberry bushes. It was a perfect spot for game, with plenty of cover to approach from behind. Will and Falcon headed that direction.

Will studied the area around the berry bushes till he found what he was seeking. A half moccasin print next to a shallow round depression in the soil showed where the hunter had knelt to take aim.

Looking across the clearing from this vantage point, the scout picked a likely spot under an oak where he could imagine a deer to have stood. A dark stain on the ground under the oak confirmed the accuracy of Will's guess. The trail of occasional drops of blood mingled with the curious halting steps of the limping man, and both led to the west.

Just then a rustling came toward Will and Falcon through the brush. They froze in place under the shadow of the oak. Falcon's gnarled hands fitted an arrow with a jagged obsidian point to his bow. He dropped to one knee and drew the bowstring back to his ear.

A moment later the Yokut chief and the white trapper both relaxed. The sound had only been Meho and Coyote. The man with the limp had apparently called his companion to rejoin him in following the wounded deer.

Together the four followed the track that was again plain to read. A vagrant swirl of air reached them. Death was on the breeze—the sickly sweet, metallic odor of decay. The three Indians instinctively fanned out across the trail, their bows at the ready. Will drew his Green River knife and moved from tree to tree, crossing open spaces with a rush, then stopping to look around. Overhead, a flight of vultures spiraled.

Ahead was an oak, seventy feet tall, with a large limb that jutted out a dozen feet off the ground. From this limb hung the bloated carcass of a deer, the deadly shaft of an arrow plainly visible behind its shoulder.

And underneath the deer was the body of a man. Scavengers had already been at work on the man's flesh, but his twisted right leg told Will that this had been the man with the limp.

Falcon knelt beside the body, taking a handful of dust from the ground and sprinkling some on the corpse. The rest he poured on his own head. In silent mourning he lifted his arms toward the sun, let them fall, then lifted them again.

Meho and Coyote stood as sentinels to this grief. They watched the surrounding area, scanning both near and far.

Will continued to search. Not far from the tree, a struggle had taken place, with torn-up earth and uprooted plants testifying to its fierceness. Then came a flattened space, where the uncoiling spirals of orange fiddleneck had been crushed by a man-shaped press. Two long streaks mutely bore witness that the other missing Yokut had been dragged away.

Will followed the drag marks to the edge of a tule swamp, where some horses had been tethered. One of the horses had shied violently, perhaps as an unfamiliar burden was loaded onto its back. The riders had then departed, heading west, skirting the outline of the swamp. *There's nothing further to be learned here,* Will thought. Or was there? He stopped and puzzled over something. One rider had been mounted on a mare. The position of the hoofprints where the animal had relieved itself made this clear.

But a mare was an unusual choice for a mount. Most riders believed stallions and mares were too much trouble and often as unpredictable as saddle animals. Geldings were the usual selection. *Of course,* Will thought, *that logic only applies to riders who have a choice.* Indians thereabouts would have to make do with whatever runaway stock they could catch.

Returning to the place of death, Will found that the dead Yokut had been wrapped in Falcon's rabbit-skin cloak. The three Indians were preparing to return to their village.

"Wait," Will told Falcon. "The other man is alive. Or at least he was when he was taken. I found where whoever did this mounted up. We can still follow."

"Which way do the tracks lead?" asked Falcon mournfully.

"To the west," reported Will, "and just as plain as day. If we were to—"

Falcon shook his head, but before Will could say any more, Meho jumped between them. He waved his arms and shouted angrily again before pushing Will in the chest, hard.

"What is it? What's he saying now?" Will demanded of Falcon, who was trying to grasp Meho's arm.

Meho roughly shrugged off the chief's grip and moved toward Will.

"He says it is a trap. He says you are here to lead us right into their clutches. I tell him to stop, not shame us. He—"

But Meho was in a blood rage, and like his namesake, the bear, could not be called off easily. He drew a wicked-looking, curved-blade knife from a deer-hide sheath that hung by his side and lunged at Will.

The trapper barely had time to throw himself to the side. The slashing knife missed, but Meho's massive shoulder crashed into Will, knocking him to the ground.

Will rolled completely over and bounced to his feet. His red beard brushed up fragments of wildflowers as he rolled.

The toolmaker rushed in again. This time Will stood his ground and let the anger-blinded man come. The American caught the upraised knife arm in both hands, and the two stood momentarily locked almost face-to-face. Will wondered if he had made a mistake, because Meho was immensely strong in his forearms and hands. But before the stout Yokut could force the blade down toward Will, the taller white man used his Mississippi upbringing to good effect.

Will backheeled the Indian, setting him up by yanking his knife hand unexpectedly down, then pushing up suddenly. Thrown off balance, Meho toppled to the sweep of Will's leg. He fell with the American on top of him and the blade of his own knife pressed across his throat.

"Tell him," gasped Will, "I could kill him now if I wanted to." After Falcon had translated these words, Will continued, "And tell him I am not leading anyone into a trap."

"He understands," agreed Falcon. "You may let him up now, Will Reed. He will fight you no more."

The two men stood up, brushing off the dirt and leaves. Will hesitated, then reversed the knife and extended it handle first toward Meho.

After Meho took the knife, Will said to Falcon, "Now let's get after the raiders."

The Yokut chief shook his head. "The West has taken him, Will Reed. If we follow, neither our tribe nor yours would ever see us again. Let us go back to camp." He gestured toward the cloaked body lying on the ground. "I have a son to bury."

CHAPTER 6

A steady stream of Indian women flowed uphill toward the mission. Each carried a single, heavy building block. A second file returned downward, carrying bundles of straw to the mixing pits.

In groups of three, Indian men milled around in mud up to their knees, stamping straw, clay, and water together to form the substance known as adobe. Another circuit of laborers piled the mixture into rawhide aprons, which they carried to the waiting wooden forms. There another set of men were smoothing off the blocks, turning the adobe bricks over to complete the drying process and stacking the completed bricks.

There was no grumbling amongst the workers, but there was no enthusiasm either. For every team of nine workers, the object was to complete seven hundred bricks as quickly as possible.

"You have gotten these miseries well organized," observed Don Dominguez to Captain Zuniga, "but I still object to your quota system. Letting these wretches quit when they have filled their allotment only makes my workers want to do likewise. I have heard that some groups finish work at midday and are allowed to do nothing all afternoon."

"It is not *my* quota system, as you well know," retorted the officer. "It has been the rule of the mission since these *desgraciados* were first coaxed into covering their naked bodies. Besides, I have already raised the quota twice, over the objections of Father Sanchez."

Dominguez snorted with derision at the name of the kindly priest. The noise he made startled the palomino horse on which he sat, causing his gelding to bump into Zuniga's bay. When the bay reared slightly, Don José's horse sidled away from it, stepping into one of the adobe mixing pits.

Dominguez shouted and swore, turning the confused horse around and around until one of the Indian workers grasped the cheek piece of the bit and led the horse to firmer footing. The Indian muttered under his breath, "*Gauchapin.*"

Dominguez overheard the word and slashed downward with his quirt, striking the man who had just come to his aid on the shoulder.

The man actually drew his arms back as if he were about to leap onto the ranchero, but two of his comrades intervened and pulled him away.

"Did you see that impertinent scoundrel?" demanded Dominguez. "He was going to strike me! Zuniga, I want that man hanged! *Gauchapin!* Spur, he called me! Hang him; do you hear?"

The spectacle of the overweight ranchero having a tantrum while his agitated horse kicked up spatters of mud on the military commander brought all work to a halt.

"Back to work, all of you!" shouted Zuniga. "Julio," he said to the native foreman, "bring that man to my office when you finish work today. That's an order." To the ranchero he replied, "Come, Don Dominguez. I will discipline that rebel personally."

The two rode on toward the shore. Dominguez turned around every few steps to curse and shake his fist at the Indians. Zuniga picked globs of mud from his uniform.

"What's the matter with you?" asked the ranchero petulantly. "We, *gente de razón*, were insulted! Why didn't you kill him right where he stood?"

"Calm yourself," the captain suggested in a quietly authoritative tone. "Should I kill a valuable worker? *You* of all people should know the *value* of every miscreant soul."

When Dominguez turned at the abrupt change in the quality of the officer's voice, Zuniga continued. "There is an important matter we are going to discuss."

He gestured toward where the *Paratus* was anchored in the bay. The ship's tender was coming ashore with some returning customers.

"When I was last on board Easton's ship to review his cargo, he asked me about a certain cove a few miles north of here. He wanted to know if I had heard any rumors about any midnight loading of . . ." The rest of the sentence was allowed to flutter away on the sea breeze.

Dominguez froze, sitting very erect in his saddle. "I don't know what you are talking about."

"Don't toy with me," threatened the officer coldly. "What you are doing is illegal. We both know that I could have you arrested and sent away in chains."

"But you wouldn't do that. We are partners," whined the ranchero.

"Partners must never have secrets from each other," said Zuniga flatly. "Never again. You should have told me, Don Dominguez. Now your avarice is going to cost you." Cold, black eyes turned fully on the rancher's face like a white shark in the channel that had selected a seal to devour.

"Agreed! Agreed!" said Dominguez too eagerly. "I was going to tell you everything. Really. You must come to my hacienda, and we can review the details. But what about Easton? How much does he know?" The ranchero was anxious to change the subject.

"Easton is not a problem. I am the only law that matters here, remember? I will take care of him if it becomes necessary," concluded the captain.

A shiver ran down Don Dominguez's neck as he heard these words.

The small boat from the *Paratus* was coming through the surf. Two sailors were rowing strongly, while the mate of the *Paratus* managed the tiller to keep the boat square to the waves. Timing the run perfectly, the boat shot forward on the mate's command and beached itself on the white sand.

The two caballeros watched as several women were assisted from the boat. Bundles containing their purchases were passed to them. The ladies waved cheerfully to the sailors, who turned the tender around and floated it out to shove off. One of the women, Dominguez noted, was the beautiful daughter of Don Pedro Rivera y Cruz.

He turned to point her out to Zuniga but found the officer already staring at Francesca. He continued staring with his shark eyes as the group of women came up the beach and passed near them.

"Good day to you, ladies," called out Dominguez cheerfully.

A polite murmur of greetings replied, except from Francesca, who walked with her eyes on the sand. Dominguez guessed she had seen his companion's hungry stare.

When they had passed, Dominguez remarked to Zuniga, "I do not think she cares for the way you look at her."

"All women desire a man's mastery," said Zuniga with a shrug. "Some conquests take longer than others; that is all. She will be mine."

"It would not be well to let her father hear you say that," advised Don Dominguez. "He would horsewhip you. Besides, I now know how to cement our partnership."

CHAPTER 7

The crackle of the flames rising above the tule-thatched hut was deafening. A thick trunk of dense gray smoke sprouted from the fire like a seed germinating into a tree of pointless destruction.

No one made any attempt to quench the inferno. To prevent the fire from spreading, those Yokuts who lived on either side of the dead man's dwelling had taken the precaution of wetting down their homes, but that was all.

Will had seen this practice before. Other tribes also burned the homes of their dead. There was a finality and absoluteness to the end of Indian life that Will found unsettling.

It was so different from the view that Will had grown up with, and that Jed Smith had also revealed in their late-night discussions around a fire—that each person was created by God for a purpose and that every life had meaning both on this earth and beyond the grave. That there was a place called heaven, where those who chose to follow God would be taken. And that those who did not choose to follow God would suffer for all eternity in hell.

But the Yokuts seemed to accept death simply as the end of life. After that, there was no more. No hope. No future.

As soon as the pyre was ignited and the first tendrils of smoke twisted skyward, the other Yokuts turned away. In fact, they did everything to make life appear as normal as possible. An ancient crone directed the grinding and leaching of acorn meal. Two hunters prepared to leave the camp in search of game. Only Will and Blackbird stood silently watching the hut being consumed.

In contrast to this morning's studied nonchalance, the dance for the dead had lasted the entire preceding night. For hours on end the women of the tribe had jumped and swayed around a campfire, while the men chanted a funeral dirge over and over. The night had been punctuated by the beating of long drums until all the listeners felt their breath and heartbeat become one with the rhythm. After hours of the monotonous pounding, Will noticed that even a temporary silence caused him to be filled with a sense of anxiety and foreboding.

Gifts of food, clothing, baskets, and tools had all been brought to the funeral ceremony but not for the comfort of the bereaved family. Instead, as each dancer reached exhaustion, the gifts were tossed onto the blazing fire.

But now, the morning after, the savage excitement of the ceremony had worn off and was replaced by a blank numbness compounded by weariness. Will watched as Blackbird stared into the dancing flames. The charred ribs of the willow framework crumpled into what had been the interior of the home.

Will walked over to the boy and put his hands on his thin shoulders.

Blackbird's hands flew up to his face, and small clenched fists ground into his eye sockets. "I am not crying," he insisted, though Will had asked no question. "It is the smoke that makes the water come from my eyes."

The scout said nothing, only stood quietly, offering the comfort of a touch on the boy's shoulders. Will was remembering himself as a young red-haired boy with freckles, about Blackbird's age. A grieving child standing beside two mounds of earth back in the red clay hills of Tennessee.

Was that when the restlessness in Will's soul had started? when he had become a loner, no longer trusting that the people he loved would always be by his side? Wondering why God could allow such a thing to happen?

Will had never given up his faith in a good God, but it had taken many years of wandering for him to come to terms with that early loss.

Now he shook his head as if to make the image of the graves in

Tennessee go away, but the hollow, empty ache remained. Even after all these years, he still missed his parents.

Will knew that Blackbird would be well cared for by his grandfather, who clearly loved him, but that would not lessen the anguish of missing both his murdered father and the mother who had died earlier.

Here was Eden, truly, but it was an Eden after Adam's fall. All the freedom to live, to hunt, to fish, to swim came to lie in the ashes of the now-smoldering hut. Jed Smith was right. Evil walked in this land, and it brought death.

What was worse, Will knew that these people had no clear picture of life beyond this patch of earth. Many Indians spoke in vague terms of a Happy Western Land, but they did not know where it was or how to reach it. Sometimes their stories told that The Beyond was a great forest in which a soul might wander forever without rest.

The Yokuts danced and chanted themselves to numbness. Then they tried as quickly as possible to put the reminders of a missing loved one behind them. It was their way of avoiding the awful question "After this life, what?"

"Father," the boy suddenly cried, "do not get off the path!"

Several adult Yokuts cast disapproving looks at Blackbird's show of grief. An elderly woman said, "Shhh! Enough!"

"Do not get off the path," the boy repeated, unheeding. "It may be dark there. There may be thornbushes and steep cliffs. If you fall from the path, how will you find it again?"

Will sat beside Blackbird and slipped an arm around the boy's shoulders.

"I am not old enough," the boy exclaimed, "to know how to track well. How can I learn to walk where the trail is dim and unknown?"

The red-bearded scout spoke in a quiet voice, yet his words echoed with strength. "I, too, have known loss. And I also know the path—that is, I know the One who *is* the path."

"What do you mean?" asked the boy.

"Blackbird, all men everywhere are fearful about what lies beyond this life. We would *have* to be afraid of it, except for this fact: God, the one you call the Great Spirit, sent His Son, Jesus, to scout the trail for us. You see, He not only took the punishment of death in place of us, but He came to life again, and He says He will show us how to walk beyond this life."

"Tell me some more about this man! He must be the greatest tracker who ever lived."

"And much more," the scout replied. "He will blaze a trail for you in this life also if you will let Him." Will turned Blackbird to face him. "Listen. I need your help as well."

The Indian boy rubbed his eyes again, then peeked out past one. "What do you mean?"

"I am going to stay with your people for a time," answered Will. "But I am ignorant of your ways. I need someone to teach me, to show me how a proper Yokut acts."

The boy straightened and squared his shoulders. "I am the grandson of a chief. My fa . . ." His voice faltered. "*I* will be chief someday. I will teach you so you need not be ashamed."

* * *

The stillness of a soft, spring afternoon was interrupted by a messenger from another camp upstream. The man, Badger by name, brought news that a party of Mojaves had come over the pass from the desert. Badger had been surrounded while hunting but had been allowed to go free in order to bring word that the Mojaves wanted a parley.

"What does it mean?" asked Will.

"Who can say?" Falcon shrugged. "The Mojaves raid the valley, robbing and killing. If they want to talk, they must want something that they cannot easily get by stealing."

The smoldering cooking fire was refueled. When it was blazing, a bundle of water-soaked reeds was placed on top to send up a thick column of white smoke that signaled the Mojaves to come down into the camp.

No more sound than the barest rustle of wind among dry leaves preceded the arrival of the desert people. Six warriors and a leader glided into Falcon's village under the watchful eyes of a dozen Yokut men. The women and children were out of sight, hiding in the tule huts.

Will stood inside the doorway of the hut he shared with Falcon and Blackbird. No one had asked him to help guard the camp, but no one had told him to stay away either. He felt a stirring at the back of his neck when the Mojaves came into view.

The desert tribesmen were taller than most of the Yokut men Will had seen. Their complexions were several shades lighter than the valley people, as if designed to blend easily into the sands of their home. They wore their hair long, even below their shoulders. Unlike the Yokuts, who went barefoot or wore buckskin moccasins, the Mojaves wore sandals made of woven yucca fibers.

The faces of the desert warriors were etched with ferocity and deep scowls. For men who supposedly had come to talk, Will noted that they had not come empty-handed. Each had a short bow made of willow branches and a short wooden club shaped like a sickle with a round handle on one end and a flattened killing point on the other.

The leader of the Mojaves wasted no time on ceremony. He addressed Falcon in words unknown to Will but conveying a tone of angry demands. His speech was accompanied by vigorous gestures to the south and the west and with an exaggerated show of surprise toward the east.

The Mojave held up all ten of his fingers and displayed them to Falcon three times. Then, as if to prove a point, he reached into a rabbit-skin pouch hanging around his neck and withdrew a knife. He flipped the weapon so that it stuck quivering in the ground between them.

Will could not help staring forward in horror—the knife standing upright in the soil of the Yokut village was a twin to the one Will had taken from Forchet.

As Will moved from the shadowed doorway of the hut, the Mojave leader took notice of the white man for the first time. The desert warrior stared at him, then bent quickly and retrieved the knife from the ground.

Will pulled the other blade from his belt and advanced with cold anger toward the Mojave. The other desert Indians had nocked arrows to bowstrings, an action mirrored by the Yokut warriors. One wrong move and a fully pitched battle would break out.

Falcon shouted a command for Will to stop where he was. Without turning his back on the Mojave, Falcon continued calling out instructions. "You will not come one step closer. You must put up your knife at once. You are not permitted to disturb the parley in this way."

"Ask him where he got the Green River knife," Will replied.

"He has already said he took it from a Mexican chief whose men attacked their village. He came here to propose that we join them in fighting against the Mexicans."

Will answered quietly, but his muscles were as tense as a coiled spring. "The truth is, he took that from Beckwith, another American and a friend of mine; after the Mojaves ambushed us without any reason!"

The two chiefs spoke together again.

Turning toward Will, Falcon said, "Sihuarro says you were spying for the Mexicans and that thirty of you were killed attacking his people."

With icy calm Will responded, "There were only twelve of us, and we never saw them till they jumped us. We traded peacefully with every tribe we met on the trail till these scorpions attacked. Tell him I said that."

"Do you know what may happen if I return your words to Sihuarro? If he chooses, he might fight you here and now to prove you have insulted him."

"Let her rip," replied Will calmly.

Falcon spoke to the Yokut guards, telling them to carefully let the tension off their bowstrings while the Mojaves did the same. Then the Yokut headman said one word to Sihuarro, very quietly but very distinctly. It was the Mojave word for *liar.*

What followed was a smear of movement. Sihuarro shifted the knife to his left hand and raised his killing stick with his right. There was a whir like an angry bee. Catching a glimpse of a blurred threat spinning toward his head, Will lifted his left arm to shield his face and nearly was too late. The killing stick smashed into his forearm, cutting a long shallow arc and nicking his ear as it completed its murderous path.

Will pressed his injured arm against his chest and prayed that its total numbness would quickly go away. From the corners of his vision he saw that the two opposing lines of warriors had closed into a circle around the fight. Then all his attention was focused on Sihuarro, who rushed toward him brandishing the knife overhead. The Mojave obviously intended to end the fight quickly with a killing stroke.

But the speed of the attack was his undoing. With a presence of mind born more of instinct than conscious thought, Will waited until Sihuarro was almost on him before ducking under the descending blade. The trapper put his shoulder into the Indian's midsection and turned the attacker's momentum to his advantage.

With the same stretch and leverage used to hoist a hundredweight of beaver pelts, Will propelled Sihuarro over his back. The Indian landed with a jarring thud but rolled into a ball and jumped up again to face Will.

Circling each other warily, the opponents looked for an opportunity to strike. Blood from the cut on Will's arm dripped from his elbow onto the dark earth. Neither fighter looked up when a condor soaring overhead shadowed the scene.

Again it was Sihuarro who could not wait, springing toward Will. This time the movement was more controlled, and the Indian's Green River knife was held low, blade upward. The blow was aimed toward Will's belly with a stab and a slash.

But Will met the move blade to blade. Using his skinning knife like a short sword, he parried the thrust in a clang of steel. What he could not parry was a rake of the Mojave's left hand that tore across his eyes.

With a cry of pain, Will threw himself to the side away from the Indian's knife hand. One of his eyes began to stream tears and immediately began to swell shut.

Sihuarro closed again, the knife straight forward. This time there was no opportunity for Will to meet the thrust and only an instant to duck out of the way. Will spun around and locked his hands on Sihuarro's wrist, but the injury to the trapper's left arm had left it still partly numbed and weak. Will used the butt of his knife handle to hammer on Sihuarro's hands.

Before he could make the Mojave drop the knife, a snakelike arm groped over Will's head. Long fingernails began probing for Will's eyes, making him squirm and duck.

The trapper smashed his skull into the Indian's face. The Mojave lost interest in raking the white man's eyes, reaching too late to cover his own shattered nose.

Putting his rough-and-tumble upbringing among river toughs to good use, Will snapped Sihuarro's knife arm upward, then yanked it down. With a mighty heave, he swung the warrior over his hip and to the ground. "Two falls to none," he growled.

The savage had apparently underestimated the white man's strength and fighting ability. Sihuarro sprang to his feet before Will could press his advantage but not so quickly as before.

Both men eyed each other, catching their breath. "I will enjoy giving your head to my dogs for their sport," hissed Sihuarro in English.

"I thought so," muttered Will. Then louder, "You'd best rethink that plan. I grew up wrestling Tennesseans and the littlest one not so scrawny as you."

The Mojave moved toward Will's left, pressuring the trapper's injured arm and blinded eye. Another lunge and a slash forced Will to circle quickly to his right.

Sihuarro repeated the move, trying to take advantage of Will's weaker quarter. A third time he made the same play, and Will stumbled, feigning a slip.

This time Sihuarro came in farther and faster. At the last instant, Will ducked the opposite direction to the feint, leaping to his left. He slashed down hard with his own blade on the warrior's forearm.

Sihuarro yelled and spun away from Will, yanking his damaged limb close to his body.

Will jumped toward him. Sihuarro made a wild, backhand slash that Will only avoided by throwing himself flat. He lashed out with his right foot as he fell, kicking hard against the Indian's knees.

The Mojave tried to leap over the leg sweep, but Will's back foot caught Sihuarro's foot, and he heaved upward with all his strength. Sihuarro fell heavily on his side, plunging his own weapon into his side between the fifth and sixth ribs. He yanked the blade out of the wound with a shriek, then rolled facedown and was still.

The fight was over. Will dragged himself wearily to his feet. He felt no particular sense of victory, just gratitude at being alive. Sihuarro lay still in the dust of the Yokut camp. The spreading crimson pool widening beneath his motionless body gave mute testimony to the severity of his wound.

Will scanned the faces of the Indian onlookers. The Mojaves reflected sullen hatred, the Yokuts a stoic indifference.

Falcon stepped forward from behind Will and stood silently at the trapper's elbow. He offered Will the Green River knife that had fallen from Sihuarro's fingers. "Take it. It is yours now."

Will accepted the knife, but still no one in the circle moved. "What's happening?" he asked Falcon. "What are they waiting for?"

"Are you not going to cut off his head?" inquired Falcon earnestly. "The others of the desert are waiting to take his body back with them."

"Your people do this?" asked Will.

"It is our custom," returned Falcon in a matter-of-fact tone. "Otherwise the warrior's spirit may return to the body and seek revenge."

"Well, it's not my custom," answered Will flatly. "Tell them to take him and go. He might still be alive. Don't they care?"

Falcon shook his head. "Even if he lives, he is a defeated warrior. He will have to fight many times among his own people to lead them again." He kicked dirt on Sihuarro's body and jerked his head toward the Mojaves as if to say, "Take this lump of earth out of here."

* * *

"Wake up, my friend," urged Falcon. "Come to the sweathouse with me. When we are purified and bathed, your wound will heal faster and not feel so stiff."

Downstream from the camp was a willow-and-tule hut similar to the Yokut sleeping lodges, except that this hut was partly sunken in the ground and the exterior was covered with a plaster of mud.

The inside temperature was already above a hundred degrees from an oak fire.

In no time Will's body cast off the morning chill, and soon he began to perspire. He wondered at the timing of this invitation—it was the first since he had come to the Yokut village. The events of the previous day seemed to have gained him a new acceptance with these people. He picked at the moss poultice bound around his wounded arm.

"Falcon," Will wondered out loud, "have I brought trouble on your people with the killing yesterday? Will the Yokuts be blamed?"

"Put your mind at rest," answered the Indian. "There is no love between the Yokuts and the Mojaves. We would have listened to their speech, then sent them home. We do not trust them, and we do not want their quarrel with the Mexicans."

"Then I may stay here longer?" asked Will.

"Of course," Falcon replied. "As long as you wish. But first, come into the stream and wash off the white man stink!"

The two men tumbled out the opening into the cool morning air. It was good that the sweathouse stood just above the creek because it gave Will no time to consider the next action. As it was, he tumbled down the bank after Falcon without stopping and plunged waist deep into icy water.

"Phew!" Will sputtered to his Indian brother. "You do this for fun?"

"Every day," returned Falcon. "We spend half our lives in the water. It is our friend."

"Maybe so," replied Will, "but it sure doesn't like me yet!"

* * *

In the days following the fight, Will discovered that his relations with the Yokuts had changed in a subtle way. No longer their guest, now he was an accepted member of the clan. The early morning plunge into the stream never became a pleasure for the scout, but he adopted it as a part of the Yokut daily routine.

Another kind of adoption took place as well. Will went looking for Blackbird and found the boy sitting beside the remains of his father's hut. The child was idly picking up handfuls of ash and sifting them through his fingers, letting the east wind blow them away.

Will sat down cross-legged next to Blackbird. For a time neither spoke. Blackbird stared into the west as if watching the minute particles of dust float beyond the sight of mortal eyes.

"Blackbird," Will called softly, "I seem to recall your promise to teach me some things. It is time that I had a hut of my own. Will you show me the proper way to build it?"

The boy was short on enthusiasm, but he was agreeable. He and the scout tramped downstream toward the marsh to select reeds for the thatch.

Will stopped beside the bank of the creek to point out a clear footprint in the sand. "What is that?" he tested.

"Raccoon," replied the boy carelessly.

"And what was he doing here?"

The Yokut youth inspected the bank, noting the way the grassy turf overhung the water and was cut back underneath. "He was fishing for crayfish." Blackbird frowned in concentration, but Will could tell that the game was becoming enjoyable.

"Did he have a successful hunt?"

Blackbird was already scanning the banks as if he had anticipated this question. At last his gaze stopped a dozen feet downstream where a fallen tree stretched across an arm of the creek.

The Indian boy scooted over to the branch and peered intently into the water. "Ah," he said in triumph. "Raccoon sat here and ate his catch. Crayfish scales show where he picked apart and washed his food."

"Bravo!" Will applauded. "What a tracker you are."

The Yokut visibly brightened at this praise. He set to inspecting every inch of the trail for other signs that he could call to his friend's attention. "Deer. Coyote. Another deer. Skunk." Blackbird called the roll of every animal footprint he recognized. He looked at Will expectantly after each identification and smiled when Will gave him a nod of approval.

Up ahead, a thick patch of gray-green horehound surrounded the base of an oak like a leafy collar around a neck of tree bark. Two does burst from this cover, sneaking off westward. They had jumped from their hiding, even though the man and boy were still quite far and could not have seen them yet.

"Look!" exclaimed the excited boy. "Let's follow!"

"Hold on a minute. Duck down behind this elderberry and watch . . ." Will inspected the surroundings, deciding at last on a buckeye tangle on a little knoll. "Watch the gully back of that knob."

A minute passed. Blackbird almost spoke, apparently impatient with this unexplained lesson. With a shake of his head, Will cautioned him to remain silent. Once again the scout pointed toward the dry wash. A moment later, an old buck, hunched so low that he seemed to be walking on his knees, came sneaking out of his buckeye hiding place.

"That old buck sent those does out to distract us, while he sneaks out the back door," explained Will.

The shine of hero worship was radiant in Blackbird's eyes as the two gathered the reed bundles for the scout's hut. Together they cut willow poles and formed these into a travois to drag the tule bundles to camp. The boy assured the scout that this was proper Yokut fashion: the willow poles would be lashed together to form the framework of the hut.

They spent the next day building the dome-shaped dwelling. It stood in line with the rest of the Yokut homes, but at the opposite end of the camp from the ashes of the boy's former home.

That night as Will and Blackbird shared a small fire in front of their finished construction, Falcon greeted them and sat. "You have done well," he said to Will in approval.

"I had a good teacher," the scout acknowledged.

Falcon nodded solemnly. "Blackbird," he addressed his grandson, "I see that you are taking your duty to our new brother seriously."

The boy did his best to return an appropriately adult nod of agreement.

"Therefore," Falcon continued, "I direct that you stay in Will Reed's lodge and continue to teach him the Yokut ways." To Will he added, "And we must give you a name. You say you met the great Cherokee Chief Sequoyah, who stood as tall among his people as the red-barked tree stands in the forest. You are tall and red-haired, so we will call you Sequoyah."

CHAPTER 8

The Indian named Donato slumped on the cord binding his wrists. He was suspended at tiptoe level from an iron hook that protruded from a wooden beam.

"You are shamming, Donato," observed Father Quintana, "and it will do you no good. Let him have five more."

"But, Father," argued the Indian overseer wielding the whip, "he has received twenty-five lashes already." He pointed to Donato's bare back, already crisscrossed with cuts from the thin leather strap. Blood oozed from the mass of raw flesh and had spattered the wall by the hail of blows.

"Do not question me, Lazario, or you will hang there next," corrected the priest. "This one has carried the punishment pole, sat in the stocks, and still he persists in sneaking out at night. No more will I listen when he pleads he will reform. This will be a lesson he will remember forever!"

Lazario had raised his arm in preparation for another whistling stroke of the whip when the chamber door opened and Father Sanchez bustled in.

"What's this, Quintana?" demanded the little round priest to the lean one. "I thought we agreed to cease beating the neophytes for minor infractions."

"Minor! This little brother," Quintana said with a sneer, "is disrespectful and willfully disobedient. He must be used as an example."

"Yes, but what kind of example will he be?"

"I will not discuss this with you in front of the prisoner and the *mayordomo.* We may exchange views later. . . . Why did you interrupt me anyway?"

"I came to tell you that Captain Zuniga is here and wishes to speak with you immediately."

"Why didn't you say so at first?" stormed Quintana, pushing Lazario aside on his way to the door. "You may take over here, and do as you will with this . . . this . . . rebel!"

Sanchez and Lazario removed Donato from the hook and laid him facedown on a rough wooden bench. "Bring me the salve from my cell—the blue tin on the shelf," the priest ordered.

When the *mayordomo* had gone to fetch the ointment, Sanchez sat on the bench beside the huddled form. He tried ever so gently to place a folded cloth beneath Donato's head, but even that slight movement caused a groan to escape the clenched teeth of the neophyte.

"Ah, Donato, my friend," murmured Padre Sanchez, "he will beat you to death next time. He is in charge of discipline, so who can stop him? Why do you persist in sneaking out?"

Bit by bit, in gasps expelled past shudders of pain, Donato told how he had visited the free-roaming Indians who lived in the Temblor range of mountains. There he had met a girl and fallen in love. But her people were preparing to move to their summer hunting grounds, much farther to the north.

"I must see her . . . convince her . . . marry me and remain here." Donato coughed.

"But why did you not tell us this before? If she is willing to become a Christian, we will welcome her among us."

"Quintana did not . . . believe me . . . said I ran away . . . to sin with the heathen."

"But if she returned with you, that would prove—"

"She would not. She says Christians are too cruel and not to be trusted."

CHAPTER 9

Another mark of how much Will was accepted by the Yokuts came when he was asked to accompany the men on a hunting trip. Falcon's wife examined his wound and pronounced him healed and able to go, and Will was eager to give up the enforced inactivity. Besides, he thought it was about time to help replenish the Yokuts' stores that he had been consuming.

Will was awakened well before dawn by Blackbird. The boy excitedly informed Will that he was also invited on this hunt. Coyote had been selected to lead the group of four, and Falcon would remain in camp. Will was without a rifle, of course, but he was a decent shot with a bow and had been honored to carry Falcon's for the purpose.

The hunters had sweated and bathed in the gray mists of predawn. More important than cleanliness, they wanted to reduce as much as possible the human scent they would carry to the hunt. The Yokuts felt so strongly about this procedure that they would not touch their weapons until the cold plunge had been completed.

A hasty breakfast of cold acorn-meal cake followed the bath. Then the four headed northeast out of the village, crossing the stream by a shallow rocky ford. Their plan was to ascend a steep ridge of granite rock that ran down to the river.

On a bench of land about halfway up the ridge, the hunting party stopped for a brief rest. Climbing rapidly to the top of a huge boulder, Blackbird gestured for Will to join him. From this vantage point, Will could see back downstream to the Yokuts' village strung out along the banks. Looking upstream, the canyon was bathed in deep shadows as it pressed against the wall of the Sierra Nevadas.

Will understood that Blackbird was proud of his home and showing off the Yokuts' domain. If the young boy grew to manhood, he would follow his grandfather to leadership of their clan. The future chief swept his arm in a semicircle from mountain shadows down to the tule bog where the stream disappeared into marsh. Next he pointed his skinny brown arm toward different marks on the horizon and began reciting a list of names. Will was not certain if the names were those of Yokuts' rancherias or of neighboring tribes.

Apparently satisfied that he had passed his self-imposed test, Blackbird made a last stab of his finger. "Tubatulabal," he said as he hopped down off the rock.

The yellow disk of the sun was climbing above the Sierras, riding on the outstretched arms of the pines on the high ridges, when the hunters began their stalk. The breeze off the peaks was dying down, but its faint trace still bore the chill of the snowy summits and the tang of the mountain cedars.

Coyote and Meho were carrying their deer-head disguises. At a spot where two ravines met, the hunting party separated into two groups. The two Yokut men tied on their animal camouflage gear, explaining that a short distance up the left-hand draw was a spring and a small meadow. The Yokuts had often successfully hunted there before, but it required a painfully slow, creeping approach.

Will and Blackbird were instructed to wait a few minutes, then begin moving up the canyon on the right. It was not as likely that deer would be found foraging in the right-hand fork, but Will would be in a position to get a shot if a deer was spooked and came over the ridge.

Will and his small partner squatted down to wait. Blackbird was doing such an intense job of scanning the brush ahead that Will took an opportunity to examine Falcon's bow.

The weapon was made of a stout piece of elderberry branch, smoothly finished. The front was rounded and the face toward the archer was flat. The flat surface had been strengthened with an application of deer sinew glued lengthwise, and deer sinew was also used as the bowstrings.

Falcon had also presented Will with pouches of arrow shafts and heads to accompany the bow. Both of these were carried by Blackbird. Over one shoulder he wore a fox-skin quiver containing the feathered willow shafts. Around his neck, hanging against his chest, was a smaller buckskin bag that had different sizes of obsidian heads attached to short willow foreshafts.

In this way the Yokut hunter could quickly change the type of killing point to suit the game being sought, and if the arrowhead broke off in a wound, the main shaft could be recovered. When Will extended his hand toward the small boy, Blackbird immediately knew what was wanted. He carefully selected the straightest and best-feathered shaft and coupled it to a newly made obsidian head.

Will nocked the arrow and practiced bringing it to a full draw. He thought it wise to imitate the Yokuts' stance with the bow held at an angle to the left across the front of his body. The trapper nodded his readiness to proceed.

The tall, sun-bronzed white man and the short, dusky Indian child made their way up the right-hand draw. Will was amused to see the caution with which Blackbird took each step, placing his bare foot carefully and stopping after each pace to watch and listen.

There had been no sound from the direction the other hunters had taken, so Will was agreeable to the slow advance adopted by Blackbird. The trapper did not want to range past the location of the other two and let the quarry sneak out behind them.

A file of quail paraded in front of them. Several birds took turns hopping onto a prominent rock to inspect the humans before proceeding. The Yokuts made a small arrowhead with projecting prongs for stunning birds, but they also had means of trapping quail in larger numbers.

When the last quail had scurried off into the chaparral, Will and Blackbird approached the stone perch. Above them on one side was a tangle of buckeye limbs and trunks. Several of the trees had blown down in the winter's storms, but with the enthusiasm always shown by buckeyes, the remaining twisted limbs were already covered in bright green leaves.

The hillside on their right was occupied with patches of gooseberry bushes. These thickets showed the dark red buds that preceded the outburst of the fruit. Higher up, the slope was dotted with oak trees, sprinkled with a few faded green leaves that had neglected to fall the previous autumn.

Marking the open area between gooseberries and oaks were bands of poppies—brilliant orange in several places and sunshine yellow in others. Will struggled to keep his attention on the hunting and off the scenery.

A quail called from the gooseberry thicket closest to the bottom of the ravine. It was answered by another hidden in the mass of buckeye branches and yet another from the growth of oaks. Will's mind did a curious double-voiced response: half his brain was still glorying in the beauty of the scene, while another part was already screaming a warning.

It was fortunate that the warning voice overrode the admiration of the view. Will yelled "Get down!" and pushed Blackbird behind a rock just as a Mojave killing stick whirred past the little boy's ear.

The throw came from the clump of gooseberry bushes only twenty feet away. The desert Indian who had hurled it was already following up the attack, charging toward Will with an upraised knife.

Will knew that the single arrow now nocked would determine whether he lived or died. The little voice also reminded him that, depending on how many other Mojaves were represented by the quail calls, he might be dead anyway.

This added worry did not interfere with his aim or make him hesitate to release the arrow. The obsidian arrowhead, as sharp as a shard of glass, pierced the warrior's chest and passed almost completely through his body. His feet stumbled over a small tree limb, and he fell face forward on the grassy turf. The arrow point protruded two feet above his backbone.

There was not a second to spend in self-congratulation. Two equally terrifying screams rose from opposite sides of the canyon. The Mojave high on the slope who had been in the cover of the oak trees broke into the open. The other attacker, waiting in the mass of buckeye branches, loosed an arrow without ever showing himself.

The downhill shot and the interference of the buckeye leaves deflected the arrow's path. It landed between Will's legs, and the stone point shattered on the rock beside which Blackbird was crouched. Cooler under fire than many a grown man, the Yokut boy had fitted another broad point to a shaft and was handing it to Will.

Will grabbed the arrow from the child but also shouted to him, "Run! Run!" and gave the boy a shove.

Blackbird slipped off the arrow pouches and made a dash back the way they had come.

Will had not fired his second arrow when another came whizzing at him from the buckeye clump. This time the Mojave's aim was true. In fact, it was too good. Directly in line with Will's chest, the arrow struck squarely on Falcon's bow. The arrow point stuck in the elderberry wood, and the impact made the bow spring out of Will's hand like a wounded animal jumps when shot.

Will's second arrow discharged wildly into the air, passing high over the attacker's head. Will knew he could not survive another shot, and he had no time to retrieve the bow. So he pulled one of the knives from his belt and charged the Mojave.

The startled desert Indian looked up to see Will leaping over a fallen trunk with a yell of his own and the gleaming knife flashing in his hand.

The Indian made a wild swing with his bow, trying to stop Will's rush or fend off the knife. The bow and the blade collided, forcing Will's hand wide of its mark. The power of his rush carried him atop the Indian, and they tumbled over into the buckeye clump.

The native's hands closed over Will's wrist, obviously intent on gaining possession of the skinning knife. Will drew back his left arm and drove a clenched fist into the Indian's jaw.

The desert dweller's head snapped back, but his grasp on Will's knife hand did not waver. The Indian twisted Will's arm inward, knotting the wrist joint. Again and again Will drove his fist into the Mojave's face. The roundhouse blows delivered in their tumbling struggle in the brush heap had little effect.

Will's inner voice reminded him of the desperate need to hurry. Only seconds remained before the last warrior came down from the oaks and finished the contest forever.

The Mojave was winning the struggle for the knife. Will's fingers were numbing and releasing their grip. He tried again to drive his fist into the Indian's face, but the Indian ducked his head against the blow. Over they rolled again, coming to an abrupt stop against a fallen buckeye trunk with the Mojave uppermost.

A savage gleam of victory appeared in the tribesman's eyes. He pushed the blade downward, ever closer to Will's throat.

From the direction of the other slope came the sound of running sandaled feet. The other attacker was nearly down the hill. Suddenly there was the twang of a bowstring and a piercing cry. This scream was followed by an angry, outraged shout.

The warrior on top of Will spun his head around at the sound.

It was just the opportunity Will had needed. With his free hand he grabbed a limb and swung it with all his strength against the Indian's head. The heavy branch crashed into the warrior's skull, and he crumbled much as the trunk had fallen in the winter's wind.

Will threw the Indian from him and jumped the opposite direction into the thickest cover of the buckeye tangle. As he peered cautiously over the trunk, he saw an astonishing scene.

The last member of the desert tribe's ambush was advancing to a kill but not toward the trapper. The third attacker was dressed in a baggy shirt that hung to his knees. He was brandishing a killing stick at Blackbird, who cowered with his back against a boulder. The grimacing warrior was walking awkwardly, limping and halting. The cause of his crippled movement was the point of a Yokut arrowhead buried deeply in his thigh, pinning the smock to his leg.

Blackbird had disobeyed Will's order, retrieved his grandfather's bow, and shot the enemy!

Will grabbed the fallen Mojave weapon and nocked another arrow. Climbing out from the jumble of brush, the scout shouted, "Hold it right there!"

The wounded Indian did not understand the words, but the

sudden English speech from a man he thought wounded or killed jerked him around. Disbelief, anger, and pain competed on his face. He slowly dropped his hands to his sides, letting the killing stick fall to the ground. His features were flat, but more startling was the fact that his ears had been cut off.

"You're not Mojave. Why'd you jump us?" demanded Will.

In a growing stain from the barbed shaft, blood spread down the man's smock in a fan shape. He stood awkwardly, all his weight on his good leg. "Please, señor," he said in clear Spanish, "you will help me remove the arrow?"

"First, I want some answers. Where'd you come from?"

"My name is Paco. I am—was—a neophyte of the Mission Santa Barbara. I ran away from the mission, and the Mojaves took me in. Please, sir, can you help me?"

"That still doesn't explain why you helped the Mojave attack us."

"But I did not, señor. I shot no arrow. I threw no club."

"You didn't come charging down the hill to wish me good luck. Blackbird here saved my life by nailing you."

The mission Indian hung his head. "It is true, what you say. But the fierce ones of the desert demanded I must prove myself true to them or they would kill me! They said a spy of the Mexicans was here and that attacking would revenge the wounding of their chief." The bloodstain had spread to the hem of the man's smock and begun to drip on the ground. He visibly paled and swayed.

"Wounding? He's not dead?"

"No, señor. Sihuarro is recovering his strength. His brother, the shaman, argues that Sihuarro was not defeated really. His spirit only sojourned in the land beyond, gathering power to return and defeat all Mexicans, all foreigners."

"So that is the reason for this raid? Sihuarro could prove it was true by having me killed?"

"Please, señor, may I sit down?"

Will made no reply, nor did he lower the arrow point from its aim at Paco's belly.

"Yes, yes," pleaded the man. "What you say is true. Sihuarro said that the raiders would kill you without difficulty and without causing war with the Yokuts."

At last Will gestured with a shake of the arrow point for the Indian to sit.

Paco crumpled more than sat, catching himself only on his elbows before he fell completely flat.

Blackbird ran to Will and, without saying a word, grabbed the trapper around the legs and hugged him tight.

Will was astonished for an instant, then reached down and tousled the boy's shaggy mop of hair. "You did well, Blackbird. You saved my life."

"I was scared," the boy blurted out. "I thought you were getting killed. Then I thought I was and . . . I never shot a man before. . . ." Blackbird made no sobbing noise, but a silent tremor went through his body.

"But you did well. . . . You were brave," encouraged Will. "Not many would have found the courage to return."

"I began to run," Blackbird said with a great sigh. "Then I remembered: I will be chief someday."

* * *

Moments later Coyote and Meho came over the ridge and descended to an amazing sight. They found Will bandaging the leg of an unconscious mission Indian while Blackbird gathered a collection of Mojave weapons from two dead warriors.

✵CHAPTER 10✵

On a small knoll, clear of the surrounding willows, Will and Falcon stood together without speaking. Falcon shaded his eyes against the glare of the westering sun, now turning an angry orange as it descended.

At last the chief volunteered, "I look for sign of Meho's return."

"Yes," Will agreed. "He said he would be back the same day he went to gather flint rocks."

That had been two days ago. When the toolmaker's lateness had first been noted, everyone said he must have found game to his liking. But now no one spoke of him at all. It was as if the Yokuts wanted to avoid thinking about what might have happened to him.

Falcon muttered something low, almost to himself. It sounded like, "The West has taken him."

"Should we not search for him?" Will asked quietly, respectful of the old man's thoughts.

Falcon rounded on him suddenly and spoke sharply. "No! The West has taken him. We will not speak of it further."

✵ ✵ ✵

"I must leave you," Will said in his best Yokut speech. He was addressing a council of Yokut elders headed by Falcon. The men were dressed formally in their buckskin vests trimmed with fur and bits of shell.

Falcon spoke. "But why, our brother of the reeds? You have shown yourself to be truehearted and brave. Why would you separate yourself from us?"

"Because, Father," said Will with respect, "as long as I remain here, your people cannot have peace with the Mojaves. I endanger your families. Blackbird might have been killed for being with me. I cannot permit this."

Falcon stood erect on the side of the fire opposite Will and waited politely for him to finish. The Indian's hair was tied into two braids and laced with milkweed string twisted with eagle down. "I would say that I owe you the life of my grandson. You are welcome to live with my household forever. If need be we will fight the Mojaves together."

Coyote followed in turn, pleading with Will to remain.

Others of the clan took turns expressing their willingness to face the threat of the desert tribe if the white man would remain.

Finally Will alone stood before the silent, expectant group. A chunk of burning oak broke and crumbled in the fire pit, tiny sparks flying up. He shook his head gravely. "My father and my brothers and my friends, I owe you very much. But I cannot remain now. I came to this land for the purpose of furs. Now I have no means to continue *that* purpose, but I have not yet found another. What is more, I must seek news of my white brothers, if any of them still live. I must go."

Among the Yokuts, when a man expressed his decision after taking council, there was no more discussion, no continued debate. It was settled.

Falcon rose to confirm the choice. "So, our brother Sequoyah will go from us. Let us smoke to bless his going."

A short-stemmed clay pipe already charged with native tobacco was lit with a coal from the fire. Falcon blew smoke to the four points of the compass and toward the sky. He then passed the pipe to Will, who repeated the motion, then returned it. The small tube of fragrant embers was passed around the circle and came back to Falcon.

From around his neck, Falcon drew a string of the fuzzy red topknots of the mountain woodpeckers. It was one of the most precious things the Yokuts possessed and a mark of Falcon's status. "Take this, my son. We know the Mexicans esteem it not, but should you wander among others of the Yokuts, they will know you for a man of honor and importance. Also, you must take my bow as your own."

Will thanked Falcon for this kindness, and the meeting was over. The council began to disperse to their huts.

Coyote drew Will aside. "There is yet one more matter to speak of. Since you spared the life of the man Paco, what do you wish done with him?"

Will had already considered this. "I would have allowed him to return to the Mojaves, but he was afraid. I know you do not trust him and cannot permit him to remain with you, so my way is clear."

"Good." Coyote nodded. "Send him away to walk alone. His cropped ears mark him as a thief. Every hand will be turned against him wherever he goes."

"That was not my meaning," corrected Will. "I will take him with me. I have explained that he has no choice."

"You are wrong," Coyote argued. "He will knife you as you sleep."

"I think not—" Will shrugged—"but I will be wary. Perhaps I will be back this way again soon, and we will see who was right."

Coyote shook his head and snorted a mocking chuckle. "If you are wrong, my brother, you will not return this way ever."

CHAPTER 11

The morning came for Will to take his leave of the Yokuts and cross the great central valley and the coastal range of mountains. A three-day journey separated the Yokuts' nation from Spanish California.

The scout awoke in the predawn grayness to the flutter of a rising east wind. The camp was perfectly still. Far off he heard a jay scolding some other creature for waking him so early. Closer by, the creek laughed and gurgled as it lapped against the roots of a thirsty willow.

Gazing at the reed-thatched ceiling took Will back to the hut in which he had been imprisoned by the Mojaves. The similarity lasted only a moment though. The Yokuts' village was too peaceful for such a disturbing comparison to last. The sense of calm and belonging carried Will's thoughts toward a dimly remembered childhood home on the Mississippi.

The trapper rolled over in the rabbit-skin blanket. He was so wrapped up in memories that the fact Blackbird was missing took a minute to register. The boy's sleeping cover was thrown in a corner of the hut, and he was gone.

Will shook off the pleasant sleepiness and pulled himself awake. Where had the boy gone and why? Blackbird knew that the scout was leaving. Why would he choose this morning to disappear?

Exiting his hut, Will began a mental list of the more likely places to search. For a few steps Blackbird's footprints showed plainly in the cleared area around the huts. Will followed them quietly, not wanting to rouse the camp. The trail was lost after a few paces in the jumble of tracks around the village.

Down at the sweathouse? wondered Will. The communal structure next to the creek was deserted this early in the morning. Will did not need to feel the ashes. The cool temperature inside told him the hut had not been used since the previous day.

The trapper searched the dark green gooseberry thickets for signs that Blackbird might have gone in search of breakfast. He found no trace of the eight-year-old until he came to the trail that they had followed into the Mojave ambush.

Discovering the next footprint, he knew that he was on the right track. In fact, he already knew the destination.

Ignoring the faint traces of the young boy's passing, Will cut cross-country toward a rocky bluff that stood out against the skyline. It was the same spot where he and Blackbird has surveyed the Yokuts' world.

"Take me with you." Blackbird made the demand without any preamble as the scout joined him on the stony ledge.

"I can't do that," answered Will. "I don't know what I'll find or how I'll be received, and I won't chance your life to find out."

"But you are going west, and I will never see you again," mourned the boy, his brown eyes searching Will's face. "It makes my heart hurt. First my mother, then my father, and now you. Take me with you."

The scout gently explained. "But what about your grandfather? He needs you, and your people need you. Besides, it's not as you've said. I'm headed west, but I'm not going to die. I'll be back this way soon."

"How can I know that you are speaking the truth?" questioned the child. "No other one who has gone west has returned."

Will thought for a moment, then drew one of the Green River knives from the leather straps that crossed the front of his buckskin jacket. "Look—I want you to keep this. I will hold its twin. Whenever you use it or see it, you must think of me and I will do the same of you. Keep it safe, because it and its brother knife must be reunited before the snow flies in the passes." He gestured toward the high mountains to the east. "Learn all you can from your grandfather about the ways of the wilderness. Soon enough you will be of an age to join me as a scout."

Blackbird nodded, but sorrow remained in his eyes. He refused to return to the camp.

When Will and Paco began their journey, Will could feel the eyes of the boy gazing down upon him, following his friend as he walked the path that led toward the ocean.

* * *

"I wish you would not do this, señor," asserted Paco for the third time in as many minutes.

Will had been trying to ignore the pleading mission Indian but decided he could not stand listening to it for another minute, let alone days.

The scout whirled around, the fringe on his buckskin leggings twirling. "For the last time, Paco, you have no choice, unless you want me to let you wander off to starve. Why are you afraid?"

"You do not understand, señor. If I go back, they will beat me to death."

"Bah," snorted Will. "You're not serious. If you go back of your own free will, they probably won't beat you at all."

"Listen to me, señor," begged the Indian, who was leaning heavily on a crutch made of mountain mahogany. "Perhaps you are right about the holy fathers, but they are not the ones who will punish me. They are not the men who did this." The stocky man stopped moving and forced Will to turn and look.

"Captain Zuniga, he cut off my ears, and this time he will cut out my heart."

"Paco, if you got your ears trimmed, it's only because you are a thief."

"No, no, señor. That is what Captain Zuniga told the fathers so they would not trust me, but it is not so."

Will gestured impatiently for Paco to start walking again, and the two men resumed their march. They were skirting the southern end of the great valley's tule bog. Over his shoulder Will demanded to know the real reason for his cruel punishment if Paco was not a thief.

"Ah, señor. It is because of what I heard Captain Zuniga and Don Dominguez plotting. They intend to push the governor to take over the mission lands. I tried to tell the fathers this, but Captain Zuniga said I was lying to cover up my thievery."

"It sounds pretty fanciful to me also," commented Will. "Let it go for now, and I'll speak on your behalf if need be. Now fill me in on the mission. What's it like?"

They camped that night in Canyon de las Uvas. Will noticed the steep hillsides covered with wild grapevines, giving the canyon its name.

Over a supper of roast rabbit shot by Will and acorn-meal cakes provided by the Yokuts, Paco gave the young trapper a sketch of life in Spanish California.

"I was born at the mission," he began. "My grandparents were of the Chumash people living at a rancheria right where Presidio Santa Barbara now stands. They lived off the sea, fishing and gathering. They made shell money and traded it with other people for things they needed.

"When the holy fathers came, everything changed. The Spaniards invited my grandparents' people to come to the mission. They were not forced to become Christian, but the holy fathers told them stories about how the Lord Jesus died for their sins and they listened. They were told that if they became neophytes they would receive clothing, better food, homes, be taught to grow crops."

"So they wanted to join the mission?" asked Will.

"*Sí*, but they had to agree to many things. If they became neophytes, they had to work for the padres and no longer could they leave without permission."

"And runaways are forced to return and are punished?" Will inquired.

"That is right. Sometimes my people tried to revolt. My father died in one such attempt. But he was not a rebel, señor. He was killed protecting the mission from others who wanted to burn it down."

"Surely your people outnumber the Spaniards many times over," offered Will, remembering his grandfather's stories about the American Revolution against the British. "Why didn't they—what's that noise?"

A low rumble could be heard in the distance. Very faint at first and harmless, like the drumming of rain on his cabin roof back on the Mississippi, the sound swelled until it resembled a continuous roll of thunder. The noise seemed to be sweeping toward them, down from the high pass.

The rumble increased in volume and tempo, reminding Will of an avalanche he had heard in the heights of the Rockies. He jumped to his feet. "I know that sound. It's a buffalo stampede. I saw one when we were crossing the plains." Unconsciously he switched to speaking English in his excitement. "This oak here is good and stout. Quick, up . . ."

Paco still sat by the fire. "Calm yourself, señor. There are no buff . . . what did you say, 'bufflers'? There are none here."

"Then what?" demanded Will.

A herd of horses swung into moonlit view. Their leader, a glossy black stallion of immense size, swept around a rocky outcropping two hundred yards away.

At the sight of the campfire, the stallion did not even break stride. He led his band in a great S curve that carried them to the farthest side of the canyon opposite the two men.

Will caught glimpses of various horse hides—dark, light, pinto—as he stood watching the spectacle. Like the sudden release of a river hitting the rim of a waterfall, the horse herd spilled past the camp. Their eyes flashed in the light of the moon; their hooves churned the sage into a piercingly sharp fragrance that filled the night air . . . and then they were gone.

Will stood staring after them.

From behind him the still-seated Paco spoke. "There you see a part of the answer, señor."

"Answer—what answer?" said Will, who had forgotten his question.

"You asked why my people and the other Indios did not throw out the Spaniards. It is true that they came with weapons and armor of iron and with gunpowder. But most of all, they came with horses from whom these wild ones descend. With such beasts they can move men and supplies in great numbers and so quickly."

"Well, why don't your people learn to ride—meet the Spanish as equals? You could catch that one herd and have mounts for seventy-five or one hundred men."

Paco looked furtive for an instant . . . the expression of a weasel surprised in the henhouse. "Oh no, señor," he said quickly and shook his head. "Only *gente de razón*, the people of reason, are permitted to become caballeros. It is forbidden for any of my people to even get on a horse."

CHAPTER 12

Don Pedro Rivera y Cruz stood on the veranda of his hacienda and watched his gardener hoeing weeds. Don Pedro's thoughts drifted back some twenty-five years earlier to a tiny garden outside the adobe walls of Presidio Santa Barbara.

The Rivera y Cruz family was of noble blood, well-known and highly regarded in Spain. But notoriety and nobility, even combined with a Jesuit education, could not ensure wealth and position for the future adult lives of thirteen children. As the tenth in line, Don Pedro's military career in the Americas had been decided long before he wore his first beard.

The ranchero rubbed his hand over his clean-shaven face, and then, by habit, up over his balding head. He thought ruefully how thick and black his hair had been when he was a young soldier.

With his good looks and confident manner, there had been no difficulty convincing lovely Guadalupe Flores to become his bride. They had been married in the presidio chapel during the first month of the year 1801. She was the first to tend the scrap of garden outside the wall of the fort, and she was in his thoughts now.

Don Pedro's military service might have been without distinction had it depended on fighting battles. Garrison duty in California was almost always peaceful.

But in a different way, Don Pedro had earned the gratitude of Spain. In 1812 both the presidio and the mission were destroyed by a cataclysmic earthquake. Don Pedro put his studies from his youth to good use. Demonstrating an amazing skill at architecture and engineering, he soon had rebuilt both structures. People far and wide recognized that the buildings were better than the originals.

At his retirement from military service, he had received a grant of land and set to work stocking it with cattle. At first there had been little profit in the sale of meat and tallow, but in time the demand for rawhide drew attention to California.

Within ten years, the first hesitant attempts at commerce with America's eastern states had grown into an active, thriving business. Valued at two dollars apiece, cowhides soon became known as California banknotes. Their proprietors became wealthy men as the young and energetic United States continued to demand more leather for shoes, boots, saddles, and harnesses.

There was only one sadness in the life of the ranchero. His wife had had only one year to share the hacienda built from the profits of his trade before she died.

Don Pedro was recalled from his reverie by the creaking of saddle leather at the front of the house. Turning the corner of the veranda, he saw that his son was mounted on the bay horse with the white blaze and was awaiting instructions.

"Ricardo, I want you to ride out to the south pasture and see how the roundup is going. The last two hundred hides are cured and stacked. It is time for us to prepare more."

"*Sí*, Father," replied the slim young man. His features duplicated those of his sister, Francesca, but in a chiseled, masculine way. He controlled the prancing horse easily and took the time to secure under his chin the strap of his flat-crowned hat.

Don Pedro Rivera y Cruz gazed upon his son with pride. "Before your return tomorrow, ride up Canyon Perdido. I have had a report that some of our cows have been slaughtered there."

Ricardo turned the bay in a circle back toward Don Pedro, the silver conchos on the tack flashing in the sunlight. "Should I take some men with me, Father?"

"No, not till we know more. It is probably the work of some travelers or Indios. Anyway, if it is only one or two dead animals and they have left the hides, it does not matter. We will not begrudge anyone meat, so long as they are respectful. *Vaya con Dios*, my son."

Ricardo had only to touch the bay's flanks with the tips of the five-inch rowels of his spurs and off they flew. Horse and rider merged into the fluid motion of water bubbling over rocks in a streambed. In no more than a minute they were out of sight.

Don Pedro again wiped his work-thickened hand over his bald head with its fringe of short white hair. How proud his wife would have been of their two almost-grown children and how fine the rancho had become.

"Miguel," he called to the rancho gardener, "are the strawberries ripe yet? Ah, no matter, bring some anyway, the ripest you can find."

To himself he sighed. "She could never wait for them to get really ready. Besides, she always said there was something magic about the first strawberries of spring." Don Pedro shook off his thoughts and turned to climb the steps back to his office.

CHAPTER 13

Will and Paco walked through the mountains on a path that wound its way past forests of oaks and piñon pines. On the trail they came to a deserted village in a hilly canyon.

Will stopped to examine the forlorn site. Collapsed reed huts encircled by a mud wall were all that was left. On a bluff above the village were some grinding holes bored into a granite slab and the remains of a rectangular foundation.

The trapper called Paco over to him. "What about this? I never saw the Yokuts build anything that wasn't round."

Paco studied the ground for a moment. Next, he squinted down at a corner of the green valley that could be seen through the canyon's mouth. A sheen of silver reflected a large lake's presence in the valley. "This place I have never been to before, but I have heard of it. There was once a great Yokut village here. The holy fathers came to this place and built a small mission. That must be the foundation. This was many years before I was born.

"Then some runaways passed through here, fleeing from Mission Santa Barbara. The military commander used this place as a fort to attack the tribes that were hiding the *huidos*, the runaways. When the Yokuts protested, he punished them also, so they all moved away and never returned. Soon the padres went away too."

Will nodded, trying to imagine what life might have been like here. "So the commander, by being so hard, chased away those that the priests had come here to seek. He made their work more difficult, not easier."

There was nothing to add to that. But it gave Will much to think about as the two pushed upward through passes that led toward Santa Barbara. Eventually they faced a high rounded ridge covered in dark green grass and dotted with oaks.

"Just across those mountains, señor." The mission Indian directed Will's gaze to a zigzag path of red dirt, streaking the hillside like a faded scar over an old wound.

* * *

The next morning they were up before sunrise. Will was eager to cross the threshold of Spanish California. He had heard stories about the richness of the mission lands and their exotic Spanish culture from a handful of English-speaking trappers who had been there before him. He had seen nothing that resembled civilization in the usual sense of the word since leaving Missouri, a thousand miles and another lifetime ago.

The rounded ridge did not look threatening, but it was steep. The path they followed was long in reaching the top as it plunged in and out of canyons and gorges.

When the scout and the mission Indian finally reached the crest of the hill, Will was out of breath. Paco said his leg was aching, and he was ready to rest also.

Will glanced back the way they had come, thinking how glad he was that the climb was behind them. He was not yet ready to look down the western slope. Many ranges had been crossed only to find another and still another looming ahead, so his enthusiasm to see what lay beyond had been tempered.

It was a shock past anything he had ever experienced to see the ocean from his perch! The land dropped away sharply below him, flattening out to a narrow coastal plain in front of a line of white sand and foaming breakers.

The coastline made an arc, and Will could see it was a bay of sorts. The mountain range on which he stood curved to plunge abruptly into the ocean some miles south of him, while to the north it faded into a rocky point in the dim distance.

Will could see islands across a narrow channel of blue water. One especially clear island lay directly before him. The length of its silhouette and the shape of its peaks and valleys showed that it was not inconsequential in size.

Paco tugged at Will's elbow when he saw the scout staring across the water. "My people once lived there."

"There? You mean on that island?"

"*Sí.* It is called Santa Cruz . . . the island of the holy cross. When the Spaniards came to this coast, one made a stop there. A priest lost a valuable silver cross while they were exploring. An ancestor of mine swam out to stop them from leaving so that the cross could be returned. The Spaniards were very impressed and grateful and decided to name the island to honor the event."

Will's first view of the ocean—in fact, of any ocean—filled him with wonder but was overshadowed by a sense of unease. There had never been a time when he had stood on the shore of a lake so vast that he could not see the farther shore. It strained his belief as well as his eyes that no matter how hard he peered into the distance, there was no trace of land. He had the same feeling of disquiet when he had left the little trading post outside Vicksburg: adrift with no farther shore in sight.

He was grateful for the islands on the near horizon. They were like a wall holding back the unutterable loneliness of the sea beyond.

"Come, señor," interrupted Paco. "Let us descend. Santa Barbara is just across these hills."

CHAPTER 14

The California morning was perfect, and young Ricardo Rivera y Cruz had enjoyed it to the full. His canter to the cattle roundup was made under the bluest of skies and billowy white clouds. He was pleased with the figure he made and with the performance of the horse he had trained.

Passing a group of Indians hired from the mission to repair an irrigation ditch, Ricardo was saluted respectfully. There was no hint of the sullenness that often accompanied their response to other masters.

Ricardo also met a *carreta* occupied by the daughters Gonzalez. The wooden-heeled cart was creaking its way toward the market. Old man Gonzalez was not a great ranchero, but he was very successful at raising beauties for marriage. Ricardo touched the brim of his hat as he cantered by, pretending not to notice the giggling that erupted.

Ricardo wondered if one of the Gonzalez sisters might one day be his mate. Since he was little he had known that his father had arranged a marriage for him, but he had not been told with whom. At the age of nineteen, he was not expected to know his future wife. Indeed, decisions about his life were still his father's to make. He had not even been allowed to begin shaving until he was eighteen and then only with his father's permission.

Thoughts about his own eventual wedding brought his sister to mind. At twenty-two, Francesca was six years past the accepted marriage age. Her betrothed, a forty-year-old don in San Diego, had died in a fall from a horse when Francesca was only fourteen. Some said he was drunk when it happened.

While a hundred other prospective sons-in-law could have been found, the death of Francesca's mother less than a year after her fiancé's had made Don Pedro reluctant to push her to marry. Don Pedro was proud of his son, but he doted on his daughter.

Ricardo shrugged, glad he was not responsible to find a husband for his sister, and rode into camp.

The roundup concluded smoothly the following morning. The ranch foreman and his vaqueros had gathered about two hundred of the rangy cows into a small meadow. With its surrounding thickets of brush and a rocky stream across one side, it was an ideal holding ground.

Some of the vaqueros were Indians. They were permitted to ride for Don Pedro only after he had applied to the government in Mexico City and was granted a special allowance. It had taken two years and much wrangling, but the prohibition against Indians on horseback had been partially lifted.

After a brief final talk with the foreman, Ricardo concluded that all was going well. By the next evening the cattle would be driven down to a section of the rancho near the ocean, where the skinning would take place.

It did not matter that a few neighbor cattle had been rounded up with Don Pedro's. They would be skinned with the rest and the hides cured; then the finished product returned to the rightful owner. This approach saved the effort of rounding up those cattle again later, as well as trying to separate out the strays. Since all the rancheros operated the same way, no one was cheated.

The ride up Canyon Perdido took Ricardo away from the ranching and farm operations and away from the traveled roads. The canyon's gnarled oak trees and tangles of brush had a wild, uncivilized appearance, though it was just beyond the sight of the grazing herds.

Ricardo had searched the canyon for strays many times. A path of sorts wound through a boulder-strewn gulch and up the slope toward the mountains. The path was said to eventually climb into the Santa Ynez Valley, but Ricardo had never ridden along it that far.

The bay shied suddenly, and a moment later Ricardo caught the stench of rotting flesh. Around the next bend of the arroyo, he came upon the partially dismembered carcass of a cow. It was lying next to a rock basin that held a small pool of water. The head and forequarters of the cow were partly covered with a pile of leaves and dirt. Someone had done a poor job of hiding their kill.

The horse's nostrils flared, and it snorted violently twice, then pranced in a tight circle.

"Easy," said the caballero to the bay, "easy."

Ricardo searched the rocks and the tree branches for a hide. Some wild beast had been feasting on the remains—that was certain. But the cow must have been killed and skinned for its hide.

He never saw the grizzly till it charged. Evidently the silver-tipped, hunchbacked bear thought the horse and rider were moving in on his larder, and he was having none of it.

The bay screamed as only a horse that has been frightened near to death can sound. It jumped straight up and lashed out with its hind feet, catching the bear on the nose and momentarily stunning him.

But the grizzly was not easily put off the attack. Lunging again, it closed its jaws over a scrap of the horse's tail and with that tenuous hold pulled the bay backward.

Truly panicked now, the horse stood almost straight up and down on its forefeet. The bay's rear hooves pounded against the bear's shoulders, but the bear hung on grimly.

On the bear's third desperate plunge, Ricardo parted company with the bay and flew off forward. Arcing through the air over the carrion pile, he landed heavily on the rocky basin and was knocked unconscious.

When he came to, he lay very still, taking stock of his injuries before attempting to move. It was the wisest decision he ever made.

Only an instant later, the hot, rotten-smelling breath of the grizzly blasted his neck. The bear began to snuffle along his legs, as if attempting to place the strong man scent.

Ricardo's mind raced with horrifying possibilities. Even if he convinced the grizzly he was dead, what if the bear decided to add him to the carrion pile?

That chilling nightmare became a bloody reality when the humpback suddenly closed his jaw over Ricardo's head and sank his razor-sharp teeth to the bone. Ricardo let out a yell almost equal to the bay's.

The bear dropped him. A deep, angry growl rumbled like an earthquake from the depths of the beast.

In the split second that elapsed between the grizzly's surprise and what Ricardo was sure would come next—the bear's decision to tear the man thing into bloody pieces—the bear jerked, as if momentarily distracted.

Ricardo scrambled away. Playing dead was now out of the question; he was only seconds away from the reality. With one hand he held his pierced and torn scalp, bleeding from half a dozen deep gashes. With the other hand he dragged himself over the rocks, crying with terror and praying that he would not pass out.

Will Reed nocked another arrow as the grizzly rose on its haunches, roaring. It swatted clumsily at the painful barb sticking in its neck.

The shaft broke off and the bear drove the point inward, sending the creature into a rage of pain. The second arrow struck low on the flank, and the bear dropped its great head to bite at its own side.

Closing its teeth over the barbed shaft and ripping it free of flesh, the silvertip bear stood erect. Flashing eyes searched for the source of the cruel flying things.

Will knew the instant the grizzly spotted him. It stood up on its haunches next to a tree at the edge of the clearing and bellowed at him, challenging him.

Will fumbled in the pouch for another arrowhead. His hand closed over one and drew it out—too small! The tiny flake of stone was only fit for killing rabbits, not this berserk hulk of killing ferocity. He scrabbled through the pouch again, coming up with another only a little larger.

Across the stone basin Will could see the injured man scrambling up a rocky ledge to safety. Time to think about his own safety. "Paco," Will called. "Paco, distract him! Throw a rock—something!"

There was no answer. The Indian was long gone.

The bear's claws rattled the granite as he dropped to all fours, ready to charge the intruder.

Unless Will did something soon, this contest was about to end! He shot a glance upward. *No tree limbs near the ground. No time to run. No way to get to the safety of the rocks.* Will's jaw tensed. If this was the end, he'd go down fighting.

As the bear rushed him, Will drew out one last arrow shaft, fitted the barb to the socket, nocked the arrow, and released.

The last arrow, a mere pinprick, also lodged in the thick folds of the bear's neck. The beast, on him now, seized the bow in its teeth, tearing it from Will.

One more swat of an enormous paw and Will would be crushed. He held his breath as the grizzly batted hurriedly at the latest arrow, striking again the first barb whose shaft protruded from the long, coarse hair.

The five-inch-long arrow, crafted of razor-sharp black glass, pushed by a ton of angry grizzly, was driven all the way in. Suddenly the bear jerked, as if its carotid artery had been sliced. Blood burst from the wound, spraying the silver-tipped fur.

The bear collapsed like a huge fur sack full of air that had been suddenly punctured. Its lips were still curled back from his fangs, and on either side of the massive jaws lay shattered pieces of Falcon's bow. The terror of the canyon lay silently in a heap at Will's feet.

Will knew there was no time to relish this unlikely victory. Turning to climb the rock face after the wounded man, he found the horseman cradling his lacerated head in both his hands. Blood streamed between his fingers, staining his hands and face. The young man's breath was coming in ragged gasps, and he did not try to look up when Will approached.

"Can you hear me?" Will asked gently in Spanish.

"*Sí,* and I think I owe you my life," the man choked between gasps.

"Just sit easy until I find something to bind your head with. We've got to get you some help fast. You're losing too much blood." Will tore a strip off the Spaniard's linen shirt. "Take your hands down now."

Slowly, reluctantly, the man did as he was told.

Will saw why the injured man had been holding on so tightly; his scalp was bitten completely through in places. White bone gleamed dully against crimson streaks. The scalp was nearly detached around half the circle of the grizzly's bite. The man's face visibly slipped, his features wrinkling grotesquely.

Trying to keep the wounded man from seeing him shudder, Will worked swiftly to wrap the scalp with linen. Searching for the least injured place he could find, Will knotted the bandage there and prayed that the bleeding would stop.

Will had to guide the man's booted feet into the cracks in the rock in order for the mauled man to climb back down. Reaching the bottom, the trapper brought the young horseman a drink of water from the pool.

"I'll make you as comfortable as I can," said Will. "My name is Will Reed. I'm a stranger here, so I need you to tell me the quickest route to get help."

"No need, señor," replied the man. "I am Ricardo. Just let me catch my breath and perhaps you can get me one more drink of that excellent water."

When Will had done so, Ricardo placed two fingers against his tongue and blew a shrill whistle. *"Aiiee."* He winced. "I never knew whistling to hurt before!"

A few moments passed and the bay horse trotted back into the clearing. Lather covered his neck and flanks and his eyes were wild, but he came obediently at his master's signal.

"Do you want me to walk and lead him?" asked Will.

"Not necessary. Lorenzo can carry both of us, and he knows the way home."

Assisting Ricardo into the high-cantled saddle, Will mounted behind him.

"If you can take the reins, señor, I think perhaps I will concentrate on not falling off again," he said to Will. Although it had slowed, blood was still flowing from the lacerations and dripping from Ricardo's matted hair.

"Señor, if it is far to your home, then we should seek help

sooner," observed Will, keeping a tight grip on the reins to prevent the keyed-up stallion from racing down the trail.

A weak voice haltingly responded, "Turn the bay . . . at the fork . . . the mission is just . . ." Then Ricardo's voice faded out altogether.

Will had heard all that was necessary. He settled himself firmly, gripping with his knees, and wrapped one arm around the now unconscious rider. "Come on, Lorenzo," he urged. "Move out."

The long-legged bay stretched out his neck and doubled his speed.

Just over the crest of a small hill, the horse broke free of the surrounding brush. Less than a mile below them to the west was the whitewashed mission. Its single bell tower glistened white against the green landscape and the blue of the ocean beyond.

Will rode directly to the steps of the mission. Small adobe houses and thatched huts crowded the square in front of the great church. It was midafternoon and the square was nearly empty.

The clattering entrance of Lorenzo and the spectacle of the buckskin-clad stranger holding tightly to the bloodied body in front of him caused instant commotion. People poured into the square from every direction; then someone rang an alarm bell.

A gray-haired man dressed in the cowled gray robe of a Franciscan padre hurried down the front steps of the mission. At the sight of Ricardo's waxy complexion caked with gore, the priest crossed himself and cried out, "What has happened? Who has murdered poor Ricardo?"

"A grizzly, Father. But he's still alive," explained Will. "Please help me ease him down."

The priest called two neophyte Indians to assist him, and the three gently received Ricardo's limp body. As they moved quickly around the side of the building, the priest called back over his shoulder, "We have an infirmary. Follow us."

Will stepped from the horse and looked around for someone to hold the bay. A young boy approached and offered to care for Lorenzo.

In front of the mission was a fountain bubbling with clear water. Will decided that what he needed more than the infirmary was a quick wash and a long drink. Stepping over to the pool, he washed

Ricardo's blood from his hands and face with double handfuls of water. Once the filth was cleansed away, Will bent over the fountain and drank deeply.

When he stood upright, he saw that everyone in the square was staring at him with undisguised curiosity. Neophytes in short tunics like that worn by Paco were standing in groups, evidently discussing him. At a long tank fed by the outflow of the fountain, mission women stopped their laundry chores to gaze at him. Across the square, a mixed group of soldiers and men dressed in short jackets and tight pants were pointing at him and gesturing. A dark-skinned priest in a gray robe stared for a minute, then hurried from the mission.

For the first time in a long while, Will was embarrassed. He was grateful when one of the Indians who had helped carry Ricardo returned and approached him. "Father Sanchez asks if you are wounded also. He wants you to come."

"No, I'm all right," responded Will. "But I would like to see how Ricardo is doing."

CHAPTER 15

"Please, allow me to pour you some more wine," Father Sanchez offered.

"No, thanks," responded Will. "It beats anything I ever tried before, though. Did you have it brought by ship?"

The pudgy friar chuckled. "Only if you mean the rootstock. We made this wine from grapes grown on our own sunny hillsides." He poured himself another glassful and sipped with an appreciative pride. "We are trying other varieties of grapes as well, but I think this will rival any zinfandel in the world."

As Will sat back from the linen-covered dining table, an Indian servant whisked away his empty dinner plate, and another removed the silver serving tray bearing the remains of a joint of mutton.

The trapper glanced down at his stained buckskin clothes. Even washed, wrung out, and dried, they still smelled of woodsmoke and carried the stains of hunting, fighting, and overland journeying. Since arriving at the mission this afternoon, Will had cleaned up and shaved, but his unruly thatch of hair and travel-weary clothing embarrassed him.

"You live very well," observed Will.

"It is surprising, isn't it, here on the edge of the world?" replied Father Sanchez. "Of course I am just the inheritor from great men of faith like Fathers Serra and Garces. When they arrived, they had to live in reed huts like the Indians. Can you imagine that? But look what has been achieved in less than sixty years."

"What about the Indians, Father?" prompted Will as a servant placed a china cup of fragrantly steaming hot chocolate before him.

"Oh, they are such children." The priest laughed. "We have all we can handle constantly checking on them to see if they have followed instructions. They are likely to run off and go fishing instead of working, but they are good-hearted, simple people. We have such a large neophyte population now that we can hire out the young men to the local ranchos for wages."

"What do the workers do with their pay?" inquired Will.

"Bless me." Father Sanchez chuckled. "You don't think such simple ones are responsible enough to handle *money*? Oh no! I meant that their wages are credited to the mission's account, of course, to balance what we purchase in supplies."

"Don't your workers resent giving up all their pay?"

Father Sanchez looked as if this were an astounding thought. "Why should they? They receive all the necessities from our hands." He glanced at his own soft, plump fingers. "No one forced them to become neophytes, señor, and we keep no secrets from them before or after they join our community."

"Isn't it true that most of those young workers are born to Christian families already attached to the mission?"

"That is correct," agreed the padre. "Sadly, the unbelievers of the interior are not as receptive as those of the coast."

"I'm not so sure that's true," responded Will. He informed the Mexican priest of the interest in Christianity he had seen among the Yokuts. "But there is something else going on as well. They seem very suspicious of your people, Father. I understand a very hostile tribe of desert dwellers is already at war with you."

"You must understand that this is a time of confusion," commented Father Sanchez. "We Mexicans have only been free of the yoke of Spain these past ten years. I am Mexican born, but many of the highest-ranking families like that of Ricardo's father are highly suspect to the Mexican officials.

"Moreover, there is much strife in Mexico itself. The military officials have so many conflicts that they have adopted harsh measures against many tribes. We hope to prosper here in California without such difficulties, but who can say?"

The padre's discussion was interrupted by an Indian servant announcing that Captain Zuniga had arrived.

The little priest frowned, the only time during the meal Will had seen him do so. "I wonder what he can want?" muttered Father Sanchez. Turning to Will, he added, "Excuse me a moment, please."

But before the friar could rise from the table, a lean man with a scarred face advanced into the room. He was accompanied by two soldiers wearing bull-hide vests and carrying flintlock muskets. This did not look to Will like a friendly visit.

"Ah, Captain Zuniga," Father Sanchez said graciously, "may I introduce my guest, Will Reed. He is the trapper from the East who rescued young Rivera."

"The American spy, you mean," said Zuniga abruptly. "Why was he not reported to me immediately? Where are his papers?"

Will answered the questions for himself, trying to smother the instant dislike and hostility he felt. "I only just got here, Captain. The good Father allowed me to get cleaned up and treated me to a fine dinner. I'm no spy. I was part of a trapping party that was attacked by Mojaves. Captain Beckwith was our leader. He had papers from the governor of Santa Fe, but Beckwith didn't make—"

"Silence!" shouted Zuniga. "I have heard enough. I arrest you as a spy. Take him away!"

Will was immediately seized by the two soldiers.

Zuniga grabbed the necklace of woodpecker topknots and ripped it from Will's neck. The captain ground it under his boot as he followed his captive toward the door.

Sanchez protested, "But he saved the boy's life—brought him here to the mission. You can't do this!"

The captain turned and remarked coldly, "You had better keep quiet, Father. Harboring a spy is treason, and traitors are hanged." He paused to let the point sink in before adding maliciously, "Just like spies."

CHAPTER 16

Will's adobe cell was exactly eight paces long and eight paces wide. After twenty or thirty trips each direction, he could have walked blindfolded and stopped with the tip of his nose one-half inch from the wall.

He actually had been blindfolded and his hands tied behind his back with cords for the march to the cell. These were removed when he was thrust into the prison. There was a tiny window in the stout oak door, but it was already night in Santa Barbara and nothing could be seen.

By feeling around the small cell in the dark, Will stumbled onto a wooden bucket, presumably used for a chamber pot. He also found a moth-eaten blanket, but its prior owners—thousands of fleas—were still in residence. Tossing it to a corner of the cell, Will spent the night pacing the bare earthen floor, thinking and scratching.

* * *

"So, Don José, now that we have him, what are we going to do with him?" inquired Captain Zuniga.

"For the time being, nothing."

"Nothing!" exploded the hot-tempered captain. "How long do you think it will be before Don Pedro blasts us from Monterey to Mexico City for imprisoning the man who saved his son? He is still a powerful man and can hurt our plans with Figueroa—perhaps even get me recalled."

The ranchero rocked back and forth on his small feet, a smirk of smug satisfaction on his face. "So, when Don Pedro demands the American's release or when a letter is sent to the governor, you will obligingly release him."

"But why antagonize Rivera first?"

Zuniga hated the condescension with which Dominguez spoke, but he was forced to listen to an explanation that dripped with it. "My dear captain, you will be at your most politically astute. You will say to Don Pedro, 'So sorry . . . just following orders . . . anxious to please you . . . completely understand.' Don Pedro will accept your apologies and be mollified at your willingness to see reason, despite your having acted in accordance with written law."

"But what is the point of this charade?" demanded the blunt man of action.

"If we win the confidence of Don Pedro, all is well. If not, well, it gives us something to hold over him."

"You mean—"

"Of course. If need be, the American will be *proven* a spy. And who is it that demanded his release against standing orders? The traitor Don Pedro Rivera y Cruz."

* * *

"Careful! Slowly now! Set him down gently!" Francesca Rivera y Cruz saw to it that her brother was carried safely upstairs to his bedroom. Then she took personal charge of tucking him in bed and changing his bandages.

Though she caught her breath at the severity of the gashes in his scalp, she bit her lip and said nothing. Ricardo protested that Father Sanchez had just renewed the compresses before allowing him to go home, but Francesca swallowed the lump in her throat and told her brother to hush and lie still or he'd be going back to the padre. He complied.

When she was convinced that Ricardo was properly attended to, she decided to ride to the mission to thank the good father and the American from the East who had teamed together to save her brother's life.

Francesca called the stable boy to put her sidesaddle on the buckskin. She had always been too impatient to ride in a slowly creaking carreta anywhere, let alone all the way to Santa Barbara. Off she cantered, leaving her father and aunt to look after Ricardo.

The ride along the curving lanes was a familiar one. Once each week Francesca devoted a day to teaching mission children how to read. Mission policy stated that the children begin work at the looms at the age of nine. Francesca felt that if the neophytes were ever to become *gente de razón,* people of reason, they needed to be able to read and write.

Although Father Sanchez applauded her assistance, not everyone believed this was a good thing. Some of her father's friends said that education made the Indians think too highly of themselves. Others thought it beneath the dignity of a daughter of an important family to befriend the Indian children. Francesca ignored both opinions, and her father could only shrug and reply, "In her heart, she takes after her sainted mother."

As she rode into the dusty plaza in front of the mission, several children were playing near the fountain. Seeing her, they dashed to greet her. "Doña Francesca," they called, "today is not the day for lessons, is it?"

"No, children." She smiled in return. "Not today. I will be back on Friday as usual. Where is Father Sanchez?"

The brown-skinned children directed her along the arched colonnade, past the front of the church. The largest boy of her class reported having seen the priest enter the *mayordomo*'s quarters on the east side of the mission. Francesca rewarded him by allowing him to hold her horse, which made him immensely proud and the envy of his friends. She hurried to the red-tile-roofed home that stood in the shadow of the bell tower. Reaching its porch, she met Sanchez coming out.

"Ah, Francesca," he called anxiously. "Your brother insisted on going home this morning, and I agreed against my better judgment. Is he all right? No sudden turn for the worse?"

"He's fine, Father," she reassured the priest. "I came to thank you for attending him. I also want to thank the man Ricardo tells us saved his life. Where is he? We want to invite him to be a guest in our home."

The chubby padre looked embarrassed and awkwardly shuffled his sandaled feet. "I did not tell Ricardo this morning because I did not want to upset him."

Now it was Francesca's turn to be concerned. "Tell him what? What has happened?"

"The American—Will Reed is his name—has been arrested. Captain Zuniga came last night and took him to the presidio."

"For what?" exclaimed Francesca. "What has he done?"

"Nothing, to my knowledge. Zuniga says the American is without papers or something. In fact, I was just going over the day's work plans with our *mayordomo*, and then I intended to ride out to your home to explain this to your father."

Francesca raised her chin in determination. "That will not be necessary. I will go home at once and tell him myself!"

CHAPTER 17

Toward dawn Will had dozed off. His weary body had slid down a wall to a seated position, and there he remained as gray light filled the tiny barred window, filtering around the cracks of the door.

The creaking of the heavy door on reluctant hinges brought him awake. Jumping to his feet, he found himself staring into the muzzle of a musket. The soldier aiming it told him to back to the opposite wall and not move until the door was shut again.

Will asked several questions of the soldier, but neither he nor his companion made any response. The second soldier set down a wooden bowl and clay jug, then slammed the stout door closed.

The bottle was full of water, for which Will was grateful, but he found it impossible to give thanks for the food. The bowl contained a mixture of cooked beans and cornmeal with a greasy scum layering the thick mush and drowned weevils floating on the top. A rancid stench attacked Will's nostrils.

He placed the bowl near the door, took the jug of water, and for the second time backed away from the entrance. *Could probably use that stuff to kill the fleas in the blanket.*

Once again he fell to brooding about his situation. He had been attacked by the Mojaves for being an accomplice of the Mexicans. Now the Mexicans figured him for somebody's spy. He berated himself for leaving the Yokuts. *Did this happen to the Good Samaritan? Maybe next time someone's in trouble it should be every man for himself!*

Will had plenty of time to wonder how serious the threat of

hanging might be. Of course, if the quality of the fare did not improve, he'd starve to death before they could hang him.

By afternoon, yellow light filled the hole of the door. Taking a deep breath, Will moved the bowl and its noxious contents to the same corner as the vermin-filled blanket.

The opening was only big enough for one eye at a time. Bending down a little, he pressed half his face into it.

He was looking across a dusty courtyard of what was evidently the military garrison. Two soldiers passed, one of them leading a mule. He made out the shadow of a tall pole, perhaps a flagpole, even though he could not see the staff itself.

"Zuniga!" boomed a voice in a no-nonsense tone. "Zuniga, where is the American? I want him out now or heads will roll, starting with yours!"

Will could see that the dusty grounds of the presidio had suddenly been stirred into a flurry of activity.

A balding man, whose obvious anger emphasized his muscular size, galloped into the courtyard. The horse he rode was as black as midnight and he led a fine gray, but the newcomer's face was flushed a deep red that spread over his bald head. The veins of his neck bulged dangerously.

Will watched him fling himself from the charger and contemptuously toss the reins to a startled soldier. The man demanded something of the soldier. But Will could only make out another booming, "Zuniga!"

Shrinking back from the large man's fury, the soldier pointed a shaking arm over the man's shoulder.

Will glimpsed the captain who had arrested him at the mission advancing into the scrap of his vision. The officer was in full uniform, almost as if he had been expecting this visit.

The volume of the shouted demands fell as Zuniga made calming gestures. Next he nodded vigorously and motioned toward Will's cell. The two men turned and headed toward the scout.

Will stepped back against the far wall. A rattle announced that the bolt holding the bar in place across the cell door was pulled free. Then the door swung open.

The large man strode directly into the small space. "You are the American who saved my son from the grizzly." The man offered this as a statement, not a question, but Will nodded anyway.

"I am Don Pedro Rivera y Cruz," stated the ranchero formally. "I am completely and totally in your debt and have come to see that you are immediately freed." He whirled to face Captain Zuniga and repeated, "Immediately."

The officer shrugged. "Of course, Don Pedro. As you wish. We were simply following the standing orders for treatment of those who arrive in our country without proper papers. I am sure you understand that—"

The ranchero waved his large hand and raised his voice again. "Enough! I want this fine man out of your—" he wrinkled his nose in disgust—"your accommodations this instant."

"But certainly," answered Zuniga, "you will accept personal responsibility for his whereabouts and behavior?"

"Yes, yes," snapped Don Pedro. "Bring my horses around now!"

Outside the gate of the presidio, Don Pedro's angry flush had faded, and he spoke apologetically to Will. "I cannot begin to express my sorrow at your treatment, Señor Reed. What must you think of our manners to take such a heroic gentleman as yourself and throw you into such a . . . such a . . . hole?"

The two men were riding side by side, Will mounted on the handsome gray. "The captain's hospitality was less than cordial," he agreed, "but I've been treated worse. If he was only following orders, I guess it wasn't his fault."

"Ha!" snorted Don Pedro. "He's up to something, that one. Currying favor with his commanding general, no doubt."

"Your pardon, señor, but are you a military man yourself? You sit your horse like one and a magnificent beast he is too."

Don Pedro's smile expressed his approval of Will's judgment. "You have an eye for horses and horsemen, eh, young man? Yes, I am retired from the army. I received my land and El Negro here as recompense for my years of service. But the young officers today . . ." He gave a contemptuous gesture with his free hand.

"And how is your son?" inquired Will.

"Out of danger, God be praised. You will see for yourself soon."

"We are returning to the mission then?"

"No, no. You are going to be the honored guest of my humble home. Ricardo was allowed to come home and is anxious to express his gratitude. But now, tell me about yourself."

The horses kept up an easy, slow canter that covered the ground in a fluid motion. Will related his experiences since joining the trapping party, the Mojave ambush, and his time with the Yokuts.

"That reminds me, señor," said Will, interrupting his own story. "I came from the Sierras with a mission Indian named Paco, but he disappeared when the grizzly attacked. Do you know him?"

"Paco is a knave and a coward. You are fortunate he did not murder you in your sleep. Give him no more thought. He certainly ran away to save his own skin. If he appears, he shall receive the flogging he so richly deserves." Don Pedro cast an appraising eye over Will's riding form. "You ride very well. What do you think of Flotada?"

"Flotada? Oh, 'massage'? Do you call him that because of his gentle rocking movement?"

Don Pedro laughed, a deep, resonant laugh that bounced off the green peaks and echoed through the oaks. "Now, yes! But you should have seen him when he was an uneducated brute. We called him Flotada because he *bucked so hard*!"

"My congratulations," offered Will. "He is well mannered now and a real looker."

"He should be, young man. Flotada is a true son of Andalusian Tordas, the Spanish grays. And—" the ranchero paused—"he is yours."

CHAPTER 18

"This is your 'humble' home?" exclaimed Will at the first sight of Don Pedro's rancho. "It is magnificent!"

A flock of pigeons swirled like a cloud of white-and-gray smoke at the riders' approach. The whitewashed, two-story, adobe building was nearly eighty feet across its porticoed front. A veranda completely encircled the home, matched by a second-story balcony.

A trio of Indian servants ran to meet the returning ranchero and his guest. Two of them accepted the reins of El Negro and Flotada, while the third, bowing low first, led the way to the main entrance.

Outside the front door was a bench. Don Pedro sat down, the servant kneeling in front of him. At Will's curious glance, he smiled and explained, "The floors in my home are polished oak. My dear wife, God rest her soul, made me promise to never wear my spurs into the house."

He gestured at Will's moccasins. "You do not have that need at present; however, we will soon have you outfitted properly."

Don Pedro led the way. An enormously tall clock with a polished brass pendulum the size and shape of a banjo graced the entryway.

The ranchero gestured toward a formal parlor as they passed it. "My family and servants would all like to meet you, but first Ricardo wishes to thank you. He is confined to his bed upstairs."

The hallway terminated in a broad, elegant staircase leading to the second floor. Dressed in his travel-worn buckskins, Will felt even more out of place here than at the mission.

Don Pedro brought him to the second doorway at the right of

the stairs. Propped up in an oversized four-poster bed was Ricardo. His head was swathed in bandages, and his color looked faded.

Seeing Will, Ricardo raised a hand in greeting. An attempted smile only brought pain to the already stretched skin of his face. "You will pardon me, señor, if I cannot rise to greet you. The good Father Sanchez, who is the only doctor we have in Santa Barbara, forbids me to move about yet."

"Señor, think nothing of it. To have met *oso pardo* face-to-face and live to tell of it! Your grandchildren will beg to hear this story over and over," commented Will.

"Yes, head-to-head even," corrected Ricardo ruefully. "And the living here to tell of it is solely due to your intervention."

Will shuffled his moccasins awkwardly. "God let our paths cross at just that instant, so your thanks are due to Him. Had you been armed and I the one attacked, you would have done the same for me." Then to forestall any further expressions of gratitude, Will asked for more details about the young ranchero's recuperation.

"The good padre stitched my scalp back so tightly that I fear I may look more like a citizen of Cathay than of Mexico. He assures me that all will be well in time, even my left ear, which he at first despaired of saving."

Don Pedro, who had been listening from the doorway, added that Will's speedy actions had saved Ricardo's manly good looks as well as his life. "If he is to make me a grandfather, it is well if the young ladies do not run away in terror when he approaches."

Turning to Will, he said, "Ricardo must rest now, but we would like you to remain as our guest for as long as you wish. The room next to this is prepared for your use and . . . you may wish . . . you will find . . . there are some articles of clothing that should fit you," he concluded delicately.

Will looked from father to son and saw the same expectantly hopeful expression. "It would be my great pleasure to be your guest."

"Good!" said Don Pedro, clapping. He appeared to regret his enthusiasm a second later when Ricardo winced at the sudden loud noise. "Shh," he instructed unnecessarily. "Ricardo needs quiet for a time."

The two men closed the door as they exited the room. "Would you care to join me in the parlor in an hour's time?" asked the ranchero. At Will's agreement, he showed the trapper to the guest room, then turned and went downstairs.

The room was the equal of Ricardo's. There was a finely made walnut armoire and matching dresser and a bed with a feather mattress that looked three feet thick. Trying to recall the last time he had slept on a bed, Will concluded that nothing he had ever slept on deserved to be called a bed compared to this. "Hope I don't drown in it." He chuckled to himself.

Neatly laid out across the silk coverlet was not just one set of clothing but multiple sets—dress pants, silk shirts, stylish jackets, undergarments. Will wondered what the correct dress was and if he could figure out what went with what. He determined to locate Don Pedro and ask for advice.

Opening the door to find his way downstairs, he bumped headlong into a young woman carrying a bowl and a pitcher of water. In the momentary jostle that followed, Will ended up catching the pitcher just before its contents spilled on the floor. "Excuse me," he said in English, then changing to Spanish, "I mean, *perdón*!"

The girl, dressed in a dark red skirt and a white scooped-neck blouse, had shining dark hair that fell softly over smoothly rounded shoulders.

Completely caught off guard, Will lapsed again into English and stammered, "Say, you're really something!"

"*Cómo*, señor?" returned the girl, looking confused.

Will watched as a rosy glow spread up the señorita's throat to her cheeks. Her complexion, like a fine porcelain cup held up to firelight, set off her lovely dark eyes.

Finally collecting himself, Will said in Spanish, "No harm done, señorita. No need to be embarrassed. Were you bringing these for me?"

"*Sí*, Señor," she murmured demurely, looking at the floor.

"*Gracias*," said Will, taking the bowl from the girl. "Would you tell your master that I'd like his advice on proper dress?"

A curious expression flashed through the young woman's eyes as she looked quickly at Will's face and then away. She pointed toward a complete suit hanging over a chair in the corner of the room. "Not necessary, señor. Perhaps that one there?"

"Ah. Yes. Just right," mumbled Will as the girl departed.

Will dressed in his new California splendor. But he found his thoughts drifting to the beautiful maid in the Rivera household.

The white serge pants went on underneath. The second pair was heavier dark green wool. They buttoned with silver barrel buttons down the outside of each leg. Because Don Pedro was wearing something similar, Will knew that the overbritches were left unbuttoned below the knee so the white trouser legs would show.

A finely woven white-linen shirt was intended to be worn under a short dark green jacket. The jacket also sported silver clasps to match the pants, but Will had noticed the clasps were left open.

White-linen stockings and glove-soft buckskin boots accompanied the outfit. Also included was a flat-crowned, stiff-brimmed black hat trimmed with a horsehair hatband braided with silver beads. Will elected to omit the hat until something could be done with his hair, which would never fit under the crown now.

Shaved, smelling of lilac water, and dressed in the fanciest apparel he'd ever touched, Will cautiously admired himself in the mirror. Around the high collar of the white shirt he knotted a black cravat. The last time he had worn a necktie had been at his uncle's funeral in Vicksburg.

Taken altogether, not half bad, he thought. *I guess that maidservant will approve.* He heard the clock in the downstairs hall strike the hour. *Now to see if the rest of the household agrees.*

Stepping onto the landing at the head of the stairs, Will saw Don Pedro awaiting him at the bottom. "*Bueno,* Señor Reed, you look splendid. Please come along and meet my family."

The sitting room was already filled with people. Seated in the middle of the group was a gray-haired woman with a rather prim expression. She was introduced as Aunt Doña Eulalia. The household matriarch inspected Will closely before suggesting her approval by extending her hand.

Gathered around her chair were the household servants, the head foreman of the rancho, and several godchildren of Don Pedro. Each acknowledged the introduction with a bow or curtsy of respect as protocol demanded for the savior of the heir.

When the formal introductions were completed, everyone seemed to relax, until Don Pedro said, "Where is Francesca? Why isn't she here?"

From the hallway behind Will a lilting female voice announced, "I'm over here, Father. Everyone was in such a hurry to met Señor Reed that I was left to put up my hair by myself."

At the first sound of her voice, Will had been startled, then embarrassed. He had mistaken Don Pedro's *daughter* for a servant. Now it was his turn to feel the heat of a flush rising in his cheeks as he tried to recall their exchange. What had he said? Had he been too forward? Was she offended?

Dressed in fine lace instead of the simple skirt and blouse worn earlier, Francesca entered the room adjusting a lace mantilla on a high comb. She looked the part of a Spanish princess. Her eyes seemed to have a mocking quality as they locked with Will's, as if to say, *The tables are turned now, aren't they?*

But she said nothing to give away the game. Advancing directly toward Will, she offered her hand in greeting, then called to the others, "All right now. Introductions are complete. Must we be so stiff?"

Taking the tongue-tied Will by the arm, she guided an instantly chattering throng into the dining room. Bustling servants soon piled a feast of monumental proportions onto the table.

A steaming tureen of *sopa de carne seca y arroz* was placed before Doña Eulalia, who stood at one end of the table opposite Don Pedro. Will and Francesca were across from each other in the middle of each side, flanked by the godchildren.

Don Pedro recited a blessing over the food; then all were seated. When the tureen's cover was raised, the tantalizing aroma of spicy jerky-and-rice soup filled the air. Doña Eulalia tasted the first portion before allowing a maid to ladle a serving into each diner's bowl.

Will found himself staring into the soup bowl, looking for the courage to raise his face to Francesca's. Since no inspiration came, he occupied himself by taking several mouthfuls of the soup. It was not until the fourth swallow that the chili seasoning took effect, causing Will to grab for his water glass.

He was afraid he had shamed himself again until he heard Don Pedro praise the mixture by declaring, "Whew! This broth is capable of raising the dead! Pass the tortillas and the water!"

Roast lamb accompanied by beans, corn, and tortillas was seasoned by the spice of conversation. Everyone wanted to know Will's history and to hear his stories.

The children exclaimed over the tales of Will's wilderness wanderings and Indian ambushes. They all complimented him on his mastery of Spanish.

Finally gathering enough courage to look at Francesca, Will found that she appeared genuinely friendly and interested, with no trace of mocking. She said sincerely, "You may protest that it was Providence that brought you to meet the grizzly, but it was your decision to face the bear when you could have thought only of yourself. *Gracias*, Señor Reed, thank you."

"In two weeks," announced Don Pedro," we will have a fiesta and invite all our neighbors to share in honoring Señor Reed."

Excited squeals broke out from the younger children around the table.

After dinner, Will managed to find a moment alone with Francesca. "I want to apologize," he said quietly, "for mistaking you for a—for a servant, I mean."

"Doña Eulalia would have scolded *me* for not correcting you at once," she replied with a sincere smile. Offering her smooth white hand to Will, Francesca said politely, "Let us say no more about it."

Then she left Will with the memory of her hand in his.

CHAPTER 19

"Most esteemed Don Pedro," began Don Dominguez.

Such formal speech coming from a neighbor, thought Don Pedro. *I wonder what is coming next.*

"For some time I have given careful consideration to a matter of great importance," continued Dominguez, "and I have decided that the time is correct for me to approach you."

"Go on," said Don Pedro cautiously.

"We are not getting any younger, you and I."

"This is most certainly true," agreed the ranchero. "Do you have a way to prevent it? Perhaps you have discovered a spring of magic water on your property such as the Indios say exists near Paso Robles?"

Don Dominguez looked offended at the jesting tone of his neighbor's reply. He ran his hands through his hair as if straightening his ruffled dignity before speaking again. "As you are aware, I have no son, no heir to my estate. I am, alas, childless."

Aware that this matter was a difficult and socially delicate one for any ranchero, Don Pedro at once became properly subdued.

"You yourself," Don Dominguez resumed, "almost lost, most tragically, the staff of your old age, Don Ricardo."

Don Pedro nodded and felt again the stab of terror he had experienced when first hearing about Ricardo's injury. Dominguez had gained his complete attention.

"Fate has played with your future in a most devilish fashion. First, your lovely daughter loses her betrothed almost on the eve of her wedding. Then you lost your sainted wife, and now almost your son. Do you not see how Providence has preserved you from the misery of Job?"

"I *am* very much aware of how blessed I am that I *still* have two strong, healthy children."

"Is it possible you have missed the divine warning within this blessing? Certainly you see that you must take steps to secure the future, even as I have?"

"What steps exactly?"

"I have decided to adopt Captain Zuniga as my son and heir, and I would like to announce this important decision at your fiesta."

"I congratulate you. You are certainly welcome to make this announcement at our festivities, but wouldn't you prefer to hold one of your own for the purpose?"

Dominguez smiled at Don Pedro. "But for the second announcement, this would be the proper procedure."

"What second announcement?"

Speaking very carefully, Don Dominguez explained, "Times are very uncertain, are they not? The Mexican government, if it can be called such, changes almost daily, except in its disregard for us Californios. We must be prepared to take charge of our own destiny."

"You wish to make a political speech at my fiesta?" Don Pedro asked, surprised.

"No, no!" corrected Dominguez. "You misunderstand me. My point is that you have been most understandably protective of your daughter. But it is time for you to secure her future and yours. My good friend and soon-to-be heir, Captain Zuniga, has asked me to petition you for the hand of your daughter in marriage."

Don Pedro's first reaction was to be offended at what struck him as a very presumptuous proposal. But on second thought, maybe it made a thread of sense. Zuniga was a strong, though not especially likable man, and he was of a suitable age to marry Francesca. Though not a landowner, if the officer were Dominguez's heir, he would inherit sizable holdings. Moreover, some Rivera property bordered on Dominguez's rancho, and if something should happen to Ricardo while he was unmarried, at least Francesca could retain the land.

"I will not give you an answer at the present, but I will think on this matter," concluded Don Pedro.

"*Gracias*, Don Pedro. That is all I ask."

CHAPTER 20

"Quiet, here he comes now," cautioned Don Dominguez to Father Quintana. "Do you understand what to do?"

"Perfectly," assured the little priest.

The two plotters were seated on a low adobe wall that edged the plaza of Pueblo Santa Barbara. They had chosen their location well: just around the corner from the cantina where Don Pedro Rivera y Cruz liked to enjoy a pot of hot, dark chocolate after an early morning ride into town.

Seeing the ranchero arrive and drop off his horse at the livery stable, the two had ample time to secure their position. Don Pedro was seated at his favorite table near the plaza and already sipping his favorite beverage when they began to speak.

In a voice just loud enough to carry to Don Pedro's ears, Dominguez began, "I just don't know what to do, Father."

"I am certain that you will do what is right, my son," soothed the padre.

"Yes, but which is correct? To carry a tale that may be only malicious rumor or to warn my neighbor against what may be a snake in the grass?"

It was clear by now that Don Pedro's ears had identified their voices and pricked up at the word *neighbor.*

"Tell me all the particulars. Perhaps I can assist you in making up your mind. Rest assured, I will tell no one."

"I do not want to slander anyone. Father, you know that."

"Rest easy, Don José; tell me the worst."

"It concerns this American, this Will Reed. As you know, Father, he came here overland as a trader in furs . . . a so-called mountain man."

"Yes, my son, go on," encouraged Father Quintana. He hoped Don Pedro was thinking the same thing.

"It has been reported to me that this is a bloodthirsty man who has killed before and will undoubtedly kill again."

Quintana made light of the accusation. "But surely he has fought his way through territory held by savages. One must not judge—"

"Yes, Father, but there is more. He lived for a long time with the Indios . . . like the Indios. He has had Indian wives and more than one, indulging in heathen and perverted customs I cannot speak of."

"Is this true, Don Dominguez? Can it be proven?"

"Oh no, Father. I heard it from . . . well, no matter . . . another wayfarer, who had no reason to lie. But tell me, Father, what would be best to do?" Dominguez stood, brushed off the seat of his dark blue trousers, and straightened his hat.

Quintana stretched as he rose and smoothed out his coarse gray robe.

✶ ✶ ✶

Though Don Pedro strained his ears, he could not make out any more of the conversation as the two men strolled off across the dusty, sunlit plaza.

Ten minutes later he was still sitting, leaning his hand on one work-thickened palm. A waiter finally stopped to ask if the chocolate was unsatisfactory.

Don Pedro peered into his cup with as much distaste as if it contained vinegar. "No, nothing is satisfactory this morning."

✶ ✶ ✶

From the window of his study, Don Pedro watched his daughter stroll slowly across the courtyard with Will Reed. They were engaged in a lively conversation, a fact which did not altogether please him. They walked like two people more interested in each other than in where they were going. Neither seemed to notice the flowers that bloomed on the trellis and lined the adobe-tiled path. Nor did they look up at the blue sky and admire the clear, cloudless weather. No. Each looked only at the other as they walked aimlessly.

Sunlight glinted on the raven black hair of Francesca as if to illuminate the vast difference between her and the copper-haired mountain man. They were a world apart: separate cultures, vastly different lives, different religions. So what was it about this Yankee that so animated the face of Don Pedro's daughter?

He frowned as he considered the question. Perhaps it was those differences that interested Francesca. Yes, that must be the explanation. The very things that drew Francesca to Will Reed now would certainly cause her great heartache if the friendship developed into anything more. She would be better with one of her own kind. Perhaps a man like Captain Zuniga?

At that moment the trapper must have said something amusing, for Francesca burst into laughter. She was enjoying herself far too much.

Don Pedro rocked onto his toes in a gesture that signified displeasure. Why did she not have a chaperone? Where was Doña Eulalia, who should have been walking within earshot of the couple?

"Doña Eulalia!" Don Pedro called his sister, but he did not leave his place at the window.

His eyes widened as Francesca stooped to pluck an orange poppy, which she then tucked behind the ear of Will Reed. More laughter.

Once again, Don Pedro called the delinquent aunt. This time it was a bellow, raising the clatter of footsteps on the stair behind him. *She'd better be here in a hurry,* he thought irritably. As Francesca's chaperone, Doña Eulalia had failed today and he would find out why.

A timid knock sounded at his door. Don Pedro called his permission to enter, but instead of his sister it was her servant girl who appeared.

He turned from his observation to glower at the poor girl. "Where is your mistress?"

"She sent me to say she is ill. She begs your pardon." The girl's hands trembled as did her voice. It was rare for Don Pedro to raise his voice in the house.

"Then you will have to do," Don Pedro said grimly. "Go tell Francesca I wish to speak with her alone. Now!"

The servant nodded, then hesitated. "Francesca . . ."

"She is in the courtyard." Don Pedro gestured out the window as if to give the frightened woman every clue as to his displeasure. "Go! Tell her to come to my study!"

Francesca's eyes were bright with amusement as she considered the poppy in Will Reed's hair. "I have often been amazed when a horse has been left to run the back pastures for a season, how much time it takes to get it presentable for riding. You have curried and combed out nicely for one so long in the mountains."

"I take it that is a compliment of sorts?"

"Proper tack. A good bridle and saddle. A few hours pulling the burrs from the mane. These help the appearance of a horse but do not always mean he adapts to civilization."

Will smiled and shrugged. "I have not always worn moccasins, you know. It's just that man and beast must adapt to their surroundings or perish."

"They say you are as much an Indian as the Indians." She turned from him as if she suddenly noticed the flowers and had to stop and consider them.

"In some ways they are as civilized as you or I."

She whirled around. "I differ with you in that opinion. They are ignorant and godless and—"

"Ignorant of the ways of the white man, but like the wild horses, they know the tracks and trails of their world better than you imagine. To them, you might be considered ignorant, Francesca."

She tossed her hair as a mare might toss its mane. Clearly she did not like his reply. "They have no knowledge of God . . . or of the church."

At this, Will did not argue. He looked thoughtfully at the sky as a blackbird sailed across it. He smiled slightly as though he remembered something . . . *someone.* . . . "You are right in some ways. Death is imponderable to them. They have no real idea of what will come after this life." He shrugged. "But they are just as much eternal souls as you and I. Just as valuable to God as a mission priest, a ranchero, or a ranchero's daughter."

"What do you mean?" she shot back, genuinely offended at his thinly veiled accusation. "That is why there are missions here."

"Jesus Christ was never brutal, never physically cruel. I have heard enough reports about some mission Indians to know that—"

Their conversation was cut short by the servant of Doña Eulalia who cleared her throat nervously behind them.

Both Will and Francesca turned to stare at her a moment before she found the courage to speak.

"Your father wishes a word with you, señorita," she ventured, looking toward the study window that framed the figure of Don Pedro.

Francesca raised her eyes toward the window and flushed.

So, Will thought, *Don Pedro has been watching us.*

"Perhaps we shall continue our conversation later, Will Reed," she said in a suddenly cool tone. Then she brushed past him, hurried across the courtyard and into the house.

Her father's silence was ominous as Francesca sat and watched him pace the length of the study. His hands were clasped behind his back, a posture he assumed when he was constructing decrees that must be obeyed the instant he pronounced them. Francesca wondered what she might have done to stir his displeasure.

Finally Don Pedro spoke. "This Americano is not one of us." His opening words were like the death knell rung out by the mission bell after someone died. There was no mistaking the somber meaning.

"No, Father." She said what was necessary and required. Understanding the deeper meaning of his statement, she pretended only to hear the truth that Will Reed was quite different than anyone else in California.

"You were talking with him." A stinging accusation, intimating that whatever they were talking about could not be entirely proper.

"About the Indians, Father."

Don Pedro frowned. Everyone knew of the immoral and inhuman practices of the Indians. Was the trapper speaking of the unspeakable to his innocent daughter? "What of the Indios?"

Francesca phrased the discussion lightly. "Señor Reed would have made a dedicated priest, Father."

Don Pedro's expression betrayed his surprise. "What is that?"

"He has simply said all the things Mother used to say about them: that they are also eternal souls."

"Who . . . ?"

Her father was wading through his confusion, and Francesca was intent on keeping him away from his reason for calling her. "Yes, Señor Reed is convinced of the great value of the savages, Father. You must talk with him on the matter sometime. Almost word for word the things Mother used to say."

She did not mention that Will had spoken of the brutality of the missions against many of the native population. Now was a time to be careful as she related her conversation with Will. If she wished to speak again with him, she must walk softly through the maze of her father's disapproval.

"I should enjoy hearing his opinion, Francesca, but—"

She interrupted what she knew he was about to say. "Yes. I thought you might enjoy hearing his viewpoint. It is good for the mind to at least look at the ways of those who are so very . . . different from us." She did not add that often one found that there were not as many differences as one thought. "Perhaps after dinner then. You and Ricardo will enjoy his company. I have other things to attend to this afternoon, so I cannot join you. My day to teach the children." She rose and kissed her father on the cheek.

Don Pedro inhaled deeply. For a moment, he looked around the room, as if he were trying to locate his lost objections. She could see him trying to put his thoughts together. What was it he was going to forbid her to do? What had he been so angry about?

"You cannot join us for luncheon?" he asked finally.

"I will eat at the mission," she explained. "You know how the children look forward to their lessons. I cannot be late."

"So much like your mother," he muttered and kissed her on the top of her head. The relief was evident on his face . . . as if whatever worries he might have had had been proven unfounded.

Francesca was relieved to slip out of the study unscathed and without any fatherly decrees ringing in her ears. *There is still some hope,* she thought as she changed her clothes. Her father might see that the Yankee was not so different from them after all!

CHAPTER 21

"What is the urgency of this meeting, and what secrecy requires my arrival at this ungodly hour?" complained Captain Zuniga to Don Dominguez.

"Quiet down," ordered the ranchero. "My servants may be awakened by the noise you are making. They may gossip all they wish among themselves, but I do not want them carrying tales to others."

"What tales? What others?"

"Something new has come up. Something that makes it more important than ever for Figueroa to favor *us* and for our other—uh—business to be more productive than ever."

"What can be so new about raising cattle? Have you figured a way to grow a second hide on a steer? Now *that* would be news." The little captain sneered.

The burly ranchero pulled himself up haughtily. "I have a mind to dismiss you and keep this all to myself."

Zuniga knew that Domiguez never joked where greed was concerned, so he was suddenly all ears. "Your pardon, Don Dominguez. What is the nature of your news?"

Dominguez's shoulders relaxed at the change in Zuniga's tone. "Yesterday a vaquero of mine chased some steers up Canyon Perdido," Dominguez said. "Last winter's rains caused a mudslide there that uncovered a dark red rock face. The vaquero did not recognize the ore, but he thought it unusual enough to bring me a sample." He handed Zuniga a lump of rock.

"So?" questioned Zuniga. "It obviously is not gold or silver. This may be the land of precious metals in old fables, Don Dominguez, but California will never produce wealth from the earth."

"Ah, but you are wrong, my good captain," asserted the ranchero. "This sample is cinnabar, the source of quicksilver."

The captain was all attention now. "Quicksilver? You mean the liquid metal used to refine silver and gold?"

"The very same," asserted Dominguez with finality. "Quicksilver grasps hold of silver and gold as eagerly as you or I. It is used to free the precious metals from the baser elements. Then the quicksilver can be burned away, leaving the wealth behind."

"So it is almost as valuable as gold?" asked Zuniga with a barely controlled squeak in his voice.

"At the moment, even more so. The gold and silver mines of Mexico are dependent on quicksilver from the state of Jalisco—"

"Which is now in turmoil because of the revolutions sweeping Mexico," noted Zuniga.

"Exactly," agreed Don Dominguez. "If we can produce quicksilver in quantity, every would-be ruler of Mexico will want us for his ally. We need not be content with a rancho in Santa Barbara. Oh no! We may soon control California!"

He leaned forward in a conspiratorial tone. "Captain, I am going to need your help more than ever before. Cinnabar mining will require many workers, and the preparation of the quicksilver is hazardous as well. We will need more Indios than ever, only not for Sonora. We will need them here!"

"And the location of the mine?" Zuniga was suspicious. There had to be more to it than this. "It is on your own property?"

"By no means! That is why the secrecy is more important than ever. Canyon Perdido is divided between the holdings of the mission and those of Rancho Rivera!"

"And what of the vaquero? What if he should wonder aloud to someone who might know what the ore is?"

The ranchero laid his fleshy chin into his palm in thought.

"It would be wise to avoid unnecessary complications. I will have Juan and Iago arrange for him to meet a most unfortunate accident."

"But of course, Don Dominguez," Zuniga said and smiled. But he didn't allow the smile to reach his eyes.

CHAPTER 22

"You like this Señor Reed." Francesca's aunt began her remarks without any preamble. She had called her niece into the parlor of the hacienda without any explanation. Francesca only expected the usual discussion of some problem with the servants or a complaint about an inferior grade of lard.

"What? What did you say, Aunt?" Francesca feigned incomprehension to cover her confusion.

"It is all right, child. Did you think that to another woman, even one my age, the signs would not be plain?"

Francesca shook her head and swallowed hard. "But Father would never . . . ," she began, trying her best to sound dutiful.

Her aunt patted the needlepoint stool she had drawn near her knees. "Sit here, child. Your father is exactly the subject I wish to speak with you about. . . ."

* * *

Doña Eulalia inclined her gray-haired head a moment and listened to the sounds of the house. It was midmorning, and the servants' duties took them all outside for the time being. She nodded to herself in satisfaction that she and Francesca would not be overheard.

"Your father loves you very much and wants your best. Never doubt that. But he cannot replace the advice your mother would have given you. Neither can I, but I must do my best. What I wish to say is this: I too loved a young man once, a common sailor. 'Not suitable,' my father said." The old woman's voice dropped.

Francesca waited patiently, then reached out to her aunt's nervously fidgeting fingers. Doña Eulalia and her niece clasped hands.

At last she found her voice again. "I made plans to run away with him. My father—your grandfather—found out. He had my sailor abducted and sent away on a galleon. I never saw him again. So," said the aunt, drawing both her figure and her voice erect, "what lesson is here? Be obedient, child. Be extremely careful to obey your father's wishes. Do not encourage Señor Reed. Be distant, cool, reserved, and if need be, rude to your young man."

Francesca looked puzzled. "But that is exactly what Father wishes for me . . . rude? . . . oh! Yes, I see." She brightened. "I must be very obedient!"

Doña Eulalia gave a deep, throaty chuckle, remembering herself as the young, headstrong girl who had loved deeply. "Just beware of looking into Señor Reed's green eyes!" she instructed. "Even I find it difficult to be properly reserved!"

* * *

In five days' time, Ricardo was out of bed despite Padre Sanchez's admonitions. "My friend," the young ranchero said warmly to Will, "I feel fine. Never better, in fact. If I am to properly celebrate at the fiesta in your honor, I must get back on my feet."

Dressed for riding but with a sombrero two sizes larger than normal to fit his bandages, Ricardo led the way to the barn. Ricardo's bay horse and the gray Flotada were saddled and awaiting them. They met Francesca coming out of the barn. Will touched his hat brim and started to speak, but Francesca turned her face from him and walked away.

"My father tells me that you ride well," commented Ricardo as Will stared after her a moment, then adjusted the stirrups and tightened the cinch.

"What? Oh, I spent some time on Cumberland ponies back home," acknowledged Will. "And when I came west, I found some pretty fair mountain horses and traded for them with the Crow and the Pawnee."

Will led the gray around the enclosure three times, then stopped to tighten the cinch again.

"Ah," observed Ricardo, repeating Will's actions with his own horse, "I see you are a true vaquero who knows the *paso de la muerte*."

"The step of death? Oh, I get your drift," responded Will, mounting Flotada. "I once had a real cinch binder of a trail horse almost come over with me because I forgot to circle him after tightening the girth. I won't forget that lesson."

The two caballeros rode out together. Ricardo wore a rust-colored suit of velvet, and Will was dressed in his dark green.

"*Mi amigo,* it feels good to be on horseback again," admitted Ricardo as they moved at a slow canter along the road.

Over two hills the riders turned aside from the road and loped across fields of orange poppies and dark blue lupines. They had no particular destination in mind; it was the joy of riding in the late-spring air that beckoned them on.

"What are your future plans, *amigo*?" inquired Ricardo.

Will had to ponder this question for a time. "I'm not sure," he said at last. "My campañeros of the trail are all gone, along with our gear and furs. Maybe I can find someone to stake me to go back and try again."

"Have you not had enough hardship for one lifetime?" asked Ricardo. "Why not stay here and become a ranchero, or if that does not suit you, a merchant like others of your countrymen?"

Will had heard of the easterners who had come to California by ship. Some had accumulated fabulous wealth and prestige like Henry Fitch, now a trader in Pueblo de Los Angeles. Fitch had married Joséfia Carrillo, daughter of a prominent San Diego family.

In the settlement around the presidio and mission of Santa Barbara, there were other Easterners. Daniel Call was making a living as a carpenter after having jumped ship from the leaky China trader *Atala* back in 1816.

It was even rumored that Don José Maria Alfredo Robinson, born plain Alfred Robinson of Boston, hoped to marry into the de la Guerra family. His Yankee business acumen, if united with the de la Guerra riches and respectability, would create a trading operation of considerable force.

Will wondered how others from the East had been accepted so

completely while he was treated with suspicion. Ricardo explained that it was the mode of his arrival that made the difference.

With their coastal network of pueblos and presidios, the Mexican government felt able to control immigration from the sea. But overland was another matter. The ranges of mountains that guarded California on the east had long been considered impassable. Now they had been breached by energetic and voracious trappers and scouts, Americans from the new United States.

In time trade routes might be established and travel regulated so the Mexican authorities would relax. But for now there was too much internal turmoil in Mexico to allow foreigners to come and go freely.

"So why don't you Californians develop the trading possibilities yourselves?" asked Will.

"It is not suitable for *hidalgos* to become merchants," commented Ricardo. His reply was without pretense or snobbery; he was simply stating the facts. "You see, my friend, there is an order to the universe. Some men are born to rule and others to be ruled; some to be merchants and others to be craftsmen. The Lord God has made it so."

"But," interrupted Will, "what about the Indians? What is their role?"

"I have given this much thought," replied Ricardo seriously. "The holy fathers believe that the Indios could become *gente de razón* by study and observation. But I no longer think this possible. They are too childlike to ever govern their own affairs or reason for themselves. They will remain servants forever."

"Seems to me I've heard that point of view from everyone except the Indians themselves," said Will, reining Flotada back to a walk.

"Enough of this talk of merchandising and Indios. I have a powerful thirst," concluded Ricardo, also slowing the bay. "Let us turn aside here for refreshment."

The cantina Corazón del Diablo was as unimposing as its name was sinister. The Devil's Heart was a low adobe structure from which most of the whitewash had peeled. The weathered bricks slumped as if a good rain would melt the building altogether. The hitching rail outside, to which three horses were already tied, looked more substantial. Will noted that one of the horses was a mare.

Inside the saloon were three customers and the proprietress. An older man was seated at a table by himself. His spurs and leather leggings proclaimed him to be a vaquero.

The other two men leaned on the slanted pine plank that served as a bar. They were dressed in badly stained blanket serapes through which their heads protruded. Their unshaven faces were close together, and they were laughing loudly at some private joke.

Just as Will and Ricardo were entering, the taller of the two coarse men at the counter spoke. In a voice meant to carry, he said to his companion, "Ugh! Hey, Juan, don't you hate the smell of cows? And have you noticed how those who herd cattle have the manners of cattle as well?"

The lips of the vaquero in the corner may have tightened at this remark, but he gave no other sign of having heard. He took a sip of his drink and set the glass back down.

Seeing Ricardo and Will, the man called Juan whispered something to his loud friend.

The first man downed his drink in one gulp and shook off his companion's restraining hand. "I hear that to keep the vaqueros docile they treat them just like the young of the herds—they make steers of them."

At this statement, the short, fat woman behind the counter excused herself, saying she needed to go to her casa for more glasses.

Still the man at the table said nothing, but the provocative play was far from over.

The loud man sauntered over to stand in front of the rickety table and folded his arms across his chest. "Say, you are a *vaquero*, a cowherd, aren't you? Tell us if it is true. Are you a toro bravo or only a poor steer?"

The vaquero threw the remaining contents of his glass into the tormentor's face, jumped to his feet, and kicked the table out of the way.

When the loud man uncrossed his arms to wipe his face with one hand, he held a long, thin-bladed knife in the other. He dropped into a fighting crouch and began to stalk the cowhand. "You are already as lean as an old steer, but maybe I can still trim you some."

The vaquero picked up the three-legged stool on which he had been sitting and held it in front like a shield.

The knife wielder lunged in, drew a sweep of the stool, then jumped to the side, slashing the vaquero's sleeve.

"Say, *amigo*, can't a body drink in peace in these parts?" asked Will mildly.

The loud man did not even glance toward the voice. "Keep out of this. It is not your fight."

"Maybe not," admitted Will, "but I think I can see it evened out some." As he walked closer to the fight, Juan moved from the bar to confront him.

"I would not involve myself, señor," suggested the fat-lipped one. "This is between Iago and the vaquero." With a smile he also drew a daggerlike blade from under his serape.

Will stopped and lifted his palms in a gesture of agreement and smiled in return.

The two combatants continued to circle warily, blood dripping from the vaquero's arm.

Will fixed his gaze on the eyes of the man facing him, then called over his shoulder to Ricardo, "You know what my uncle taught me about situations like this? He said if a man insists on fighting bare knuckles, oblige him. If someone gets the drop on you with a rifle, give him what he wants. But do you know what he said to do if someone pulls a knife?"

Will pivoted his shoulders slightly to the left as though turning to see Ricardo's reply. Halfway through the pivot, he spun sharply back toward the right, his right hand doubled into a fist the size of the head of a sledgehammer. With his arm at its fullest extension, he backhanded his fist solidly against the ear of the man guarding him.

"He said I should break his arms," Will concluded, following up the right by stepping through with his left, flush on Juan's nose.

Already staggering sideways, Juan flew backward against the bar. His arms bounced straight over his head from the force of the impact. The knife jumped out of his hand and landed on the floor behind the bar.

At the sudden commotion, Iago, the loud one, looked around

to see the cause. This was all the vaquero needed. He swung the stool hard toward Iago's face.

Iago recovered to bring the point of his knife up to ward off the blow, but the stool knocked the blade from his hand.

"Things are looking a whole lot more even now," commented Will.

Juan grabbed a bottle from the bar and took a clumsy swing at the scout's head. Will caught the bottle in middescent, turned his back into Juan's rush, and, lifting under the man's armpit with his other hand, flipped the cutthroat onto the floor.

Will stepped across the prostrate body with his right leg, keeping Juan's arm on his own left side. Dropping to his knees, Will fell onto Juan's chest. At the same instant he bent the man's elbow backward over his thigh. There was a loud pop and Juan screamed once, then passed out.

At the scream, Iago looked back, startled. It was clear he had never intended this to be a fair fight. Now that his accomplice had been dispatched, the coward bolted out the door.

"Your pardon, señors," apologized the vaquero, dashing past Ricardo and Will in his pursuit of Iago.

Outside, the failed assassin had already reached his buckskin mare and untied the reins when the vaquero reached his zebra dun. In an unhurried manner, the cowboy took down his reata and shook out a medium-sized loop.

As Iago clambered aboard the saddle and spun the mare to flee, a floating ring of braided cowhide settled over his shoulders. When the rope reached its end, Iago burst backward out of the saddle.

"What was that about, anyway?" asked Will, who had followed the men out of the cantina.

The vaquero shrugged as he coiled the reata in hs hands. "*Quién sabe?* Who knows, señor? Perhaps this one—" he gestured toward Iago—"had been drinking bad liquor and it made him crazy."

Will studied the scruffy villain now seated sullenly in the dust and trussed up like a chicken. "I don't know," he wondered aloud. "He seemed bent on picking a fight with you. You sure you don't know him?"

"No, señor," said the old vaquero emphatically. "These are not vaqueros, not even *jinetes*, the expert riders, I have seen before. They are likely *ladrones* from the cantinas of Pueblo de Los Angeles, robbers fleeing the law."

Ricardo was dragging the motionless form of Juan from Corazón del Diablo and depositing him in the dirt next to his partner. He awakened once, gave another scream from the pain of the shattered arm, and promptly passed out again. There was no need to tie him up.

A troop of horsemen headed by Captain Zuniga clattered toward the cantina. Zuniga reined to a sudden stop and threw up his hand to halt his squad of soldiers. "There was a murder reported here and I—" he stopped midsentence and looked with surprise from Will and the vaquero who were standing, to the dust-covered prostrate forms of Iago and Juan.

"No, no murder," corrected Will, "an attempted one, though. Your arrival is very timely, Captain. You can relieve us of these two snakes."

"I am in charge here," barked the little captain, fairly launching himself from his horse. "Once again, Americano, I find you involved in suspicious circumstances. How do I know that you are not robbing these caballeros!"

The gray-haired cowboy who was no taller than the captain and even thinner, jumped in front of Will and confronted Zuniga. "These caballeros—" he pointed at the two men groaning in the dirt—"are *rateros*, criminals! I, Diego Olivera, declare it to be so!"

"You watch your tongue, old man, or I will arrest you *and* this Americano. Now be quiet while—"

Once again the captain was interrupted. This time it was by the voice of Ricardo, speaking from the door of the cantina. "Captain Zuniga, I can vouch for what took place here. These two provoked a fight with Señor Olivera, and *my good friend* Señor Reed only took part to see that it remained fair."

The captain's eyes hardened and glittered with anger. He visibly fought to control his emotions. The result was a hideous half smile, half grimace that when added to the scar on his cheek made Zuniga look especially evil, Will thought.

"Ah, Don Ricardo, I did not see you there," said the captain awkwardly and in an entirely different tone.

What was going on here? Will wondered. Why the change?

"Apparently not," concluded Ricardo. "Now, are you willing to take *my* word for what has happened?"

"*Sí,* of course," mumbled the officer. Ordering his men to take charge of Juan and Iago, Zuniga turned and announced to the old vaquero and Will that they were free to go.

The cowboy only snorted as a reply, and Will shook his head in disgust.

As he and Ricardo mounted their horses, Will could not resist calling out, "By the way, Captain Zuniga, how did you know that a murder had taken place here?"

The soldier snapped rigidly upright as if ordered to attention, then said woodenly, "The proprietress ran to where we were resting our horses by the stream and said that she feared a murder was *going* to take place. That is what I meant."

Will's instincts told him the man wasn't telling the truth. So did the man's eyes. There was something about this whole scene that just wasn't right.

Will and Ricardo gathered their horses and began to head back toward Casa Rivera y Cruz. Within a few hundred yards they were overtaken by Diego Olivera. "Señors," he called, "wait a moment, please."

They had reined up just under an arch of cottonwood tree branches that laced together over the roadway. "In the confusion, I did not properly thank you," Diego began.

"Not important," responded Will. "They needed to be taught a lesson, and I suspect they got it."

The older man drew himself up proudly in his saddle. "You are both gentlemen and I am but a poor vaquero, yet I am indebted to you. Please accept from me this token of my debt."

Diego untied a small leather pouch that had been hanging behind his saddle. "I note that you are a fine horseman and your beast is a true caballo bravo. Will you accept from me these spurs, as I see you have none?"

Will glanced at Ricardo, who nodded, silently saying, *Do not wound his pride.* Will smiled amiably, and the old vaquero passed over the pouch.

"Should you ever need my service," Diego pledged, "you have only to send. I am employed by Don José Dominguez. *Vaya con Dios!*" He clapped his own spurs to his horse and shot away from the young men, waving a final salute over his shoulder as he went.

* * *

The spur that fell from the pouch was made of finely worked silver. Will sat on the veranda of the Rivera hacienda examining the old vaquero's gift.

The engraving on the curving side piece was almost worn smooth from years of service, but the spur retained the soft gleam of high-quality metal. The rowel was four inches across and carried twelve blunted points. The broad leather strap that fit over the instep of Will's boot and the twin chains that went underneath showed the care of frequent oiling and polishing.

"Ah, my friend," said Ricardo as Will tried on the spur, "you look like a Spanish vaquero now—let us see you with the other spur in place."

As Will shook the other spur free of the bag, a lump of rock also fell out. It was a dark red fragment of stone no bigger than the scout's thumb. He held it up and inquired, "What do you suppose this is?"

"I cannot say. A good-luck piece, perhaps?"

"If that's true, then I should return it to Señor Olivera. He may have forgotten it was in there."

Ricardo agreed but added, "Why not wait until the fiesta? Señor Olivera will most certainly attend, and you can return it then."

"That's a good idea," Will replied, "and since these spurs are too valuable to use every day, I'll keep them in the bag for now."

Ricardo took a moment to reexamine the rock fragment. "I have seen something like this, but I cannot remember where." Shrugging, he handed it back to Will, who placed it with the spurs in the pouch.

CHAPTER 23

"You seem very quiet this evening, *mi amigo,*" commented Ricardo as he and Will walked through the fig orchard at the rear of the hacienda.

Will stopped and leaned his hand on a slender tree trunk. He studied the silver piping on the seam of his dark blue velvet trousers. Still without answering, he raised the sleeve of the jacket and pulled at the cuff of the white silk shirt. "Ricardo," he said at last, "do I look like I fit in your society?"

"Most certainly," agreed his friend. "You appear as a true caballero bravo, only bigger and red-haired, of course."

"And do I express myself clearly in your language? Have I butchered too many phrases? Have I done things that are offensive?"

"What is this about?" Ricardo asked slowly. "Has someone been rude to you or critical of your speech? He will have to answer to me!"

Will grimaced, making a face between a frown and a silly grin. "That is the problem. It is not a he; it's a she."

"What?" demanded Ricardo.

"Your sister. Don't misunderstand—she has never been anything but polite. But I fear I have offended her."

"What do you mean?" asked the bewildered ranchero, looking back through the trees to the lighted outline of Francesca's window.

"Ever since a conversation we had . . . I meant no disrespect . . . I can't even remember what I said . . . she has been cool, distant. All we talked about was Indians and—"

"Say no more," instructed Ricardo. "It is not fitting that a gentleman such as yourself has to explain. I am certain you said nothing improper. I will speak with her and if she does not behave better, I will have Father instruct her." The young man strode purposefully back toward the house.

"Wait, Ricardo," Will called after him. "I didn't mean for you . . ." But his friend had already reentered the hacienda.

"Father," began Ricardo, bursting into Don Pedro's study, "I wish you to speak with Francesca."

Don Pedro was studying a map of the rancho, planning the location of another watering pond for the cattle. "Eh? What's that?"

"I have spoken with Francesca about the way she speaks to Señor Reed. She gave me a most disrespectful reply. In fact, in words better suited for a mule skinner, she told me to mind my own business."

The elder ranchero stood and clasped his hands behind his back. "Is your sister too forward with the Americano?" he questioned, concern flitting across his brow.

"On the contrary, she has been rude to him. Señor Reed is a fine gentleman, a brave one who saved my life. He must be made to feel welcome in our home. She fails to uphold the courtesy of the house of Rivera y Cruz."

Don Pedro looked confused. One hand remained clenched behind his back while the other passed over the dome of his head. "Certainly, our hospitality cannot be questioned. Señor Reed is our honored guest. I . . . ah . . . I will speak with her."

Francesca repressed a smile as she watched her father pace the length of his study. His hands were clasped behind his back; his attitude once again was that of the great ranchero considering how best to pose his decree.

"Father," Francesca ventured timidly, although she did not feel timid. "I wish you would not pace so. It makes me feel as though I have displeased you in some way."

Don Pedro frowned, continuing his walk to the window overlooking the courtyard.

Francesca remembered it was the same place where he had stood when he'd seen her talking so pleasantly with Will Reed and been displeased.

Slowly he turned to face Francesca. "Daughter, I do not understand your behavior," he said at last. Indeed, the tone of disappointment was inherent in his words.

Francesca opened her eyes wider, pretending her innocence. "Whatever have I done, Father?"

"Ricardo has told me—"

"Ricardo!" she scoffed in mock anger. "What does he know about my affairs?"

Don Pedro held up his hands to silence her, a gesture she meekly obeyed. "Now, now! It is not only Ricardo who has noticed, but I myself have observed your behavior."

"My behavior?"

"Coolness. To our guest."

"Guest?"

"To Señor Reed you have been—" he frowned and rolled his hands as if to make the right words come forth—"you have been more than cool. . . . You have been rude."

"I? Rude?" she protested, while feeling a sense of exhilaration. The days of coyness had paid off! Now, instead of instructing her that she must not speak to the American, her father was about to reprimand her for aloofness and command her to pay *more* attention to their guest. "But, Father, he is a stranger. You said it yourself . . . quite different than us. Whatever is Ricardo talking about?"

"I realize it is difficult at times to be polite to one so . . . unlike us. His manners are American. His speech is clumsy, but he is the man who saved your brother's life."

Now it was Francesca's turn. Imitating her father's gesture, she raised her hand slightly. "You need not say more, Father. I was not *aware*. . . that I might be offending him. Or being rude. I will try and do better. Really, Father, I will try and make up for it. I was not thinking of Ricardo or the great debt we owe."

The change in Don Pedro's countenance was marvelous to behold. He beamed, as if proud of the way he had raised her to be a proper hostess no matter how difficult the task. "Your mother would be pleased." He smiled.

After kissing him lightly on the cheek, Francesca ran upstairs to bathe and change for supper.

✶CHAPTER 24✶

Ricardo enthusiastically described the planned events of the fiesta, explaining in detail the succession of trials of skill and courage that would occupy much of the day.

"And will there be a shooting match at this fiesta?" inquired Will.

"There will be the exercise of the *lazadores*, the ropers, and games of *raya* and once and—"

"Do any of those involve shooting?" persisted Will.

Ricardo looked dubious. "I doubt that a contest of firearms is planned. Most of the sports are from horseback and—"

"That'll work," said Will. "I'm a fair hand with a horse but not even close to your vaqueros with their reatas. If I can get a rifle or a brace of pistols, I may be able to show you people a few things."

"We have nothing suitable in the hacienda," responded Ricardo thoughtfully. "Nothing but an old fowling piece. But I know where we may obtain something for you."

✶ ✶ ✶

The rowboat beached on the white sand below the little community of Santa Barbara belonged to the *Paratus*. It was left onshore for the use of customers whenever the trading ship was in port.

"Ahoy, Captain Easton," called Ricardo as he and Will rowed toward the ship.

"Who's that?" responded Easton, glancing over the deck rails. "Well, welcome aboard, Señor Ricardo. Come up and introduce me to your friend."

The pair climbed a rope ladder to the teakwood deck of the vessel. The fact that Ricardo was a frequent visitor aboard *Paratus* was evident by the ease of manner with which he and the captain greeted each other.

"And this is obviously the American we've been hearing about from the ladies," acknowledged Easton with a nod in Will's direction. "You're certainly a long ways from home," Easton said in English.

The scout took an immediate liking to the trader's hearty handshake and broad smile.

"*En Español, por favor,*" requested Ricardo.

"But of course," agreed Easton, switching easily to Spanish. "And no pirate dialect today either."

At Will's puzzled look, Ricardo explained that the captain put on a swashbuckling act that appealed to the ladies of Santa Barbara. "Billy adopts an air of mystery and danger because it's good for business." Ricardo laughed.

"Don't give away all my secrets," requested the pirate merchant with mock ferocity, "or I'll be forced to cut out your heart and feed it to my pet shark!"

"Actually," said Will, "we are here on business." He proceeded to explain his intention of demonstrating a mastery of sharpshooting on the day of the fiesta.

"I think I have just what you are after," responded Billy. "Wait here." He disappeared belowdecks for a minute, returning with a walnut case inlaid with teak and mahogany. He presented it, unopened, for both men to see the quality of the workmanship, then raised the lid with an expert salesman's touch.

Inside was a matched pair of dueling pistols. Their half stocks were made of polished walnut, and the octagonal steel barrels gleamed.

"These are .50 caliber and as you see were made as percussion models, not converted flintlocks."

"They are beauties," agreed Will, hefting one to feel the balance.

He drew a bead on a masthead to check the sights. "But too expensive for me, I'm sure."

"Nonsense," said Easton. "Take them as a loan. I'll back you in a gentlemanly wager or two and win enough for you to keep them as a gift."

"You place a great deal of confidence in someone you've never seen shoot," observed the trapper.

"You came cross-country living off the land, didn't you? What better recommendation might I need? Come below and we'll get powder and shot."

Ricardo said he preferred to remain on deck to watch the white clouds pile up on the peaks behind Santa Barbara. Will understood. The breeze out of the northwest was refreshing, and the earlier ocean calm had been replaced by small, dancing waves.

Easton escorted Will down a companionway, then past stores of trade goods. "We can't take long. The way the wind is rising, we may have to slip our cable and run out behind the islands till this blows over."

Easton stopped in front of a double-locked cupboard. "Heard you lived with the valley Indians for a time," he said in English. "Was anything bothering them?"

"The usual tribal feuds, but I think I know what you're asking about. They had a curious way of talking about their people being 'taken by the West,' but then shutting up tight as a clam. Never figured out what they meant."

Easton's ponytailed hair bobbed as he nodded. "I thought as much. I've come across some late-night shipping going on at a little cove north of here . . . and the cargo wasn't hides or tallow."

The trader offered no further explanation of his mysterious words. He took a key on a string from around his neck and commented, "Powder's here in the Santa Barbara."

"Santa Barbara? Same name as the mission? Why is it called that?"

Easton regarded Will with a questioning look. "Not up on your Catholic saints, eh? Saint Barbara is the lady in charge of sudden calamity—explosions, for instance."

Opening the locker, the trader removed a keg of powder and a sack of lead balls. These he passed to Will, along with a small tin of percussion caps. Reaching into the back of the locker, Easton moved some more kegs around and came out with a cloth-wrapped package. Will could see several more similar packages. "There's also this," he said.

When unwrapped, the object revealed was a brand-new Hawken rifle. Will whistled sharply between his teeth in admiration.

"Fifty caliber, same as the pistols," noted Easton. "Only this will carry three hundred and fifty yards and still knock down a grizzly or a man."

"Maybe I'll win the prize at the fiesta and be able to buy this," said Will.

"Nobody else knows I have it," said Easton, rewrapping the gun. "Let's keep it that way, all right?"

"Whatever you say," agreed Will.

"If you find you need it sooner than that fiesta, you know where to come," the trader concluded, securing the locker.

"Why would I need it at all?" asked Will, frowning.

"You just remember what I called the powder magazine and that'll do for now," concluded Easton. "You had best get to shore. I'm going to have to get this ship under way."

* * *

Sensing a need for more courage than it had taken to face grizzlies or hostile Indians, Will had finally worked up enough nerve to take direct action with Francesca. After supper, he caught her by the elbow and asked if she would care to "walk a piece."

To his surprise, she agreed with no hint of reluctance. Saying that she needed a moment to collect a shawl from her room, she left Will standing by the front door.

When she descended the stairs with the shawl draped around her slim form, he politely offered her his arm, and she accepted it graciously. For a time they strolled in silence in the fig orchard. It was all shades of silver from the light of a full moon, sailing over the surrounding hills like a brilliantly lit ship cresting a dark wave.

Will knew what he wanted to say, but he was so pleased by

his initial success that he did not want to take a chance on ruining it. "Francesca," he finally said, "I'm afraid I was rude to you and offended you. If so, I'm sorry. I'm a plain speaker and I value that in others, but I had no right to be critical."

"Say no more, Will Reed," she said gently. "There was no offense for you to apologize for."

A hint of lavender wafting from Francesca electrified Will's senses. "But . . . but I sounded abrupt when I spoke about the treatment of the Indians. I did not mean you personally, of course. I meant that their path . . . if we want to show them a path . . ."

Francesca had turned to stand in front of him. Will's great rough hands engulfed her diminutive smooth ones. Her chin jutted up toward his, and there was amusement in the sparkle of moonlight reflected in her eyes.

"Hang it all, Francesca," Will complained. "Here I claimed what a plain speaker I am, and now I can't get words to even come out of my mouth right!"

She smiled up at him then, a dazzling smile of genuine affection and promise. "I understand that mountain men are men of action and not of words."

✱CHAPTER 25✱

Will and Ricardo rode out together to take part in the preparations for the fiesta. In Will's honor, a bull-and-bear fight was to take place.

The bull, a huge cinnamon red toro bravo, was already pawing up the ground in a corral adjacent to the fiesta grounds. The proud bull tossed his head and charged the fences at the slightest provocation by passersby. When they jumped hurriedly back, he would clash his four-foot-wide dagger-tipped horns against the posts as if saying, *I dare you to step in and fight me.*

Ranchero hands were busy reinforcing the stockade and sprucing up the grandstands from which the high-ranking guests would watch the action.

The purpose of today's journey into the canyons above Santa Barbara was to procure the other combatant for the contest. Will and Ricardo, accompanied by six vaqueros, were going to capture a grizzly bear *alive.*

Will wasn't sure he approved of this venture, especially when the idea was coming from a man who had nearly lost the top of his head to the crunch of a bear's jaws. But the vaqueros had made their preparations for the capture as calmly as if securing a half ton of ferocious fury were an everyday occurrence.

The line of riders began to sweep across a hillside from a little creek that circled its base up to its crest. Will and Ricardo rode behind to observe, although the young ranchero chafed at not being in the action. His father had made him promise not to take part; not because of the bear but because he might reinjure his head if thrown from his mount.

The vaquero highest on the hill got the first view of the next arroyo over. He gave a shout of discovery, then a moment later a cry of "*la osa*" in disappointment.

As they rounded the ridge, Will could see down into the canyon. At the bottom, along a stony creek bed, was a large mother bear accompanied by two cubs. The riders began to whistle and shout and slap their reatas against their leather chapedero leggings.

The mother bear stood erect at the noise and gave a sharp *wuff* in alarm. The cubs darted across the creek and into the brush, encouraged by a swat from this mother when one did not move fast enough to suit her. When the cubs were safely across, she too dropped down and rushed after them.

The riders watched until the trio of grizzlies disappeared over the next ridge to the east. As the vaqueros advanced again, Ricardo explained that it would never do to take back a she-bear, although her ferocity in defense of her cubs might be legendary. To pit a female bear against a male bull—what if the bear should win? "Unthinkable," Ricardo remarked, shaking his head.

Several canyons farther on, a vaquero in the middle of the line called out a warning. He said he'd seen the head and shoulders of a great silvertip bear rising from a thicket of sugar sumac on the hill opposite them.

A low, marshy area in front of the thicket was an ideal capture ground. Shaking out their tallow-smeared reatas, three of the vaqueros trotted their horses in a wide circle to get behind the bear and drive him into the open. The other three, backed by Will and Ricardo, slowly advanced to the edge of the clearing.

When the riders on the slope were in position, they began making noises to move the bear downward. "Hey, *oso*," they called. "We have come to invite you to a fiesta!"

Will and the others did not have to wait long. A few minutes passed before a huge, humpbacked *oso pardo viejo* crashed through the brush. At the last clump of willows opposite the waiting riders, the grizzly threw up his head and sniffed the air. Clearly he did not like something. He shuffled his feet and swung his head from side to side.

The flapping, yelling sounds coming toward him down the slope were enough to finally convince the great bear to move into the open. Out into the marshy space he swayed and halted again at the sight of the advancing riders.

Immediately the huge bear stood erect, roaring his defiance. He made an almost human gesture of looking over his shoulder as if plotting an escape, then reckoning himself surrounded, he prepared to do battle.

Six riders advanced cautiously toward him, their mounts betraying nervous excitement by stamping and snorting. The vaqueros tried to close the circle evenly, constricting the circle all around.

The bruin, gray-muzzled and slavering, turned slowly around, judging each rider's approach like a boxer looking for an opening.

"El Viejo," one vaquero muttered. The title was repeated by the others. This was not just *an* old grizzly but *the* old bear of the mountains. Never captured, never bested in a fight, he had disemboweled half a dozen horses and mauled four men—two of them to death.

At last one of the riders, anxious for the glory of being the first to secure a reata to El Viejo, allowed his palomino to get in advance of the others.

Instantly the great bear charged.

The vaquero waited coolly, then cast a perfect loop around the grizzly's neck. Two turns of the braided cord were taken around the horn of the saddle as the palomino reared and spun.

The huge bear sat back on his haunches and resisted the pull of the line. This was expected and was the reason why the reatas were covered in tallow. An *oso pardo* could pull in a horse and rider like a man landing a fish, unless the cord was greased so the bear could not keep a firm grip.

Two other vaqueros quartered the bear, preparing to add their loops to the capture. But El Viejo had not reached his advanced age by doing the expected. When he found that he could not draw in the horse, he simply turned his massive head to one side and bit through the taut rawhide with a snap.

The grizzly immediately charged the nearest of the approaching riders, and this time the panicked vaquero made no attempt to cast a loop. It was all he and his bay horse could do to avoid the bear's rush. Even a miraculous leap to the side did not spare them a rake of El Viejo's claws, lacerating the man's leg and the horse's flank.

But the circle of riders continued to close in. The lazadores, three men of great experience with the reata, timed their approach to arrive together. Two loops were flung to snare the bear's head. His parted jaws closed over one, but the other settled around his neck, choking him. The third man flung his loop and captured El Viejo's front paws.

Will rode out to take the place of the man who had been injured. The scout and the remaining vaquero urged their mounts toward the struggling bear. He was attempting to free himself from the noose around his neck by upward thrusts of his bound paws.

Will and the vaquero watched for the bear to lift a hind leg to move; then Will encircled one of the bear's hind legs with a rawhide loop. An instant later the bear moved his other hind leg. The vaquero swung his rawhide loop. With little urging from their riders, the well-trained horses pulled stoutly back on the reatas until the grizzly was stretched out on the ground.

The coil around El Viejo's neck was kept tight, to choke off his wind. No one dared dismount his horse until they saw that the massive beast was unconscious. The mounted men were enough to keep the bear spread-eagled on the marshy ground, but the injured vaquero was busy tending his leg and his limping horse.

So although he had made a promise to his father, Ricardo was called on to get off his horse and secure the bruin's muzzle and paws with stout rawhide straps so the reatas could be released before the grizzly choked to death.

But just as Ricardo bent to secure a strap around the bear's jaws, the mammoth grizzly lunged upward! He had been shamming and was not unconscious at all!

The bear brought his bound paws toward his muzzle, obviously intending to catch Ricardo's leg between his murderous claws and his ponderous head.

Whether it was only instinct or a flicker of motion that caught Will's eye, he never could say. But the American's shout of warning came just in time. The young rancher flung himself backward from the bear's clutches and landed sprawling in the mud.

All the vaqueros immediately tightened their reatas around the grizzly's neck. This time they waited longer to make sure the bear had passed out. No one approached the grizzly until a few pokes from a long stick, which they knew would make any bear angry, proved him unconscious.

The bear was trussed in three times the normal number of rawhide straps and loaded aboard a bull-hide sled to be dragged back to the hacienda. The wounded man rode double behind another vaquero so his injured bay could be led carefully homeward.

Everyone noticed and commented on how close Ricardo's escape from this second *oso pardo* had been. From the sweep of the bear's claws, his boot had been slit from top to heel, just missing shredding the leg within.

CHAPTER 26

The morning of the fiesta, dawn was rosy-tinted over the slopes east of Santa Barbara and the wind unusually serene.

Will was up early, laying out his changes of clothing for the day's events. He had been told that tradition demanded at least three different outfits be worn in the course of the day: green for the *paseo*, the parade that would start the festivities; dark red for the afternoon's contests of skill and bravery; and black with silver for the evening's grand ball.

Will had donned the forest-colored suit and was attaching the emerald green sash when he remembered the spurs given to him by Diego Olivera. Will had removed the pouch from the top drawer of a nightstand. He pulled apart the drawstring and upended the contents onto the bed. As the spurs tumbled out, so did the curious lump of red ore. Will wondered again about the rock, then shoved it into his pocket, intending to return the piece to Olivera during the fiesta.

The scout picked up the spurs. He was going to carry them out onto the veranda before putting them on, so the rowels would not gouge the floors as he walked.

That was when he noticed the blurred spot on one of the shanks. While all the rest gleamed evenly, a jagged outline on one limb surrounded an area that looked smeared with a thumbprint of grease.

Will tried polishing the spot to see if it would come off, but all his rubbing and buffing produced no change in the appearance. *Must have been like that a long time,* he thought. *Strange I didn't notice the other day.*

Inspecting the outline of the faded area, another thought struck him. Will reached into his pocket and fished out the chunk of stone. By the early light coming through the bedroom window, Will studied the spur as he turned the dark rock over and over in his hand. At last he found a surface of the stone that looked familiar.

Will fitted the edge of the rock against the blurred area of silver. The outline was a perfect match. *What do you suppose makes that happen?*

He puzzled over this curiosity for a minute before returning the ore to his pocket and picking up his hat. As he headed downstairs he thought, *Another thing to ask Olivera about his lucky rock.*

* * *

"How will we know when to release the bear?" asked Iago.

He and Juan maintained a healthy distance between themselves and El Viejo's enclosure. Sometimes the bruin demonstrated his savagery, roaring and tearing at the ground and the bars. But now, as at other times, he was dangerously quiet, waiting to rear up and plunge a raking claw through the fence.

"I will maneuver the Americano right into the gate," answered Captain Zuniga. "One of you must watch from under the stands and signal the other to open the gate." He pointed to the darkest corner under the seats. "In the meantime you must hide there."

"This *oso pardo* is already very angry. He will crush the Yankee like an eggshell. But where will he stop?"

"That is not our concern. We can blame whatever happens on the Indios and be rid of the interfering Señor Reed at the same time." Zuniga looked at the pink streaks lighting the eastern sky and at the dark mass of the hulking grizzly. He rubbed the scar on his cheek thoughtfully. "Yes, it will all work perfectly. Now go, and be certain you stay well hidden!"

* * *

Will stood on the veranda of the Rivera hacienda, watching the bustling activity of the courtyard. Grooms paid particular attention to their equine charges, currying and brushing the manes and forelocks and tails till not a single tangle remained. A twelve-year-old Indian made the rounds of all the horses' feet with a bucket and a brush, polishing the hooves until they gleamed in the sun.

From the balcony of the hacienda, a vaquero dropped a weighted reata. He allowed it to twist slowly until all the kinks had been removed from the braided line, then coiled it carefully up again.

Francesca came out of a door at the far end of the house and stood, not noticing Will. She was, he thought, the most beautiful woman he had ever seen. Her lustrous dark hair was gathered up on her head and pinned in place with a high comb. A fine lace shawl draped her ivory shoulders, while a silver cross on a black velvet ribbon sparkled at her throat.

It seemed to Will that all the clattering noises of the courtyard were suddenly replaced by a rushing. It reminded him of the sound a swiftly plunging river makes as it echoes out of a mountain gorge. He stood entranced, staring at Francesca as if seeing for the first time the goal for which he had been searching.

CHAPTER 27

Will and Ricardo sat in their ringside seats, which meant staying mounted on their horses while watching the roping.

A big Chihuahua steer was loosed into the arena, and a moment later an Indian vaquero, mounted on a line-back dun, raced after him. Four lengths into the corral a loop of reata floated over the animal's head.

The dun set his heels and dug in, even as the roper was completing the second dally of braided rawhide around the high, flat horn. The lazadore expertly flipped the slack out of the reata so it would not get under his mount's hooves.

An instant later the dark red steer hit the end of the cord and was jerked completely off his feet. The roper, who had carried a length of rawhide pigging string in his teeth, vaulted off the dun. He hog-tied the steer before the long-horned animal had even twitched, let alone gotten back to his feet.

Ricardo waved his sombrero, and there was a round of "Bravo!" and "Well done!" from most of the other riders. A few sat silently, looking sour.

"What's wrong with those men?" asked Will.

"Pay them no mind," suggested Ricardo, straightening his hat. "There are some who still dislike it that my father has trained Indios as vaqueros, and they are perhaps jealous."

Almost as if overhearing this remark, one of the unimpressed men rode forward into the starting position. As Will watched, the lazadore shook out his reata and tied the end fast to the horn of his saddle.

"I thought you weren't supposed to tie the reata," observed Will.

Ricardo was shaking his head. "It is still done by some. Father won't permit it. He says the impact when the steer hits the end of the line is too hard on the horse unless the cord can slip a little around the dally."

The vaquero in the starting gate glanced over where the Indian lazodore who had just roped was coiling his reata. His scowl gave a clear message: *I'll show you how it's done.*

When the rider nodded, another rangy steer was prodded from the pen, and the vaquero went flying after the beast. His sorrel colt was young and eager and fast, and the loop of reata left the roper's hand in only two strides.

But the vaquero's haste proved his undoing. He had made his cast before the steer had settled on a course. At the moment of his throw, the lean, grouchy steer veered in front of the sorrel, almost under the horse's nose.

It was the vaquero's misfortune that his throw was good. The loop settled over the steer's neck even as the startled sorrel spurted *ahead* of the steer. All the frantic yanking and sawing on the bridle by the vaquero had no effect, and the horse plunged on until he, not the steer, hit the end of the reata.

There was the sound of bursting rawhide and the exclamation of shock. The hard-tied line and the hard-charging colt combined to snap the saddle and its occupant backward off the horse.

The vaquero hit the ground with a sickening thud. Then as his mount kicked itself free of the girth, he came within inches of having his head reshaped. The horse raced off, still kicking, across the corral.

The roper picked himself up slowly. Everything seemed to be working and no bones appeared to be broken. Dusting off his leggings, he turned around to retrieve his saddle and the audience burst into laughter. He had split the seat out of his trousers!

Will and Ricardo rode around the side of the corral toward the open field, where other contests of riding and roping were being held.

"Do you suppose that last vaquero learned something today?" asked Will.

"Perhaps. But he will not like it that he was bested by an Indian *and* made the fool. He may have learned not to tie his reata, but it will not make him treat the Indians any better."

Will pulled Flotada to a stop and pivoted in his saddle. "Ricardo, explain something to me. Spain's soldiers were in the New World for three hundred years, and many raised families with Indian wives. If most Mexicans are part Indio themselves, why are they so hard on the California tribes?"

"It is not the amount of Indian blood that matters. A family name that goes back to Castille or Aragon is our source of pride." Ricardo swung his arm in a sweeping circle around the fiesta grounds. "You see the Indios haul water, stack firewood, drive cattle, and tend the fields. We—my father and I—treat them well, but they will never be *gente de razón.* They are like beasts of burden. Some are more clever than others and trainable but not ever fully civilized."

"What you mean by *civilized* might change how you view the Indios, but does that give anyone the right to kill them or make slaves of them?" asked Will.

"Oh no!" exclaimed Ricardo. "Only those who willingly join the mission family have requirements placed on them that they must keep. Slavery is illegal and murder is still murder!"

"I wish I were as certain of that as you." Will shrugged. "The Yokuts were terrified of something to their west, and I don't think it was sharks or whales."

* * *

The large grassy field next to the enclosure for the bull-and-bear combat event was bordered on two sides by oak trees. They provided shady seating for the onlookers.

Francesca and Doña Eulalia were busy organizing the massive amount of food that would be a major part of the fiesta. The quarters from four entire dressed steers were hanging in cheesecloth over the limbs of an oak. A barbecue fire presided over by three cooks was already blazing, and the first of hundreds of pounds of meat was sizzling on the spits.

"Wasn't that a grand *paseo*?" observed Margarita, a friend of Francesca's.

"You can't fool me, Margarita," teased Francesca. "You did not see the parade! You only had eyes for the younger son of Don Alfredo."

The girl being teased blushed until her ears turned pink. She retaliated by blurting out, "You should not talk, Francesca! I know one who was watching you!"

"Well, what of it?" Francesca countered. "Didn't he look splendid?"

"Oh yes," agreed Margarita. "And so masterful with his horsemanship. Aren't you excited to see how well he does in the contests?"

"I wonder what he will choose to wear for the *lazo*. I don't think his customs require so many changes of clothing."

"Well, of course he won't change," responded the girl. "He must wear his uniform until changing into the dress one for the grand ball."

"Uniform?" puzzled Francesca. "What are you talking about, Margarita?"

"Ah," countered the younger girl. "The question is *who* are you talking about?"

"Girls! Girls!" interrupted Doña Eulalia, clapping. "The guests will be coming around for their midday meal soon, and we are not close to ready. Francesca, run and check the *pasole* to see if it is seasoned properly. Margarita, you come with me. We must speed up the making of the tortillas."

* * *

Across the field, the contests for *lazadores*, ropers, and *jinetes*, or riders, were continuing.

"Trust Flotada." Ricardo laughed. "He knows what to do even if you do not."

"What is this game called again?" inquired Will.

"It is *once*—you know, eleven. If father would permit, I myself would show you how it is done. But I will be here applauding!"

Will and his gray horse took their position at the end of a line of riders waiting a turn to compete. Will held Flotada a little to one side so he could watch the proceedings.

When the course was clear, each rider set out at top speed toward a bare patch of ground about fifty yards away. After reaching the edge of the bare space, each jinete did his utmost to set his mount back on its haunches. The parallel skid marks produced by each animal's hind legs looked like the number eleven, *once.*

A pair of boys too young to take part ran out to measure the length of the skid. Each rider got three chances, the best mark counting for the final competition. The vaquero ahead of Will moved up and prepared his horse at the starting line.

"*Vámenos!*" he shouted to his white-painted bay. Horse and rider flashed across the ground to the edge of the cleared area. A jerk on the reins and the horse obediently sat down abruptly.

A plume of dust obscured the action, and then the boys called out, "*Viente-dos!*"

"Twenty-two feet!" exclaimed the rider behind Will. "Aiyee, he will be the winner for certain. My eighteen is outclassed."

Will approached the line with Flotada. A wave of a handkerchief announced that the marks had been smoothed out and the scoring zone was clear. As Ricardo had taught him, Will moved his boots slightly so the loose chains on each spur made a tiny jingle.

Flotada was immediately alert. He flicked his ears back toward the sound, then forward toward the goal, all attention on the business at hand.

The scout's barest tap of the great rowelled spurs was all Flotada needed to bound forward with a great leap, as if crossing a bottomless canyon. In three strides the gray was already at top speed and running as if his life depended on it.

Will could see the clear space coming up quickly. He knew that he would have to anticipate the edge or they would fly past. He raised himself in his stirrups, preparing to gather his weight on the reins and . . .

Flotada needed no more signal than the shift of weight. His great gray body gathered beneath him till Will's spurs almost touched the ground on either side. The scout found his face next to the horse's head as they slid.

"*Viente-cinco!*" called the boys as Flotada trotted back to the end of the line.

Some of the competitors who had not passed twenty feet on their first attempt now withdrew, leaving Will and six others.

"Well done, señor," complimented the jinete in front of Will.

"Not since the great days of Diego Olivera has a rider reached twenty-five feet."

"Olivera," repeated Will. "Do you know him?"

"*Sí,* señor," responded the rider. "We both worked for Don Dominguez."

"You mean you no longer work there now, or he does not?" asked Will. "In any case, will he be here today?"

The vaquero's face clouded in a deep frown. "No, señor, he will not be here today . . . unless his caballero spirit insists on one last rodeo. He was found dead, only these two days since."

"Dead!" exclaimed Will. "How did he die?"

"His throat was slit as he rode night herd, señor, and—"

A flash of sunlight gleamed off the polished side piece of Will's spur.

"Those spurs, señor." The vaquero's eyes narrowed. "Where did you get them?"

"From Olivera. He gave them to me. Listen, I can't explain right now. Where is Captain Zuniga?"

Will rode out of the line of competitors and circled the field looking for the captain. He found him by the barbecue fire, talking with Francesca.

"Zuniga!" Will demanded, vaulting from Flotada on a sudden stop that would have won the contest for certain. "Olivera is dead. Have you interrogated those cutthroats to see if they had a third accomplice? What were they after? Why were they hounding the old man?"

The captain had not turned to face the scout for any of these questions. Francesca's eyes widened at the raving torrent from Will.

Zuniga at last slowly turned around. "You are very rude, Americano," Zuniga said. "If you wish to discuss police business,

I suggest that you come to my office next week." He began to turn away.

"Just a minute," demanded Will, closing his powerful hand around Zuniga's elbow. "Pardon me, Francesca, but the captain and I need to have a talk."

"Of course," Francesca agreed. "I need to attend to other guests as well."

The captain shook off the restraining hand and warned darkly, "Never touch me again, Americano. And never interrupt my conversation unless you no longer have a use for your own tongue."

Will was not impressed and stood with his hands on his hips. "I want answers, and I want them now. Who killed Olivera? What are you doing to find out? Who hired those criminals, and why were they after Olivera in the cantina?"

The officer smirked and puckered his thin face as if he smelled something bad. "You have a lot of questions, Americano. Too many that are none of your business. Just so that you will leave me alone, I will tell you: I don't know who hired those men or why, but perhaps they succeeded after all. They escaped from the presidio three nights ago."

"Escaped!" ground out Will. "How convenient. Left no trail either, I suppose."

"I do not like your tone. You will apologize at once."

"Apologize," snorted Will, "I'd sooner—"

Ricardo had followed Will's hasty departure from the contest and now stepped between the two men. "Will, no unpleasantness. This day is in your honor after all. Your pardon, Captain. We will discuss this with you at a more appropriate time."

Will stood staring into Zuniga's face. The squinted green eyes of the trapper locked with the shark expression of the soldier.

At last it was Zuniga who turned and walked away.

CHAPTER 28

Will watched Zuniga saunter off toward the plank tables, which were groaning under the weight of the noon meal. Will noted to whom the officer spoke and his manner, following Zuniga with his eyes as if the captain were a wild animal the trapper was tracking.

"Zuniga is a strong man and bad to cross, my friend," cautioned Ricardo. "And he is not without support from some rancheros because they agree with his toughness toward the Indios."

"It is not strength when a man brutalizes those who cannot defend themselves. And it is not toughness to leave a murder unsolved while two likely killers escape."

"Just so, but do not provoke the captain if you can help it. He has a reputation for dueling to the death."

Will turned to his friend and said seriously, "Ricardo, sometimes the quality of a man is just as apparent by his enemies as by his friends. I won't be looking to start a fight today, but Zuniga will bear watching."

"*Bueno,*" Ricardo agreed with seeming relief that the matter was temporarily at rest. "Let us address ourselves to the food. We almost had a victory of yours to celebrate in the *once*, and now we should fortify ourselves for the afternoon's events."

The pair joined a group of fiesta-goers who were picnicking. Francesca invited Will to sit down while she prepared a plate of food for him. Ricardo was attended to by all three Gonzalez sisters.

✲ ✲ ✲

Captain Zuniga had the appearance of a man strolling in the enclosure of the corral, walking off the midday feast. He wandered around the stockade until he was satisfied that no other fiesta-goers were present.

The officer stopped directly in front of the stands with his back to the platform. He kicked idly at the dirt with the toe of his boot and remarked over his shoulder, "Iago, can you hear me?"

"*Sí*, we hear you," came the whispered reply.

"Get ready!" Zuniga hissed in return. "It won't be long now!"

✲ ✲ ✲

After consuming barbecued beef, beans, and tortillas, there were ripe strawberries for dessert. The ladies retired to a nearby tent while the men returned to a similar structure provided for them.

Will swapped his green suit for one of burgundy trimmed in black leather. He was saving the black suit finished in silver for the grand ball in the evening. He also picked up the wooden case of dueling pistols he had borrowed from Billy Easton.

Some of the guests had taken advantage of the break in the events for a midday siesta. In fact, this idea, combined with the warm sun and hearty fare, so appealed to Ricardo that Will had to remind him that it was nearly time for the shooting exhibition.

"I won't need Flotada to do the shooting for me," he joked. "I can handle this part myself."

When Francesca rejoined them, she linked her arm through Will's and together they led a procession toward the corral. Halfway there, Don Pedro was seen approaching on his flashy black horse, and the group stopped to wait for his arrival.

At Don Pedro's side rode Don José Dominguez, as grouchy as ever in his tight boots. A deep scowl appeared on his face at the sight of Will's and Francesca's linked arms.

Francesca's father tossed his hat back on his head and mopped his forehead with a silk handkerchief. He was handsomely dressed, as befitted the host of the fiesta. The rust-colored jacket he wore was trimmed in gold, just the reverse of his gold brocade vest with its rust-red piping.

The flowing tail of the sash that wound around the waist of his trousers carried the tones of burnt orange and gold down into a matching saddle blanket. He and the horse seemed to be made of one piece of workmanship.

"Good day, children," he called cheerfully. "I'm sorry to be late. Don José wished to discuss some business with me. Is everything to your liking?"

A chorus of "*Sí, bueno!* Most excellent!" responded to his inquiry.

"And where is this procession going? Surely it is too early for the combat of the great beasts?"

Ricardo left his three doting companions—Consuelo, Juanita, and Arcadia—and stepped forward to explain. "We are going to the corral for a contest of marksmanship, Father."

Don Dominguez managed to look even more sour than before. "I suppose this is a Yankee invention."

"Pleased to make your acquaintance too," said Will, his eyes twinkling.

"Bah! No real man cares for anything but horsemanship," argued Don José. "Why not let the Americano try his hand at *correr al gallo* if he wants to show off?"

"What's this about a rooster?" asked Will.

Ricardo explained that a rooster was buried up to its neck in a pile of sand. The object was to gallop past at full speed, lean down from the saddle, and pull the fowl out by the head.

"Of course, the Yankee may not have the stomach for our sport," needled Don José. "Seems he'd rather play with guns."

"Of course I have the stomach for it," retorted Will. "You can put the pot on to boil right now."

"Boil? Pot? What nonsense is this?"

"To cook the dumplings that go with the chicken, of course!"

Laughter broke out from the group. Don José's face turned red.

"If this is to be a contest, then there must be a challenger," demanded Ricardo. Facing Don José Dominguez, he continued,

"Since it is you who issued the challenge, Don José, will you ride or do you have a champion to propose?"

Don José's smile glittered brittlely. "Captain Zuniga has already agreed to ride against the Americano."

The captain was approaching on his lanky bay.

"To make matters more interesting," continued Dominguez, "I wish to propose that the course be laid out right in front of the gate into the corral."

The strategy behind this suggestion was plain: After leaning out of the saddle to grab the rooster's neck, a rider would have only a split second to sit upright again or risk being smashed against the stockade fence. A timid rider would be distracted by the upcoming obstacle and unable to concentrate.

At this point Don Pedro intervened. "I cannot permit this. Señor Reed is my guest and has never engaged in this sport before. It is not fitting to put him at such a disadvantage."

"I completely understand," said Zuniga through thinly veiled sarcasm. "I would not wish to embarrass anyone, especially the day's heroic guest . . ."

The scout's response was to step off Flotada without speaking and set to work tightening the girth and checking the bridle. As everyone waited to see what would happen, Will completed his preparations and stepped back on the gray. At last he spoke. "The way I was raised, a man who's still talking when he should be getting ready usually loses."

The little officer visibly swayed in his saddle as if the raging anger seen on his face were surging through his body. If he responded at all verbally, he would fall into Will's cleverly worded trap, yet if he stepped down to tighten the bay's cinch, he would be seen as following the American's lead.

Zuniga took the only course his pride would permit. He urged the bay forward without speaking, as if to say, *What are we waiting for?*

The black rooster protested loudly and violently when two Indians tried to place him in a shallow hole in front of the corral. Dominguez swore at them to hurry up and cursed them for being fools and cowards when the rooster flogged and pecked and clawed them.

At last the two men finished and climbed the fence with twenty other mission Indians to watch the contest. Behind them the captive grizzly snarled and growled, rearing to swat the air. He was answered by the deep bellow of the bull from the enclosure across the corral.

The rooster, now buried to his neck, was silent, but his gaze darted around wildly. He pecked furiously at the ground as if he could make it release him.

"The passes will continue until one rider is successful, or until the other is unwilling or unable to continue," declared Ricardo. "Now, who shall go first?"

"Captain Zuniga," blurted out Don José before anyone else could speak.

Zuniga settled his hat back on his head. He urged his horse toward the rooster with a jab of his spurs that made the bay spurt forward. The captain leaned far to the left out of the saddle. Holding his body parallel to the ground, his shark eyes fixed on the rooster's head.

The bay horse ran true, and Zuniga's small fingers were closing over the rooster's neck when the captain glanced ahead at the fast-approaching stockade fence. He jerked upright in the saddle, pulling the horse up right before they reached the fence. In his left hand he clutched nothing but air. The rooster was still buried in the sand.

At Will's touch of the spurs, Flotada leapt forward. The scout leaned even farther from the saddle than Zuniga, his fingers almost brushing the ground as he and the horse flew over the ground. Will hooked the rowell of a spur in the girth. He trusted the horse to run straight and true without any correction from his rider.

Nearer to the rooster they swept and closer to the corral fence. Flotada corrected his path, moved nearer in line with the target, then straightened out again.

The wall loomed ahead. Will's hand was open and on course with the rooster. His fingers closed, grasped, pulled—the scout's body snapped upright just before Flotada reached the fence.

Will looked down at his hand to discover that he clutched feathers. The rooster was still buried in the sand. Will trotted Flotada back to the watching group. Some of the Indians hopped off the stockade and fanned out to watch the next attempt.

Zuniga spent longer preparing for this run. The little captain tightened the girth on his bay and checked the straps of his spurs. When he remounted, he nervously shifted his weight, testing the cinch.

As the bay sprinted down the course again, Zuniga hooked the spur of his right foot onto the saddle horn. His body hung downward alongside the horse with his head almost touching the ground.

The horse raced across the space, and the officer's hand closed over the rooster's neck. His grip and the surging power of the bay combined to pull the flapping chicken free of the sand.

Zuniga's free hand reached up to grasp the saddle horn to pull himself upright. He began a triumphant swing of the rooster so all could see that he had not missed again. That he was, indeed, the winner.

With Zuniga halfway back into the saddle, the bay horse shrieked in alarm and plunged to a stop that jolted the officer's handhold loose. Next the horse reared, flipping Zuniga's spur off the horn and plunging him to the ground. The black rooster squawked and fluttered free.

The horse screamed again, terrified, as El Viejo, the massive grizzly, confronted him in the middle of the open corral gate. The trumpet of fright was cut off midshriek as the lumbering grizzly smashed a blow to the bay's head, breaking the horse's neck.

"El Viejo! *Oso pardo!* The grizzly is loose!" Shouts erupted from the crowd, and the people scattered in confusion like a frightened nest of ants.

Will's first reaction was to get Francesca to safety. At a tiny signal from his rider, Flotada whirled and raced toward her. The vagrant thought flashed through his mind that he had warmed up for this necessary rescue only a few moments before.

Gesturing for Francesca to lift her arms, Will leaned from the saddle and swept her up behind him in one fluid motion. Flotada sped to the corner of the stockade, where the high posts were occupied by Indians who had scrambled to safety.

Will handed Francesca up. He shouted to them to keep her safe.

One of them replied, "We will protect her!"

Spinning the gray around, Will took the reata from the horn and shook out a loop. Other vaqueros were racing in toward the great bear from all around the rodeo grounds.

The first of the lazadores was already flinging his loop at the grizzly. El Viejo stood erect, roaring his defiance and slashing the air with his great claws.

Will saw Zuniga scramble out of harm's way and leap up to scale the stockade. From the speed of his escape, the wiry officer appeared unharmed.

El Viejo took the coil of ungreased reata that had settled around his neck and pulled it toward him. The horse at the other end of the cord was jerked sideways and gave a panicked neigh. The vaquero was forced to draw a knife and slash downward, parting the line.

The grizzly dropped to all fours and charged. Two more vaqueros dashed in to try to distract the bear. He took no notice and pursued the first horse and rider, rising from his crouching lunge to slash at the horse's hindquarters.

Without the greased rawhide cords, the vaqueros were in great jeopardy from the enraged bear. With his terrific power and cunning, he could keep pulling in hapless riders. The ropers who had charged to recapture him only a moment earlier now drew back a safe distance from the snarling El Viejo. The bear rushed toward a knot of riders, scattering them.

Will knew the grizzly was intent on one thing only: heading back toward the wild canyons where he lived. And he wasn't going to tolerate any interference.

In line with his escape was the feasting area of the fiesta and a group of terrified women and children. The grizzly was aimed straight at them.

Will shouted to Ricardo, "Slow him down some, any way you can!" Urging Flotada to his greatest speed, the scout galloped back to retrieve the case of dueling pistols that sat abandoned in the dust. The pistols had already been loaded in readiness for the marksmanship exhibition. Will knew that the demonstration he was about to give went way beyond what he had planned.

The American thrust one pistol in the sash around his waist and the other he held in readiness. Flotada reversed direction, running flat out behind the track of the grizzly.

Ricardo and the other vaqueros were having no success distracting the bear. No matter how they charged at him or made futile casts with their reatas, El Viejo never swerved or slowed except to bite through a lasso and force a threatened lazodore to abandon it.

Will pushed Flotada to overcome the horse's natural instinct for safety and run in close along the bear's flank. The stouthearted gray obliged, and soon the pair had overtaken the grizzly.

Will leveled the pistol at a spot toward the back of the bear's skull and cocked the hammer. Even though the explosion of the pistol followed the click of the hammer by only a second, the click gave enough warning to El Viejo to swerve toward the horse.

Flotada jerked to the side and spurted past the bear as Will's shot clipped the grizzly's ear and creased his head.

One shot left and only thirty yards before the bear reached women and children too petrified to run. Will and Flotada raced ahead of the bear, crossed in front of him, and stopped directly in his path.

Shooting downward at the bear was risky at best because the shot could glance off the bear's ponderous skull. So he jumped from the horse and slapped Flotada out of the way.

Will dropped the discharged pistol and drew the other from his sash. He cocked it and drew a bead on the bear. It took only a count of two for the range to close and Will fired.

The lead ball entered the grizzly's gaping mouth as he roared his charge. In what was the best shot the young trapper ever made, the bullet pierced the bear's throat and tore out the back of his skull.

El Viejo's rampage turned into a crashing roll like a giant furry cannonball bouncing along the ground. The bear's carcass smashed into Will, bowling him over. The scout ended up half under the dead grizzly. One great paw was flung across Will's chest in the appearance of amiable companionship.

Captain Zuniga was yelling something as he jumped down from his perch on the corral. As Will struggled to free himself from the monster's weight, he could not hear what was said, but he could see the officer waving his arms and gesturing for his squad of soldiers to join him.

At Will's whistle Flotada rejoined him and Will remounted.

Ricardo rode up.

"What has got Zuniga all worked up?" Will asked.

"He says that the Indians let El Viejo out on purpose. He is mad! He is yelling that they were trying to kill him."

* * *

"Now what?" fumed Dominguez. "You looked like a fool who needed to be rescued, and the Americano is now a hero to everyone, not just the Riveras."

Zuniga's eyes went cold, and his hand closed over the hilt of the dagger he carried in his sash. Not surprisingly, the complaints from the blustering ranchero stopped abruptly. "May I remind you," hissed the officer in tones that left no doubt about his willingness to enforce respect by a knife thrust, "that I was the one nearly killed today. What happened to those idiots in the corral? I will cut off their hands and feet after I gouge out their eyes!"

Dominguez, who believed the captain would do exactly what he said, tried to shunt the officer's wrath aside. "Yes, they *are* fools! They claimed the gate did not open when they pulled and then sprang open by itself! But don't destroy them now, not tonight! We still need to move cargo while everyone is preoccupied with the dancing."

Zuniga thrust his half-drawn dagger back into the red velvet sash. "All right, but after the cargo and the Americano are both disposed of, they are mine to deal with."

Don José Dominguez was happy to agree.

CHAPTER 29

The scent of honeysuckle was on the light breeze that blew down from the hills and wafted into the great tent. Where only a grassy field had been for the daytime events, an enormous canvas pavilion had sprung up to house the fandango.

Will, now dressed in his grand ball outfit of midnight black and silver, was standing outside the tarp by one of the guy ropes. He watched scores of Indians carry plank sections into the tent and assemble them into a dance floor.

Dear God, he prayed, *how I thank You for sparing my life today. And Francesca's.* At the remembrance of sweeping her into his arms and carrying her to safety, a shiver ran down his backbone. *What if I had not been close enough to save her?* He shuddered. It never occurred to him to marvel that he felt more dread at the prospect of her death than he did his own. *How have I come to feel this way about a woman I just met?*

The grass rustled behind him, but his distracted mind dismissed it as a stray puff of wind stirring the canvas door flap. From inside the tent came sounds of guitars tuning up for the first dance, the *jota.*

Will was dazzled by another memory: After his fight with the grizzly, Francesca had run up to him and thrown her arms around him. Even when she at last pulled back, she still gripped his arms and held him locked within the embrace of her eyes. *Never leave me,* her eyes had said. *Never frighten me like this again!*

Could it be possible that she felt the same way about him that he did about her?

A scurrying sound reached the scout's ears. It was the soft press of furtive human footsteps.

Will whirled around, his hands involuntarily grasping for knife or pistol, neither of which were there. "Who is it? Speak up!"

"Not so loud," requested an urgent whisper. "Señor Reed, it is me, Paco."

"Paco! Come into the light. What are you doing skulking out there?"

"Shh, Señor Reed! Captain Zuniga will have me killed if I am discovered."

Will started to argue, then decided that the fear he heard in the mission Indian's voice was real enough. He stepped away from the lighted tent into the shadow around one of the oak trees. He was soon joined by a flitting shape dimly recognizable as Paco.

Even in the faint light, Paco's clothes were obviously ragged. The Indian's face was gaunt, and his eyes were hollow.

"Tell me what this is all about," Will ordered in a low, hoarse voice.

"The grizzly today, señor. It was no accident! I was there, under the stands. I saw it all. It was Zuniga and the ones called Juan and Iago."

Will started at the link formed by that trio of names. "Go on."

"They were supposed to kill *you*, but I fixed the great beast's gate so it would not open when they pulled."

"But why me? I mean, what are those three mixed up in?"

"It is not just the three," corrected Paco. "The fat ranchero Dominguez, he is in this also."

"In what? What do two murderers, the captain of the presidio, and a ranchero have in common?"

"Slaves," murmured Paco. "They are selling captured Indians to Sonoran mines. At first it was mission Indians accused of crimes, but to prevent suspicion—"

"Can you prove this?" interrupted Will. "I can't go flinging accusations like this to Don Pedro or anyone else without proof."

"Prove it yourself, señor. I heard them say that they have cargo to move tonight. If either Zuniga or Dominguez leaves the fandango, follow and see for yourself."

* * *

Francesca tried for the third time to catch Will's eye as they swirled past each other on the dance floor in the motion of the *jarabe.* Each glance she gave him went unanswered, as the scout always seemed to be looking somewhere else.

Anxiety caused her face to flush and her heart to beat faster. The warmth of the air in the tent made it natural for countless fans to appear, and Francesca covered her dismay behind vigorous fanning.

At the end of the music, Francesca moved deliberately to where a square of canvas had been rolled up to admit some of the cool evening breeze. . . .

* * *

Will turned around once before he discovered where Francesca had gone, then spotted her and maneuvered through the crowd to rejoin her.

"You seem very preoccupied, Will," Francesca said with concern. "Were you perhaps injured by El Viejo after all?"

"No, Francesca, I am all right. It's just—"

At that moment, Don José Dominguez, who had been in deep conversation with Zuniga near the doorway of the tent, stepped outside and disappeared.

"Excuse me," Will said hurriedly. "I'll explain later, Francesca."

"But, Will . . . ," she began to blurt out.

Too late. Will had already ducked through the tent flap and into the night.

Outside, the air was much cooler and moist with the first tendrils of fog drifting in from the channel. Will circled the canvas, ducking his head and murmuring an apology as he bumped into a pair of lovers kissing in the shadows.

The tracker melted into the sheltering fringe of trees and approached the line where the horses of the guests were picketed. A reata was strung between two trees and secured to them by stout iron rings. This cord formed the temporary hitching rail to which the lead ropes were tied.

Flotada recognized Will's scent and nickered a soft welcome. At the sound, Will froze in the darkness and knelt down so he would not present a man-shaped outline.

Hoping the horse would remain silent, the scout peered out from behind the sheltering tree trunk toward the line of horses. Midway down the row he saw Dominguez untie his mount and swing aboard to ride off.

Will noted the direction the ranchero had taken, and as soon as Don José was out of sight, he followed on Flotada. Will rode bareback, with a hackamore improvised from the lead rope. He did not want the silver fittings on the tack to give him away by their jingle or by a flash in the moonlight.

With his hat pulled low over his face, Will plucked the silver buttons from his jacket and stuffed them into his pocket. The gray horse and rider dressed all in black moved like a specter over the California countryside.

The ranchero was riding at an easy trot, not hurrying, and Will easily kept pace with him. The scout reined to a stop every so often to listen for a change of direction, but the hoofbeats continued up the coast, angling toward the ocean. Dominguez never gave any sign that he suspected he was being pursued.

It was an hour's ride before the smell of salt spray and the low rumble of the breakers announced that the trail had arrived at the Pacific. Following was suddenly much more difficult as the crunch of the waves on the sand covered the sounds Will had been tracking.

Ahead there was a light. It came from a promontory that stood higher than the strip of sandy beach. The American knew no habitation existed in such a place, and his instincts told him this was the destination toward which Dominguez was headed.

Trusting that the noise of the surf would drown out his approach, Will rode around the landward side of the hill. He dismounted in a brushy gully back of the knoll and left Flotada ground tied.

When the scout had crept across seventy-five of the hundred yards that separated him from the light, he heard voices.

Loudest and very angry sounding was Dominguez's. "You fools . . ." Will could make out. ". . . him! Zuniga ought . . ."

Will had reached the windowless rear of an adobe structure. It looked like one of the hide warehouses in which the rancheros stored cured leather in readiness for shipping. He removed his boots so they would not crunch on the gravel and slipped cautiously around the side of the building.

Now the words of the conversation were clear. "Don't make any mistakes," Dominguez was saying. "This will be the last shipment to Sonora. We'll blame the grizzly attack on the mission Indians and use that excuse to round them up. Once our own mine is operating, we'll be too powerful for anyone to care if we increase our workforce with some wild Tulereños."

A mine? thought Will. *And what was that about the Tule people?*

A growly voice that reminded Will of the cutthroat known as Iago asked, "What about the Americano?"

Dominguez replied, "We'll kill him and blame that on the Indians too. In fact, we can take care of Don Pedro and his son the same way!"

So it was true! Indians were being taken as slaves. Whatever else the scheme involved, the certain threat of death now hung over Will, Don Pedro, and Ricardo.

Will wondered what his next move should be. He knew that he still could not go back and accuse Dominguez without proof—not as long as Zuniga was the law. The scout strained his ears as he continued to gather information.

"The schooner will send in the boat when we signal. How many are left in this lot?"

Iago replied to Dominguez's question. "A half dozen after the two that died on the way here. But one that is left is an old man nearly dead, and there is a muchacho who won't be good for much."

Will was very near the opening of the shed. The wooden plank door stood ajar. A heavy beam that had been used to bar the door from the outside lay on the ground. He stooped to pick up the near end of the beam. His first thought was to trap the conspirators inside and bar the door.

Silently Will lifted the heavy timber. The light of the lantern inside the building flashed around as the slavers inspected their captives. Ready to slam the door shut and drop the timber in place, Will raised the bar to waist height.

Suddenly the back of his neck prickled. He pivoted sharply with the heavy beam and swung it against the adobe of the shed like a housewife swinging a carpet beater.

What he had caught between the oak timber and the wall was not carpet but a man. It was Juan, the desperado whose arm Will had broken in the cantina.

Juan's shattered arm was tied across his chest in a dirty bandanna. From the other hand flew the knife he had intended to use on Will. The scout thought he heard the man's other arm crack in trying to ward off the unexpected blow, but whatever the damage to his arm, Juan was crushed against the bricks of the shed. He collapsed to the ground with a moan.

Will spun back around and tried to jam the beam against the door. Too late! It crashed outward, and Iago and Don José tumbled through.

"The Americano," growled Iago, holding a knife and launching himself at Will.

There was time to fend off one slash with the beam; then Will threw it away because it was too clumsy and slow. Iago slipped aside as the timber crashed down.

Will had no blade with him, but he bent quickly and retrieved one of his boots. Reversing it on his hand, he presented the great rowelled spur toward Iago's face.

Will was grateful that Dominguez was a coward at heart. The fat ranchero hung back in the doorway, content to let his henchmen do the fighting and take the risks.

And taking on Will Reed involved some risks, even though Will didn't have a knife. When Iago stepped in and thrust his knife forward, Will drove his booted fist up under Iago's blade arm, knocking it aside. He followed this move by raking the spur across Iago's face. Three parallel gouges appeared as if by magic, welling full of blood that was black in the dim light.

"Get him," ordered Dominguez.

Iago circled in front of Will, trying to force the scout out of position and trap Will's spur hand against the wall. When the American saw what was intended, he snapped his arm up, letting the heavy boot fly, rowell points first, at the cutthroat's eyes.

As the man ducked, Will stepped quickly toward his assailant, and a perfectly timed left cross met Iago's chin. The murderer staggered back, his vision unfocused. The gleam from Iago's dagger showed that he had dropped his knife hand.

Will followed the blow to the chin by stepping through with a right into Iago's chest. Now the man's eyes bulged and he choked for breath.

Will grabbed Iago's arm and knocked the knife from his hand by smashing it against the adobe wall. He was winning the fight.

Just then ten thousand stars fell out of the Santa Barbara sky and hit Will on the head. Or so it seemed to him as he slumped to the ground.

* * *

When Will came to, his wrists and ankles were bound; he was on his stomach with his hands and feet tied together behind his back. His first thought was that Dominguez had joined the fight after all, but he was wrong. It was Zuniga.

While Will was lying facedown in the dirt at his feet, the captain explained how Will had followed Dominguez from the fiesta, and he in turn had followed the American.

"Why are we wasting time?" demanded Iago, wheezing. "Let me slit his throat and throw him into the sea!"

Dominguez disagreed. "No, not here. We can still make it look like the work of the Indios. We should load this cargo at once and get away from here." Then a new thought seemed to strike him. "Wait! I have heard that the Americano is a great lover of Indians. What could be more fitting than for us to send him with them? No questions are asked at the mines, and no one ever returns."

Zuniga and Iago gripped Will's arms and roughly tossed him into the warehouse.

Will landed more softly than he'd expected. There was a body underneath him!

"Stay here," Zuniga ordered Iago. "We'll go to the beach to signal the boat." He nodded toward Dominguez, and they headed for the beach.

Iago shut and barred the door, then stood guard outside.

The body Will had landed on grunted but made no other sound. The scout apologized in Spanish.

"Sequoyah!" piped a thin treble voice.

"Blackbird! No! Is that you?" gasped the American, switching to Yokut.

"Yes," Blackbird whispered, a sob catching in his throat. "Oh, Will Reed! Grandfather and I were captured while gathering herbs. These awful men forced us to march across the mountains with almost no food and only a little water. We were thrown into this prison two days ago."

"Where is Falcon?" Will asked, trying to peer through the darkness.

"Grandfather is very sick," the boy continued anxiously. "He can barely move or speak. Grandfather. Grandfather. Can you hear me?"

There was no response.

CHAPTER 30

A short while later Will heard the voices of Dominguez and Zuniga returning from the beach. Dominguez was cursing loudly as he flung open the door to the warehouse. "That no-good . . . he calls himself a captain! He is a coward—a coward! A little breeze springs up, and he must hoist a signal that says 'cannot land.'"

Zuniga was more pragmatic. "He does not want to be caught on a lee shore and get beached here."

"Bah! Now we have to guard these wretches for another day. Iago," Dominguez said testily, "you must stay here. We'll be back tonight."

"And the Americano?" Iago asked, drawing his dagger by way of suggestion.

"No, not now," Dominguez flung back. He swiveled toward Zuniga. "Captain, you and I will use this ride to speak of what is best to do with Señor Reed and Don Pedro. If we plan this properly, since you are the law, you can name me as executor of Don Pedro's property."

"And guardian of his daughter?"

"Exactly so," the ranchero agreed, "and I in turn can start calling you son-in-law as well as son!"

Both laughed as they left the warehouse. Iago stepped outside with them.

When Iago did not return, Will struggled with his bonds, but without result. "Blackbird," he whispered, "do you think you can undo these knots with your teeth?"

Will was facedown in the darkness, so he couldn't see the boy's response, but he knew that Blackbird would do his best.

Sure enough, the boy immediately went to work on the thong that pulled the American's hands down toward his ankles. It was slow going. Even though Blackbird was not trussed up like Will, his hands were tied behind his back.

Long minutes seemed to pass while Blackbird worked on the knots in the inky blackness of the adobe building. At last the length of leather strap came undone.

Now Will could sit up and move a little in order to put the bindings on his wrists into a better position for Blackbird to work. "Hurry. If Iago comes in to check on us, we'll never get another chance."

It was nearly daybreak when the rawhide that secured Will's hands was loose enough for him to strip it off. He pulled his wrists free, shaking his hands to restore some feeling to them.

Will had begun to work on the cords holding his feet when he heard a noise outside the shed. There was no way to pretend to still be bound, and even tearing feverishly at the leather, the trapper could not get his ankles untied in time.

He jerked himself upright, falling hard against the adobe brick wall next to the door. Leaning alongside the opening, his muscles coiled like a snake's preparing to strike. His hands were clenched for the single, two-handed blow he would have one chance to make.

The door opened but only a crack. Then it creaked wider apart, but still no one entered At last it was pulled all the way open, admitting the dim illumination of predawn, but no one stepped across the threshold.

Positioned against the wall, Will could not see where the guard stood. Drops of sweat clung to the scout's forehead as he struggled to keep his body tense.

"Reed," a voice called out in English. "Will Reed, are you in there?"

"Easton!" shouted Will, lurching out of the warehouse. "Thank God it's you. How did you find us?"

"Paco here," said Easton, indicating the mission Indian standing behind him. "He watched Zuniga trailing you and followed him. After you got locked up for the night, he came to fetch me."

"But that's ten miles each way and three trips. How could you do that on foot?"

Paco grinned slyly. "I told you it was forbidden for my people to ride. I did not say we did not know how." He went past Will into the warehouse and with a smirk added, "I will untie the rest."

"And what happened to the guard?" asked Will.

"Iago?" responded Easton. "He never sticks around for a fight unless the two-to-one odds are in his favor. Too bad though. I think he has gone to warn Dominguez. We may be heading into trouble if we go back to the hacienda."

"Not if," Will pointed out sharply. "Don Pedro and Ricardo and . . . Francesca are in danger."

"Thought you'd feel that way," said Easton, tossing Will a burlap-wrapped bundle.

"What's this?" asked Will. When he pulled the twine, a buckskin suit and a new Hawken rifle tumbled out.

"Never met a man who could fight best in unfamiliar rigging," Easton answered.

Paco reemerged from the adobe. "Señor Reed, the Yokuts want to go home. But the old man is very bad. Even if they carry him, I don't think he will make it back to their valley."

"Please, Will Reed," begged Blackbird, "you must help my grandfather."

"Try not to worry, Blackbird. I'll see that he gets tended to." Will said to Easton, "We'll take him to Father Sanchez at the mission."

"Mate, we'll be headed straight into their hands," cautioned Easton.

"No matter," said the grim-faced scout. "It's time to take down the evil in the West."

✶CHAPTER 31✶

It was an odd-looking procession that rode into Pueblo Santa Barbara. Will in his buckskins rode on Flotada with Blackbird behind him. Billy Easton was riding a mule. Falcon was carried on a travois pulled behind Paco's horse.

Paco looked nervously around as he rode. At the first sign of observers he jumped off the horse and walked alongside.

They reached the mission grounds without incident, but several onlookers witnessed their arrival, including Father Quintana. Blackbird and his grandfather were entrusted to the safety and care of Father Sanchez. Will and Easton mounted again to ride out to Don Pedro's rancho.

As they were leaving the mission compound, they were met by a quick-marching file of twenty soldiers and Captain Zuniga.

Zuniga's uniform buttons gleamed in the sun, and the feathered plume of his hat waved in the wind. "Halt. Señor Reed, I again place you under arrest." Zuniga gave a negligent wave of his gloved hand to order his soldiers to form a line blocking the exit from the square.

"What am I charged with this time, Zuniga?" asked Will. "Does what I know about you make me a spy?"

"Silence!" shrilled Zuniga. "You are charged with wantonly murdering the man named Juan and with stirring up rebellion among the Indios."

"And how do you explain your dealings in slaves and your intended plot to assassinate Don Pedro Rivera y Cruz?" asked Will pointedly.

"Lies. The ravings of a spy desperate to save himself," retorted Zuniga. "Guards, take him."

"Not so fast there, Captain," suggested Billy Easton, a Hawken rifle across his saddlebow. "I have seen your warehouse and your human 'cargo,' and I confirm what Reed here says is the truth."

"Easton, you are charged with smuggling and trafficking in slaves. Soldiers, seize them both," ordered Zuniga.

"Wait!" shouted Don José Dominguez. He stood on the red-tiled roof of the priest's quarters. Beside him, pointing a rifle at Dominguez's quivering face, was the mission Indian Donato. "They killed Iago! Captain, tell your men to give up their weapons or they'll kill me, too!"

Atop the roofs around three sides of the square stood fifty stony-featured Indians. Most were armed with bows, but others had firearms.

Zuniga gave an animal-like scream of rage. He raised the pistol he was holding and fired it at Will. The lead ball passed under Will's arm and flattened itself against the courtyard fountain as Will and Easton jumped from their mounts to take cover.

A rifle boomed from the rooftop, then another and another. The whiz of arrows being discharged filled the air with the buzz of angry, death-dealing bees. Flotada clattered across the courtyard in confusion. Easton's mule bolted, was struck by a stray bullet, then fell over on top of a soldier.

Two of the soldiers went down with arrow wounds. The others took cover behind the adobe watering tank as a rain of arrows and rifle balls pattered around them.

Behind the fountain, Will waited, reserving his fire until Zuniga rose up with a musket. Will's shot crashed into the bricks just below the captain's head, lacerating his face with flying scraps of adobe.

"Stop! You must stop!" shouted Dominguez from the rooftop. "Listen to me! It was Zuniga! Zuniga caused this to happen!"

Aiming through eyes blinded by adobe dust and anger, Zuniga rose and wildly fired at the roof. His shot pierced Dominguez's throat. The ranchero clutched at his neck even as he toppled from the roof to land with a thud on the pavement below.

Will fired at the same instant, and his shot hit the captain square in the chest. As Zuniga fell, three arrows and two lead balls pierced him, including one fired by his own soldiers.

At that moment, Father Sanchez came out of the mission. His arms upraised, he walked boldly into the center of the square and shouted, "Donato. Lazario. You others. In the name of Christ, stop this killing at once!"

Miraculously, rifles and bows were lowered. No more shots were fired. The revolt of the Indians of Mission Santa Barbara ended almost as soon as it had begun.

* * *

The group gathered in the parlor of the hacienda of Don Pedro Rivera y Cruz included Will, Billy Easton, Father Sanchez, and Ricardo. Together they were sorting things out.

Will drew a leather pouch from his pocket and out of it dropped the small lump of dark red stone.

"Cinnabar," exclaimed Don Pedro. "Is that what all this is about?"

"And, Father," added Ricardo, "at last I remember where I have seen such ore before. It comes from the Canyon Perdido on lands shared by us and the mission."

The little council took in the implications of that thought; then Will asked, "What is going to happen to the mission Indians?"

"They have run away into the hills, but they will return when they find out that they are not going to be punished. The two soldiers who were wounded are recovering, and the only two killed, Dominguez and Zuniga, were guilty of goading the neophytes into rebellion and enslaving both neophytes and valley Indians."

"And what about Father Quintana?" asked Don Pedro.

"He also has fled," reported Sanchez, "and it would be best for him if he never returned."

"What will happen if Governor Figueroa decides to step in?" asked Will.

"I do not think we need to worry about that," suggested Don Pedro. "You see, I have today received notice that I have been appointed the governor's representative."

"That's it then, I guess," said Will. "Tell me, Father, how is Falcon? Is he going to live?"

"Live?" Father Sanchez chuckled. "That old man is as tough as bull hide. He has already been telling me what herbs are missing from my medical garden! By the way, the child tells me that he and his grandfather want to return here after visiting with their people. It seems that someone has told them about a certain path—a trail that leads straight to our heavenly Father—and they wish to learn more."

CHAPTER 32

Francesca was standing on the balcony of the hacienda, watching the sun set over the sweeping coast of California. A breath of clean summer breeze twirled her fine dark hair and rustled the pleats of her skirt.

Will and Billy Easton were in the courtyard below, and both looked up at Francesca standing there.

"Reed," Easton said, "your place is up there with her, so let's keep this good-bye short."

"Thanks for your help, Billy, and for the use of the Hawken."

"You keep that," Easton said, refusing the weapon Will offered. "Call it a wedding present, since I won't be here for the ceremony." Easton grinned.

"Oh? Will you be back this way soon?"

"Doubtful," replied the pirate figure. "Things would be a bit uncomfortable for me around here when people start asking where the Indians got those rifles. Anyway, my job is done."

"What job was that?"

"Looking into the situation here in California on behalf of President Andy Jackson. He sent me. I am the American spy."

With that, Billy Easton doffed his hat in a gesture of farewell and was gone.

The Year of the Grizzly

American Will Reed and his family have been owners of a sprawling rancho near Santa Barbara, California, for the past sixteen years. Life has been good and peaceful.
But trouble is brewing between the American military and Mexican banditos. Both are determined to grab the wealth of central California's cattle ranches for themselves.
And the Reed family rancho lies directly in the path of their greed and lust for power. . . .

This book is for Luke.

CHAPTER 1

The clanging of the church bells in the twin towers at Mission Santa Barbara rolled lazily over the canyons and hillsides. As the deep-pitched cast-iron voices announced the hour of noon, Will Reed looked up from the flank of the calf he had roped and wiped a buckskin-gloved hand across his sweaty forehead.

He pushed the stringy curls of his dark auburn hair out of his eyes and gestured for his seventeen-year-old son to hurry up with the branding iron. "*Vamos,* Peter! Just this one more, and we can break for mealtime."

"Coming, Father," the thin, serious youth replied. Peter removed the glowing brand depicting the *Leaning R* of the Reed family from the blazing coals of oak and applied it to the calf's hide. The hot iron sizzled on the hide, bringing a bleat of complaint from the calf.

After its ears were notched in a pattern to indicate the year 1846, the red calf was allowed to scamper out of the corral and rejoin the rest of the herd.

"Bueno!" shouted the short, round-bellied man who opened and shut the corral gate. "That makes a dozen so far. Young Pedro has the makings of a real vaquero."

"Paco—" Peter laughed at the heavyset mission Indian—"you've said the same thing every roundup since I was five and using my reata to catch Mother's geese. When will I *be* a real vaquero?"

Clearing his throat at the question, Will scowled. "Be careful what you wish for. The other branding teams will do twenty calves to our twelve, and the roundup lasts for weeks."

"And I would be with them if you and Mother did not make me study geometry and practice writing letters!" complained Peter.

Will swatted the dust from his leather chaparejos with a swipe of the stiff-brimmed hat. "What can we do with such a maverick?" he asked Paco, grinning. "His grandfather is a university-educated engineer, but all this whelp can think about is horses and cows!"

Paco shook his head in mock despair. "It must be the other side of his nature coming out. His father, it is said, came across the wilderness from America and put the Spanish caballeros to shame with his riding and roping. And his *ojos verdes,* his green eyes! They say he was *muy enamorado,* a great lover, to win the hand of the flower of California, Francesca Rivera y Cruz."

"Enough!" Will shot back. "It is too hot for such windy tales. Besides, they will have heard the bells at home, and dinner will be waiting. Come on!" He led the way to where his steel gray horse stamped and fretted in the shade of the tamarack trees next to Peter's buckskin and Paco's mule.

"What is disturbing the horses?" Peter began.

Another peal of church bells interrupted him.

"What can that be? Is it a fire?" the boy asked.

His father shushed him to silence, and the three men listened to the discordant jangling—not the clear tones of the single bell but a confused and uncertain sound, as if a pile of scrap metal were being dropped onto stone pavement. Underneath it all, a muted rumbling grew, like the passage of a distant stampede.

"It's an earthquake!" shouted Will. "Get away from the horses!" A sharp, convulsive twist in the ground beneath him knocked him off his feet. It tossed his son and Paco into the plunging and rearing mounts, and the horses scattered.

A sickening corkscrew motion, like a square-rigged ship facing a quartering sea, followed the initial shock. Across the plain, Will could see the waves of tremors rolling like ocean swells.

Paco tried to stand just as another crest passed, but was flung outstretched onto the ground.

"How long till it quits rolling?" called Peter from where he hugged a tamarack's trunk.

"*Quien sabe?* Who knows?" the Indian replied. "The hinges of the earth are turning, and El Diablo, the devil, is riding out of the underworld."

✯ ✯ ✯

Don Pedro Rivera y Cruz reached across the heavy oak-plank table toward the clay jar of olives. The jar, as if possessed with a mind of its own, edged away from his fingers. "What mischief is this?" he muttered to his daughter, Francesca, who was tasting a kettle of simmering bean-and-barley stew.

Then the shock wave hit, and the earthenware pot rolled off the table and broke on the floor.

"Earthquake!" he shouted.

Above the *hornillo*, the brick oven, a crack appeared in the plaster of the whitewashed adobe cookhouse. As Francesca stared in amazement, a spiderweb of lines branched and forked, like a chain of lightning spreading up the wall.

When the rippling net of cracks reached the top of the wall, it exploded in a cloud of plaster dust that showered onto the dark-haired woman. Another tremor hit, flinging her sharply against the edge of the oak table, knocking out her breath and throwing her to the floor. The *hornillo* shattered, filling the air with smoke and swirling soot and littering the dirt floor with hot coals. Francesca slapped at the smoldering embers that rolled onto her long skirt.

The crack in the wall widened, and globs of mortar fell from the seams between the adobe blocks. The beams of the roof creaked and groaned, and the heavy brick wall leaned inward, threatening to collapse at any moment.

Don Pedro, somehow still on his feet, crossed the small room with a leap and yanked his daughter out of the wreckage of the stove and flung her toward the doorway. She landed half in and half out of the opening, just as the wall split apart with a crack like the noise of a rifle shot, and the adobe blocks began to fall.

The ranchero had no chance to escape himself. He lunged for the floor and rolled under the stout wooden table. Fragments of heavy clay slabs rained down, and a roar came from the earth underneath the cookhouse as the roof collapsed into the interior of the building.

* * *

Francesca's roll through the doorway was accelerated by another spasm of the earth. She tumbled over and over in the yard between the tall wood-frame ranch house and the adobe cookhouse.

When at last the ground stopped spinning, Francesca was facing away from the cookhouse. "Father," she called as she stood slowly, fighting the dizziness, "are you all right?"

Turning toward the block building, she screamed and tottered forward. The structure had completely shattered and fallen into a shapeless mass of rubble. The roof beams protruded from the wreckage like the ribs of a whale carcass.

"Father!" she screamed again and fell to trying to shift the great blocks of clay from where the entry had been only moments before. Francesca strained to lift a single brick free of the pile and found that she could not. The ruins seemed to have locked together into a solid mass.

Even when she found a single wooden post that would reluctantly move when she pulled with all her strength, she was forced to stop when another heap of blocks tumbled into the newly made opening. With an anguished cry, Francesca clawed at the fragments of bricks, tossing them aside. Her nails tore and bled in her frenzied struggle to locate her father. She called his name again and again but received no answer.

Simona, the cook, and her husband, Luis, came running out of the main house.

"Help me!" Francesca pleaded. "Father is buried somewhere underneath and I cannot free him!"

Luis looked at the mound of adobe before glancing at Simona. He shook his head sadly.

"No!" Francesca yelled, denying the dreadful suggestion in the unspoken thought. She pounded her fists on the unrelenting bricks. "No! Father! Father!"

* * *

The turn of the earth's hinges brought rockslides and avalanches to the hills around Santa Barbara. The peaks rimming the coastal plain sprouted spirals of dust, as if the mountains had broken into a hundred fires.

Will suddenly thought of Francesca and their house. How well had it withstood the quake? His concern multiplied when he recalled his insistence that their new casa be built in the wood-frame manner of his upbringing rather than the adobe construction of California.

The horses and the mule and the herd of cattle had run from the terror of the tremors and stampeded in all directions. Will could not locate his mount. The only animal of any kind still in sight was one lone steer. The rangy, rust-colored Chihuahua longhorn shook his head angrily and pawed the ground like a fighting bull. Angered at the unexpected movement of the earth, the steer charged at the only target of blame it could find—the two-legged man creatures.

The powerful animal first lunged at Paco, who fled to the safety of the tamarack tree beside Peter. Together they climbed its spindly branches. There was barely room above the height of the steer's head for both to cling to the narrowing trunk. The steer's horns clashed against the tree, and he gave a bellow of challenge for them to come down and fight.

The crash of the heavy headed beast against the slender tree was like the force of another earthquake to the man and the boy. A few more such blows and they would fall beneath his hooves.

Will slapped his hand against his chaps to attract the animal's attention. He did not have time for this disturbance right now. At another moment the predicament might have seemed humorous but not when he so desperately wanted to check on things at home.

The flapping leather caught the steer's interest, and he charged. Will coolly inspected the distance to the nearest tree and the space between him and the safety of the corral fence. Both were too far to risk turning his back on the raging animal, so Will stood his ground, expecting to throw himself aside at the last possible instant.

When the separation between Will and the onrushing steer with the wickedly pointed horns was no more than three body lengths, the earth shook once again—an aftershock, a concluding exclamation point to punctuate the power of the original quake. No wavelike rolling motion this time but a single sharp jerk of the land.

Will felt as if a rug were being yanked out from under his feet. His knees flew upward, and he landed abruptly, sprawled on his back in the path of the steer. Paco and Peter were both jolted out of the tamarack.

Fortunately, the tremor played no favorites; the charging animal was also knocked from his feet. His front legs collapsed under him as if he had run off an unexpected cliff. The force of his rush drove the steer's muzzle solidly into the ground.

When Will got to his feet again, the steer was still struggling to get up from his knees. The ranchero watched the beast warily, but the animal's blind rage was gone. In place of the infuriated pitching of his horns, he shook his great head uncertainly, as if trying to clear it.

Still staggering, the steer tottered off toward the creek bottom in search of others of his kind. He moved slowly, testing each footstep carefully before committing to it.

Will called out to Paco and Peter to ask if they were all right, then whistled a sharp signal.

He was answered at once by a familiar neigh. Flotada, his gray gelding, trotted obediently back into sight. The horse's flanks were lathered with a nervous sweat. He rolled his eyes and trembled at Will's touch, as if the quivers in the soil had flowed upward into his body.

Will replaced the bridle and tightened the cinch, then shouted for his son and Paco to retrieve their mounts and follow as soon as possible. A slight touch of his large-rowelled spurs put Flotada into a gallop.

As he rode, Will saw the signs of the devastation caused by the quake. A stone fence bordering the road was knocked to pieces, and the earthen dam of a stock pond had collapsed and drained out all its water. Will urged the gray to greater speed, until only one hill stood between him and the ranch building. He ran a hand through his red hair and shuddered involuntarily as they passed the crest. He was afraid to see what lay before him.

To his surprise and momentary relief, the two-story wooden home seemed completely untouched. Then the curve of his route brought the rear of the estate into view. He drew in his breath sharply. Where the adobe cookhouse had stood, there was only a mound of debris. At this distance it wasn't even recognizable as having been a building. Beside the ruins two figures stood unmoving. Lying across the heap of blocks was a splash of color that resolved itself into a familiar form. Will's senses spun, and even though the earth was still, he reeled in the saddle.

Francesca! Will jabbed his spurs into Flotada's flanks, and the gelding cleared twenty feet in a leap straight down the hill, lifting his rider over four rows of grapevines and plunging directly across the flower garden.

Will abandoned the horse's back in midgallop and threw himself toward Francesca's body. He gathered her in his arms, and she began to sob.

His wife's disheveled dress, tearstained face, and bloodied fingers told him all he needed to know. Taking her firmly by the shoulders, Will tenderly set her aside, giving her to Simona and Luis to hold. He lifted a great block, then seized the projecting end of one of the roof timbers and used it to lever up a mass of the rubble.

A shaft of light penetrated into the heap of adobe and landed on a corner of the oak table. One edge was raised slightly—a clear space of no more than ten inches in height was left above the dirt floor. In the small crevice, the top of Don Pedro's bald head could be seen, covered with ashes, dirt, and plaster grit.

Deeper into the pile Will dug until he had uncovered the tabletop. Bending his muscled back and lifting with all the strength of his six-foot-three-inch frame, he raised the broad oak table and tossed it behind him.

He stooped to grasp his father-in-law and pull him free, then stopped with a fierce intake of breath.

Francesca cried out again, "Father!" and started forward, but Will gestured sharply for Luis to hold her back.

With the tabletop removed, the truth was plain. The lower half of Don Pedro's body was not merely imprisoned by the fallen bricks; it was crushed beneath them.

The old ranchero's eyelids fluttered. He was still alive! Will could not imagine how it was possible. A ragged breath escaped Don Pedro's lips, no stronger than the faint breeze that stirs the cottonwood leaves.

Will held his stiff-brimmed hat to block the sun from his father-in-law's face. The change in light brought Don Pedro's eyes fully open. He struggled to focus them for a moment; then a look of recognition came over his face. "Will," he said softly. "Francesca . . . is she all right?"

"Yes," Will reassured him, "she's fine. Save your strength, Don Pedro. We'll soon have you out."

Even as he spoke, Will knew it was hopeless. He could see in the old ranchero's eyes that he also knew the truth.

Don Pedro shook his head slightly. "Before my body . . . is . . . released from these clay bricks, my spirit . . . free from its clay." His voice faded and his body stiffened with a spasm of pain, but he fought it down fiercely. "Your fine new home . . . does it still stand?"

Will assured him that it did. "The wooden frame took the shock. It was not damaged."

Don Pedro gave a nod of satisfaction. "You were right . . . not use adobe," he wheezed, his breathing more forced and shallow now. "Old ways . . . passing. No *quedan ni rastros* . . . no vestige will remain."

"Papa," Francesca pleaded, "don't leave us!"

Don Pedro rallied once again at the sound of Francesca's weeping. "Kiss them all for me," he said. Then loudly, "I love you, children. . . ." His words dissolved in a fit of coughing that left a pink froth on his lips.

Gesturing with a twist of his head for Will to lean close to him, Don Pedro instructed, "Move the stones now, and let me pass."

When Will complied, a smile washed over the ranchero's features. His eyes opened wide, and he stared upward into the bright blue California sky.

CHAPTER 2

The dirt was soft and deep along the country lane that wound through the northern stretches of the great central valley of California. The four mules kicked up the earth underfoot in little explosions of red dust, even though the four travelers were moving slowly.

The lead rider was an Indian named Two Strike, a Delaware who scouted for the United States Army. He was dressed in a blue woolen shirt and army-issue trousers, but he was clearly Indian. Two shiny black braids rested on his shoulders. Just as clear was the fact that he was a scout. He paid constant attention to the marks in the dust made by previous travelers, and his searching eyes roved continuously.

Following Two Strike were two men dressed in buckskin shirts and trousers and caps made of animal skins. The first was the younger of the two, Anson McBride by name, nicknamed Cap. The other man, wearing the garb of a trapper from the High Lonesome, was Tor Fowler.

Fowler was tall and angular, hawk-nosed and sharp-chinned. As the Indian scout's eyes swept the path ahead, Fowler's senses registered the brush and trees on either side and silently monitored the road behind. It irritated him that the last man in the column kept up a running monologue of comments and criticism about the dust, the slowness of the travel, and the unnecessary caution.

The talker's name was Davis, a settler who had arrived in California by wagon train. He seemed to think that he could tame the West like he handled store clerks back home in the States—just complain loud and long enough, and things would be run more to his liking.

"Hey, Fowler, what's that Injun up to now?" Davis demanded.

Tor Fowler reined in the mule and stopped in the shade of a cedar. Two Strike had abruptly turned off the road and ridden up a hillside above the track to scan the countryside. He stared especially long and hard at their back trail.

"Reckon he's doin' what Captain Fremont pays him for," responded Fowler.

"Huh!" Davis grunted, gesturing toward the hill with his rifle, where the Indian continued to peer into the distance. "He looks right impressive, don't he? 'Cept, what's he lookin' for? Ain't no Mex within miles of here. Ain't that right, McBride?"

McBride, the youngest member of the Bear Flag brigade, looked worried. "I ain't sh-shore. We st-stayed on this road a long t-time, an' maybe we oughta get off it."

"Well, excuse me!" blurted a disgusted Davis, slapping his shapeless felt hat against a thigh covered in greasy, patched homespun. "We ain't gonna get back in two days ner two weeks if that Injun stops ever' mile for a look-see . . . an' now this half-wit thinks we should go skulkin' through the bushes all the way to Pope's ranch an' back." His railing stopped when Tor Fowler fiercely yanked his mule around and rode toward him.

Fowler's eye bored into Davis's round, pudgy face. He hissed in a low, ominous tone, "How'd you 'scape gettin' your hair lifted before this, Davis? Don't never call Cap McBride half-wit again, hear? He's got more sense than you, stutter or no."

Fowler watched as Davis tightened his grip on the Colt revolving rifle. But any reply Davis thought of making never made it past the knife edge of threat on Fowler's sharp features.

"All right, all right," Davis muttered. "No call to get riled. You mountain men is so touchy. I just want to get on with it. Thunderation! Them Mexicans will be busted and the war clean over 'fore we get back into it."

"I don't think so," Fowler replied.

"What's that mean?"

The buckskin-clad trapper lifted his chin toward the knoll above the road where the Indian scout still posed. "That scout . . . he just give the sign for riders comin'."

"T-tor," Cap McBride said, "do we r-run or f-fight?"

Looking to the Indian scout again before replying, Fowler said, "Fight, I reckon, unless we can parley. Two Strike says there's riders ahead of us too."

Fowler had already selected the brow of the hillside that overhung the road as the place to fort up. A lightning-struck cedar had slabbed off, and part of its trunk rested against some rocks near the edge of a cliff. The steep banks and the thick brush back of the spot made the location defensible, at least for a time.

At Fowler's urging, Cap McBride led the mules farther up on the hill into an elderberry thicket. Fowler ordered him to remain there to keep the animals quiet while the other three men prepared for battle.

Fowler, Davis, and the Delaware crouched down behind the cedar-log rampart. Davis groused about "skulkin' an' hidin' from the cowardly Mexicans" and made a great show of his eagerness for a fight.

Fowler thought briefly of correcting the settler, reminding him that these were native Californians fighting on their home ground and that the Americans were the invaders, but he decided it was a waste of time.

Also ignoring Davis's rumblings, Two Strike coolly set about inspecting his weapons. The Indian carried a short-barreled gun, .66 caliber. Fowler saw the scout carefully lay the rifle in the fork of a tree branch and set his powder horn and a row of cast-lead balls in a seam of bark beside it. Two Strike also examined a razor-sharp hand axe, checking its edge before thrusting it back into his belt.

Fowler's rifle, bought at the Hawken family gun shop in St. Louis, rested comfortably across his forearm as it had for thousands of miles. He had carried it across the Rockies more times than he could count. This expedition to California was his third trip in the employ of Captain John Charles Fremont. The Hawken had stopped marauding Pawnees, killed grizzlies, and saved Fowler's life more than once.

Fowler watched with amusement as Davis dithered around, looking up the road in one direction and then peering down in the other. The settler alternated between declaring that nobody was coming, spoiling for a fight, and maintaining to the air that the approaching horsemen would be other Americans anyway, since the Mexicans were too scared to face the Bear Flaggers.

"You got that thing loaded?" Fowler asked dryly, indicating Davis's Colt revolving rifle.

"Huh? Sure enough—fire six times to your one. I bought this new just before I come west with Grigsby's train."

"Ever shot it? You know them newfangled things is dangerous."

Davis looked to Fowler as if swelling pride might overpower good sense, but the echo of cantering hoofbeats kept him quiet. All three men lowered themselves behind the log as the mounting noise of a large number of horsemen approached.

A dozen riders cantered into view and stopped just below the embankment where the Americans had paused not ten minutes before. Peeking through a heap of bush above the level of the cedar log, Fowler examined the troops riding in columns of two.

They were a mixed lot, Fowler judged. The two leaders seemed to be a fair sample of the rest of the group. One man was dressed in knee britches of fine cloth and sported a stylish flat-crowned hat. The tack on his well-groomed bay showed silver conchas at every joint and fitting. The man himself was broad of face and pleasant in appearance.

The other man at the front of the group was the complete opposite. His clothing was shabby, and he wore a red bandanna tied over his shoulder-length hair and knotted at the back of his neck. A wisp of scruffy beard clung to his chin. The red horse ridden by this second man was a fine tall animal, but a stained old blanket covered the saddle frame. As the sorrel danced about in the roadway, the mark of Sutter's brand could be seen on its flank.

Stolen, I'll be bound, Fowler thought.

The rest of the riders were divided between these two extremes—some were well-dressed young caballeros, and others were lean and hungry-looking men with knife-scarred faces. In only one respect did the groups match: none had modern-looking weapons. Some carried old-style muskets and obsolete flintlocks. The rest were armed with lances or pistols only.

The lean man with the scraggly beard spoke loudly enough that the watchers on the hill could hear. "Don Carillo," he addressed a well-dressed, middle-aged man in Spanish, "the trail of the American dogs stops here. They have either turned aside into the woods or doubled back. I told you we should have moved faster. We must find them and exterminate them."

There was a general murmur of assent from the group, but the man addressed as Don Carrillo disagreed. "Juan Padilla, we wish to capture the Americans, but it is more important to interrogate them, find out their intentions than to execute them, and General Castro has so ordered. Please remember this."

"Bah!" spat Padilla. "If you have no stomach for this business, then go back to the women. All *true* Californios wish to teach these rattlesnakes a lesson they will never forget."

"You dare speak thus to me?" countered Carrillo. "You saloon keeper!"

This is getting interesting, Fowler thought. A little dissension among the Californians would make a worthwhile report to Captain Fremont.

"Don't puff up with me, señor rich ranchero. Remember, I was elected cocaptain of this troop of lancers."

As Tor Fowler listened intently to the troop's next move, he heard the sound of a single-action hammer being cocked and turned his head. Davis had risen from his kneeling position to slide his over the top of the log. It was aimed right at Carrillo.

Fowler threw himself toward Davis, but it was too late. The roar of the .66 caliber rifle discharging deafened both men as they crashed against the trunk of the tree.

Don Carrillo reeled in his saddle and dropped like a stone to the dusty roadway. "*Emboscada!*" the horsemen shouted, and the battle was joined.

Two Strike's gun fired, and a lancer threw up his hands and screamed. A flurry of shots replied from California muskets.

Fowler rolled back to his position, picked out a man aiming a pistol, and fired.

A third horseman clutched his leg, and Padilla shouted, "Retreat, *amigos*, retreat!"

The fleeing horsemen fired a few shots back over their shoulders, but none took effect. They soon disappeared out of sight around a bend of the road.

Exultant at this victory, Davis jumped up on the cedar log and yelled catcalls after the Californios. "Look at 'em run! What'd I tell you? They won't even stay to fight. Did you see me drop that fat one? Right through the brisket and—hey, why'd you jump me?"

Fowler seethed with rage. It was all he could do not to club the ignorant settler where he stood. "You cussed fool! You may have killed us all. Now get that popgun reloaded and get ready."

"Ready for what? We won. Didn't you see? They run off with their tails betwixt their legs."

"They'll be back. By now they figured out that they heard only three different guns, and they know right where we are." Fowler stopped suddenly as he heard a distant rumbling and saw a swelling dust cloud floating above the trees. Both the pounding noise and the swirling haze swept nearer.

When the rank of riders reappeared, they were six abreast, all bearing lances at the ready. The shafts may have been old and dull from disuse, but the triangular steel points glittered in the sunlight. The churning mass of men and horses surged forward like a single spike-toothed beast bent on the destruction of the Americans.

In contrast to the now-cowering Davis, Fowler stood upright and took careful aim. At extreme range he fired and saw a palomino horse stumble but come on. He remained standing still, reloading mechanically as he picked out his next target.

When Two Strike fired, a Californian slumped forward. His lance struck the ground, pitchpoling the man out of his saddle and under the hooves of the onrushing horses.

Davis fired all six chambers, hitting nothing. His fingers fumbled as he tried to reload, and he scattered percussion caps across the tree trunk. Two chambers received no powder but got double charges, and two got powder but no shot.

Fowler ignored him.

The wave of riders swept closer, urging their mounts up the steep bank without hesitation. The second rank of six spurred past the bend of the road, then wheeled to attack from the other direction.

A lancer's plunging bay reached the top of the embankment. Instead of jumping over the cedar log, the caballero turned sharply and rode along it, lance point at the ready.

Fowler fired, and then, with no time to reload, used the Hawken as a club and knocked the lance head aside as the Californio charged past.

Out of the corner of his eye, Fowler saw Davis futilely squeeze the trigger on two misloaded chambers. After the two empty clicks, Davis threw the Colt away and fled up the hill toward the mules.

At the opposite end of the fallen tree, Two Strike faced a musket with his hatchet. As the rider cantered up the brow of the embankment, the Delaware leaped at the horse's head. It reared up, eyes rolling in terror, and struck out wildly.

One of the flailing hooves knocked Two Strike to the ground. As the Indian struggled to his feet, another Californio rider appeared above the barricades, his pistol aimed at the scout's head.

Two Strike gave a defiant yell and spun the hand axe at the attacker. He missed, and the shot pierced his heart and sent him hurtling down the embankment.

Just that suddenly, it was over.

Fowler lay on the ground, a lance thrust against his throat. Then, flanked by lancers and followed by a third man with a musket aimed at his head, Fowler stumbled down the embankment and was forced to kneel in the churned dust of the road. Beside him lay the bodies of the leader of the Californios, Don Carrillo, and another man.

Raising his head wearily at a new noise from the hillside, Fowler saw Cap McBride prodded down the hill.

"Q-quit stickin' me," Cap protested. "I'm a-g-goin'."

Glad to see that Cap at least appeared unharmed, Fowler asked, "What happened? Did they get Davis?"

"N-no!" Cap said with disgust as he was likewise forced to his knees. "He weren't even hurt. He r-run up and kicked me out of the way and r-rode off with all the mules!"

"*Silencio!*" the man known as Juan Padilla shouted. He spurred his prancing sorrel in a tight circle around the kneeling men.

"Four Fingers," Padilla said to the rider who had killed Two Strike, "how many did we lose?"

"Two killed and four wounded, Capitan," was the report.

"All right," said Padilla abruptly, "shoot that one first." He indicated Cap McBride.

"Hold on!" erupted Fowler in Spanish. "He wasn't even in the fight, and anyway, you don't shoot prisoners!"

"Not all at once," sneered Padilla, shaking Davis's Colt rifle in Fowler's face. "You we may tie to horses and pull apart. What do you say to that?"

Tor Fowler pleaded for the life of his friend, who was being dragged toward the earth bank at the roadside.

"Prepare to fire," Padilla ordered.

"See you in g-glory," Cap called to Tor.

Musket fire rang out, and McBride toppled face-first into the road.

With an anguished groan, Fowler dropped his head to his chest, anticipating his own death.

Then he heard riders approaching at a gallop.

"What is the meaning of this?" boomed a commanding voice at the head of the newly arrived troop.

"Ah, General Castro," whined Padilla, "we were ambushed by Americanos, but we have defeated them."

"Padilla," Castro warned, "do not trifle with me. By whose order are you executing prisoners? Answer me!"

"Don Carrillo's," Padilla lied. "He who was murdered by the first treacherous shot."

"Well, no more," Castro demanded. "The remaining prisoner is coming with me."

CHAPTER 3

Northward, the dark green heights of the rounded peaks shimmered in the haze. To the south, a curious trick of the atmosphere caused the low hills of the island of Santa Cruz to loom over the settlement of Santa Barbara as if only a short swim away instead of twenty-five miles offshore.

The grass-covered knoll that overlooked Don Pedro Rivera's rancho was itself a tiny island, set between the mountains and the sea. Francesca thought for perhaps the hundredth time that it was in just such a place that she fully understood her father's love of California and his desire to remain and never return to Spain.

As a young girl she had often climbed to this very location to dream of her own future. Through the changing seasons—from wildflower spring to peaceful summer and on into blustery fall and gentle winter—she had grown into a reflection of the beauty and charm of her California home.

The breeze off the ocean was rising, and it ruffled the black lace veil covering Francesca's face as she stood beside her father's newly dug grave. An obelisk of pink granite already marked the spot. Don Pedro had lovingly dedicated this hilltop years earlier when Francesca's mother had passed away.

Her father and mother had come together to the knoll to take the children on outings, to plan the building of their house, and to speculate on their future and that of their chosen homeland. Now they would lie together, side by side, in that place of beauty and peace.

Francesca was flanked by her tall, broad-shouldered husband on one side and her slender son on the other. Their three other children, all younger than Peter, were away at the missionary school in Hawaii. Beside Peter stood sixteen-year-old twins Ramon and Carlos Carrillo—Peter's two best friends and the godchildren of Will Reed. Across the grave from Francesca was her brother, Ricardo, and his family—his wife, Margarita, who had been a good friend of Francesca's since childhood, and their stair-step brace of six children.

At the foot of the grave, a small man in the garb of a Catholic priest led the group of bereaved in the Lord's Prayer. The cleric's diminutive stature and dark brown skin and eyes displayed his Indian heritage.

The small circle of family was surrounded by a much larger group of mourners that included Don Andres Pico, the governor's brother, and Don Abel Stearns. Stearns, a Yankee-born trader, had been living in Southern California for almost twenty years and was reputed to be the richest man on the West Coast. He was so widely admired and respected that he had been named subprefect of the pueblo of Los Angeles.

When the service concluded, Don Andres and Stearns drew Will aside.

"Don Will," Don Andres said, "we hate to intrude upon your grief, but serious matters have arisen that require that we speak with you."

"Don't fence with him," said Stearns gruffly. "Straight out, Reed, do you know anything about this ragtag bunch of Americans calling themselves the Bear Flag Republic?"

"Only the same rumors that everyone has heard—some American adventurers are proclaiming independence from Mexico. I also understand that some U.S. Army officer has been encouraging them, but again, it's only hearsay."

"Exactly!" Don Andres burst out, his elaborate side-whiskers bobbing. "It's all hearsay and rumor, promoted by General Castro in Monterey. Listen to this official proclamation." He extracted a folded paper from a deep side pocket of his frock coat and read: '*Countrymen, arise. Divine Providence will guide us to glory.*'"

"You see," Stearns explained, "we in the South believe that this fuss may be a pretext for General Castro to increase the size of the militia, ask Mexico City for more troops, and subdue all of California with himself as dictator." Stearns wiped perspiration from his broad forehead with a silk handkerchief and loosened the knot of the black cravat tied below the stiff-winged shirt collar.

"This is all very interesting," said Will, looking to where Francesca stood hugging Margarita, "but why tell me? You are, as you say, intruding on a time of sorrow and I have never been interested in politics."

"Quite right," apologized Don Andres, bowing.

"Hold on," Stearns said in a no-nonsense tone. "Let's get it all said at once; then he can give us a straight answer. Will you go see the American captain and find out the truth? Fremont's his name, and he's been across the Rockies with surveyors and mountain men like yourself. You two should speak the same language."

"No," said Will with finality. "It does not concern me or mine."

The guard almost shot Davis before recognizing the shambling, gasping form that lurched out of the darkness. The round-faced settler's clothing was torn and full of burrs and foxtails. He was weaponless and walked with a limp, clutching under his arm a crutch improvised from a tree branch. His face was streaked with blood and his hair matted with dried gore from a gash that cut across his forehead and angled up into his scalp.

The guard alerted the camp of the Bear Flaggers. He caught the swaying Davis and led him to the watch fire. Whistling a low exclamation over the settler's injuries, the sentry pressed a cup of coffee into Davis's hands, then brought a bucket of fresh water to wash the wound.

By this time a crowd had gathered around the scene.

"What happened, Davis? Where are the others?" asked Andrew Jackson Sinnickson. Five foot ten and solid as a brick wall, Sinnickson was the leader of this group of the Bear Flag Party.

"Dead," said Davis, shuddering with the horror of the memory. "The Mexicans jumped us. I fought my way clear, but they killed all the others. It was terrible. There must have been fifty of 'em. 'Kill all Americanos,' they was yellin'!"

Sinnickson scanned the blackness of the Sierran foothill night. "Double the sentries and put two more men on guard around the horses."

"Got shot in the head," Davis said, indicating the scalp wound. "Shot me clean outta the saddle. I crawled into some bushes and hid out all last night and hiked back here today."

There was instant acceptance of this story, although the truth was less dramatic. When Davis had ridden away from the fight, he had looked over his shoulder for pursuers once too often and turned back just as the racing mule had run under a low tree limb.

"Tor Fowler and Cap McBride and the Injun all dead?" asked Sinnickson, shaking his head in sorrow and disbelief. "Well, it can't be bloodless now. Grigsby, you and Merritt best ride on over to Captain Fremont and tell him what's happened. Tell him the country's up, and we are requesting the army's aid. Davis," he continued gently, "can you remember any more that might be helpful—anything at all?"

Davis tried his best to look noble and heroic but only partly succeeded, since he winced at the touch of a washrag on his forehead. "We stood 'em off to start with—yessir, turned 'em back. Ouch! Watch it, will you? An' I heard Fowler say that I had killed a feller name of Carr-ill-o or Ka-reyo or somethin'."

"José Carrillo? Why, he's a rancher in these parts and supposed to be a moderate man. Was he with them?"

"Right enough," Davis concluded. "He was their leader."

* * *

Captain John C. Fremont ran his slender fingers nervously through his wavy brown hair, then plucked at the top brass button of his dark blue uniform. "So you say hostilities have begun?" he asked Sinnickson, the black-haired leader of the Bear Flaggers.

"Yessir, and it wasn't us who started it, neither. Oh, we had rounded up some horses and made some plans defensive like, but now it's a real shooting war. We've even had reports that General Castro is advancing against us with a force of six hundred. We need your men and your leadership, Captain."

Fremont looked at Marine Lieutenant Falls. "This puts me in an awkward position, doesn't it, Lieutenant? You see," he explained to Sinnickson, "war is imminent between the United States and Mexico over the annexation of Texas, but it has not yet begun. If I, as an officer of the United States Army, allowed my troops to be used against the Mexicans, I would be committing a breach of international diplomacy."

Sinnickson looked uncomfortably nervous. His prominent Adam's apple bobbed several times before he spoke. "But you can't leave us without protection. We're American citizens, after all. Why, the bloodthirsty Mexicans shot and killed three men in cold blood without any provocation. They may attack our women and children next! You've got to help us!"

Clearing his throat politely, Lieutenant Falls waited for Fremont to acknowledge him.

"What is it, Lieutenant? You have a solution?"

"Yessir, I think so," the short, round-shouldered officer said in his whiny voice. "If Mister Sinnickson would step out of the room for just a moment?"

After Sinnickson had obliged, Falls continued. "Sir, the exact wording of the verbal instructions for you from Secretary of State Buchanan was that you were to render aid to American citizens in the event of actual hostilities. Do you hear the wording, sir? Not in the event war is declared but hostilities. Isn't that what has just happened, sir?"

Fremont brightened visibly. "You're exactly right. My duty is plain. Lieutenant, ask Mister Sinnickson to come back in and the others as well."

When the group of Americans calling themselves the founders of the Bear Flag Republic had assembled, Fremont explained his conditions for assisting them. Fremont was to be the absolute commander, with all others subject to his orders.

"The first order of business is to capture General Castro. We must strike quickly and not give them time to gather their forces. Those Californio leaders who have already surrendered will remain in custody at Sutter's Fort. From here on we need to move too rapidly to be encumbered by prisoners."

* * *

Trading ships of many nations—French, Russian, English, and American—had all plied the California waters for decades. Some were legally approved by the Customs House in Monterey. Many more were smugglers' crafts, anxious to take advantage of eager buyers and hundreds of miles of unpatrolled coastline.

As commerce increased, countries encouraged the fair treatment of their citizens by shows of naval might. The British and the Americans in particular kept Pacific squadrons cruising the length of California. It was even rumored that Britain might accept upper California in payment of old war debts owed by the Mexican government. Of course, officially, Britain had no interest in any stretch of the Pacific Coast south of the Oregon territory, and her ships were supposedly present as observers only.

The appearance of Her Britannic Majesty's ship-of-the-line *Juno,* caused no little stir when it anchored off Santa Barbara. Although not as impressive as the eighty-four-gun British frigate, *Collingwood,* which was also sailing in California seas, the *Juno*'s three decks bristling with cannons were an imposing sight.

"What do you make of it all, Father?" Will Reed asked the small-statured priest who had spoken at Don Pedro's funeral. "First Governor Pico arrives from Los Angeles with eighty armed men and now this warship."

The two watched from the white-sand beach in front of the sleepy coastal town as *Juno* sailed into the lee of the point before turning sharply upwind and letting go the anchor with a show of British precision.

"My friend," said the little dark brown man, "as to the governor, there is no reason I should know any better than you. Yet, as regard to the English ship, I believe I have the answer."

The ranchero waited for the explanation as the priest debated about saying more. "You always think more than you speak, Father," Will urged him good-naturedly.

Resuming his reply with a grin and a shrug, the priest offered, "I have been informed by my superiors that a certain priest, a Father McNamara, is to be expected here. As his last location was reported to be Mazatlan, where the British fleet has been anchored, I have followed the rabbit tracks to the rabbit hole and come up with a rabbit."

"Father Francis—" laughed Will—"there are times when you still sound more like Blackbird of the Yokuts than you do a Catholic priest!"

"I am proof," said Father Francis modestly, "that one may be both."

"And you said your visitor's name is Mik-Na-Mee-Ra . . . is he Yokut also?"

"No." Father Francis shook his head, smiling. "Another tribe . . . Irish."

Three gently waving lines of white breakers separated the landing of Santa Barbara from its anchorage. Will and the priest watched as the small boat, called the captain's gig, was fitted out and two men, one in the robes of a cleric and the other in a naval uniform, were rowed ashore.

"And will you be entertaining the visitor?" Will asked.

"No," said Father Francis. "Since attacks by the shaking sickness and by the Mojave tribes have moved my people into desolate hills, they have many needs. I go now to serve them."

✶CHAPTER 4✶

The gold braid on General Castro's uniform was frayed and faded, and one of his tunic buttons was missing. Even his muttonchop whiskers and gray hair looked thin and threadbare.

His voice was not worn out, though, as he shouted in English at Tor Fowler with a bellow like an angry bull, "Where is Fremont going? What are his plans?"

Fowler was seated in a stiff wooden armchair, his hands bound behind his back with rawhide strings. The chair's legs were uneven, so Fowler rocked forward and back with each blast of the interrogation.

"Don't know, General," he answered truthfully. "I signed on to hunt meat for the camp and to keep track of Injun sign. Never was any call for anybody to tell me nothin' important."

Castro seemed impressed with the frankness of Fowler's reply and changed topics. "How many men are armed? What about more troops?"

With a look of complete sincerity, Fowler lied, "Man, General, you just can't believe it! Must be close on a thousand in camp already, and I heard the lieutenant sayin' that General Kearny was comin' with a thousand more."

Castro rocked back on his heels as if he were the one seated in the wobbly chair. Worried consternation skittered across his face, and his bushy eyebrows pulled together. The effect was so comical that it took all of Fowler's poker-playing ability to keep from laughing out loud.

Switching to Spanish, the general addressed the scrawny killer, Juan Padilla, who stood at his elbow. "What do you think?" the general demanded. "Is he speaking the truth?"

"We have seen nothing like a thousand men, General," Padilla replied. "But let me tickle his ribs with this—" he drew a knife halfway out of the dirty sash knotted around his waist—"and I'll have the truth soon enough."

Castro made an abrupt gesture to Padilla to put away the blade. "He may prove useful as a hostage later. In any case, you do not know this breed. His kind live with the Indians and think like them—they will die without speaking and spit blood in your face at the end."

The first rifle shot came just as General Castro's camp was stirring for breakfast. Tor Fowler had spent an unpleasant night, unable to swat the cloud of mosquitoes that feasted on him. He was standing, tied with his back to an oak tree, his wrists fastened by a rawhide strap that encircled the trunk. At the whine of the bullet and the report of the gun, he sat down abruptly and slithered around to put the oak between him and the firing.

The Californios bolted out of their tents and rushed for their stacked weapons. The first man to reach the muskets was dropped with a rifle ball through his leg, and the rest suddenly elected to flop on their stomachs and crawl. Three men ran toward the corral of horses, but two were picked off trying to climb the rail fence, and the third crouched behind a post.

General Castro stormed out of his quarters shouting commands. As Fowler watched, Castro attempted to buckle his sword belt around his middle before hitching up his suspenders and got tangled up. A bullet clanged into the hanging lantern in front of the general's tent, and he dropped, sword and all, behind the oak chest that contained his belongings.

In quick succession, two bullet holes were added to the trunk's fittings. One split a leather strap and flipped the loose end up in the air. Another neatly punched out the lock.

The Californios were returning fire with their muskets, but it was plain that the Americans were out of range of the older weapons. Buckskin- and homespun-clad figures could be seen walking upright between the trees at two hundred yards distant. A blue-garbed man with a white bandanna tied over his head was waving men into positions.

"Whooee!" Fowler yelled. "Go to it, boys! Hammer and tongs!"

Another bullet clipped a branch above Fowler's head and knocked some leaves and bark down around him. "Hey, General," he called, "how about untyin' me?"

Castro scowled at him and shouted for his men to circle behind the corral and saddle up.

Working the rawhide binding, Fowler sawed the tie back and forth in an attempt to set himself free. The Californios were feverishly occupied, so escape never looked more likely than now.

Sixteen lancers made a crawling circuit of the corral and managed to saddle their mounts among the jostling and milling horses. Fowler figured that they would make easy targets riding through the gate, since it was too narrow to allow more than one at a time. But he had not counted on the Californio's resourcefulness—or their horsemanship.

With a shout of defiance, four jinetes, expert riders, jumped their horses over the corral fence without bothering about the gate. These were followed by four more and twice again four until all sixteen riders swept across the camp and the open pasture toward the Americans. The tiny pennants on the lance heads waved like flags when the horses jumped, then fluttered in front of the riders when the weapons were leveled for the charge. Fowler looked on with satisfaction as the lancer galloped into the hail of rifle bullets now being fired with renewed intensity.

Back and forth Fowler continued sawing at the leather tie until his wrists were bloody. "May have to cut this tree down before I get loose," he muttered to himself.

Another fusillade of shots made Fowler sneak another view around the tree trunk. Two riders were shot out of the saddle. When one horse was hit, he made an end-over-end roll at full speed. The power of the charge was broken short of the American positions, and the riders were forced to seek shelter in the trees bordering the pasture to try to regroup.

The action by the lancers had succeeded in drawing the Bear Flaggers' attention away from Castro's camp, giving the general time to organize a second wave of horsemen to go in with muskets while he and the rest of the Californio troops withdrew south toward San Francisco Bay.

Still sawing feverishly at the leather strap, Fowler heard another flurry of shots, and two more thudded into the tree behind which he hid. He yanked with all his strength on the rawhide and jerked up as another bullet unexpectedly hit the binding, freeing him instantly.

The mountain man wasted no time trying to untie his ankles. With his feet still bound together, he began crawling quickly toward a clump of yellow mustard brush beyond the edge of the camp.

Fowler just reached it when he heard the unmistakable sound of a hammer click. A cold barrel poked him in the ear. It was Padilla with the Colt rifle captured from Davis. "I would like very much to kill you," the wiry little man said with a twisted grin, "but General Castro says you are to come once again with him."

* * *

The solid wooden wheels of the ox cart bumped violently over the rocks and dropped with a thud into every pothole. Tor Fowler wished that his captors had tied him into the carreta standing up instead of sitting. As it was, each bounce sent a jolt up his tailbone like being thrown from a mustang onto a granite boulder. Fowler was being transported with the cavalry troops' supplies: sacks of beans, spare saddles, General Castro's trunk, and one prisoner, all clumping along together.

Fowler listened with amusement to the groaning complaints of the ungreased axle. Without their Indian servants, these Californios seemed incapable of the least effort that required manual labor. He had heard it said that if a task could not be done on horseback, then they would not do it at all. At any rate, not one of these horsemen had attempted to grease the axle, even though a bucket of tallow for that purpose hung underneath the carreta.

The cart bumped down a track that ended at a broad expanse of dark water. Fowler guessed it was San Francisco Bay, although he had never seen it before.

General Castro rode up the column on his white horse. "Padilla, take the prisoner and your men and go across the bay. I want Fremont to think that I have gone that way also, but my men and I will ride south from here, driving before us such horses as we can find and recruiting some more lancers."

"Couldn't we sweep around the road and attack Fremont's flank?" Padilla asked. "Do we have to run, General?"

Castro looked thoughtful. "It is the best strategy at present until we have raised the whole country and that cursed snail Pico sends us more men. We are not ready to face Fremont's thousand."

Tor Fowler had to duck his head quickly to hide his smile.

Lieutenant Falls stood on the shore of San Francisco Bay not far below the town of San Rafael. He was noisily sucking his buck teeth as he shook his head with displeasure. "It's a bad job," he remarked to Davis. "Castro and his men have escaped across the bay. Now they'll have a chance to regroup—perhaps fortify San Francisco. What I wouldn't give to know his plans."

The breeze blowing across the water was tossing choppy little waves onshore. Gusts danced on the wide expanse in playful patterns. The wind rippled a stretch of surface half a mile wide, leaving smooth and undisturbed swaths on either side. The passing clouds floating overhead contributed to the show of shifting light and shadow, dividing the waters of the bay into green and blue areas that changed with each moment.

Shading his eyes with a dirty palm, Davis peered across the bay. "What's that?" he asked at last.

"Where?"

"Yonder, straight across from us. See that white patch? First I thought it was a wave and then I figured it for a cloud, but now I reckon . . ."

Falls confirmed his guess. "It's a sail, and it's headed right this way, too. Let's get out of sight and see where she lands."

The two men hid themselves behind some rocks above the makeshift pier that served as a landing for San Rafael. It was not long before it was apparent that the triangular sail on the little sloop was tacking so that it would arrive right in front of them.

As the single-masted ship spanked against the tops of the waves, drawing closer to the shore, Falls could see that two men paced the forepart of the deck and a third handled the tiller.

"Slide out toward the road," Falls ordered Davis. "Bring back as many of our boys as you can round up quickly, but do it quietly. Stay out of sight till I holler, in case they've got a bunch belowdecks. But when I yell, come on up and take 'em."

The fore-and-aft sail fluttered in the breeze, and the small ship lost headway but not much. The last two tacking movements swung the boat away from the pier and back parallel to the shore. Falls thought that the pilot was going to run alongside the end of the dock, leaving his escape route ready for a quick departure. The sloop's motion toward the pier looked like a fleeing bird swooping toward a tree branch. The two men on the forward deck had taken places along the rail on the landward side.

The sail dropped and the sloop coasted up beside the wharf. The first man jumped over the rail and landed cleanly. He pivoted to catch a carpetbag that the other tossed to him. Then it was the second man's turn to leap. His foot snagged some rigging and he tumbled onto the planks of the dock, but he was up quickly as the boat continued to glide past the pier.

The ship's departure was as abrupt as its arrival. Falls watched as the lone remaining figure hoisted the sail taut again and put the tiller over. The two men left standing on the dock each raised a hand in farewell, but the steersman did not acknowledge them. The sloop stood out into the bay sharply, as if dropping off the passengers had been an interruption to the important business of sailing.

Falls drew his pistol and cocked the hammer, glancing down to check the percussion cap. The two Californios moving up the pier were young and carried no weapons openly, but Falls was not taking any chances of running foul of something hidden in the carpetbag.

A moment passed. In the brief interval the sloop was out of range to be hailed into returning, but the men had not yet reached the landward end of the pier.

Stepping out from his place of concealment, Falls leveled his pistol at the chest of one and commanded, "Halto! Or whatever means stop in your lingo."

Startled by the lieutenant's sudden appearance, the pair who had been talking and laughing paused midstride and were silent. They made no attempt to flee. Both lifted their arms in token of surrender, one holding the carpetbag awkwardly at shoulder height before he set it down.

Lieutenant Falls looked from one face to the other and thought he was seeing double. They were twins, about sixteen or eighteen years of age. Dressed alike in black knee breeches and short black jackets with silver trim, the brothers matched down to the silver buckles that decorated their boots.

"Señor," said one, tentatively lowering his hands and stepping forward.

"Get back there!" snarled Falls, "and keep your hands up!" The round bald patch on the lieutenant's head turned bright red when he was angry or scared; it was crimson now.

"Señor," the young Californio meekly tried again, "we speak English. Please to tell us what is wanted—what have we done?"

"I'll ask the questions around here, and you'll answer right sharp if you know what's good for you. What are your names?"

The one who had already spoken continued to reply. "I am Ramon Carrillo, and this is my brother Carlos."

The twins glanced at each other, and then Ramon said, "The manner of our arrival was not of our choosing, señor. The captain, he was afraid to come at all—we had to pay double—and even then we had to jump because he would not stop."

"Yeah? What's he afraid of?"

"He said some crazy Amer . . . some foreigners had caused some trouble on this side of the bay, and he did not wish to get mixed up in it."

"Davis!" Falls bellowed, "bring 'em on down. We caught us some spies!"

"Oh no, señor," protested Carlos. "We are coming to visit our uncle, who lives near Commandante Mariano Vallejo in Sonoma."

"Vallejo, eh?" Falls scratched his thin gray mustache. Davis and half a dozen men with rifles ran up and surrounded the Carrillo brothers. "Well, Vallejo is already our prisoner, and his rancho and his horses belong to us. What do you say to that?"

The twins said nothing at all.

Falls, certain that their silence proved their guilt and puffed up with pride at the capture, ordered the carpetbag dumped and the brothers searched.

"Lookee here, Lieutenant!" Davis exclaimed as he drew a folded sheet of paper from Ramon's jacket pocket. "Some kinda handbill or somethin'."

"Lemme see that," demanded Falls, snatching the paper from Davis. Falls scanned the printing; then, since he could not read Spanish, he announced the only thing he could make out for certain. "It's signed by General Castro hisself!"

"Well, go on, Lieutenant," requested one of the other soldiers of the Bear Flag brigade, "read it to us."

"It says . . ." Falls paused before plunging ahead. "It says for all Californios to take up arms and kill Americans! Yep, that's what it says. Men, women, and children, it says, kill 'em all. Burn their homes, take their belongings, run 'em clear out of California. That's what it says!"

Ramon and Carlos both reacted with horror. "Oh no, señor!" they exclaimed in unison. Then Ramon continued. "It calls on Californios to forget their past differences and band together to fight the invaders, but it says nothing about—"

"There, you see?" said Falls triumphantly. "They admit it! Out of their own mouths, you heard 'em. They were sneakin' across the bay to organize a counterattack—probably to slaughter us all in our sleep!"

"String 'em up!" growled Davis.

"Drown 'em like mongrel pups," suggested another.

"Run!" yelled Ramon, pushing Falls to the ground. He lowered his shoulder and ran into the midsection of a second of his captors before a rifle butt clubbed him to the ground.

Carlos threw himself off the pier and into the chilly waters of the bay. Striking out strongly, he was swimming along the shoreline when the first rifle ball struck him in the back. When the second and the third crashed into his head, he sank without a splash.

"Davis," Falls said as they stood over Ramon's unconscious form, "name Carrillo mean anything to you?"

"You bet," said the settler, rubbing the half-healed wound on his forehead. "Carrillo was the name of the leader of the bunch that jumped Tor Fowler and me . . . I killed him," he concluded proudly.

"Well, what do you know? This scum here is some kin to that feller." Falls nodded, nudging Ramon with the toe of his boot.

"What do you want we should do with him?"

Falls considered for a moment. "Captain said we got no time for prisoners. Drag him over in that gully and shoot him. And remember, they was spies and assassins!"

* * *

Tor Fowler had a theory about pain. He believed that one could withstand anything by concentrating all thought somewhere else. It seemed to him that pain could not rob a man of his reasoning without his agreement. If he would just ignore it, then he could go on functioning and surviving.

He had tested his belief before, once when a barbed Pawnee arrow had to be cut out of his back. Another time he had hobbled ten miles across a range of eight-thousand-foot peaks on a newly broken leg. *Keep on thinking and live, or give in to the pain and die.* In Fowler's mind, it was that simple a choice.

But he had to admit that the present torture put a whole new slant on pain. He was hanging facedown, spread-eagle, by rawhide straps around his wrists and ankles. The straps were tied over the rafter beams of an adobe hut so his body sagged under its own weight and tore at his shoulder joints. His breathing was labored and slow.

Concentrate! Ignore the pain! Fowler forced himself to review how he had gotten to this place. But he had almost lost track of how many times his captors had moved him, by forced march on foot and in the carreta and most recently in the smelly hold of a little trading sloop.

They had thrown him headfirst into the bilge of the small ship and carried him across the bay to the tiny, dirty settlement of Yerba Buena. Upon arrival, Padilla had ordered that Fowler be trussed up like a ham hanging in a smokehouse.

Now that Fowler thought about it, there was one thing to be grateful for. The Apaches practiced a similar torture to what he was undergoing now but with an additional refinement: they hung their victim's head downward over a slow fire.

✶CHAPTER 5✶

Will and Francesca were invited to a reception honoring Father McNamara and the *Juno*'s captain, Blake. The evening's festivities were held at the property of the Irish doctor Nicholas Den.

Den stood at the front of the receiving line, obviously enjoying his role as host and introducing the rancheros and merchants to Father McNamara and the warship's captain.

At the opposite end of the row of dignitaries was Governor Pio Pico. With his politician's smile firmly in place on his coarse features and his ample girth stuffed dangerously into a formal black suit, Pico managed to look jovial and imposing at the same time.

Nicholas Den fairly bounced with the importance of the occasion, and as often happened when the small curly-haired Irishman got excited, his Spanish took on an improbably Irish brogue. "Don Will and Doña Francesca Reed," he intoned with a ferocious rolling of *r*'s.

McNamara spoke a cultured Spanish as befitted a well-educated man. "Charmed, Doña Reed," he said, bowing. "Don Reed . . . American, yes?"

"Mexican citizen these last sixteen years," replied Will. "And you . . . Irish, like the good doctor here?"

"Aye, but a long way from home, and a long time away as well." McNamara was a large man, as stout as Governor Pico, but a head taller. He had pale skin, much freckled from the California sun. His short brown hair was balding in the crown, and Will thought he looked like a woodcut of Friar Tuck in a book about Robin Hood.

"Father McNamara is here to speak with the governor about Irish colonists coming to live in California," interjected Den with excited self-importance.

Father McNamara shrugged off the comment. "Ireland, my homeland, has many starving folk and not enough farmland to feed them, while I hear that California has plenty of good soil for willing hands to cultivate. But I am really here on a mission for the church."

Will and Francesca passed down the row and reached the governor. The Reeds had met Governor Pico many times before. While Will did not entirely trust the politician, he had at least a grudging respect for the man who governed as a Californio first and not as a high-handed representative of the government in Mexico City.

"Eighty soldiers escorted you here, Governor?" Will inquired.

Pico, beaming through his thick lips at a row of señoritas coyly peeking at him from behind their fans, pretended at first not to hear. But he could not ignore the topic when Will continued. "Two years ago we took up arms against a governor who brought his army with him from Sonora, and we kicked him and his men back south again."

Pico's stubby fingers plucked at the gold and black-onyx watch chain draped across his expansive stomach. A flicker of a frown passed across his brow before he answered lightly, "You will remember that I also participated in the ouster of Governor Micheltorena. Now another man's ego may have gotten too big for him, but I assure you, it isn't mine."

"So you believe that the stories of the American invasion are exaggerated by General Castro for his own purposes?"

"It remains to be seen how much of the present crisis is General Castro's invention. But rest assured, Don Will, whether to put down rebellion or to corral General Castro, my men and I are ready to march." His words were uttered in a light, almost careless tone, and he made a sweeping gesture with both arms, like a bear hug, as he said the word *corral.*

"And the timely arrival of the good captain and the British warship," added Will, indicating Blake, who was listening without comment. "Does that event also have something to do with the crisis?"

"Purest coincidence only." Pico laughed, holding his ample sides as if to keep the humor confined. "The *Juno,* on which Father McNamara was coming to visit me, put in at San Pedro, only to hear that I was on my way here. Captain Blake was kind enough to sail on to Santa Barbara instead of making Father McNamara await my return to Los Angeles. Ah," he interrupted himself, "I see dinner is ready."

And Pico walked away.

"Hogwash," muttered Will to himself in English.

"Cómo?" asked Francesca, looking cool and beautiful in her white dress. "What did you say?" Her eyes were twinkling, and Will knew she had not only heard his comment but understood it as well.

"*Nada*—nothing, really. I am just wondering what is so important about a scheme to bring in Irish settlers that Pico would lie about it."

"How do you know he is lying?"

"Because," Will said, pausing in the doorway and leaning close to Francesca's ear as he pretended to straighten the red sash knotted around his waist, "Blackbird—Father Francis—told me that Father McNamara was expected here. That means Governor Pico and the Irish priest planned to meet here in Santa Barbara all along."

Enormous quantities of food greeted the guests as they entered the dining hall. Quarters of beef, roasted over oak-coal fires, were sliced into huge steaks and heaped on round wooden serving trays the size of wagon wheels. The Indian servants who carried the trays around the dining hall staggered under the weight of them.

Fragrant mounds of *arroz con frijoles*—rice and beans, seasoned with chili peppers—were accompanied by steaming heaps of freshly baked corn tortillas. The diners sampled the zinfandel wines from two different mission vineyards. Some were from vines already over fifty years old.

At length the still-heaping platters and serving bowls had been carried around a final time, and the last filled-to-capacity guest had refused even one more helping. The pewter dishes were cleared away, and the tables and chairs pushed back to make room for the musicians to come in and tune up.

Will and Francesca went for a walk in the plaza, as did several other couples. "You won't get sleepy before the dance, will you, Señor Reed?" teased Francesca.

"Not a chance, Señora Reed," Will asserted earnestly. "What with you being the most beautiful woman present, I'll have to be on my guard that some young caballero doesn't sweep you away."

"Impossible!" she said, stretching up to kiss him quickly. "I am holding on to the most dashing and handsome man here, and I won't let him go. I saw the eyes that shameless Julieta was making at you."

"Huh!" Will scoffed. "Making eyes at old Pico, I shouldn't wonder, or that British captain."

"I do wish Peter could have come this evening," Francesca reflected. "He will be sorry he missed the dancing."

"He is being sensible," Will argued. "Since he is leaving tomorrow to join the twins in Sonoma, he needed to stay home this evening to prepare. You know, he is writing out a list of instructions for the care of his herd of cattle during his absence. I like to see him taking his responsibilities seriously."

"So like his father," Francesca murmured.

"And his grandfather," Will added. "Don Pedro would have been proud."

The first notes of the *jota* sounded from the band, calling the strolling couples to the dance floor. Will noticed the glint of a tear in Francesca's eye. He guessed that the swirling mixture of violin and guitar conjured up for her visions of the Aragon of her ancestors. No doubt the mysterious strains that drew from the Moors and the gypsies called to her mind the Spain she had never seen, only heard about in the stories of her father's youth. Now she would hear them no more.

The inner circle of ladies faced the outer circle of men. Clapping and energetic footwork punctuated the *jota*, the dance that translated as "little details." Pio Pico capered around the dance floor, sweating profusely.

At the next break in the music, Will made his way to the punch bowl. The laughing governor was there ahead of him, with a young señorita hanging on each arm and every word. "Quite a nice fandango, eh, Governor?" said Will in a cheery, offhand way.

"Most excellent," Pico agreed. "Nicholas certainly knows how to entertain. For being a little chino, a curly-headed Irishman, he has become more Californio than many who were born here. Not like some foreigners who think to bring their own culture and force it upon us."

"Perhaps the new crop of Irish will fit in as well," Will observed.

"No doubt, no doubt," said the governor, looking anxious to return to the dance floor where the strains of a waltz could be heard.

"Isn't it curious that Father McNamara says his plan is of little importance, yet it could not wait for your return to Los Angeles?"

Pico looked annoyed. "I don't know what you are trying to suggest, Don Will Reed, but this is a strange line of questions for a man who told my brother and Don Abel Stearns that he had no interest in politics."

"Let us say that I have no political *ambition*," said Will, stressing the last word while staring into Pico's flushed face. "But that does not mean I lack concern for my country."

"Which country?" shot back Pico. "Mexico or the United States?"

"California," Will retorted, bristling.

A cry from the musicians' corner rang out over the laughing crowd. "The bamba! The bamba!"

Applause and still greater laughter greeted this announcement.

Three wicker hoops the size of small wine casks were placed in a cleared area of the dance floor. Three young señoritas stepped forward, and each stood inside a hoop. Each was handed a glass of water to balance on her head.

A single guitar began to slowly strum a rhythmic progression of measured notes and minor chords. The girls dipped gracefully and carefully brought the hoops up to knee level. The tempo of the music increased as each dancer moved first one ankle and then the other in a succession rapid enough to keep the hoop from slipping down. The glasses jostled, but not a single drop of water was spilled.

Faster and faster went the chords as the crowd picked up the beat by clapping. Each girl bent quickly and gave the hoop a spin; the flashing ankles and pointed slippers were joined by the whirling of the bands. One girl, trying to keep up the pace of footwork and manage the spinning hoop, overbalanced and the water glass tumbled off her head. A groan came from the audience, but it changed to a cheer as the dancer recovered quickly enough to catch the glass before it struck the floor.

The two remaining girls were well matched, and the spectators placed wagers on which would last the longest. The noise of the crowd and the music and the clapping rang loudly, drowning out all other sounds.

Then, through the rear of the milling throng, Will spotted his son Peter, accompanied by Will's friend Paco. He was pushing through the crowd, calling, "Father!"

The crowd, grumbling, parted reluctantly, jostled by the interruption.

Paco shoved two onlookers roughly aside and received angry glares in return. Someone muttered about Indios who did not know their place. Another uttered a threat of punishment.

The music was reaching a climactic moment when Peter pushed into the inner circle of the audience and yelled to his father and mother on the other side, "Ramon and Carlos are dead—killed by the Americanos!"

The music jerked to a halt. The crowd noise died away gradually, and then as the message sank in, one of the dancers screamed.

In the abrupt silence that followed, the shattering of the water glasses on the stone floor seemed to ring on and on.

* * *

The slash of the leather strap across Tor Fowler's back made him jump and yank against the rawhide that tied him to the roof beams. He grunted in pain when the blow landed, but otherwise he made no sound. The sweat of his torture gathered in the tightly knotted furrows of his brow and dripped from the end of his pointed nose onto the black earth of the floor.

Juan Padilla, a former saloon keeper, had beaten Fowler before, but this whipping was particularly savage. Padilla was matched blow by blow by his accomplice Four Fingers. In between lashes the two men reviled Tor, telling him he deserved death for what the Yankee pigs had done.

The mountain man was grateful that the cutthroats did not beat him in silence. Even though he did not understand what they were talking about, it helped him to ignore the pain as he tried to cipher their accusations.

He gathered that some of the Bear Flaggers must have killed two young Californios . . . in cold blood, from the sound of things. This news gave Padilla an excuse to be even more cruel than usual.

Finally the pace of the blows began to slacken, as Fowler knew it would. The Californios had eventually tired of their activity and stopped the beating. Fowler knew what was coming next and braced himself for it.

The knots securing the rawhide ties were let go and he was dropped, face-first, onto the floor. Padilla kicked him twice in the ribs and told him to crawl back to his corner, but Fowler could not move. The Californios grasped him roughly and pitched him back to the wall like a discarded cowhide.

Sometime later, an old crone of an Indian woman entered the adobe hut. She brought Fowler a pan of brackish water and a shallow bowl of thin barley gruel. The woman, who never spoke much less answered questions, fed the broth to Tor like she would a baby and held the tin of water to his thirsty lips. It would be several hours before he could use his arms again.

* * *

"It does not require the gift of prophecy," Father McNamara declared to Governor Pico, "to foresee that California will not remain part of Mexico forever . . . unless some defensive measures are undertaken."

"Yes, yes," responded Pico impatiently. "Everyone agrees that the American invasion is real and not merely an invention of General Castro's. But what do we do now?"

McNamara looked pointedly at the stoic face of the British Captain Blake and finally received a nod. "Give us one square league, four thousand acres, for each family and we'll plant a hedge of Irish Catholics strong enough to keep the Methodist wolves at bay."

Pico's bulging eyes turned inward toward his bulbous nose, and the strain of mental calculation took place. "You want me to deed . . . four *million* acres of land? That's preposterous! In all the area around all the existing pueblos and missions, there is not that much unclaimed property!"

McNamara shook his head and in an ingratiating tone replied, "It is not necessary to disrupt your fine coastal cities. My people are people of the land, willing to settle in the harsh interior. What is it called . . . the valley of the San Joaquin?"

"But it is completely uncivilized . . . a country of wild Indios and wild beasts!"

"Exactly," agreed McNamara. "Ideal for both our purposes, don't you agree?"

Pico pondered. "For such a large transaction, I must confer with the territorial assembly—"

"By all means," the priest concurred. "Only remember, the wolf is at the door, howling to be let in among the sheep. May I suggest at least your tentative approval while the details are being worked out?"

Pico nodded eagerly and stuffed his too-small, European-style top hat down onto his large head. He bustled from the room, shouting for his carriage driver to bring the *caretela.*

Father McNamara turned to regard Captain Blake. Broad smiles painted both of their faces.

"He doesn't yet understand how completely he has just thrown his lot in with us, does he?" Blake said.

McNamara shook his head, still smiling.

"But the assembly?" Blake questioned. "Will he be able to get them to agree?"

"Without question. Exchange worthless, unoccupied land for a buffer of one thousand settlers between the ravenous Americans and these pitiful remnants of bygone Spanish glory? My dear captain, we could have asked for forty thousand acres for each family and they would still agree."

Captain Blake nodded. "Of course, it doesn't really matter that it will take a year or more to arrange such a colony. The first twenty

British subjects will want protection from the American invaders, and the British navy will be honor bound to oblige."

"And what better way to aid and protect than to seize the ports?" McNamara said. "Will it be difficult to locate twenty volunteers for such a project . . . facing wild Indians, wild beasts, wild Americans, and wild Californians, I mean?"

"You have only to ask," Blake replied. "I have *already* dispatched twenty sailors whose ill health made them eager to exchange their shipboard labors for a little time spent living off the land."

"Captain," Father McNamara asked with delight, "where did the governor put that bottle of excellent California brandy? I think a toast is in order."

* * *

"Don Abel Stearns wishes to speak with you, Father," reported Peter from the head of the stairs.

Will, who was digging through an old sea chest in the attic of his home, turned at the interruption. "Did he say what he wanted? I am in a terrible hurry, Peter."

"I know, Father, and I told him so, but he insists that it is important."

At that moment, Will's hands grasped the leather-wrapped parcel he had been seeking. He stood up with the rolled bundle. "All right . . . now I have what I was looking for. Tell him I'll be right down."

Don Abel was admiring the clock on the mantel of the Reeds' fireplace. Will gestured for him to be seated in a chair made entirely of cattle horns lashed together with rawhide. Will sat across from him.

"Don Will, I know you are anxious to go north and locate the killers of Ramon and Carlos Carrillo, so I will be brief."

Will acknowledged the accuracy of Don Abel's statement with a nod but said nothing and waited for the merchant to proceed.

"I want to—how can I put this?—I want to encourage you to go to Captain Fremont with an open mind."

"An open mind about murdering children?" Will burst out. "What are you saying?"

"No, no!" cautioned Don Abel hurriedly. "I mean, I am certain that Fremont is an honorable man and that he will also want to punish the offenders. I hope you will give him a chance to investigate."

"And I hope it will already be done and the murderers under arrest!" snapped Will. "If Fremont has any control at all over that rabble, he should have captured the killers already."

"Correct, correct," said Stearns, "but please remember that the future of this land is properly with the United States and not with Mexico. We don't want Captain Fremont to think that our sentiments run any other way."

"Is that what this visit is about?" Will snorted, standing up abruptly. The leather-covered bundle fell off his lap and spilled its contents: a fringed buckskin jacket and leggings from Will's days as a mountain man. "You think I might make Fremont rethink his support for the revolt? You know what, Stearns? You're absolutely right! If I find out that he or any of his men had anything to do with the murder of the Carrillos, I am going to tell him that all Californios, Yankee or Spanish, will resist him and the so-called Bear Flag Rebellion to the last drop of our blood!"

"You cannot be serious," Stearns responded. "We want to belong to America—peacefully, if possible, but by armed conflict if necessary. How can you, an American yourself, feel any differently?"

"Stearns—" Will towered over the hawk-nosed man—"you have had your beak in the account books for too long. You cannot see anything but stacks of silver reals. Get out of my house."

Stearns went without protest.

Will stood glaring at his back as he left, and his son, who stood in the entryway, closed the door behind Don Abel with somewhat more force than was necessary.

"Peter, I am leaving you in charge of the herds," Will said.

"But I want to go with you," his son replied. "They were my friends."

"I know," Will agreed, "that it is hard for you to remain behind, but it is important. Paco is a crafty *mayordomo*, and he will help you do what is required."

CHAPTER 6

Six days after the terrible news about the twins' deaths had reached Santa Barbara, Will Reed stood on a hill overlooking the little settlement called Yerba Buena. Located on the tip of the peninsula that formed the western enclosure of San Francisco Bay, it was not much more than a miserable collection of shacks. Initially it had sprung up around a Hudson's Bay Company trading post but had never grown into a thriving city.

The small harbor that provided the anchorage for Yerba Buena was a cove on the eastern shore of the peninsula, just below the ramshackle town. The only oceangoing ship anchored there was a Russian vessel from Alaska. Its rigging looked dull and in disrepair, and an air of greasy neglect hung over it.

Will arrived seeking answers but found no one to provide them. All the Mexican authorities had fled southward, including General Castro and his men. Evidently, the *alcalde* of Yerba Buena had abandoned his post and taken to his heels. Some said he had heard that the Americanos not only killed children but took captured officials and skinned them alive.

No one seemed to know anything about what had actually happened to the Carrillo twins. Leidesdorff, the American vice consul, was conveniently absent. Robert Ridley, the captain of the port and a Britisher who had adopted California as a home, was likewise ignorant of what was happening north of the bay. The Americans had been victorious, it seemed, and all of northern California now belonged to them.

Will made up his mind to cross the bay and seek out Captain Fremont, the American commander. He would demand an explanation of the deaths of the brothers and insist on knowing what was being done to catch the murderers.

But no one would take him across the water. Trading sloops and fishing smacks were available for hire, but no Californio captain was willing to risk coming in range of the American rifles. Will had even offered to pay the captain of the Russian vessel for passage, but the oily-looking officer had only stopped stuffing his face with rice and beans long enough to say that the matter would have to be referred to Sitka and that a response would take six weeks.

In frustration at his wasted day, Will rode Flotada to the windy heights above Yerba Buena as the sun began to set. He stared hard across the straights. Shielding his eyes against the glare on the water, Will traced the line from the cove below him to the far shore, lit in gold and orange by the reflection of the sinking sun.

He noticed a sail on the horizon. As Will watched, the small craft, no bigger than a whaleboat or the shore launch off a trading vessel, tacked on its course toward the peninsula. The ranchero decided that here at last was someone who had braved the trip to the farther shore at least once and could perhaps be persuaded to go again.

Will started down from the heights, leading Flotada by the silver-worked bridle. He paused on a slightly lower ridge, expecting to see the boat veer around toward the harbor.

Instead of coming to land at Yerba Buena, the vessel grounded directly below the old presidio of San Francisco. Twelve men armed with rifles jumped from the boat. They held their weapons aloft to keep them dry as they waded through knee-deep water, picking their way over rocks to the shore. The last to step from the boat was a young clean-shaven man with a thin face and wavy brown hair that showed around the edge of the blue cap he wore. He was dressed in a blue shirt and a fringed buckskin vest.

The men formed into two columns and hiked up the hill toward the presidio. The young man, who was apparently the commander, walked between the two files, carrying a rolled-up banner. As Will watched with disbelief, the leader stepped to the center of the compound of tumbledown, crumbling adobe walls and unfurled an American flag. As the twelve men stood respectfully still, the commander evidently spoke some official words that Will could not hear. *Taking possession,* Will thought, and he shook his head at the audacity.

Will's approach to the gate of the old fort was stopped by a man in the uniform of a United States Army lieutenant. There were two guards with the officer, one wearing a long, loose coat of deerskin, knotted around his waist with a rawhide tie. The other had on a shirt of homespun above the dark knee breeches of a sailor and no shoes.

"Hold it right there," ordered the lieutenant. "Who are you, and what do you want?"

Looking past the odd assortment of men, Will could see small groups of men clustered around the antique brass cannons with which the presidio was armed. The clangs of hammers rang in the evening air as the squads of invaders set to work spiking the ancient guns.

"Maybe you didn't hear me? Or is it that you only *habla Español*?" said the lieutenant roughly.

"I speak English or Spanish as needed," Will replied, "but I only speak *with* the commander—take me to him."

The army officer stepped up a pace and studied Will from his flat-crowned hat to his tooled cowhide boots and silver spurs. "What do you know?" the bucktoothed little man observed to no one in particular. "He dresses Mex and talks American. What are you, anyway?"

"Why don't you stop wasting my time?" said Will angrily. "My name is Will Reed. The two young men, Ramon and Carlos Carrillo, reported killed by the Americans were my godchildren. I am here to find out who was responsible."

The lieutenant looked over his shoulder. Will followed his gaze to the man returning to the small boat waiting at the shore.

"Will Reed, eh?" the lieutenant repeated with a sideways glance from his beady eyes. "Stubbs," he ordered, addressing the man in the sailor pants. Then, "Bender," he called toward the other man. "I think he's a spy. . . . Take him, boys!"

"Yessir, Lieutenant Falls!" they responded immediately and stepped toward Will, closing in from both sides.

But Will surprised them by jumping straight for the lieutenant. Bearing the lieutenant to the ground, Will jammed a knee hard into the officer's belly. Falls doubled up with an explosion of breath and feebly waved for help.

Stubbs grabbed Will from behind, pinning his arms to his sides. Will let himself be yanked upright, then stomped down with all his force on the attacker's bare foot, raking his spur down the man's shin at the same time. With a howl of pain, Stubbs let go of his hold and clutched his wounded leg while he hopped around on the other.

Grabbing his Lancaster rifle, Bender swung it around toward Will. Too close to bring the gun to bear, Bender tried to club the ranchero with it.

Will seized the barrel of the rifle with one hand and clamped his other fist firmly over the hammer to prevent the gun from being fired. A tug-of-war began in earnest, but Will's extra height and superior strength were winning the battle for possession almost at once.

Bender began screaming for help.

It took a moment for the terrified shouting to penetrate the ears of the squads still pounding away at the two-hundred-year-old cannons. Peering through the gathering gloom, the raiding party was astonished at the spectacle at the gate. The lieutenant was still on the ground, fumbling with the flap of his holster and gripping his stomach. Stubbs was also sitting on the ground, holding his lacerated knee and moaning. Meanwhile, a big man in Californio dress wrestled for Bender's rifle.

"Help!" yelled Bender again. "We caught us a spy!"

Just then Will saw the others drop their hammers and reach for their weapons. He drew Bender onto his tiptoes with a jerk upward on the rifle. Planting his boot in the middle of Bender's chest, Will kicked the shorter man backward twenty feet.

Just as Will swung into his horse's saddle, Falls freed his pistol from its holster and fired. The .54-caliber ball hit Will just below his right elbow. The impact almost flung him completely over the off side of Flotada. He reeled in the saddle, snagging the rowel of his spur in the cinch as if riding a bronco. The gray bounded off toward the village of Yerba Buena.

* * *

The door of Fowler's adobe-hut prison creaked open. Someone stood in the doorway, but Tor Fowler did not raise his head from where he again hung face downward by the rawhide straps. The pattern of his imprisonment was set, and he no longer feared torture or expected rescue.

The mountain man knew that Padilla was carrying on with the torture only because he had the power and enjoyed inflicting the pain. There was no real expectation that Fowler would furnish any important information. Fowler also knew that Padilla would stop short of killing him. As long as General Castro wanted Fowler kept as a hostage or for a future prisoner exchange, his life was safe.

A blow on the side of his head swung Fowler against the adobe bricks, and his skull bounced off the wall. Muscles that he had thought already numbed to pain awakened at the renewed violence.

A second clout on the head set Fowler's body rocking in the rawhide thongs like a tenderfoot riding a green-broke colt. His moccasined feet thumped against the back wall of the hut, and his angular frame began a corkscrew motion.

The third blow whizzed past his ear but did not strike him. Fowler's mind could not grasp why this was so until he heard Padilla's voice, so slurred and thick with drink that the words were almost incomprehensible.

The missed swing had spun Padilla completely around. He tripped over his own feet and sprawled on the floor. Tor's face dangled only a few feet overhead.

Padilla mumbled, "Gonna slit your throat, gringo." The Californio pulled his long knife from the sash around his waist and waved it clumsily underneath Tor's nose.

Fowler forced himself to speak calmly and reasonably. "General Castro will not like this—not one bit. You know he told you to keep me safe."

Padilla's unfocused eyes followed the arc of the glittering blade as he waved it in a gesture of denial. "No, no, gringo," he said in a surprisingly soft voice. "*No importante.* The general would not want me to let you escape. If you are killed escaping, what can he say?"

Fowler believed that Padilla, when sober, was capable of any evil. He seemed totally without conscience. He stopped at nothing, except for fear of punishment. Now it seemed that drink had taken that last restraint away.

The cords suspending Fowler left him hanging at just the right height to have his throat cut. As soon as Padilla could stagger to his feet, it would all be over. Unless . . .

Fowler recalled the blows of a moment before. His feet had brushed against the adobe wall. He was that close, and the leather straps had more slack in them now. For his plan to work, Padilla needed to be standing close by. Fowler thought he knew just the appeal that would work.

"Do not kill me," Fowler pleaded. "If you took me back to Captain Fremont, he would pay you gold. Two hundred dollars."

Padilla shook his head. He jabbed the point of the blade into the earth and tried to lean on it but fell back. "Bah! No scout is worth that to his commandante. I am tired of wet-nursing you, gringo. Make your peace."

"Wait!" Fowler said urgently. "Listen to this. I know where there is gold hidden—more gold than you ever dreamed off—taken off a rich ranchero that we killed."

Padilla's spinning eyes steadied, and he blinked slowly and deliberately as if trying to wake up. "Another Yankee lie to save yourself."

"No, I swear it. Only one other man besides me knew of it, and he's dead. If I die, it'll be lost forever. Don't you know the Valdez rancho? The old man's gold is buried, and I know where. Let me down and I'll give you half."

When Padilla halted, Fowler knew he was considering. Don Valdez was known to be a wealthy ranchero.

Padilla finally stood clumsily and took a step toward Fowler's head. "Do you know what will happen if you are lying, gringo?"

"Yes," said Fowler urgently. He kicked his feet upward hard

and bent his body in the middle, ignoring the sudden tearing in his muscles.

Fowler's feet contacted the rear wall, and he pushed off with every ounce of force left in his abused carcass. As the forward motion began, he ducked his head. Directly on target, Fowler's thick skull connected with Padilla's face, which had been only inches from his own.

The single blow propelled Padilla backward through the air, until the flight was cut short by the other adobe wall. Padilla hit heavily, and Fowler heard a crack as the Californio's head struck the bricks.

Between the impact of Fowler's head used as a battering ram on Padilla's chin and the short arc of the Californio's body that ended against solid adobe, Padilla was unconscious before his frame pitched forward into the dirt.

Now, how to get free before someone else came or before Padilla was awake again? Otherwise Fowler had only postponed the inevitable.

* * *

The outcry of pursuit rang in Will's ears, and several more shots were fired after him into the gathering twilight. One splintered against the bricks of an old well just as he rode past, but no other came close.

The shooting fell silent. The Bear Flaggers were too busy running after their quarry to reload. But their speed on foot was no match for Flotada. The great gray horse bounded over a gully and turned up a *barranca.* The narrow canyon between the two hills dropped mount and rider below the sight of the pursuers as if they had disappeared into the earth.

Will trusted his horse's instincts to keep him away from the chase. His own senses were dulled with the shock of the wound. *God, help me,* he prayed. *Please don't let my life end this way. Not with Francesca and the children wondering what has become of me . . . never knowing. . . .*

The horses of the inhabitants of Yerba Buena were scattered and haphazardly placed. Few streets existed at all, straight or not. The gray horse sensed the need to hide their trail, and he darted from crude hut to adobe home, turning corners without Will's commands. Flotada changed directions three times, always when some structure was between his master and the panting pursuers.

Yerba Buena appeared deserted, as if, after hearing gunfire ring from the direction of the already rumored invasion, those who lived in the little community by the bay had elected to stay indoors. Flotada turned two more corners, then entered a narrow passage between a larger building and a small adobe shed.

The last abrupt change of direction proved to be too much for Will's precarious hold. His spur's rowel snapped free of the cinch, and he tumbled out of the saddle. Making a last grab for the apple of the horn was futile. He swung his injured arm in a desperate attempt to hang on, but his nerveless fingers brushed uselessly against the leather. He fell heavily onto packed earth.

Flotada stopped immediately, pawing the ground in an anxious declaration of their need to get farther away. Will tried to rise, pushing himself up on his good arm, then falling back when it collapsed under him. Flotada stamped again and whinnied softly.

Squinting against the pain, Will caught sight of a wooden door hanging from leather-strap hinges. The opening led into a hut that seemed to be a shed or storeroom. "Have to do," Will muttered to himself.

He dragged himself upright with the last of his strength, knowing he would not be able to remount the horse. It was all he could do to yank his Hawken rifle free of the leather scabbard and slip the pouch containing powder and shot from around the barn. The world swayed in a dizzy, looping spiral. "Go! Go!" he roughly urged the horse. "Get on with you!"

He flicked the cord of the shot pouch at Flotada, smacking it sharply across the horse's rear. The unexpected rebuke turned Flotada's own nervousness into flight, and Will could hear the gray cantering off down the hill.

Will did not wait to watch the animal's departure. He tucked the rifle awkwardly under his good arm and held its stock pressed against his side as he faced the sagging wooden door.

Will kicked it inward and thrust the barrel of the rifle forward into the room. When no protest erupted, he stepped inside and leaned wearily against the planks of the door as he shut it behind him.

It took his eyes a while to adjust to the darkness of the shed. Then he swung the rifle around and fumbled with the hammer to be certain it was cocked.

The unconscious figure of a man was crumpled against the wall of the hut, almost under Will's feet. He looked and smelled drunk. But it was not this man that riveted Will's attention. He focused instead on a buckskin-covered form that hung suspended in the center of the room like a recently slaughtered deer hung up to be bled.

Will could feel the creeping numbness of the shock and pain of his wound sweeping over him. Even reminding himself about the grim chamber in which he had taken shelter did not enable him to shake off the deepening weariness. He was just about to surrender to unconsciousness when a groan escaped from the hanging figure . . . the carcass that Will had thought was a corpse!

The noise pulled him awake with a start. "Who are you and who did this to you?" Will asked in horror.

The man's head jerked upward, his eyes snapping open in the gloom at the question Will had asked in English. "Please get me down, mister!" the man sputtered.

Will searched the folds of his sash for his knife, but it had been lost during his wild ride.

"There . . . on the floor by his hand," the man urged. "Hurry!"

Will found the blade, and with the backhanded slash of his uninjured left hand, he severed the rawhide that held the man's feet. The man cried out as the sudden extra weight hit his shoulders, and his legs refused to hold him up.

"Sorry," Will muttered.

"Just get me loose."

Another awkward backhand sweep of the knife, and the man dropped to the earth with a thud and a groan. He lay so still for a time that Will wondered if the man had died. Will's own body had now expended its last reserve, and he sank to the floor himself, cradling his wounded right arm.

At last the man rolled over onto his back. "I hope you got somethin' to cover that snake there in case he wakes up. Else I'll have to crawl on over and slit his throat like he was fixin' to slit mine." When

Will did not acknowledge this gruesome warning, the man called to him again, "Hey, friend, the name's Fowler. You all right?"

Through pain-leadened lips, Will said, "Will Reed. Arm's broke . . . shot . . . I'm all played out."

Fowler whistled his dismay.

CHAPTER 7

The sun was finally sinking after a dusty, daylong cattle drive. Peter Reed stood in his stirrups and scanned the hills ahead of the trail. He paid particular attention to the gap up ahead toward which he and the Reed vaqueros were moving the herd. The upper reaches of Canyon Perdido touched the wilderness heights of San Marcos Pass.

Grizzlies were not as plentiful as they had been in years past, or so Will Reed had told his son. Of course, according to Will's campfire tales of the early days, every canyon had held an *oso pardo gigantesco,* a great ferocious bear. In legend, each weighed over a thousand pounds, and the track of every clawed foot measured eighteen inches in length! Peter chuckled as he recalled the shuddery excitement of his father's stories.

Still, Peter kept a watchful eye on the places where the live oaks, called *encinas,* grew the thickest. Beyond San Marcos Pass, the land was wild and rough and little known to the Californios, whose ranchos hugged the coastline. The other side of the mountains was a place of coyotes, rattlesnakes, condors, and a home from which the grizzly stirred to raid the cattle ranches. Somewhere up ahead lay the seldom-used trail that Peter's father had followed in first coming to Santa Barbara.

Peter could see no immediate danger threatening the herd of two-year-old steers, so he reined aside and waited for Paco to catch up. Already taller at fourteen than the short-statured Indian, the difference in their heights was exaggerated by the mounts they rode. Peter's *grulla*—crane-colored—gelding towered over Paco's mule.

"I saw you looking over the ground before we brought up the herd," commented the Indian. "It is well to be watchful in this country. It is a place of bad medicine."

The boy looked curiously at the *mayordomo.* "You speak like one of the Wild Ones instead of like a good Christian, Paco. Are you superstitious?"

"No, only cautious," Paco replied, crossing himself. "I think that evil is real and does linger in some places . . . places it would be best to avoid if it is possible, but which should on no account be entered blindly."

"Why here?" Peter questioned, gesturing toward the slopes covered with coyote brush and chaparral. "This canyon looks no different from many others hereabouts."

"My mind remembers this place," Paco said, reining up and pointing toward a tree-topped mound near the rocky wall of the canyon's mouth. "It was just there that Don Ricardo, your uncle, was almost killed by an *oso pardo* before your father saved him."

Nodding his acquaintance with this piece of family history, Peter said, "I have seen the scars on Tío Ricardo's forehead, *sí.* But the story did have a happy ending. Besides, it brought my mother and father together. Surely you do not believe that the spirit of the bear lingers here."

"No, no." Paco shook his head. "But it is not just the bear. You see, I was also present on that day. I heard your uncle scream . . . saw your father face the *oso grande* alone, and . . . I fled."

The boy hardly knew what to say or how to respond to this. "I never heard that," he said at last.

The Indian said solemnly, "Don Will is a good man, a great man. He told no one, and have I not been his *mayordomo* these ten years past?"

In a bend of the canyon, a trickling stream had collected in a pool deep enough to water the herd. "We'll camp here tonight and push over the pass tomorrow," Peter announced. Then he looked at Paco with embarrassment. "That is, if you agree, *mayordomo.*"

"No," Paco chided, all the uneasiness of the earlier conversation left behind, "you do not appeal to me for approval. Your father put you in charge of this drive. You have made your decision, Don Peter. If I have comment, I will offer it, but as it happens, you have chosen well."

The other vaqueros brought up the herd and set the leaders to circling. The forward motion soon ceased, and the rangy cattle fell to browsing the grass on the banks of the creek.

Paco pointed out a particularly handsome reddish brown colt in the *caponera*, the string of horses. "What do you think of the retinto-colored one? The one there with the curly coat?"

Peter knew that the question was not a casual one. His education in horsemanship had begun as a two-year-old, when his chubby legs had stuck straight out from the horse's back and Paco had walked alongside to hold him upright. Questions about an animal's conformation or habits or training were a kind of test and game that Peter enjoyed playing with Paco.

The retinto with the curly coat had a long, sleek body and long legs to match. The arch of his neck and the set of his shoulders indicated good bloodlines for a horse that would rein well. The colt's large eyes were interested in his surroundings, and he pricked up his ears when a steer splashed into the creek to cross and graze on the other side.

Peter considered all the factors and gave his judgment. "When he comes into his own, he will be one to ride all day without stopping, and he seems attentive."

"Good," Paco confirmed. "You saw that he has *amor al ganado*—cow sense. It cannot easily be taught, but a horse that comes by it naturally will leap on the trail of one steer and never lose it."

"And now, *mayordomo*, why did you call my attention to him in particular?"

"Because, *hijito*, little son, he is broken to the *jaquima*, the leather noseband, but has not yet worked in the bit. Your father and I wish you to school him."

Mentioning Peter's father made the request into a command. It meant that Will and the head vaquero had planned this lesson before the drive had even begun. Peter knew that the schooling would not be the horse's alone.

* * *

By the time the camp was set, the herd settled, and the simple supper of beef jerky and hard biscuits finished, the Milky Way glowed in the California sky.

The night herds were posted, and Peter was drifting off to sleep when the first sliver of the full moon crept above the ridgeline. As if at a signal, a mountain lion screamed in the *barranca*, upstream where the canyon narrowed into a rocky gorge.

Peter's eyes snapped open, and he slapped his hand down on his blanket over the saddle carbine that rested beside him.

"Gently," cautioned Paco from his bedroll nearby. "You will frighten the cattle more than señor puma."

Apart from a lone bawling steer, the herd remained quiet. There was none of the confused snorting and bellowing that foreshadowed a stampede.

"How far away was that?" Peter asked.

A drowsy reply confirmed that Paco felt no danger. "Far enough. The horses will give the warning if he gets near enough to scent. You may depend on it. Of course . . ."

"Of course what?" Peter demanded.

The sleepy afterthought was slow in coming. "Of course, if the lion calls near our camp again tomorrow night, we will have to hunt him."

"Why?"

"Because," came the slurred answer, "on the third night, he will be hunting us." On that cheerful thought, Paco drifted off to sleep.

Peter was counting another set of a thousand stars when it was time for him and the *mayordomo* to go on watch.

* * *

It was the strangest kind of three-way race, and only one of the contestants even knew about the contest. Tor Fowler studied the unconscious Padilla and the silent figure of Will Reed. Fowler's arms and legs were shot through with fiery pains as circulation returned to his numbed limbs.

Inch by agonizing inch, Fowler stretched out his arms. He dragged his uncooperative body toward Will Reed's weapons. Two feet more to go . . . one foot . . . a half. Fowler's fingers closed around the stock of the Hawken rifle. But the weight of Will's body held the rifle prisoner, and Fowler could not jerk it free.

The knife must be his objective then. The room was pitch-dark, and Fowler scrabbled in the filth of the hut's floor. He found Padilla's knife near the end of Will's outstretched hand.

Using the weapon to assist him, Fowler plunged its blade into the earth and pulled himself up to it. When the dark mass that was Padilla stirred and groaned, Fowler redoubled his efforts. Like a sailor climbing the tallest mast in the midst of a raging gale, Fowler drew himself hand over hand toward his enemy.

When Fowler was an arm's length away, Padilla's eyes flickered, then opened. For a moment they focused on nothing at all. Then Padilla screamed in terror.

Fowler knew what Padilla saw: the dark shape of a wild beast with blazing eyes and raking claws that had crawled out of his worst nightmares and was coming to rip out his throat!

Padilla fumbled for a weapon but found none. He gave a bleat of panic and threw himself backward against the adobe wall just as Fowler stabbed the knife downward.

Fowler struggled to stand. A guttural animal noise came from his throat as he slashed the air again and again. He heard a rustling from Will Reed.

Padilla hurriedly groped his way along the wall to the door. Twice he pushed futilely against it.

Fowler's blade sliced both the Californio's legs with a sweeping slash. The wound, not deep, was the goad Padilla needed to escape. Throwing his weight against the ramshackle door, he burst it from its strap hinges and fell out into the night.

* * *

The mountain man lit an oil lamp and held it aloft. "Come on, man," Tor Fowler urged Will. "We've got to get us both some doctorin'."

Will shook his head. "Not together we can't. You can go back to the army for help, but they want to capture me . . . maybe kill me."

"That's some kinda mistake, you bein' American and all. Why would we be mad at you?"

Will reached up with his good arm and let Fowler help him stand. A swirl of dizziness swept over him, but it passed quickly. "Do you know about the Carrillo twins?"

"Do I? I should say so!" Fowler agreed emphatically. "I was beat plumb near to death while bein' told what child-killin' murderers us Yankees is! But personally, I never met 'em. Reckon it happened after I got took."

Will nodded. He pulled the sash from around his waist with Fowler's help and used it to fashion a sling to support his wounded arm. "Those boys were my godchildren. I came here from Santa Barbara to get to the bottom of what happened."

"Well, what *did* happen? How'd you run foul of our folks?"

Will explained the circumstances at the presidio and how the lieutenant had been at first hostile and then belligerent.

"That's Falls," Fowler grunted. "He's as useless as a saddle made for a grizzly and just about as likely to get somebody kilt. Fancies himself a real military hee-ro headed for politics . . . hopes to hitch onto Fremont's star."

"Then you understand why I can't go back with you."

"No sucha thing," Fowler insisted. "Falls, see, he ain't Cap'n Fremont. The captain is an ambitious man, but he knows what he's about. 'Sides, him and me been in some rough scrapes before, and I saved his bacon. He'll be bound to hear your say if I tell him to."

Will was still doubtful, but he agreed that his arm needed attention. What was more, it was to see Fremont that he had ridden all the way from Santa Barbara, and here was a man who could make the connection.

"All right," he said at last. "On one condition. Don't tell anybody except Captain Fremont who I am. Ask him to come and see me at the cantina down the street."

But the two men had no more than stepped into the dirt lane when they found themselves surrounded by a squad of soldiers.

Lieutenant Falls presented a carbine at point-blank range at Will's stomach, remarking with obvious satisfaction, "Fowler. Good work. Escaped *and* captured the spy!"

"Not so, neither," protested Fowler. "This fella saved *my* life, and—"

"Poor man is deranged," Falls observed to the marines. "Take the prisoner away."

"Lieutenant," said Fowler, "I'm warnin' you. This is an important fella with a secret message for Captain Fremont. Ain't nothin' better happen to him!"

Falls regarded Fowler and Will with a look compounded of suspicion and cautious self-interest. "Captain Fremont has already departed, leaving me in charge. All right, lock him up." Then he added in a grudging tone, "*Just* lock him up."

Will knew that protest was futile and that any further attempt to fight his way clear would get him shot on the spot. He let himself be led away quietly.

✶CHAPTER 8✶

Peter yawned into his morning cup of coffee and stared at the tin platter of cornmeal mush without taking a bite.

"Eat! Eat!" Paco scolded. "One cannot conduct the cattle drive, without nourishment."

The curly-haired retinto was caught and brought to Peter for saddling.

"It is a perfect time to try him with the bit," Paco said. "He was first bitted up exactly one month ago, and now it is time to advance his schooling. Every true vaquero knows that the best reining *caballos* are given the bit in the full of the moon."

Peter examined the mouth of the reddish brown gelding before turning to the canvas on which were displayed the various bits. The boy chose a silver-mounted bridle. Attached to it was a mild-curved mouthpiece called "the mustache of the Moor" from its drooping shape. In the center of the crossbar were two barrel-shaped rollers made of copper.

"*Bueno.*" Paco nodded. "Exactly the bit with which the retinto has been standing each day in the corral."

The curly-coated horse took the metal bar in his mouth without objection, and soon little whirring noises could be heard. The colt was spinning the copper barrels with his tongue, indicating his contentment.

Peter saddled the horse with care, tightening the center-fire cinch and leading the animal around in the small circle known as the *pasos de la muerte*, the steps of death. Many a rider had come to grief when a cinch-binding horse came over backward as the rider's weight was added to the saddle.

Removing the silk *mascada* scarf from around his neck, Peter tucked it into the bridle over the horse's eyes as a makeshift blinder. He did not know if this precaution was necessary, but it was a point of honor to discover the colt's personality and secrets without asking too many questions.

Stepping lightly into the stirrups, Peter mounted and settled quickly into the high-backed, apple-horned saddle. The retinto stood perfectly still in the clean morning air and flicked his ears back toward his rider. Peter adjusted his grip on the reins and nodded for Paco to remove the scarf.

The spur chain jingled once as Peter tapped his heel against the colt and urged him into a walk. The horse wheeled left and right in response to Peter's directions, and Peter found no trace of obstinacy or rebellion as the horse worked in the bit.

"Shall we start the herd moving?" Paco inquired.

"*Por favor.* I'll take the colt across the canyon and back to work on his rein. We won't want to try him with the cattle until tomorrow."

"*Bueno,*" Paco agreed, "and perhaps you may be able to bring back meat for the camp." He handed Peter a rifle and gave a nod of affection and approval.

The colt took eagerly to the trail, trotting across the creek and looking around him with an intelligent interest. Peter followed the twisting path away from camp and started the horse up the climb that led out of the canyon and onto a mesa beyond.

A pair of finches chattered in the buckthorn brush. The boy instantly recognized their noisy calls and was reminded of the childhood tales his mother had told him. The finch's red breast, Francesca had said, was caused by blood dripping from the brow of the crucified Christ. A pair of the small birds, so the story went, had flown to the head of Jesus on the cross and plucked out the crown of thorns one by one. God allowed the blood to permanently stain their chest feathers as a remembrance of the time when men had no pity on the

Lord of glory, but two of the least members of creation showed compassion for their Maker.

Both Peter and the rust-colored horse turned their faces toward the twittering in the scrub. The colt nodded toward their perch, seeming to acknowledge the finches' greeting.

"Ah," said Peter, "so you know the story also? We will be compadres, you and I. Also, I like your curly coat. I think your name should be Chino—Curly. What do you think?"

The trail reached the mesa rim and leveled out as it angled across the plateau. The brushy undergrowth thickened, with gooseberry patches replacing the coyote brush. As Peter scanned the dense growth, his attention was drawn to a clump of heavy thorned cover at the base of a huge boulder that jutted out of the landscape like a stone sailing ship set on end.

Peter's gaze traveled past the location, then flickered back again, and he studied the berry thicket intently. Was it a rabbit in the brush, or perhaps only the flitting of another small bird that had caught his notice? Both horse and rider stopped, searching for the unseen animal. Slowly the camouflaged outline of a deer bedded down behind the gooseberry thicket took shape. Peter stepped off Chino's back and carefully lifted the Hall saddle carbine out of its scabbard.

Dropping the reins to the ground, Peter stood away from the colt and took aim. He cocked the hammer while judging which branches were actually antlers and where the point of the buck's shoulder was located. The boy took a deep breath and let it out slowly, then took another and held it, just as his father had taught him.

The boom of the .60-caliber rifle shattered the morning stillness.

At the explosion, the buck leaped up from the bushes as if by the release of a spring, but Peter had no chance to judge his success. Behind him, Chino reared and plunged, reared again and came down on the reins. The colt jerked away from the abrupt tearing in his mouth, breaking the bridle and scattering silver conchas across the hillside.

The horse snorted with fear as Peter lunged at him in a grab for the reins. Chino reared again and struck out with a forefoot, and Peter threw himself backward onto the ground and out of the way. The colt whirled then and ran off, back the way they had come.

Peter sat up and watched the horse's flight. He kicked himself mentally as he retrieved the fallen rifle. The hammer had broken off, and the stock had two deep scratches in it. From the dirt near a broken piece of rein he picked up a silver ornament and tossed it morosely up and caught it.

What would Paco say? Worse, what would his father say? Peter knew better than to fire a gun next to an untried colt. He should have tied the horse to a stump and moved away before firing, but the horse's good nature and cooperative spirit had made Peter careless. Carelessness got people killed, his father had taught him. Well, Peter might wish he were dead, but he was not, so he had better pick up what he could and hike back to the herd and face the consequences. Peter hoped that the colt would find his way back, or else the boy would be in even bigger trouble.

With the broken rifle over his shoulder and two dusty silver conchas in his pocket, Peter turned to follow the vanished horse when a thought struck him. He had fired at the buck, but he did not know whether his bullet had struck the animal or not. The boy fervently hoped that his shot had been successful so that he at least would not have to go back empty-handed.

Peter returned to the location from which he had fired the shot. At first he could see no trace of the buck. He placed his feet in the same tracks again and sighted along the rifle barrel toward the gooseberry patch. Nothing was stirring there now. He swung the barrel slowly to the left, tracing the buck's leap and trying to remember where his last glimpse of the deer had been.

He hoped he had either killed the animal cleanly or missed it completely. Now that he was afoot, he doubted if he could trail the buck if it were only wounded. Anyway, he had no weapon with which to shoot again.

Walking toward the brush pile, Peter circled it on the uphill side, in the direction of the buck's leap. He looked in each clump of thorns and weeds as he passed but saw no sign that the deer had ever been there, much less been shot. Peter glanced back at the point from which he had fired, judging the correctness of his course and the amount of distance he had covered.

He was far beyond where he believed the animal could possibly have been when he saw it: a single drop of blood glistening on a shiny gray-green gooseberry leaf. An instant's excitement that his aim had been true gave way to remorse. He had let the deer get away wounded, after all, to suffer and fall victim to some predator.

In a last attempt to locate the buck, Peter set up a stick beside the telltale drop of blood, then backtracked to where he had last seen the deer. Turning around once more, the boy sighted up the hill in a straight line from where he stood, past the marker stick . . . and saw the deer, lying still.

It had come to rest in the crevice formed by a slivered chunk of the granite boulder.

Peter walked slowly up to the dead deer, thinking about what he must do next. He could not carry the entire deer back to camp, but he could manage to take a hindquarter back with him. Perhaps there was even some way he could use the broken reins to hoist the remaining meat out of the reach of scavengers until it could be retrieved later.

Standing over the buck, Peter was mentally preparing himself for the gutting and cleaning that must come next in order that the meat would not spoil. He knelt over his boot top to withdraw the hunting knife he carried there.

When he stooped to draw the blade, he heard the tiniest whisper of a sound, directly over his head. Peter's head snapped up.

He found himself looking into the pale, amber eyes of a mountain lion.

His direct gaze caught the big cat's. The cougar regarded him from near the top of the boulder, where it lay in the shadow of a rocky ledge, and snarled . . . not a scream or earsplitting roar but a low, menacing rumble that ended with a coughing sound. The cougar snarled again, louder this time, and flashed a threatening glimpse of spiked fangs.

Peter understood the mountain lion's anger. It had not been on the rock above the brush-choked ravine by chance. No, it too had been stalking the buck until Peter had stolen the kill. But the lion did not intend to part with his meal without a fight.

Very slowly and deliberately, Peter stood erect and began backing away from the base of the boulder. He recalled what he had been taught about never turning his back on a lion. Cougars hunt by stealth and surprise and will attack even humans from behind, given the opportunity. The boy placed each step carefully. He did not want to glance away from the mountain lion, not even for an instant, but he could not risk tangling his foot in the brush and taking a tumble, either. Peter remembered the *Leatherstocking Tales* read to him by his mother. It seemed that Cooper's characters were always falling down when pursued, and Peter did not want this to happen to him.

The lion shifted on its perch and stretched out a great paw toward the deer carcass in an unspoken statement of claim. Then, as if reaching a decision, the cat jumped lightly down from the boulder. It looked once over its shoulder at the dead deer, then fixed its yellow gaze on Peter and began moving slowly toward him.

The boy had backed up about halfway across the brushy slope when he found himself against a tangled gooseberry thicket so dense that he could not push through it. The lion was still padding toward him, but Peter could not risk turning to look for a path across. Instead he began to move sideways, crablike, hoping to come to a clearer place where he could resume his getaway.

A crashing of branches from the upslope direction drew the attention of both the lion and the boy. A light breeze was blowing up the little draw, or the cougar might have scented the second intruder sooner, but there was no mistake now. Ambling across the brush piles and smashing them down with total disregard for the thorns was a large sow grizzly with a very small cub alongside.

The bear was evidently following the blood smell from the buck, for she was moving with purpose directly toward the carcass, pausing only to sniff the air and correct her course. The lion lashed out an angry snarl that ripped through the morning stillness like a saw blade through lumber.

Giving a *wuff* of alarm and swatting the cub to get it behind her, the grizzly stood on her hind legs. She shook her massive head and peered around through squinted eyes, the very picture of a myopic matron refusing to take any nonsense.

Peter looked around with alarm. There were no trees near enough to climb that the bear would not be able to reach him first. In fact, the only place of safety close by was the granite monolith, and the lion stood between him and the rock. Peter crouched down right where he was and hoped that he would escape the humpbacked bear's attention.

So far the plan seemed to be working. The mother and cub were still zeroed in on the scent of the deer, and the lion demanded the grizzly's notice by letting loose another full-throated scream. The mother bear snarled and growled in reply and dropped to all fours to charge.

The lion jumped back toward the rock ahead of the grizzly's rush and grabbed the deer by the hind leg. The cat tried to drag the carcass away, but the antlers wedged in the crevice of the rock and would not budge.

The bear charged with a bellowing roar and swung a paw at the lion in a blow that would have crushed the cougar if it had connected. At the last possible instant, the cat gave up its hold on the deer leg and leaped over the fractured chunk of rock. The two opponents glared and snarled at each other, no farther apart than the width of a tabletop. The lion's ears were flattened against its skull, and it roared and hissed its defiance of the bear.

Peter rose and began to back away again from the scene. He would have no better opportunity than right now to make himself scarce. The grizzly had grasped the deer, her superior weight drawing it free of the crack in the rock where the lion had failed. The cat snarled and slashed and threatened, but the bear, unperturbed, was bent on drawing in the prize.

The boy might have been able to withdraw from the confrontation had it not been for the curiosity of the bear cub. Since Mama had forced the cub to stay back out of harm's way, he had cast around and come across Peter's scent. The grizzly cub shuffled and sniffed his way over the bushes, directly toward the retreating boy. Peter stumbled into a heap of dried gooseberry brambles that crackled underfoot. As if suddenly noticing the absence of her baby, the mother bear whirled around with the mangled body of the deer hanging limply from her jaws.

The rush of the grizzly toward Peter made her earlier charge toward the lion look like a peaceful stroll. With the momentum of an avalanche, she galloped across the mesa, her mouth full of venison, bellowing all the while for the cub to get out of the way.

Peter was certain that this was his finish. Then, out of the corner of his eye, he saw a streak of tawny lightning. The lion had given up the idea of trying to retrieve the buck, but it was not going to leave empty-handed either. The bear cub squalled as the mountain lion's fangs closed around his neck, and the cougar went bounding away up the slope.

The charging grizzly stopped abruptly and skidded into a sudden turn, reversing direction. In her distress at this new development, she dropped the deer carcass from her grasp and tore off across the mesa in pursuit of the cougar and the stolen cub.

CHAPTER 9

"Whew," muttered Peter, wiping his face with his *mascada.* "A deer, a lion, *and* a grizzly. It is true, what Paco says, *'Cuando Dios da.'* When God gives, He gives with a full hand!"

The deer carcass was too mangled and chewed to be worth bothering with. The order of business now was to rejoin the herd and relocate the missing colt—with the saddle still intact, he hoped.

Peter started back across the mesa, pushing aside the coyote brush and retracing the spidery line of the trail. In a hundred yards, a thought struck him and he stopped to consider.

By now the herd was probably already on the move, going farther up the canyon toward the high pastures. If he followed his own trail back, he would come in way behind the location of the next night's camp. This plan would have been reasonable on horseback, since a mounted man can travel farther and faster than a drifting herd of cattle. But on foot, that was another matter altogether.

Peter decided that an angle toward the northeast would cut into the canyon of the *jornada.* Trail drives are noisy, dusty affairs with slapping leather and plumes of airborne dirt. Once striking the correct arroyo, Peter believed that he would have no difficulty locating the camp.

Taking his bearings, Peter turned so the sun was just ahead of his right shoulder before he started up the slope. He picked out a peak on the horizon that was directly in line with his nose and began hiking.

It was still before noon, but the air was already shimmery with the heat. Cicadas singing in the brush stopped when Peter's shadow passed over them and resumed their buzzing when he trudged on.

The broken and useless rifle slung over his shoulder was a weight he would gladly have traded for a canteen of water, but he knew better than to leave it behind. A couple hours' walk, that was all. With a little luck, the story of his encounter with *la osa* and *señor puma* just might protect him from punishment. He hoped so. To a young caballero, the reception he would get arriving in camp on foot was going to be punishment enough.

The canyon that appeared over the next ridge when Peter crossed it was narrow and deep. It had no stream flowing in its rocky depths so could not be the one the herd was following.

By now the sun was directly overhead, and it was impossible for Peter to set his course by it. He concluded that it did not really matter, since he had to cross the *barranca* anyway and certainly would find the right canyon just over the next ridge.

But the next ridgeline revealed only another narrow, dry arroyo, clearly still not the right one. Worse, while Peter could descend into the canyon, ascending the near-vertical wall on the opposite side was not possible. He would have to follow the canyon farther along to locate a way out of the steep embankment.

Walking through the age-old sand of the dry wash, Peter found himself following a looping path. Flash floods had carved the deep canyon, but in slicing through the sandstone layers they had gone around other, harder material, turning the streambed into a tortuous serpentine. Far above him, through gaps too high to reach, Peter could see towering sandstone columns sculpted by the wind into strange, wavy sentinels.

Peter wondered how far off course he must be. This forbidding landscape did not have the appearance of pastureland. The wall on his right by which he had descended into the canyon dropped lower and lower as he paced along. The bank receded to a low berm, and the hills on that side retreated as the width of the canyon expanded into a small valley. Peter continued hiking, almost oblivious to the newly flat terrain on that side, for his attention was focused on the north.

In fact, his decision to climb out of the floodwater's path was not made because he thought of reversing his course but because he hoped to get a wider perspective of the barrier he faced.

Over the bank of the dry streambed at last, Peter found himself on a level plain covered with small gray-green brush. The flat stretched away to the south and east until it merged with the hazy brown and yellow streaks that were the vague outline of distant hills.

The low bushes crushed when he walked over them, giving off a pungent aroma, not unpleasant but penetrating. *Sage,* he thought, *like Mother uses in the kitchen.*

The boy now knew that he had completely missed his rendezvous with the herd. He had somehow overshot the mark and would have no choice but to backtrack his own trail. But a great concern came first. Peter recognized that he needed water—and soon. The way back was a long distance to a stream.

Ahead, a line of cottonwoods presented the possibility of moisture. If not a pool, perhaps at least a spring. Peter changed his direction to line himself directly with the little clump of trees.

For a long time, Peter trudged across the sage-covered field. He amused himself by watching his shadow flow over the brush and the ground-squirrel mounds.

The boy was not alarmed at his predicament. The nights were not cold enough for the lack of a fire to be a problem, and tomorrow he could retrace his steps. He regretted having refused Paco's advice. He wished now he had eaten breakfast. Still, water was the pressing issue. Tomorrow he would probably meet someone looking for him, and there would be food.

Glancing up from his shadow and his thoughts, Peter corrected his course slightly and checked his progress toward the group of trees.

The dark dots on the horizon grew into tree shapes. The images wavered with the heat waves reflected off the red soil. The upper half of each tree appeared to be floating, while the lower half had disappeared.

Floating alongside the trees were two brown domelike bodies that hovered above the ground. Peter stared and squinted, trying to determine exactly what he was seeing. In appearance, the forms were like two extremely large brown bears, sleeping near the line of trees.

The recent experience with the bear and the lion made the boy cautious. If there was water near the cottonwoods, then it could very well be a place where grizzlies came to drink.

Peter stood inspecting the shapes, then advanced a little and studied them again. A change in the light and shadow revealed a third domed shape and then a fourth and a fifth.

Understanding flooded Peter's mind, but he did not know whether to be relieved or more anxious. The group of rounded images shimmering in the afternoon sun were huts—the dwellings of a tribe of what Peter called the Wild Ones . . . Indians.

There was no turning back. Peter needed water and he needed it now. That an Indian rancheria existed by the line of cottonwoods meant a certainty of finding water, and Peter meant to have it.

The dome-shaped huts grew in his vision and increased in number as he got closer. They were oddly placed in irregular groups. Peter was curious as to why he saw no people out and about. The afternoon was wearing on, but it was not late enough or cool enough for the people to stay indoors. *Perhaps this is a deserted village,* Peter thought. *I hope they didn't leave because the water ran out.*

No dogs barked at his approach, no horses stamped, no children played, no adults watched him, and yet . . . Peter had the eerie feeling that the village, though clearly deserted, had only recently been abandoned.

At the edge of the cleared ground that marked the collection of huts, the village was tucked into a fold of hillside where a rockfall released a spring. There was not enough water to run down the creek bed, but there was a trickle of the precious liquid that dripped steadily down from the ledges and filled a good-sized pool. The overflow of the pond made its way downstream only a few yards before it was swallowed by the thirsty sand. It was barely enough to supply a village of this size and keep the trees alive as well. Perhaps the people *had* moved on.

Peter went directly to the spring. He eyed the stagnant basin with its covering of yellow-green scum and turned to the rocky ledge. Cupping his hands beneath the seep, Peter waited patiently for a handful of water to drip into his grasp. He drank it greedily, waited for his palms to refill, and drank again.

His eyes glanced downward as he waited for his hands to fill the third time. At first nothing seemed out of the ordinary, but then his mind focused on what his eyes saw: there was a footprint directly under the drip of the spring. In the sandy verge of the pool was the imprint of five large naked toes.

Staring at his own feet encased in soft leather boots, Peter came to the inescapable conclusion. Not only was there at least one other person around the camp, but the dripping water would have obliterated the print in no more than ten or fifteen minutes. Whoever it was could not be far away.

Peter tried to backtrack the trail, but other footprints could not be seen. Beyond the line of the cottonwood trees, a dust devil danced and hopped its way over the sage. The dry, thin dirt would not hold a print long against the sweeping breeze, except in a sheltered place such as near the rocks.

The way the wind swished through the camp, there was no true lee side to be sheltered, and no more distinct prints met Peter's eye. He circled one hut, then another and a third without finding any evidence of another human.

"*Hola,*" he called. "Is anybody here?"

There was no answer but the rustle of the leaves. Discarded baskets and tools lay scattered about. An odor of decay assaulted Peter's nose, and he did not enter any of the buildings.

Next to the third deserted hovel was a circular heap of rubble where a hut had burned to the ground. Most of the ashes had been blown away by the wind, but fragments of charred timber remained. Peter studied the location for a moment, then went past another abandoned structure, which also had a burned-out hulk beside it.

He passed another hut, buzzing with a cloud of flies, and two more burned spaces. The boy thought how strange it was for the village to suffer so many fires yet not lose *all* the buildings. He stood beside a fifth burned place and examined the debris. A broken clay pot was overturned in the center of the rubble. Peter idly kicked at the shard with his toe.

The pot fragment rolled over to reveal a human skull. Its empty eye sockets appeared to stare at Peter. Even without the lower jaw there seemed to be a malicious grin to its expression.

Peter ran toward the edge of the camp, passing standing huts and burned-out ruins without looking. He did not stop running until he was beyond the last of the domed houses and was outside the village next to a long, low mound of earth.

He forced himself to stop. His breath was coming in ragged gasps and his heart was pounding in his ears. What was he afraid of? Old dead bones could not hurt anyone, nor was Peter a child to be frightened anymore by Paco's ghost stories about headless vaqueros and haunted caves.

He dropped onto the mound next to a discarded deer hide to rest and think, to regain the composure that he thought an almost-adult should have. He laid down the broken gun and reviewed the situation: some disaster had hit this village, with multiple fires that had claimed at least one victim. Also, as lately as a few minutes before his arrival, there had been some person—not a ghost but a living, barefoot human—walking in the camp. *Now what?* he thought.

As if in answer to his unspoken question, the earth beneath him moaned. Not a quick groan like Peter had heard when tree limbs rub together in a windstorm, but a long, drawn-out sigh of misery.

Peter jumped up from the mound. From the highest part of the long barrow of earth, near its center, a puff of smoke drifted up. At the same time, the deer hide lying on the ground stirred and shook as if something were coming out. *The demon caballero riding forth!*

Adult composure or not, Peter was *not* remaining to see what actually came out of the ground. He was already running back toward the spring when he remembered the rifle.

It was a credit to Peter's discipline, if not his courage, that he turned around and raced back to reclaim the gun. He had just reached it when the deer hide shook itself free of some clods of earth that had rolled on it, and it flipped open to reveal a tunnel into the mound. Peter stood transfixed as a small bony hand appeared and was followed by a sleeve of coarse gray cloth and then the familiar small form of . . .

"Father Francis!" Peter cried with relief at the sight of his father's friend. "What are you doing here? And what is this place? Where is everybody?"

The priest was just as dumbfounded as the boy. "Don Peter," he said, brushing off his robe and standing up to look around. "Is your father here?" His face was lined and drawn and his expression anxious.

In a few clipped phrases, Peter explained how he came to be lost and wander into the village.

The priest shook his head with a sorrowful expression. "You cannot remain here, Peter. It may cost you your life."

"Why? What is it?"

"Smallpox," came the weary, toneless answer. "The village is dying. I alone am able to care for the people calling for water in their dreadful fevers." And then the priest explained further.

Only a month earlier the village had been thriving. Bustling with the summer activities of preparing hides and gathering chia seeds for meal, the Yokuts had welcomed a group of twenty British sailors who said they had come to settle.

Always hospitable, the Yokuts noted that the sailors were sickly and weak, and many exhibited small sores and pockmarks. The Indian elders had done what they could to supply the needs of the newcomers and treated them with such medicine as was known.

Two weeks later, the first of the Yokuts fell ill. The next day two more and the following day six. The traditional Yokut ceremony of burning the bodies of the dead inside their huts with all their belongings had been carried out at a pace that accelerated daily. What prevented the *rancheria* from being totally reduced to ashes was only that no people remained who were strong enough to carry out the cremations. Only Father Francis was untouched by the disease, and he was too busy caring for the sick and dying to bother with the dead, now piled in two of the remaining huts.

"Only two of the Britishers died," Father Francis said, "but the rest fled—back to their ships, I suppose."

"Why have all the sick people gone into the hole in the ground?"

"It is our way," Father Francis replied. "The sweathouse has always been our cure for sickness, and now all who are left alive have gone there."

Peter looked around at the dusty valley and the slight frame of the careworn priest. "You need help. I will stay to aid you."

"God bless you, my son," Father Francis said sincerely. His body swayed as he made the sign of the cross. "But it cannot be. I will not risk your life—" He stopped suddenly. "Perhaps God has sent you here for a greater purpose than you can know." The priest retreated abruptly into the bowels of the earth.

When he emerged again a moment later, he had a tiny bundle wrapped in doeskin. Father Francis stood before Peter, who watched curiously as the priest tucked back a fold of soft white hide to reveal the face of a baby.

"His name is Limik—'Falcon,' the same as my grandfather," Father Francis said. "He is only two days old. My cousin's baby."

"But his mother?" asked Peter.

The priest shook his head sadly. "She will not live another night. I despaired of keeping this little one alive, but now I see that heaven has sent you for that reason."

Peter drew back sharply. "Me? You want *me* to care for this baby?"

A strand of fluff from a cottonwood tree drifted out of the sky and landed across the baby's nose. Impulsively, Peter reached over to pluck the strand away. Limik, who had been gnawing on his fist, opened his hand and grasped Peter's little finger in a grip surprisingly strong.

The young ranchero gulped. "All right. What do I do?"

* * *

The lines of white surf had already disappeared, and the red-tile roofs and whitewashed adobe walls were fading into the backdrop of dusty green California hills as the *Juno* sailed away from Santa Barbara.

Father McNamara and Captain Blake regarded the receding shoreline. Blake said gloomily, "I do not relish having to report to Admiral Seymour on the complete failure of our mission here."

Father McNamara was more sanguine. "Tut, Captain, it is not

your fault that events proceeded so rapidly. Who would have foreseen that the Americans would be prepared enough to achieve their seizure of San Francisco, San Diego, and Monterey, all within one month? They will be lounging about the pueblo of Los Angeles and wandering through Santa Barbara in another week."

"But the scheme to colonize!" Blake exclaimed, dashing his fist against the taffrail. "It should have worked!"

"Yes. It is a pity that your sailors were not able to perform as expected. But let me cheer you up with another plan that I expect to lay before Admiral Seymour."

"What might that be?"

"Ah, a capital scheme to be sure . . . controlling the crossroads of the Pacific, I call it. Tell me, Captain, have you ever been to the Sandwich Islands, discovered by the inestimable Captain Cook? I believe in the native tongue the land is called Ohwyhee. . . ."

CHAPTER 10

The boom of the twelve-inch cannon echoed around the Santa Barbara roadstead. The arrival signal rolled past the mission, up San Marcos Pass, and back again.

The report reverberated in the ears of Nicholas Den as he sat in his counting house. The curly-haired Irish ranchero was reviewing columns of figures for "California banknotes." Each entry represented cowhides worth two dollars, American. "What ship can that be?" he muttered to himself. "Julio," he called to his Indian servant, "fetch my telescope."

Den's eyes crinkled at the corners in the pleasant anticipation of some trading to be done. He climbed the stairs to the flat roof of his office two steps at a time. "Could it be the *Juno* back from Monterey in only a week? If it is, they'll be wanting twenty head or so for meat."

"Don Nicholas," said Julio, handing him the spyglass, "I do not recognize this ship. She is a frigate, *sí*?"

"Not so fast," corrected Nicholas Den, snapping open the brass telescope and fitting it to his eyes. "We'll know in a moment. She must be one of Admiral Seymour's—" he gasped—"that's not a British ship—they're flying the Stars and Stripes . . . she's American!"

The word spread quickly through the settlement and into the countryside beyond, bringing a crowd of curious onlookers to the beach.

"Can you make out the name of the vessel?" someone asked Don Nicholas.

"She's swinging around now . . . yes," he said. "The *Congress*."

The small boat being rowed ashore from the frigate looked to be in danger of swamping. Besides the six sailors manning the oars, there were ten men carrying muskets with the muzzles held rigidly upright, one dressed like an officer, and two midshipmen.

As the boat swept onto the sand, two of the sailors jumped overboard to guide the boat farther onto the shore. When the little vessel was beached, it was dragged past the high watermark. Only then did a distinguished-looking passenger get out.

The man who stepped out of the boat onto the Santa Barbara landing was no taller than Don Nicholas and thinner of face and body. He was wearing the full dress uniform of a commodore of the United States Navy. Despite the warm late-summer temperature, every brass button of his double-breasted coat was secured, right to the high, stiff collar worked with gold. His gold epaulets glinted and gleamed in the sunlight as he proceeded directly to where Don Nicholas stood. The two midshipmen followed.

"Sir," he said formally in English, "I am seeking the *alcalde* of this place, Don Nicholas Den. Can you help me locate him?"

"It depends," Don Nicholas replied, shifting uncomfortably. "What do you want him for?"

"Why, to announce my arrival and give him my compliments," the youthful-looking man with the aristocratic nose said with a touch of sarcasm. "No matter . . . I have other pressing business. Mr. Mitchell, if you please."

"Fall in!" commanded one of the midshipmen in a high, nervous treble.

Leaving the six sailors beside the boat, a double file of men with muskets escorted the naval commander and two midshipmen from the beach.

Don Nicholas and the crowd of curious Barbareños followed but at a respectful distance. After all, the soldiers' muskets were fixed with bayonets, and their field packs and grim expressions suggested that they meant business.

The main thoroughfare of Santa Barbara was little more than a muddy track more suited to *carretas* and oxcarts than to precise military formations. And proceeding along it also meant wading across Mission Creek.

The formation followed the rutted highway directly to the old adobe presidio. There were no Mexican soldiers present, since the remaining few guards had been withdrawn when Governor Pico had retreated to Los Angeles only a few days before.

The courtyard was empty except for a forgotten goat and a flock of chickens pecking in the dirt. The whole fort had an air of dilapidation and abandonment. The slumping adobe walls could have been deserted for a century instead of only a week.

The commodore looked around uncertainly, as if wondering how to demand the surrender of a town when there was no opposition. "Mr. Mitchell," he said at last to one of the midshipmen, "I'll have our flag run up the flagpole, if you please."

"Begging your pardon, sir," apologized the middie. "But there is no flagpole, sir."

The young American officer tugged on his bushy sideburns and frowned. "All right, then, we'll just march until we find one!"

After slogging down narrow lanes even more rutted than the main highway, the detachment of troops halted in front of a two-story adobe casa. It looked like many other nondescript tan brick buildings in Santa Barbara, with one notable exception: it had a flagpole. The slender mast was actually a semaphore staff that its owner, Don Nicholas Den, kept to exchange signal flag greetings with ships in the harbor.

"Mr. Mitchell, you will post the colors," ordered the commodore.

The middie saluted sharply and called the detail to attention. The red, white, and blue of Old Glory was soon hoisted to the peak.

Much whispered commentary erupted from the crowd.

Don Nicholas stepped forward in protest. "Sir, what do you think you are doing?"

"Well, señor *alcalde*, mayor. You *are* Nicholas Den, aren't you?" inquired the commodore.

Don Nicholas stumbled back a pace. "How did you—?"

The naval officer brushed the question aside in favor of answering the earlier challenge. "I am Commodore Stockton of the United

States Navy. Inasmuch as the United States and the country of Mexico are now at war, I am hereby taking possession of the Santa Barbara presidial district."

* * *

As soon as the word of Commodore Stockton's invasion reached the Reed Rancho, Francesco ordered her gray barileno mare saddled and set off for town. No word had come from Will or news about him. But he had gone seeking Americans, and it was to the Americans that she would go for information.

Stockton had set up his headquarters in Nicholas Den's office and was proceeding to treat Santa Barbara as conquered territory. Francesca was stopped by a sentry outside Don Nicholas's doorway, but that did not prevent her from overhearing the conversation within.

"And I expect you, Don Nicholas," a high-pitched, nasal voice was saying, "to be responsible for keeping the peace. I will be departing shortly to continue the campaign, but I will leave Midshipman Mitchell and Lieutenant Falls, along with a platoon of marines."

"Commodore," an unhappy-sounding Don Nicholas sputtered, "I must protest! How can you force me, a Mexican citizen, to administer the laws of a foreign invader? It is against all the rules of the civilized world!"

"Civilized world be hanged!" the nasal voice retorted. "I intend to see that order is maintained in Santa Barbara, by force if necessary. If you wish such an unfortunate consequence to be avoided, you will do your utmost to make certain that the citizenry remain cooperative and peaceable."

The finality of both words and tone left no doubt in Francesca's mind that she had just heard the last pronouncement on the subject.

"Now," the voice continued in a quiet volume, "as to quarters for my men. Your own rancho, Dos Pueblos, is just outside of town. Is that correct?" A short man in a crisp blue uniform paced in front of the doorway.

Don Nicholas sputtered again and choked. His bulging eyes and beet-red face gave a good imitation of a man suffering apoplexy. But he was saved from responding by a marine guard announcing that a lady wished to speak with Commodore Stockton.

The officer spun on his heel to face Francesca. The words that he did not wish to be disturbed were on his lips, but Francesca watched him check himself and saw his gaze inspect her face and figure. Striking a military pose with one hand behind his back and the other grasping his jacket lapel, the banty rooster of a man addressed her. "What may I do for you, señora?"

Seizing on the interruption, Don Nicholas said smoothly, "May I present Doña Francesca? Her husband is an American, and their rancho is even closer to Santa Barbara and more spacious than my own humble casa."

"Wonderful," said Stockton, eyeing Francesca. "Your husband is American? Where is he? Is he in favor of our, uh, activities?"

Francesca fixed the commodore with a steady gaze of her dark eyes. "It is about my husband that I have come to see you, sir. My husband, Don Will Reed, went north some time ago to inquire into the reported deaths of our godchildren, Ramon and Carlos Carrillo. I have not heard from him since. Do you know his whereabouts or if he made contact with the American commander named Fremont?"

Stockton's face grew grim. "I know something of the death of the Carrillos. I must tell you, madam, that they were executed as spies, and if your husband had any connection—"

"They were *not* spies!" Francesca snapped. "They were barely older than my own son! And what of my husband? Do you know of him?"

"Know *of* him? Yes, I know of him . . . he attacked Captain Fremont's landing party in Yerba Buena. He is a prisoner, madam, and after trial will face further imprisonment—or worse."

Francesca groped for the office chair into which Don Nicholas guided her. "You cannot mean it," she murmured, shaking her head. "It cannot be so."

Stockton looked stern. "Don Nicholas, under the circumstances, I think it entirely appropriate to adopt your suggestion. Lieutenant Falls and half the troops will be billeted at the Reed Rancho."

Staring at the wood-planked floor, Francesca bit her lip and held a lace handkerchief to her eyes. She said nothing at the outrage and barely heard Don Nicholas inquire, "And the rest?"

"I think that some should remain closer to the center of town. Yes, I'd say the remaining troops can bivouac right here in your office building."

* * *

"They are thieves and cutthroats, these Americanos," declared Simona, the cook in the Reed household. With one infant on her hip and a toddler trailing after, Simona helped Francesca stash the most precious household belongings into a large trunk. Luis, her diminutive vaquero husband, was already hard at work digging a hole in the floor of the stall reserved for the master's horse, Flotada.

Silver table service, tea sets, goblets, and candelabra were wrapped in delicate lace and linens. All the weapons, including table knives, were placed into the trunk lest the Americanos carry out their threat to arrest every citizen caught with a weapon of any kind.

Francesca warned Simona, "Tell Luis that these Americanos are greatly afraid of vaqueros. They know how accomplished our men are with their reatas and now have made the rule that anyone with a reata will be publicly whipped or arrested. We will bury the reatas in the trunk as well."

"They are loco!" fumed Simona as she hurried out the door. "If Don Will were here, they would not treat us like prisoners."

Francesca was secretly relieved that Will was not here, even if it meant he was in jail. Certainly he would not stand for the endless list of regulations that the American Lieutenant Falls had imposed upon the "conquered" people:

BY ORDER OF THE AMERICAN COMMANDER LT. FALLS

1. Shops will be closed at sundown.
2. No alcohol will be sold.
3. A strict 10 PM curfew will be enforced.
4. No meetings to be held.

5. No two people may be on the street together.
6. No assembly of more than two people.
7. No carrying of firearms.
8. No carrying of reatas or tailing of steers.

American Commander Lt. Falls will act as civil judge in the absence of Commodore Stockton. All violations of the above regulations are punishable by whippings, imprisonment, or death. Houses may be searched if a suspicion of wrongdoing exists.

Written in English and posted on the wall of every shop and home in Santa Barbara, the regulations were then read aloud in Spanish from the rooftops. Clusters of astonished citizens had listened, then looked at one another in the realization that anyone standing among a group of three or more could instantly be arrested and punished.

The crowd had simply evaporated. No doubt every Santa Barbara resident had hurried home to do the same thing Francesca was doing now. Every valuable would have to be hidden. The new laws were not laws meant to protect from harm. They were simply designed to grant absolute power to the strutting little tyrant who would soon be moving into Francesca's own home.

Simona returned with the reatas, which she wrapped in a sheet and placed at the top of the chest. "Luis says he understands why the Americanos fear our skill with the reata. But why have they made a law against the tailing of steers?" She shook her head at the madness of such a proclamation.

Francesca expelled a short, bitter laugh. "Perhaps these Americano cows have tails beneath their uniforms. Perhaps they have seen the way our vaqueros can flip a steer by simply cranking its tail. No doubt this Lieutenant Falls is afraid Luis will crank the man's tail, and he will live up to his American name."

That explanation was as reasonable as any, since the whole list seemed to border on insanity.

"Don Reed would tail this strutting calf if he were home! Did you see Falls parade around as though he were some handsome *mayordomo* on a prancing stallion? His teeth poking out from those thick lips! And he has only half his hair. Skinny neck and a potbelly, too! A very poor specimen of Americano, if you ask me. It is a good thing we know Don Reed, or we could think them all piggish and pitiful and . . . *loco*!" She finished where the conversation had begun.

"If he is loco, then perhaps he is also very dangerous, Simona." Francesca closed the trunk and snapped the lock closed. "I have heard my father speak of men such as this Lieutenant Falls before. He sees danger in every look and believes that each whispered word is about himself. He feels that he is much despised—"

"And so he is!"

"Ah, but he does not believe that such hatred is justified. His whole existence depends on fighting some personal enemy. For this reason, men like Falls work very hard at making enemies of all men. It is a twisted mind. A twisted and dangerous life." Francesca glanced worriedly out the window. "We must be careful, Simona. He has made himself the law. If we offend him, we are subject to his revenge."

"The fact that we were here first offends him."

"Think of your children. Smile and keep silent until someone sane returns to put an end to this madness." She was glad that Peter was in the hills, relieved that Will was far beyond the reach of this little madman. She would pray for Will's release and safe return but not if homecoming meant greater danger!

* * *

The company of eight marines rode toward the Reed Rancho as Francesca and Simona stood on the porch. Luis hurriedly spread straw to cover the turned earth in Flotada's stall.

On the shoulder and rump of every horse, Francesca recognized the brands of the finest ranchos in the country. She was justified in burying her belongings. These vile men took what they wanted.

Simona noticed the brands at the same moment. Through gritted teeth the plump cook declared, "Thieves and cutthroats, Señora Reed. They should be riding wild burros! American pigs!"

"Whatever you say," Francesca reminded her, "say it with a sweet smile. They do not speak our language, but this Lieutenant Falls fancies himself to be both judge and lawgiver. No doubt he studies the expression on our faces even now." She raised her chin slightly and smiled like a gentlewoman welcoming guests to the hacienda. There would be no trace of the bitter resentment of this violation . . . not a hint of the disdain she felt for the pitiful little Americano lieutenant. He flapped awkwardly against the saddle and tugged at the reins of the magnificent horse he rode.

"It is pathetic to see when the horse is finer than the one on his back," said Simona in Spanish. Her face was also a reflection of genuine hospitality as the riders approached.

"The horse should be riding Señor Falls, I think," agreed Francesca. "The animal knows more than the man in this case."

The eight marines pulled their mounts to a halt before the porch. Francesca and Simona both curtsied in unison.

"Good afternoon, madam," said a breathless Falls as his nervous horse pranced about the yard and fought the harsh tugging on the bit. "You have prepared for us?"

"Welcome to the Reed Rancho, Lieutenant," Francesca said graciously. "I have moved my belongings to the servant quarters. You and your men are welcome here. My husband, who is an American also, will be pleased that you have chosen our home to reside in during your stay."

"Your English is quite good," said Falls, jerking the horse around in a tight circle. "I will thank you to speak only English in the presence of me and my men at all times."

"But my servants do not speak your language, Señor Falls. What if I must speak to them in front of you?"

"Well then . . . you will provide us with a proper English translation in such a case. We cannot have you Mexicans conniving behind our backs, can we?"

With a gracious nod, Francesca agreed. "As you wish, señor."

"And I am not a *señor*. I am no Mexican, madam, but an American officer."

Again the nod.

Then Simona asked in Spanish, "What does this *cabro* say, Doña

Reed?" She continued to smile demurely at the officer, who was unaware that *cabro* meant goat.

"May I explain to my servant what you have just told me?" Francesca asked.

"Tell her," Falls ordered.

Francesca did so in Spanish. "The *cabro* says that I am to speak only English to him and give him the translation of every Spanish word uttered in his presence."

"*Sí,*" replied Simona with a nod at the American. There was no change in her expression. "*Caporal de cabestros.*" She uttered the salute "Captain of Oxen" with respect.

"What did she say?" Falls demanded.

"She calls you Captain of Horsemen, an honored title," Francesca answered. Indeed, the word for *oxen* was quite close to the word *caballero,* horseman. "Does the title please you, Lieutenant? If so, it is a simple title for my servants to use. Their tongues cannot master the difficulties of your language, I fear."

With a self-satisfied smile, the Captain of Oxen set his muddy boots in the home of Will and Francesca Reed.

CHAPTER 11

Tor Fowler was leading a gray horse as he approached the guard outside the adobe-block hut—the same hut in which he had lately been held. Will was now confined there. An iron gate had replaced the wooden door. "Davis," Fowler said, staring at the guard as if in disbelief, "is that you?"

Davis hastily put down a tin plate of beans and wiped grease from his whisker-stubbled chin. "Hello, Fowler. I heerd you was back." Davis appeared nervous.

"Yup," Fowler agreed. "You know that feller in there," he said, pointing to the hut. "He saved my life."

"I heerd something like that." Davis nodded. "But he's a turncoat what's to be sent to Sutter's with the other prisoners."

Fowler studied Davis's face intently so long that the settler fidgeted, shuffling his feet. "What're you lookin' at, anyhow?" he demanded at last.

"They tell me you was nearly killed, shot in the head, escaping. Same time I got took prisoner. That so?"

The smallest mark remained on Davis's forehead. A twitching hand rubbed over the spot and traced around it as if pretending the wound were larger. "Yup."

"Got you promoted too?"

Davis bobbed his head. "Corporal of Californie Volunteers, ever since we took care of them Carrillo assassin fellers." Then as if drawing renewed confidence from remembering his rank, he demanded, "What do you want here, Fowler?"

"Hear that?" Fowler asked, jerking his chin toward the cannon-fire salute. "Captain Montgomery is comin' ashore to read a proclamation. Probably be a regular fiesta after."

"So?" said Davis unhappily. "I got to guard this here prisoner." He hefted an army-issue musket. "And I don't need no help from you."

"Thought you might like to go on down to the party and leave me on guard a spell." Fowler's voice sounded surprised at Davis's hostility. The barest droop of an eyelid over a gray eye was directed at the doorway.

"What kinda fool you take me for? Everybody knows you favor lettin' this fella loose!" A move closer by Fowler made Davis draw the musket up to chest height and cock the hammer back. "That's far enough."

Fowler held up both empty hands, palms outward. "Whatever are you scared of, Davis?" he said innocently, taking one more pace nearer.

Davis backed up a step, and his shoulders touched the iron gate across the door. "I'm warnin' you." He raised the musket to his shoulder.

From behind him, Will Reed's hand shot out through the grating and grasped the barrel of the musket. The gun erupted with a roar, striking nothing, its blast blending with the rolling cannon fire. Will yanked back hard on the weapon, pinning the settler by the neck to the metal frame.

Fowler took one step as Davis's eyes began to bulge and his hands waved frantically. Fowler raised the fist that had been hidden by his side and threw a haymaker in an overhand arc toward Davis's nose. Within a second Davis had gone limp, and Will let him slip to the ground.

"That was for Cap McBride and Two Strike," Fowler muttered, rummaging through Davis's pockets and coming out with the key to free Will.

"Thanks," Will offered, emerging into the sunlight. "Now tell me where that fellow Falls has gone, and we're all square."

Fowler shook his head. "I'm still comin' with you. Nothin' left for me around here. Castro's moved south; Fremont too. I figure there'll be a fight round Santa Barbara somewheres."

Will started. "My home! What about Falls?"

Gray eyes locked on green. "Left by ship," Fowler said. "Fremont sent him ahead to Santa Barbara to cut off Castro's retreat."

* * *

A crowd of spectators gathered on the dirt field that passed as Yerba Buena's public square. Russian sailors, whaling men, Frenchmen off a merchant vessel, and American traders all jostled for a better view, but there were few Californios. The Spanish-speaking residents mostly stayed indoors.

Those who stood before the customs house could see boats being lowered from the United States ship *Portsmouth*. Seventy black-hatted sailors rowed ashore at Clark's Point at one end of the arc of Yerba Buena cove.

To the brittle noise of one drum and the shrill prattle of one fife, the files of men marched to the square. Down came the Mexican flag, and the Stars and Stripes was hoisted in its place.

But the banner at which a small knot of Californios was staring was neither of these. At the rear of the crowd stood Juan Padilla, flanked by a dozen men. Their wide *poblano* hat brims were pulled low over their eyes, and under their serapes they held pistols. The flag at which Padilla directed his attention was a white sheet with a red stripe along its bottom edge. The crudely lettered words *California Republic* paralleled the stripe. In the center of the flag was a hulking shape meant to be a grizzly bear.

One of Padilla's friends made an obscene comment and the men laughed, the sound covered by the cheering of the rest of the crowd.

"Looks like a *cochino prieto*, a black *pig*, to me," Padilla added.

"What do we do now, Capitan?" whispered Four Fingers hoarsely. "Do we ride south to aid General Castro?"

"We ride south," Padilla agreed. "But we go only to aid ourselves! *Vamanos!*"

* * *

Peter stopped pounding the chia-grass seed long enough to gather up the tiny wailing Limik and rock him for a moment. "Just wait a bit. I'll have food for you soon."

Still holding the baby, he stirred the pounded seeds into a gourd bowl half full of water. Using a pair of wooden tongs, Peter picked up a clean round stone that had been heating by a fire of mesquite wood. He dropped the stone into the bowl of porridge and stirred it until it began to steam.

"You are hungry all the time, Limik," he said, "but that's all right because you will grow up strong." Peter dipped his finger in the porridge, then let the baby suck the thick gruel.

Limik wrinkled his face as if to say that the meal was not altogether to his liking, but he continued eating.

"I know we need milk, but there is nothing I can do about that now."

Father Francis stumbled out of the sweathouse. His robes were drenched in perspiration, and his brown complexion had turned almost as gray as his robes. He was exhausted.

Stooping beside the trickle of water from the spring, Father Francis splashed a few drops over his own face, then thrust a gourd under the flow to let it fill.

When the bowl was nearly full, he turned to go back to his charges but stopped beside Peter and the baby as if he had just seen them. A weary smile played across his face, and his eyes lightened just a touch. He stretched out his hand as if to place it on the baby's head, then drew it back quickly without contact. "They say this sickness is spread by the touch," he croaked.

Across the plain, up from the canyon, four swirls of dust appeared. At first they seemed to be nothing more than dust devils in some curious parallel flight, but soon they resolved into riders, coming at a hard gallop. Peter pointed them out to Father Francis.

The priest shaded his eyes and squinted, then asked, "Can you make them out, my son?"

Covering Limik carefully in his doeskin wrapper, Peter laid the baby down on a hide, then hopped on a ledge of rock. "The lead rider is on a tall mule. It looks like . . . Paco!"

In a few minutes the Reed *mayordomo* and two vaqueros rode into the Yokut camp. They had brought Peter's horse, Chino, with them.

"Peter! *Hijito,* little son! Where have you been?" Paco managed to sound angry and relieved in the same breath. "Your horse wandered in without his rider, and we found not only *oso* tracks but also puma tracks over yours. Now here you are, miles away from . . . what is that?"

The flow of questions and rebukes ceased abruptly as the thin wail of baby Limik rose from the bundle on the ground. Paco's mule snorted and cross-stepped sideways as a small brown arm broke free of its doeskin wrap and waved angrily in the air.

"Father Francis," Paco said, "where are all the Indios? And how long has Don Peter been here?"

Father Francis waited patiently for the stream of words to subside before explaining. When he had finished, the two vaqueros had purposely backed their mounts several paces toward the edge of camp and Paco was looking nervous.

"So you see," concluded the priest, "Don Peter was sent by God to serve the needs of this little one. And now that you have arrived, Paco, you must take them both back to Santa Barbara at once."

"But what about you?" Peter blurted out. "You alone cannot care for everyone."

The gray robe, once a perfect fit around the sinewy arms and legs of Father Francis, appeared to have grown. The folds of coarse cloth swallowed up the little man. "No, there are very few left now . . . I will manage."

At that moment the cowl slipped backward, exposing the drawn features of Father Francis. And in the hollow of his neck, at the base of his throat, Peter saw a single yellow dot.

The priest's eyes met Peter's. "Peter, my son, do you remember what follows the rodeo, the roundup?"

Peter looked surprised at a question that seemed so out of place, but he answered respectfully, "*Sí,* what follows is *de escoger y desechar,* the choosing and the discarding."

"Just so," Father Francis agreed. "You and I have both been chosen, Don Peter, but we must go to different fields for a time."

The boy bit his lip. "Will I see you again?" he managed to say.

"Of course," replied Father Francis, smiling once more. "In the

Rodeo Grande. Isn't there always a *parada de escojidos*, a parade of the selected ones? We will be there together, you and I."

A deep saddlebag was taken from Paco's mule and emptied of its provisions: jerked beef and small sacks of rice and cornmeal. The pack was lined with rabbit fur, and baby Limik was carefully tucked inside. The bag was secured to Paco's saddle, and Peter mounted Chino. "I will miss you," the young ranchero said to the priest.

"*Vaya con Dios,*" Father Francis said softly. "Go with God."

* * *

It was inevitable that the American officer Falls would become the object of quiet ridicule on the Reed Rancho as well as in the town of Santa Barbara. Greeted by young and old alike as *el cabro,* "the goat," the salute was always uttered in such a respectful tone that the little tyrant did not catch on. He was told—and believed—that *cabro* meant "leader."

"*Buenos dias,* El Cabro," said priest and mission Indian and schoolchild alike. "Good day, you goat."

He always nodded his too-large head in acknowledgment, although he did not speak.

Later he ordered Francesca to let it be known that he liked this title better than the one that meant Captain of Horsemen because it was shorter and easier for him to keep track of.

This small conspiracy among the citizens somehow helped to ease the tension of the almost intolerable oppression. When a runaway steer tore through the main street of Santa Barbara and was halted when a vaquero tailed it to the ground, El Cabro Falls carried out his threat and had the vaquero publicly whipped. From windows and doorways, citizens watched the whipping with hostile eyes. Forbidden to gather together for solace or action against such injustice, they comforted themselves by smiling and greeting El Cabro at every opportunity.

Each new outrage was met with this quiet inner resistance. Not every Americano could be so loco! After all, Señor Reed was a kind and good man. Certainly this Lieutenant Falls was some sort of aberration, a *diablero,* a demonic lunatic who would sink back to hell before the summer was past.

Falls added the proclamation that there would be no church services. Visits to the mission were restricted to one worshiper at a time. The citizens complied, entering the sanctuary one person at a time, lighting candles one at a time, until all the prayers and all the candles added up to one great hope—that soon the oppression of *el cabro* would be lifted from the tiny village.

CHAPTER 12

It was late when Peter and Paco rode into the sycamore-bordered lane that led up to Casa Reed. The two vaqueros had accompanied the young ranchero and his *mayordomo* only as far as the mouth of the canyon before turning back to rejoin the herd.

Baby Limik was sleeping in his makeshift cradle. Fed not an hour before on a mixture of chia gruel and cow's milk, he was content to be rocked by the gentle motion of the mule.

"Wait a moment," requested Paco, gesturing for Peter to stop. "I must walk a bit or my leg will stiffen completely."

"I thought you said vaqueros were too tough to notice a little thing like a kick in the shins," Peter teased.

Paco was not amused. "Next time *I* will mind the reatas and *you* may milk the wild cow! That hurts!"

"It was all for a good cause, and anyway, there won't be a next time. Mother will know of someone to nurse the child, probably tonight. *If* we don't dawdle too long in getting home."

Remounting the mule, Paco said, "You know, young Pedrito, you have a cruel streak about you." Then the weathered *mayordomo* leaned over to check the slumbering infant. His gruff voice was softer when he said, "We must take good care of him, Don Pedro. He is our godchild, you know. Perhaps the last of all his people."

Peter shuddered at the remembrance of the terrible loneliness and stench of death that clung to the Yokut village. "Come along then," he said with fervor, "let's get home."

The lights of Peter's house had just come into view around a bend in the lane when a voice from the darkness ordered in English, "Halt! Who goes there?"

"Quien va? Quien es?" called Paco, echoing the same challenge in Spanish.

"Halt or I'll shoot," came the order again.

"Wait, Paco!" cried Peter. "Think of Limik!"

It was a timely reminder. Paco was on the verge of spurring the mule and riding down the voice from the shadows.

"Get down and lead your animals," came the demand. "Walk on up to the house there, nice and easy-like."

The metal triangle hanging on the porch for calling the vaqueros to meals began an insistent ringing. There was a muffled stir of cursing and swearing, the thump of boots running onto the hardwood porch mixing with the flap of bare feet.

"That's far enough," called the sentry from behind Peter and Paco.

On the porch Peter could see a disheveled array of soldiers in various stages of undress. Some stood with uniform blouses hanging out, and others wore suspenders over bare chests.

In the center of the group posed a little man with round shoulders. A rumpled ring of hair stood straight out all around his crown as if he had slept standing on his head. He held a pistol in front of his bulging potbelly. "What is this, Hollis? What have we got here?" demanded the little man.

"Well, sir, Lieutenant Falls, sir, I caught these two sneakin' up on the house."

"We were not sneaking!" Peter corrected. "This is my home. What are *you* doing here? And where is my mother?"

"Ah, the coyote pup!" said Falls, snorting. "I'll ask the questions here, sonny boy, unless you want the same treatment your father got!"

* * *

The Americanos of Commodore Stockton had stolen every ham from the smokehouse of Will Reed before they sailed away. The commodore himself had tasted a fresh-cooked slice of the stuff and declared that Señor Reed's mind might be addled from living among the Mexicans, but that only a truehearted American knew how to smoke a ham so well.

Lieutenant Falls, however, had a different impression of the Reed family. He envisioned a different purpose for the empty smokehouse. Adobe walls and slit windows made it a perfect jail. . . .

✱ ✱ ✱

Francesca Reed faced off on the porch with the pompous little man who held his pistol tight at the back of her son Peter's neck. "This is madness! You cannot take my son prisoner in his own home!"

"He has broken the regulations, madam, and he is my prisoner!"

Conscious of the cold steel against his flesh, Peter did not speak or move. He kept his gaze riveted on his mother, whose eyes burned with fury and indignation at the injustice.

"But he did not know your rules. How *could* he know them? He has only just returned home!"

Oblivious to her protest, Falls licked his buck teeth in thought and then began to recite his orders. "It is plain as anything. He broke the rules. Out after ten o'clock. Carrying a weapon. Traveling with a companion. Strictly against the rules."

Baby Limik, being nursed by the cook, gave a contented cry from the parlor.

Francesca gestured toward the sound. "Traveling with this child, señor! Bringing this baby home that it might be cared for! He has told you how he and Paco came to be on the road so late! Are you a man without reason?"

Again Falls ticked off the broken rules. "On the road after ten o'clock. Traveling with a companion. Carrying a weapon . . . I can name another dozen regulations broken if you like, madam. Enough to get this boy of yours strung up. Neither Commodore Stockton nor any other American will doubt my reason in this. Your son is plainly a menace. A danger to me and my men here!" His eyes flared as he said these words.

Peter could tell that the man actually believed what he was saying. His mother was standing face-to-face with a madman who hid his insanity behind rules and regulations and imagined threats. Peter looked at her with an expression like his father's, telling her that she must tread gently. Here was a coiled snake, prepared to strike. Like a rattler, Lieutenant Falls perceived any step too near as a danger and a challenge to his petty tyranny. And there could be no doubt that he would kill without provocation if he believed he was being threatened.

"I insist that my son's case be heard by Commodore Stockton! You are the commandante, but the commodore is the governor." She played to his self-importance now, submitting to his imagined authority while appealing to a higher authority to decide the issue.

The ploy seemed to placate Falls. He stepped back a pace from Peter, removing the muzzle of the weapon from his neck. "Now you see, madam, I am only doing my job. Rules are rules. I obey authority, and so must you. If the rules are broken, it is my job to enforce them. It is for Commodore Stockton to interpret the fate of your son, whether he is hanged or imprisoned. Rules are rules, you see. My duty . . ."

Francesca had seen enough to know that Falls, when pushed, was quite capable of executing his own interpretation and judgment of the rules. A chill of fear coursed through her. "If Peter gives his word of honor that he will not run away, may he not remain your prisoner in this house?"

To this, Falls shook his head. "I already explained to you, madam, that prisoners would be confined to the smokehouse. He's lucky I do not simply hang him and this Indian from that oak tree and be done with the bother. Commodore Stockton would not question me if I did. They broke the rules. No matter whose son he might be. No matter. Men have been known to use the cover of carrying a child as hostage to protect themselves when they intend to do harm to the authorities."

Francesca saw the madness . . . the conniving . . . the questions flashing through Falls' eyes and beginning to form in his mind again. How might she stop them from taking root? She stepped closer to Peter, admonishing him as though he were a child caught in a prank. "Well, then, Peter, you shall have to stay in the smokehouse. The Commandante Falls must obey authority no matter what he circumstances, even though the rules were violated in innocence. But he is not an inhumane man—simply an officer forced to do some distasteful things. He will allow me to feed you and Paco and bring you bedding. You must go along to the smokehouse. You and Paco. It is the law, and we must obey as Commandante Falls obeys."

Falls flashed his teeth in a proud smile. He squared his sloping shoulders, placated by her soft voice and seeming compliance. "Well, now, madam," he said in a chivalrous tone. "I see you have some sense. You understand I am just doing my job."

"I would like to walk beside my son to the jail." Francesca took Peter's arm. "I have not seen him in a while and would like company if only for these few moments. A mother's wish, Commandante Falls." She said this so sweetly that he did not deny her.

Even so, he still held the pistol aimed squarely at the back of Peter's head as they marched out to the smokehouse.

* * *

The little bay horse Will had purchased near Yerba Buena for Fowler to ride could not keep up with Flotada. Will, now dressed in his buckskins, chafed at the delay. The farther south they rode, the more it sounded as though the war would soon be on the front doorstep of his home, if it was not already.

With Yerba Buena and Monterey both controlled by the Bear Flaggers, return to Santa Barbara by ship was out of the question. Will's splinted arm was bound tightly to his chest, but it was his own impatience that caused him the greatest irritation.

Once again it was necessary to rein in Flotada, whose easy canter ate up the miles, to allow the winded bay to catch his breath. "Fowler," Will said, "either I need to go on alone or we need to get you better mounted."

Tor Fowler slowed the laboring brown horse to a walk. "We can't afford to get parted," he said firmly. "You'd be in trouble with an American outfit or with them Mexes that held me prisoner, either one. Besides, I can't go back till we meet up with Fremont and explain . . . I'm a deserter, see?"

"All right then, it's a change of mounts that's needed. We'll see what we can find."

They rode along the Salinas River, south of Monterey. The course of the streambed would eventually lead them into the heart of what the old Spaniards had named the Temblor, the earthquake range. But the part through which they rode was a wide, dusty valley, dotted with oak trees, small ranches, and occasional grizzly bears.

A wisp of smoke from one of the branch arroyos drew Will's attention. "Let's see if we can do some quick trading," he called to Tor and turned aside into the canyon.

A hot breeze swirled the smell of smoke down to the riders. But there was something else on the wind besides smoke, something that made Flotada snort and stiffen his knees in his trot as though protesting their course.

The ranchero sensed the tension in his spirited horse and caught the need for caution in approaching the ranch. Fowler carried Will's Hawken rifle, while Will clenched a pistol in his left hand along with the reins.

The dwelling was on a bench of land above the canyon. Motioning for Will to halt his horse at the near approach, Tor rode past on the trail till he flanked the home at another gully.

Will heard the perfectly imitated plaintive song of a dove: low note, middle note, three sustained low notes. So realistic was the call that Will waited for the sound to be repeated just to be certain it was really the signal.

Then, putting the spurs to Flotada, Will urged the gray into instant movement. Up the trail they sprinted, then turned aside to climb a bank at the last second so as to appear from an unexpected direction.

The ranch house was a smoldering ruin. The roof had been burned, and its collapse had pulled down two of the adobe walls. In the dirt of the cleared space before the door lay a dead man. Flies buzzed around his face and swarmed thickly on the dark blood that pooled under his chest. In his hands he clutched no weapons, only beef jerky and a stack of tortillas. The shattered remains of a clay water jug were scattered around.

"He was bringing them something to eat when they shot him," Fowler said angrily. He stepped off the bay, which he tied to a corral post. The gate had been yanked free of the fence, and the tracks of five or six stampeded horses showed in the dust. "Run off all the stock, too," Tor concluded.

Examining the dead man while Fowler went into what remained of the house, Will called, "This man's been dead only since yesterday. They may be only hours ahead of us."

Fowler stepped back out of the ruined adobe and circled around the narrow bench of land, checking behind the corral fence.

Will saw him stop beside a row of trees, then turn away suddenly and lean on the rail as if sick. "There's a woman here," Fowler said. "They . . . she . . . she's dead, too."

Two mounds of earth stretched side by side beneath the shade of the nearby live oak. "Best we can do for now," Will said, putting the shovel in the ground at the head of one grave. "We still need to find you a better horse. We'll get somebody to fetch the priest and tell their kin."

"I bet the devils who did this are running off all the stock," Fowler observed. "From their tracks I'd say a dozen men were here. They could be raiding all the ranchos hereabouts and driving a herd along with them."

Will saw Flotada's ears prick forward, and the horse gazed pointedly toward a willow grove below the hillside. Indicating for Fowler to be silent, Will stepped next to the trunk of the oak. Laying the pistol across his splinted arm, he drew a bead on the center of the grove.

When he glanced back toward Fowler, Will saw that the mountain man was already ghosting from tree to tree down the slope. In the patches of light and shadow thrown by the willows and the oaks, Fowler's tawny buckskin form was zigzagging, lionlike, from cover to cover.

Fowler was no more than halfway down the slope when Will

heard a rustling in the willows, followed by the nicker of a horse. Both men froze, guns at the ready.

A riderless buckskin horse limped out of the brush. It was a tall lineback buckskin with a dark mane and four black legs. Fowler and Will still watched the willows intently until certain this was no trick. At last the flinty-faced scout approached the gelding and slipped a rawhide string around his neck. The horse stood patiently waiting, favoring a foreleg and holding his weight off it.

"This'd be one the cutthroats rode in here," Fowler remarked, pointing to the outline left by a sweat-soaked saddle blanket. "Left him 'cause he's lamed."

Will inspected the horse's brand as Fowler ran his hands gingerly down the injured leg. "I know this brand," Will remarked. "This is one of Mariano Vallejo's prize animals from his ranch near Sonoma."

"Well, lookee here," Fowler said, picking up the hoof and digging into the sole with his sheath knife. A jagged shard of clay pot fell out into his hand. "Probably came from the busted water jug when they killed that feller. Reckon he'll be sound again now."

The horse planted his forefoot firmly on the ground to indicate that Fowler's conclusion was correct.

"Get your stuff and get mounted," Will said. "You won't have any trouble keeping up now."

CHAPTER 13

The herd of horses being driven along left a trail as plain to the two experienced trackers as a well-marked roadway. The tracks headed south, keeping to the washes and gullies, out of sight of the main road and following the line of hills.

At one point the trail forked, with the milling mass of horses being diverted into low-lying pasture near a spring. The tracks of three horses with riders, noticeable because they stayed three abreast and did not cross one another's paths, continued on.

"I 'spect they left the others hereabouts with the stolen stock while them three reconnoitered up yonder," commented Fowler, waving his arms toward a hill that loomed ahead.

"It could be worse than that," Will observed. "Seems somebody in that group knows this country like I do. There's another rancho just over that rise."

The American scout and the California rancher exchanged looks. Each saw mirrored in the other's strong features his own grim thoughts: *What will we find across the hill?*

The two men checked their weapons and separated at the base of the hill to again make their approaches from opposite directions.

Will's route led to a low-lying saddle. There was very little cover once Flotada had climbed out of the cottonwoods and mesquite along the creek bottom—almost bare hillside with a few clumps of brush and granite boulders. Will dismounted, tied the gray horse to a tree branch, and crept up the hillside. If his memory served, he had told Fowler, the ranch was on the other side.

Tor Fowler saw all this from his vantage point high on the hillside to the west. He and the buckskin had climbed almost straight up the slope before moving toward the ridgeline that lay between him and the ranch. Fowler watched Will's cautious progress up the bare hill of dry grass and foxtails. Automatically his eyes traced Will's probable path from boulder to boulder until it topped the rise.

There, at the summit of the hill in a small cluster of rocks, a flash of light caught Fowler's eye. It could have been sun glinting off a patch of quartz or an outcropping of mica, but as he watched, the flash was repeated. This time he could detect movement as well. Fowler was certain he was looking at the reflection off a gun barrel.

The watcher was obviously posted to guard the hillside up which Will was sneaking. Even if he had not seen Will Reed yet, there was no way the ranchero could cross the largest bare space near the ridgeline without being spotted and shot.

Fowler could fire a warning shot of his own that would alert his friend, but if the other murderers were nearby it would bring them all into the action. "Ain't no kinda choice," he muttered to the buckskin. "Come on then, hoss. Let's go down there to help him."

As fast and as noiselessly as possible, Fowler and the buckskin plunged down the slope. As they went, he was grateful that the sun was westering. Its descent toward the hills behind him would make him harder to spot if the guard should glance his way.

The next time Fowler had a clear view of the ridgeline, he had dropped too low to see Will. But the scout could guess his friend's whereabouts. The watcher in the circle of rocks was standing now, swinging his rifle from point to point as he covered Will's approach, holding his fire till he was certain of killing range.

A woodpecker hammered on a hollow tree nearby, marking the passing like the ticking of a fast-running clock. Fowler knew that the explosion of a rifle would soon be the chime that ended the hour, perhaps marking the death of Will Reed as well.

Flicking the reins against the buckskin's rear with a loud pop, horse and rider exploded downhill toward the waiting assassin.

Fowler began screaming at the top of his lungs to distract the watcher, who stood to draw a bead on the unsuspecting Will.

The figure in the rocks whirled around, obviously startled by the spectacle—a tall apparition whose leather clothing blended with the animal he rode until both appeared as one. The charging beast thundered down the hill, as unstoppable as an avalanche and just as deadly.

Firing one futile shot that came nowhere near Fowler, the guard made no attempt to reload. He threw down his rifle and fled. Tor was behind him at once, the buckskin's pounding hooves right at his heels.

The man was brought up against a rock, his sombrero gone and one sandal missing.

"Don't even twitch," Fowler ordered, leveling the rifle across the saddle horn, "unless you figure having a big hole in your chest would make for interestin' conversation."

"No *hablo inglés,* señor," the man said, holding his empty hands aloft.

Fowler noted the ragged, cutoff, homespun trousers and the single remaining hemp sandal. "Hey, Reed," Fowler yelled, "come up here pronto!"

Will soon appeared atop the ridge.

"Somehow I don't figure this feller for one of them horse-thievin' murderers," Fowler said.

A few moments of conversation with Will in Spanish explained the true situation. The *paisano*, whose name was Feliz, was guarding against the *return* of the horse thieves. They had raided the rancho only the day before. "My brother, he is shot at the door of our casa, but he manages to wound one of the *ladrones,* the robbers. They do not see me, and they ride away when we start shooting. We think perhaps they will circle back and try again, and so I watch."

Will asked if they could have food and water. He explained about what they had found at the neighboring rancho.

Feliz gasped. His face hardened. "My brother is only a little wounded. He can stay to guard our rancho, and I will ride with you. We will hang those *malditos* or shoot them down like wild dogs. Give me but an hour, and six will ride with you."

* * *

News of Padilla's bandits reached the Reed Rancho when a half-starved young vaquero stumbled out of the mountains in search of refuge. Instead, he was captured by Falls, refused food or water, and forced to march at gunpoint to the rancho.

He collapsed on the steps of the servants' quarters as Falls glared at him. "He pretends not to understand English." Falls did not dismount from his horse as Francesca and Simona rushed to aid the half-conscious vaquero.

"*Agua,*" begged the prisoner, who was no older than Peter.

"Hey, there!" Falls commanded as Simona brought the drinking gourd. "He can have water after he explains who he is and where he comes from."

Francesca stared at Falls and took the gourd from Simona. Never taking her eyes from the little tyrant, she held the water to the lips of the vaquero, who drank eagerly.

"It is not wise to defy me, madam," warned Falls.

"He will not be able to tell you anything unless he drinks."

Falls dismounted, took two steps, and kicked the gourd from the man's hands. "If he wants any more he will tell me what I want to know."

Holding the young man's head, Francesca spoke to him softly, carefully explaining the presence of Falls.

The vaquero licked his parched lips and laid his head in Francesca's arms. "The Americanos here," he croaked. "And the bandits of Padilla just to the north. Both . . . they take what they wish. Rape our mothers and sisters and kill . . . everyone . . . except I alone escaped." He closed his eyes. His chin trembled with emotion.

Was a vision of horror replaying in his mind? Francesca wondered.

"*Por el bien del país* . . . Padilla claims he kills for the good of the country. Just as this one." He opened his eyes to glare at Falls. "This *diablo huero,* the white devil who denies me water."

"Is Padilla coming this way?" Francesca asked as Falls leaned closer, trying to comprehend if their conversation contained some treachery.

"He goes where he wishes." The vaquero closed his eyes again as though he had no strength to hold them open.

Francesca instructed Simona to prepare food and draw water to soak the vaquero's bloody feet.

Falls stomped onto the porch. "You must tell me in English what you are saying! What is this Mexican spy telling you, madam! I demand to know the truth!"

"He is the only survivor of an attack by a bandit troop headed by a villain named Padilla." She answered honestly, but Falls had already made up his mind. He had written his own tale of how the half-dead young man came to the Reed Rancho.

"Lies, I am certain. It is obvious . . . he is a survivor, all right, but no doubt he has survived a battle against our American forces! Look at him! Mexican! You cannot expect me to be such a fool as to believe that there is some rogue Mexican bandit on the rampage in the north, killing his own people?" He snorted his derision at such a thought.

"Think whatever you wish, El Cabro!" Francesca snapped, smoothing back the vaquero's matted hair. "Look at him! He is in no condition to lie!"

"Unless he has been on the run from our American forces and now finds himself my prisoner. Reason enough for a Mexican to invent such a tale!" He called to the guards at the smokehouse. "We have another prisoner! On the double!"

Francesca leaned over the vaquero protectively. "He is injured! He needs food and care or he may die! I cannot allow you to do this! We will care for him here!"

Falls placed his boot on the arm of the limp vaquero. "You cannot allow me, madam?" He sneered at her defiance. "You question my authority?"

"I question your humanity!" Francesca spat. "And your sanity in such a case!"

Simona emerged with a plate of corn bread and a bowl of cold soup.

Falls struck the tray from the hands of the startled cook. "I did not give permission for him to be fed. Unless he tells the truth, he shall not be fed, madam! That is the final word."

"And if he has told you all there is to tell?"

"Bandits? Absurd! He has met this fate at the hands of my countrymen. He is fleeing justice and thinks I am stupid enough to believe that he should be allowed to stay in a house and be fed and nursed to strength so he can kill us when our backs are turned! I am no fool, madam."

"He must be fed."

"In our little jail, perhaps. When he confesses, perhaps. When I give my permission. Then . . . perhaps, madam, he will be fed. Now stand back from him or you shall find I can be a harsh man . . . even with stiff-necked women." He clenched his fists as though he would strike her.

Simona pulled at her shoulder. "*Por favor,* Señora Reed!"

Francesca lowered her eyes and moved away from the unconscious vaquero. He was half dragged, half carried to the smokehouse and thrown in like a sack of potatoes. Then the door was slammed shut and locked again.

CHAPTER 14

The rounded slopes covered with dense chaparral trailed streamers of wet, gray fog.

"I smell the ocean in this mist," Fowler said. "Is it that near?"

Gesturing toward the west, Will Reed indicated the line of hills. "No more than fifteen—maybe twenty—miles that direction. Reminds me of home."

What Will did not say was that home was always uppermost in his thoughts and had been for the endless miles of riding. He wished he could see across the intervening space, see Francesca and know that she was safe and their home untouched by either the lunatic Falls or the evil-hearted Padilla. Will comforted himself more than once on the foresight of having sent Peter out of harm's way. *They are in Your care, God. Protect them. Let no harm come to them,* he prayed with each passing mile.

Behind the two Americans rode a score of vaqueros and rancheros gathered from the valley as the men rode south. All agreed that the safety of their families was more important than the politics of nations or the nationality of the perpetrators. They were bound together by their honor to rid the countryside of malditos and ladrones, evil men and thieves. *Por el bien del país . . .* for the good of the country.

Will shook himself out of his reverie. "Below this pass is the little mission town of San Luis Obispo. We'll get food and rest the horses there, then press on south. With hard riding and God's help we can make Santa Barbara by tomorrow."

Down the slope they rode until the mission came into view. The church sat on a knob that stood out in the surrounding bowl of green hillsides and jagged rocky outcroppings. One wing of the building, two stories high, stood at right angles to a low colonnaded portico. The mission and the church looked peaceful—a decided contrast to the uneasiness in Will's heart.

With only a mile of green pastures edged in yellow bee plant and mustard weed yet to cross, several other riders emerged from the cottonwoods bordering the small creek below the mission. The mounted men obviously intended to challenge the progress of Will's group. The newcomers spread out in a line directly across the rancheros' path. Will called a halt and both sides studied the other intently.

After a long moment Fowler announced, "It ain't Padilla. There're buckskins on that tall fella, and the others ain't dressed Mexican neither. Yup, they're Americans."

There was a hasty conference with Will's band of riders. "What will you do, Don Reed?" he was asked. "They are your countrymen."

Will shook his head. "California is my country. We did not come to fight the war to decide which nation will rule. We will not fight these men if they will let us pass. But if they will not—" he shrugged—"then see to my family after."

Holding aloft a saddle blanket in token of parley, Tor Fowler and Will rode across the field toward the waiting line of men. As they drew closer, Fowler glanced at Will's sling-bound right arm and commented, "Get ready to make a run for it. I recognize that tall, skinny fella. That's Andrew Jackson Sinnickson, one of the Bear Flag leaders."

"That's close enough, Fowler," ordered the swarthy-complected Sinnickson when the men were still twenty yards apart. "I never figured you for a traitor."

"Sinnickson," Fowler replied, "me and Will Reed here got a story to tell you. You have the reputation of being a fair man. What say you listen first and make up your mind after?"

Fifteen minutes later Sinnickson asked, "God's truth then, Fowler? Davis lied about who started the fighting, and Falls murdered two youngsters in cold blood, but right now you're trailing a gang of cutthroat Mexicans?"

Will answered for them both. "That's it. There's wickedness on both sides, and it looks like Santa Barbara and my family are about to be caught in the middle. Will you let us pass?"

Pondering for a minute, Sinnickson dropped his head in thought, like a great carrion bird perched on a limb. At last he said, "Pass, nothing. It's time the grizzly banner stood for what's right. We'll ride with you."

* * *

After an hour of rest and some food, the riders who had followed Will Reed and Tor Fowler from the north were ready to continue southward. But when they rode out of the grassy bottomland dedicated to Saint Louis the Bishop, their numbers had swollen from twenty to forty.

Behind the leading rank of mountain men in tawny buckskin rode the oddest collection of fighters California had ever seen. Elegantly dressed rancheros astride impatient stallions were flanked by frontiersmen in loose coats of leather tied with rawhide strings. The untrimmed hair of the rough trappers escaped their drooping hats, and their wiry beards were a sharp contrast to the rancheros' smooth faces. Raggedly clothed *paisanos,* the simple farmers and ranchers of California, rode their short, stocky horses next to stony-faced Indian scouts.

If the California Republic was to have any meaning, Sinnickson had explained to the group, all men who desired to live peaceably had to be able to receive justice and oppose evil, wherever it was found.

Will was grateful for the strength of men at his back, but as they rode, his thoughts all lay on what he would find ahead.

* * *

Simona nursed baby Limik as Francesca prepared the evening meal for prisoners and guards as well.

"Every day you fix supper for these Americano pigs," Simona said indignantly. "Let me prepare it, Señora Reed, and I shall add a drop or two of something special to their beans. Then we shall see how well they are able to guard the smokehouse!"

"You think I have not been tempted to do as much?" Francesca sighed as she dished up the corn bread. "Then I imagine what that devil Falls would do if he suspected we poisoned their food. No, Simona. We must try to outsmart Señor *Diablo Huero*, Lord White Devil, until Will returns. My good husband would want us to stay calm and outthink this fellow until he can put things right. Then I believe this Lieutenant Falls will find himself in grave trouble with the Americano leaders. If we can last . . ." Her brow furrowed. "I must hold my tongue with this beast."

"He is *muy peligroso*, very dangerous, Señora Reed. I am frightened to think what he might do."

Francesca nodded and tucked Will's Bible into the pocket of her apron. The condition of the young vaquero imprisoned with Peter had worsened since yesterday, and Peter said he begged for a priest. Falls had forbidden one to be summoned, but surely Peter could comfort the young man by reading from the Holy Scriptures. She had bribed the guard by making a fine berry cobbler. Falls had ridden into Santa Barbara. Could they object to her giving the Bible to Peter?

"Who goes there?" The youngest of the two marine guards challenged her as she approached the smokehouse.

"I have brought your supper," Francesca answered sweetly.

"I smelled that corn bread coming before you got halfway here," called the second guard cheerfully. They were pleasant enough with Francesca, but she knew they were much like dogs, wagging happily until the moment their master ordered them to attack.

"Simona and I made a cobbler for you today." She offered them the heaping plates, then waited silently as they unlocked the door of the smokehouse.

"You'll have to show us your pockets, ma'am. Them's the rules, and Lieutenant Falls will have our heads if we don't follow them."

She pulled the pockets of her apron out for them to examine and produced the well-worn Bible. "My son has asked for his father's Bible to read in these long days of his confinement. Surely you cannot object."

They thumbed through it, exchanged glances, and shrugged. "It ain't like it's a weapon, now, is it?" Stepping aside, they let her pass into the gloomy interior of the cell.

The sweet scent of woodsmoke and ham greeted her. Peter and Paco were against the far wall. The young vaquero, who was called José, lay on a blanket in the center of the enclosure. In spite of the thick adobe walls, the air was close and too warm. The light from the guards' lantern shone on the haggard faces of the prisoners. Francesca was forbidden to speak in Spanish. Violation of this order would be reported in spite of berry-cobbler bribes, and Falls would punish the prisoners by withholding their food.

"Two minutes, Missus Reed," called the guard.

Two minutes. Just long enough to kneel and check José's weak pulse.

"Has he eaten since yesterday?" Francesca asked Peter.

"Only a bite. I think . . . he wants to die, Mother. This Padilla is very bad. José tells us that his sisters and mother were . . . murdered. And I think he has given up all hope."

Francesca gave Peter the Bible. "You must find hope here. Read to him. This is our only comfort, Peter. Your father would say the same if he were here. This is our best weapon."

Peter held the Bible to the light. He nodded and embraced the book. "All men seem evil to me now, Mother. All . . . the Americanos of my father's homeland. And men like Padilla, who are from my own country. Who is for us, Mother? And who is for the innocent ones . . . like baby Limik? These days the darkness seems to consume everything."

"It has always been the same, Peter." She touched his forehead as though she were tucking him in. "There have always been men like Lieutenant Falls who make themselves grand by bullying others. And there have always been those like Padilla . . . and the British who brought plagues upon a gentle people without a thought or care that their whole world has vanished now."

She passed the plate of food to Paco. "God's Word is filled with such stories. Injustice. Evil. But I tell you this, Peter, the Lord is still God and these men will stand before His judgment. Sometimes that is the only hope we have left to cling to in this world."

"Thirty seconds, Missus Reed," came the warning.

"*Es la hora de rezar,*" she whispered. "It is time for prayer, Peter!"

"What was that you're saying, Missus Reed? You speaking Mexican, are you?" The lantern behind her was raised higher.

"Just reminding my son to say his prayers," she replied with a strained cheerfulness. She kissed Peter on his forehead. "Pray, Peter. Pray that the Lord will deliver us from evil just like you carried the baby home to our care."

The boy nodded. "Yes, Mother, I will."

"*Time!* Out you go, Missus Reed. Visiting is over!"

✶CHAPTER 15✶

Two of Mitchell's sailors and a pair of Falls' marines were deeply involved in their game of horseshoes. The score was three games to two in favor of the marines when the clatter of hooves and swirling dust alerted them to the approach of horses.

All reached for their rifles in alarm at the racket, but it was difficult to feel very apprehensive. After all, Santa Barbara had been peaceful under Falls' restrictive rules. If the Barbareños were not happy, at least they had not shown open hostility. Still, it was best to be on guard, so no one relaxed until the new arrivals appeared as a herd of horses only, rather than a troop of mounted men.

The American sailor on guard duty on the outskirts of the parade ground next to the old presidio gave the order to halt, but in the mass of milling animals it was unclear where there were humans to hear the command. "Halt!" he ordered again when a rider at last came into view.

The rider was openly carrying a knife. Its handle could be seen protruding above the sash around the rider's waist.

✶ ✶ ✶

Four Fingers was disgusted with the blue jacket's tone. "*Qué dice la vaca?* What does the cow say?" he muttered. His right hand crept downward to the reata, and he shook out a loop on the side of the horse where the guard could not see.

The sailor raised the still-uncocked weapon to his shoulder and repeated the order to halt.

The hand that gave Four Fingers his name flashed over the neck of his sorrel horse. The loop hit the guard in the face with such force that he must have wondered if one of his friends had thrown a horseshoe at him.

In the next second the loop flipped around the guard's shoulders, pinning his arms to his sides. Before his rifle even hit the ground, the sailor was jerked off his feet and dragged across the parade ground.

"Ha!" shouted Padilla to Four Fingers, waving his sombrero. "Bring them on, *amigos*," he yelled to the other riders. "Stampede!"

The herd of thirty stomping, kicking horses veered sharply onto the parade ground, scattering the sailors and marines. Two shots were fired, but neither hit anything.

Padilla drove his strawberry roan directly at a fleeing marine. *"Golpe de caballo!"* Padilla exulted as the horse's shoulder struck the American in the back and knocked him down on his face. *"Golpe de caballo!"* he called to his comrades. "Strike with the horse!"

Four Fingers spurred his mount toward the abandoned fort. The Americans were fleeing in that direction, and Four Fingers wanted to deny them the shelter of the crumbling adobe walls. The pace of his red horse was slowed by his kicking and crow-hopping at the weight of the still-struggling man being dragged behind. Four Fingers never slackened his gallop, but with a nonchalant air, he loosened the dally around the horn and let the reata slip to the ground.

Two of the stampeding horses jumped the torn and bruised figure without touching him, and he hugged the earth and remained flat on his belly.

The slight delay had given two of the Americans the chance to reach the cover of the presidio. The pair still had their rifles, and once out of the immediate terror of the stampede, they began a deliberate and methodical process of firing and reloading.

The battle of the parade ground was over suddenly. Padilla wheeled the roan toward the edge of the field as soon as the firing started. He waved his Colt revolving rifle, and the others joined him there, out of the effective range of the Americans' weapons.

Gesturing for Four Fingers to ride to his side, Padilla said to the other banditos, "Keep the herd here, *amigos*, and watch that the

Americanos do not break out. We will find out the strength of the Yankee dogs in the pueblo and return here for you."

As he and Four Fingers set off on the short ride into town, Padilla complimented his second-in-command. "That was a marvelous cast you made, *amigo*. Truly you are a *lazadore bravo*!"

Four Fingers made a deprecating gesture. "Not so good, Capitan. I did not hit what I was aiming for."

"You caught the gringo completely around his body," argued Padilla. "What more would you have?"

"Ah," sighed Four Fingers, "I was trying for his neck!"

* * *

The afternoon heat was stifling as Francesca carried the midday meal to the smokehouse jail.

The chains on Peter's ankles had been forged by the Santa Barbara blacksmith only yesterday. Francesca blinked back tears of fury as the door of the smokehouse slammed shut, leaving her son and Paco in utter darkness.

"I will come back with supper for you," she said in Spanish, breaking the English-only rule of Falls.

"And a lamp, Mother." Peter's voice sounded small yet unafraid.

Falls nudged her hard, away from the slit window. "You are to speak only in English, madam! I have spoken to you about that before. This prisoner is already under suspicion. How do I know if he is passing you some information? Perhaps some word from the enemy."

Francesca whirled around to face Falls, her patience finally at an end. "And who is the enemy, El Cabro? *Qué grosero!* How insolent you are to speak of enemies when you sleep in the bed of my son and he is chained to the walls of his father's smokehouse! You steal our food and then lock my son into this place as though he were nothing more than meat! I ask you again, El Cabro: Who is the enemy in this country? It is not Peter. Nor Paco. Nor myself. It is not we who have stolen and persecuted and even forbidden the gathering to worship God!"

Her outburst appeared to have startled the little man. "What I do I do for the sake of my duty," he sputtered. "For the good of the country." He drew himself up. "You are ungrateful, madam. I could have this upstart hanged for a spy. No one would question my decision. I have executed others no older than he for the good of the country, and no one questioned—"

"Por el bien del país!" she scoffed.

"English, madam!"

"For the good of the country, you say? I have heard this lie before. You know nothing of this country or of our ways. You have seen our land and desired to take it."

"And we shall have it, madam. No matter if you wish it not to happen. You and that traitorous husband of yours, who is also rotting in jail in the north!"

Silenced, Francesca suddenly felt sick. "What do you know of my husband?"

He chuckled. A low, mocking laugh, as though her pain was his amusement for the day. "He went to investigate the execution of two young spies, did he not? Two spies no older than your son, madam. Executed for the good of the country."

"Ramon and Carlos . . ." She faltered, looking at a man whose soul was the blackest she had ever known in a human. "It was you . . . you killed them."

Falls shrugged, unconcerned. "The country is full of spies . . . and former Americans. Traitors. Like your husband, madam. Perhaps like your own son?"

The threat was clear. What he had done to others he would do again. Perhaps he had also murdered Will. "Why are you here?"

"I thought my purpose was obvious, madam." He gestured toward the door of the smokehouse. "To hang the dead meat over a slow fire before it spoils and stinks up the land. I, madam, am a patriot. Here for my country. We will have no opposition left when the task is complete."

"*Usted es un diablero lunático!* You are a demon lunatic!"

Lieutenant Falls studied the angry woman standing in front of him. The woman who had dared to call him a demon lunatic. "Perhaps I am, madam. But I am efficient, am I not?"

Her accusation amused him. He was not surprised at her outburst any longer. She was a wife and a mother, after all. No doubt she knew the twins he had shot in the north. And she was not an American. She could not understand that this land must be joined to the United States at all costs. And he hoped to personally benefit from it as well.

"I do not believe all Americans are so cruel as you," she hissed at him. "You do not do this for the sake of the land. You kill and bully because it gives you great pleasure to do so. The rest is only an excuse. Fear God, you demon. His judgment is true."

To this Falls laughed. "So, it is as I suspected, madam. You are a little hypocrite yourself. You have opposed me all along." He stepped near. "Well, now that puts a different light on the relationship. Does it not? No more pretending." He grabbed her arm. "Now we can maybe get to know each other a little better. On honest terms. Come along with me."

Francesca cried out as he pulled her toward the bushes.

From inside the smokehouse he heard a shout—a shout from her son for him to stop. To leave his mother alone!

The woman lashed out at Falls, kicking him hard in the leg. She dug her nails into his arm and struck his face as he tried to kiss her.

"You think I care?" He enjoyed her struggle, slapping her hard across the cheek and jerking her hair until she screamed from the pain.

✶ ✶ ✶

Helpless in his prison, Peter slammed his fists against the adobe walls. The ring of his chains echoed like the thrashing of an animal caught in a steel trap.

"Let her go! In the name of God! Let my mother go!" he yelled over and over again.

✶ ✶ ✶

Again Francesca struck at Falls, this time drawing blood. He twisted her wrist, bringing her to her knees. Touching his cheek, he looked at his own blood and then wiped it on her face as she wept.

"Do not do this to me!" she begged. "Do not dishonor me!"

"Hear how she whines." He showed his teeth. "I have not enjoyed such sport in a long time, madam. Yes! Fight me! Fight me, then! You will not be laughing behind your hand when I am finished with you!" He gave another hard twist of her wrist and hooked his fingers in the lace collar of her dress. "I enjoy an honest fight, mada—"

Behind him stood a determined figure. Simona.

And the large iron skillet in her hand came down on his head and rang like a gong when it connected.

The eyes of El Cabro rolled back in his head. He swayed above Francesca for an instant, then collapsed in a heap on the ground.

Simona gave his head another solid blow with the skillet for good measure. She towered over him as Francesca scrambled away, standing far back from his motionless form.

"*Un mulo muy malo!*" Simona declared. "A very evil mule, this animal!" She flourished the skillet and turned to her mistress. "He will learn not to turn his back on a woman with a skillet!"

At the sight of Francesca's swollen cheek, Simona's confident demeanor vanished. "Oh, Doña Reed! If only we had not buried the guns, I would shoot this devil myself!"

Francesca embraced Simona. "You have done well. This fool did not imagine to banish frying pans from Santa Barbara! You have tailed the steer, Simona! Now we must get the keys and release Peter and Paco, then decide what we must do before the other Americanos come back!"

The bells of the mission clanged wildly as Francesca and Simona struggled to free the prisoners from the smokehouse.

"I will keep trying, Simona," Francesca said. "You go see what this alarm is about."

Up the lane ran a ragged band of marines. There was only a handful of them, and half had no weapons. "Lieutenant! Lieutenant! The Mexicans have busted loose in a rampage down to the—where's Lieutenant Falls?" Hollis demanded of Simona.

"*Cómo?*" she said, all innocence. "*No hablo,* señor."

"Blast it all, woman! Uh, *donda esta* Lieutenant Falls? Falls . . . you know, El Cabro?"

"Ah, *sí,* El Cabro." Simona nodded. With her frying pan she gestured down the hill toward town.

"You mean he ain't here?"

From around the side of the hacienda nearest the smokehouse came the sound of a hammer pounding against links of chain.

"What's goin' on in there?" Hollis wondered aloud. "Come on," he said to the six other panting soldiers. "Let's check around here real quick. Somethin' ain't right."

They rushed toward the smokehouse, with Simona loudly protesting in Spanish that El Cabro had left. They found the smokehouse cell open and Francesca hammering at the chains that bound Peter's legs.

"Hold it right there," demanded Hollis, leveling his carbine at the group. "What have you done with the lieutenant?"

From the oleander bushes came a slurred reply. "I'm right here." Out of the brush staggered Falls, holding one hand against the back of his head and swearing loudly when he stepped into the sunlight. Two lines of blood had trickled from his scalp around to the corners of his mouth, painting him with a grotesque smile like a monstrous clown.

"These lousy Mexicans tried to kill me," he said. "We're gonna shoot 'em all right now. Line 'em up against the wall." He gestured toward the smokehouse with his gore-covered right hand.

"Lieutenant," said the young marine, "we was just run out of Santa Barbara by a gang of armed Mexicans. Mitchell's holed up down at the mission, but the rest of us couldn't make it there, so we hightailed it up here. We think they'll be comin' after us, too."

Falls glanced around at the rancho. "Too few of us to defend this place. We'll retreat into the hills. Make 'em pay to get at us."

"What about these prisoners, sir?"

"Lock 'em up again," Falls said, "all except this one." He grasped Francesca roughly by the arm with his bloody hand. "She's comin' with us."

* * *

Padilla and his men arrived at the Reed Rancho with a pack of horses and mules piled high with plunder. From the top of one hastily wrapped canvas protruded a golden candlestick.

"Ah," said Four Fingers in an admiring tone as he looked at the Reed home. "I will enjoy getting acquainted with this house."

"Later," Padilla snapped. "First we take care of the Americano soldiers. We know they came this way."

* * *

The prisoners locked in the smokehouse were calling for help. Peter was yelling the loudest of all. "Get us out of here! The crazy Americano lieutenant has taken my mother and gone up to the canyons with her."

"So?" said the man outside the smokehouse. "How many men did he have with him?"

Why did he make no move to unlock the cell? Peter wondered. "No more than six or seven," he told the man. "Let me out—I must go help my mother."

"Is she pretty, your mother?" asked the man. He didn't wait for the answer. "Don't worry, boy, I will help her myself."

Peter didn't like the sound of the leer in the man's voice.

CHAPTER 16

Padilla led the charge through the arroyo that led up toward the Santa Ynez mountains. The hill rose abruptly, much steeper, and the bandits gained on the Americanos. Just past a line of live oaks, the gang broke into the open to a hillside covered in dry brownish grass and brush that reached to the horses' bellies.

Above them the long slope was mostly bare of trees, except for a grove of oaks about halfway up. The last two in a line of blue-clad soldiers could be seen disappearing into the shadows under the trees.

"We have them!" Padilla waved his Colt rifle in an overhead arc. "At them, amigos!"

But even mounted as they were, the incline of the hillside and the thick brush made the uphill attack slow work. Before the bandits had closed even half the distance to the trees, shots began to ring out from the Americanos' position.

A slug whistled past Four Fingers' ear, and another maldito took a bullet in his thigh.

Padilla was still urging the men onward when the rifle fire seemed to converge on him. In quick succession one slug cut his reins, striking the roan in the neck; a second went through his hat; and a third struck the horn of the saddle. He wheeled and sawed the useless reins as the horse gave a terrified scream and began to topple over.

Kicking his feet free of the stirrups as the roan fell thrashing to the sloping ground, Padilla leaped clear, keeping his rifle uppermost as he landed. Lying in a prone position, he returned the gunfire, getting off three quick shots before sliding down the hill to rejoin his men.

"Now what, Capitan?" Four Fingers wanted to know. "The gringos have the advantage. Why don't we leave them, the cowardly pigs, and return to more important business?"

"No!" Padilla insisted. "Do you want it said that we could not take care of a pack of Americano curs?"

"I do not care what someone says to me if he is willing to take my place and be shot at. Ayee! That one bullet burned my ear, it came so close!"

"That's it!" Padilla exclaimed. He felt the breeze that was blowing in from the sea. "Perfect."

"What are you saying?"

"Give me your *piedras de lumbre*, the flint and steel," Padilla demanded. "We'll burn them out!"

The wave of riders that swept around the Reed hacienda completely encircled the house. Paco cautioned Peter to make no noise that would give away their presence until it was known who these men were.

Still shackled, Peter wrenched around and pressed his face against the narrow crack in the boards of the smokehouse door and tried to make out the identity of the newcomers.

It was confusing. Some were dressed like his neighbors and relatives in Santa Barbara. But just as Peter prepared to call out to them, a wild and fierce-looking American came into view.

One ruffian, who had his arm bound in a dirty bandanna and the hems of his clothing trailing buckskin fringe, jumped off his horse amid the crowd. The man vaulted the steps to the back porch of the house three at a time.

Peter was about to yell a protest, then checked himself and gasped: This backwoodsman was riding Flotada!

Then Peter heard a familiar voice yelling, "Francesca! Francesca, where are you?"

"Father!" Peter called, pounding on the wall of the smokehouse. "Father, over here!" But his cries went unheard. Amid the din and chaos of the milling horses, no one could hear the boy's shout.

Frustrated, Peter watched through the crack as his father conferred with another man dressed in frontier leather. Will gestured angrily at the ground torn up by the pawing horses, then pointed up and down the coast. It took no words for Peter to understand the anguish that the muddled trail caused the man who was desperate to locate his family.

"Father!" Peter shouted again. Exhausted, he sank against the wall. No one was coming. They were all about to ride away without ever knowing that he was there. "Father," Peter said once more, his voice barely above a whisper, "help me."

Suddenly the noise outside the smokehouse subsided. At first Peter thought his father and the other men had left. Then he heard the footsteps coming across the hard-packed earth directly toward the prison.

Peter held his breath. With a roar and a deafening clang, a single shot took the lock off the smokehouse door.

When the dust had cleared, Peter saw his father standing in the doorway, silhouetted against the bright light outside.

* * *

Leaving Sinnickson to bring the rest of the troop of riders, Will mounted Flotada with Peter behind him. Over his shoulder Will called out, "I can get ahead of them, head them off."

Even with the double burden, the mighty gray horse sprang away from the trail and up a steep ridgeline, leaving behind all the others except one. At his side, stride for stride, galloped Tor Fowler on the buckskin.

The wind of their passage whipped away words like the spray over the prow of a ship under full sail. Peter dug his fingers into his father's shoulder and pointed toward a thick, black column of smoke rising from the arroyo and snaking upward toward the heights.

Will nodded sharply, and Flotada instantly caught the clashing fears of both riders. What if they were too late? The trustworthy steed, in whom the blood of his Andalusian forebears still ran true, redoubled his efforts and thundered up the mountainside.

* * *

The first wispy tendrils of drifting smoke reached Francesca's nose before Falls had recognized the threat. He was still posturing in front of his men and bragging. "The Mexicans have no stomach for fighting. Pretty soon Mitchell and the rest of our boys will venture out from town, and we'll catch these bandits between us."

It had taken only a moment for the thick, dry underbrush to catch fire. Then a heap of chaparral blazed with an explosion like a bucket of coal oil thrown onto a blacksmith's forge, and the flames raced up the hill.

"We've got to get out of here!" said the marine named Hollis. "Quick!"

Still Falls hesitated.

"Come on, Lieutenant! We can't stay here!"

"Wait," said Falls. "I've got to think. If we go out of the cover of the trees, they'll ride us down."

"No time for thinking, sir. If we stay here, we'll be cooked alive like roosting pigeons."

"Wait," demanded Falls again. "Don't they know they're endangering the woman's life? Don't they care?"

"They are *bandits*, like the boy José tried to tell you," Francesca hissed. "Now let me go while there is still time." She gestured up the hill. "There is a place of bare rock. We can find safety if we hurry."

A thick cloud of brownish gray smoke began to roll through the grove of trees.

"We got to go, Lieutenant," Hollis repeated and took Francesca's arm. "C'mon, ma'am. You show us the way, and I'll help you up."

"No!" Falls snarled. "She's my prisoner. It's a trick to get us killed. Don't you see? A trick!"

Hollis ignored him and started to ascend the slope with Francesca. A heavier wall of dense smoke poured across the hillside like a wave of dirty seawater.

Falls snapped back the hammer on his carbine and fired at Hollis.

Beside her, Francesca felt Hollis's grip tighten suddenly . . . then fall away. "Go on," he choked out to her. "He's crazy." The marine slumped to the ground.

Francesca ran through the trees, reaching the clear hillside at the top of the grove. The sound of gunfire, mingled with the roar of the inferno on the hillside below, swept toward her. She blundered into a gully, gagging and coughing from the smoke and struggling to fight her way clear of the brush.

A swirl of wind parted the column of fumes overhead. In that instant Francesca could see the barren pinnacle of rock that was her goal, and she corrected her course toward it. Another bramble-choked gully appeared across her path and Francesca hesitated, not sure whether to force a way across or look for a way around.

In that instant of hesitation came a noise from behind her. Out of the wall of smoke stumbled Falls, his face a mask of soot and dried blood, his clothing torn. He had lost his rifle. His eyes glinted with a frantic light, like a rabid wolf's, a demonic figure come to life from the painted panels in the mission church.

Spirals of flame lit the pall of smoke behind him. Incoherent ravings rumbled from his mouth, and he prepared to spring toward Francesca.

Francesca raised her arms to ward off the leap of the American lieutenant. In the next instant she felt her arms surrounded and pinned to her side.

But it was not Falls' loathsome embrace that grasped her around the middle—it was the expertly cast reata of her son, who stood on the pinnacle of safety above her head. "Hold tight, Mother," Peter called.

Beside her son was her husband, pulling her to safety with mighty yanks of his strong left arm. "Hang on, Francesca. We've got you."

Francesca felt herself being lifted and swung over the gully, away from Falls and away from the flames. Looking up in amazement, she saw Will, her son, and a third man she did not know reeling her upward with mighty pulls that raised her a yard at a time.

* * *

Falls made a futile jump after Francesca that sent him sprawling into the midst of the brambles. He floundered for a minute before pulling himself, torn and bleeding, to the other side.

Emerging from the chaparral without an instant to spare as the flames raced through the gully, Falls began to climb the rock face. Behind him the heat of a thousand furnaces charred the back of his uniform and singed the hair on his head.

The lieutenant was halfway up the stone strata when another figure appeared behind the wall of flame.

Padilla, fleeing from the forty horsemen who had caught him in his own trap, had hurriedly reloaded his rifle and was ascending the ridgeline right on the heels of the flames, in hopes of escaping the riders. He did not know the American lieutenant but saw in the lieutenant's form someone who was standing in the way of his escape.

Padilla raised the Colt revolving rifle to his shoulder and fired. At first it seemed to have no effect on the climber, and Padilla wondered if he had somehow missed. He aimed and prepared to fire again but stopped as the lieutenant began to peel away from the rock face.

Little by little the American's hands and feet let go, and his body crumpled backward. He turned a somersault, and his carcass crashed into the blazing brush of the arroyo.

Glancing around quickly, Padilla searched for a spot where the fast-moving flames were already dying down and he could cross to the other side.

Suddenly a bullet struck the ground near his feet. The shot had come from above!

Throwing his head back in disbelief, Padilla saw Tor Fowler reloading a rifle on the knoll above him.

The cursed Americano! Padilla would finish him now, before the fool even had a chance to reload. He threw the Colt up to his shoulder, drew a bead on the front of Fowler's buckskin shirt, and pulled the trigger.

The hammer landed squarely, exploding the percussion cap. The powder of the cylinder under the hammer ignited with a roar . . . and so did the next cylinder and the next and the next in uncontrolled chain firing. The frame and the barrel of the Colt disintegrated, taking Padilla's face and arms with them. With an unearthly scream, Padilla toppled forward and rolled into the inferno in the gully, stopping only when his corpse bumped against another body in the flames.

* * *

The shot intended for Tor Fowler hammered into the stock of his rifle, near the ground. The weapon flew out of the mountain man's hands but did not distract him from seeing Padilla's end.

"I told Davis them rifles ain't safe," he muttered as he watched the two bodies disappear into the roaring flames. He shook his head. "Not even havin' company for their trip will help where them two is goin'."

EPILOGUE

Will regarded Tor Fowler on his prancing buckskin horse. "You're a good man, Fowler. Why not give a pass to the rest of this war and stay here in Santa Barbara?"

Fowler shook his head. "I figger to clear my name with Captain—no, *Governor*—Fremont," he corrected himself. "'Sides, mebbe I can speak up for doin' right by you Californios."

"Why don't you ride with us?" Andrew Jackson Sinnickson asked Will. "The three of us together might convince both sides to leave off fighting."

"Sorry," Will said, his good arm around Francesca.

Peter stood close beside him.

"But do what you can," Will said. "Enough innocent folks have been hurt already." He gestured toward the infant Limik, sleeping in Simona's arms. "When the shaking out is all over, come on back and we'll build something good. *Vaya con Dios.* Go with God."

Shooting Star

Andrew Jackson Sinnickson, a leader of the Bear Flag Rebellion in 1846, had helped carry California from Mexican to American ownership. He had locked horns in Santa Barbara with Jack Powers, the first and worst of the California bad men. Then gold is discovered in 1848. Hordes of treasure seekers flock to the wild land, hoping to make their fortune. What they discover instead is a harsh lawlessness and exploitation . . . with Powers and his bandits having the upper hand. But Sinnickson is determined to not let Powers win. . . .

For the great-grandson of
Andrew Jackson Sinnickson,
H. T. (Tommy) Turner,
with love and thanks

PROLOGUE*

Shiloh, Arkansas
September 24, 1910

The gold case of the old Rockford pocket watch lay open beside the huge stack of manuscript pages heaped on the old man's desk. Soft ticking provided a gentle rhythm behind the urgent scratching of pen against notepaper. The watch hands swept across the ivory face, as if to remind the writer that time was passing too quickly for him. And time *was* running out. Only a thousand pages of his life had been written, and surely it would take ten thousand more to tell the whole story!

He paused and glared at the watch. No, it was not the timepiece that was the enemy but Time itself. The old man cocked a bushy eyebrow and tugged his drooping mustache as he recalled how he had come to carry the watch, the heavy gold watch chain, and the California-minted ten-dollar-gold-piece watch fob. It was one of the children's favorites—a tale they never tired of hearing—but the old man had not yet put the story down on paper. He had held off writing it, as though he could bribe the watch and slow down the steady forward movement of its hands.

"And when I've written about you, old friend," he often whispered to the timepiece, "then I'll shut your golden case and send you to Jim to carry. I shall lay down my pen at last, and you may mark the hour of my passing as just another tick of your cycle."

* *As taken from the prologue to* A Thousand Shall Fall

The watch made no promise in return, as though it did not care if the story of the pocket watch and chain and fob were ever written.

But there were other tales to tell.

The dark eyes of the old man flitted to the black, fist-sized paperweight that prevented the wind from scattering the legacy in the heap of papers before him.

It was the story of this stone that the old man now struggled to recount. The most important story of his eighty-six years was in that hunk of iron and nickel in stone! It had saved his life when he was twenty-six years old. It had given him the gift of sixty more years to live. It had made possible the sons and a daughter and grandchildren to gather at his knee and beg, "Tell us the story of the star, Grandpa Sinnickson! Tell it again!"

For sixty years he had hefted up the stone and cried, "Well now, children, listen up! This may look like just a black rock to you, but it's more than that. It ain't gold, but it's more than gold. This ain't an ordinary stone—no sir. This is a star! Yessir, you heard me right! A star! Straight from heaven it came, blazing across the sky on the darkest night of my life. With a tail of fire a mile long, it screamed down to earth and saved my life in a most miraculous way. Listen up now, and I'll tell you about it. For it is the truth, and I stand alive here as witness to it."

And then his grandchildren would pass the star from hand to hand. The eyes of young and old grew wide at the story of danger and death and the miracle of the falling star.

Perhaps of all the stories, this was the most often repeated. This was the most important tale to be written down because it had made all the rest of his life possible. . . .

The shrill whistle of the Hartford train echoed across the valley of Shiloh, interrupting his reverie.

The old man peered at the watch a moment. "Late again," he grumbled, snatching up the timepiece and striding to part the curtains of his bedroom window.

Just above the golden tops of the autumn trees, a dark gray plume marked the progress of the locomotive. Far across the valley, the row of birch trees trembled and swayed as if to bow toward the train.

"The boys are playing in the trees again," the old man muttered. Glancing at his watch again, he whispered a warning: "You're late, boys. Get on down. Get home before your father gets wind you're having a good time. Hurry home now, boys!"

As if they heard his distant heart, the two small boys in the birch trees began their descent. Bending the slender trunks low, they rode the treetops to the ground and tumbled onto the field.

The old man mopped his brow in relief as he watched the two red-shirted figures dash up the hill toward home. Perhaps their father, who had no timepiece, would not know they were late.

For a long time the old man stood at the window and stared across the dusky fields at the birch trees. He had planted those trees with his own hands. A tall, straight row of birch trees for his grandsons to climb and ride. Too bad their father did not believe that small boys were created to climb and whoop and laugh.

Samuel Tucker would leave a legacy of harshness, of distance and cruelty, for his sons. It was for this reason that their grandpa, the old man, worked day and night on the tales of his own life.

Clicking the watch face closed, he turned from the window and returned to his task. Filling his pen with ink, he tapped the nib on the blotter. It was easier to tell the story aloud than it was to put it down on silent paper, so he whispered the words as he wrote at the top of the page:

> *"For Grandson Birch*
>
> *"From Grandfather Andrew Jackson Sinnickson:*
>
> *"Already I have written one thousand pages, yet I find I have come only to my twenty-sixth year. This may be the most important tale of all my legacy, however, as in it I learned by the miracle of a falling star how God delivers those who trust Him. Read on, Birch, for it is a story you seem to not tire of. Perhaps one day you will have children of your own whom you may read these words to. Then you will tell them early what I have learned late: A thousand shall fall at thy side, and ten thousand at thy right hand; but it shall not come nigh thee. . . ."*

✶CHAPTER 1✶

Jack Powers. Now there is a name to frighten children into behaving. "Straighten up!" the Californio mothers would say, "or Jack Powers will get you!"

Long before Joaquin Murrieta rode into legend on a flashy stallion named Revenge, and much earlier than Black Bart ever penned his first poem, Powers was well-known and feared. From the Southern California cantinas of the City of Angels to the miners' hovels of Angels Camp in the Sierras, Powers had a name as the genuine article—the first and worst of the California bad men.

I first crossed trails with Powers in the sleepy sunlit presidio town of Santa Barbara. Powers was a sergeant in Stevenson's regiment—New York boys, they were—that had been sent to garrison Santa Barbara against rebellion in the spring of 1847. They were a crude, cutthroat band right from the beginning. Recruited straight out of Hell's Kitchen and the Bowery, the regiment drank their enlistment bonus and did not sober up till they were a day and a night out of New York Harbor.

By the time the stinking tub of a transport had dropped her hook off the point, the toughs of Company F had had three and a half months of hardtack and green salt beef to regret their decision to enlist. They came ashore sober, angry, and spoiling for drink and fight. Powers was the worst, because he intended to give them plenty of both and make a profit in the doing.

Sergeant Jack Powers was supposed to be in charge of discipline for Company F. That's like setting a diamondback rattler to ride herd on a nest of sidewinders. Within a week of Company F's arrival in Santa Barbara, there were two dozen new cantinas selling rotgut liquor to the soldiers. Within two weeks, every one of the cantinas was paying extortion money to Powers. This added cost of doing business, the cantina owners reasoned, was better than having their places burned, as happened to two who resisted, or being found floating facedown in the ocean off Goleta, as with a third.

For all that, I might still have avoided tangling with Powers if I had not been visiting my friend Will Reed and I had not volunteered to accompany his cook, Simona, into town that fine April morning.

My paint mare, Shawnee, was stepping out right smart, enjoying the salt breeze off the big water. I had to hold her in check to keep from outpacing the squawking and groaning oxcart. "Simona," I said, "haven't you got any way to make that beast go faster?"

"No, Señor Andrew," she said, "he always gets where he is going."

She added a comment about how this ox could find his way to and from town without any guidance, but her words were almost lost in the most frightful wail yet from the solid wood wheels.

"Don't you folks ever grease those wheels?" I asked.

"*Sí,*" she said, "but you can hear Señor Carreta asking for more."

"What do you mean?"

"Listen, señor," Simona said with a straight face. "He says, '*Quiero sebo; quiero sebo.*'" Her words were a perfect mimic of the high-pitched squawk of the cart. "I want tallow; I want tallow," and she laughed right in my face.

Well, I got to laughing too—the sort of laugh that comes from purely feeling good. When I get tickled like that, my laugh isn't exactly quiet either.

We were passing one of those canvas cantinas that had sprung up since Company F's arrival, and just then a knot of unshaven, red-eyed, slack-jawed drunks fell through the door flap and out into the street. They reminded me of a squirming pile of maggots tumbling all over each other, except these maggots were halfway dressed as United States soldiers.

The one who landed uppermost in the heap squinted up at me and said, "What are you laughin' at, you dirty Injun?"

Now I never was one to get riled easily, especially not on account of some drunk's slurred comment. As my Cherokee father used to say, "You can win a dispute with a skunk, but in the end you will smell like him."

So I leaned over out of my saddle and real gentle-like said, "'Pears to me you fellas already got all the trouble you need. I'm just passing by."

I was fixing to let it go at that when a big, red-haired lunk with a sunburned face got up from the pile. He looked at Simona heading down the road and then he said to me, "What's that perty woman doin' with somebody as ugly as you? Hey, señoreeter," he called, "come on back and get to know a real man."

Sometimes even a skunk puts his nose where it doesn't belong. Then it doesn't do any good ignoring him and hoping he'll go away. Best to run him off at once. I wheeled Shawnee around and put her into a parade canter, a slow gallop, with her legs churning hard.

I headed right into that heap of blue-jacketed maggots. Shawnee knocked one over with her shoulder while stomping on another. I kicked the third one out of the way and sent him sprawling over a guy rope. "Now lie there and listen," I advised them. "Señora Simona—that's missus to you—is a nice lady. Drunk or sober, you'd best not be insulting her where I can hear it." As I spoke, I dropped my hand to the coil of rawhide whip looped around my saddle horn.

That was when I first laid eyes on Jack Powers. The tent flap was flung back and a spruce-looking uniformed man with a big nose and a fleshy face stepped out. In one hand he held some cards. In the other fist was a Paterson Colt, and its .36-caliber barrel was pointed right at my breastbone. "Hold it right there," he ordered.

"Ease up a mite, Sergeant," I said. "I didn't really hurt your boys any. I was just teaching them some California manners."

"Get down off that horse," Powers ordered with a sneer. "You're under arrest for assaulting soldiers of the United States Army." To his men he added, "Pat, Ed, get up from there." Then he repeated his order to me.

I turned Shawnee so as to step down with my back to those men. I will tell you plain, my spine half expected a slug any second, but I needed to hide my whip hand as I shook out the lash.

"C'mon, hurry it up," I heard one of the drunks growl. He grabbed hold of one of my buckskin leggings. That's how I knew when to turn, because with that red-haired soldier right between me and Powers, the sergeant wouldn't dare shoot.

A flick of my whip got Powers around the wrist of the hand gripping the gun. The Paterson discharged into the air and flew over into a patch of weeds.

I reversed my grip and drove the twelve-inch, hickory-wood handle into the forehead of the red-haired fellow, and he dropped like a stone.

Shawnee was dancing and kicking up dust, and when the other two soldiers tried to close with me, she cut one of them off. It was too tight a space for lash work now, so I stabbed the drunk named Ed in the gut with the hickory handle. His breath gushed out, and as he doubled over, I hooked my left fist into the point of his chin. My shoulder—the one that had caught the lance tip in the last battle of the war with Mexico—didn't like that and let me know it, but the blow served its purpose.

The third soldier circled out of range of Shawnee's hooves and tried to come at me with a knife. I needed to hurry. I could see Powers cussing and scrabbling in the dust, trying to recover the revolver from where it had landed in the mess of prickly pear cactus.

It's amazing how much force you can put into a twelve-inch piece of hickory if you've a mind to. I smashed one blow over the soldier's knife grip, then backhanded the man across the nose.

Powers was approaching with the pistol, so it was needful to turn my attention back to him. This time I let the popper on the bullwhip do my talking for me. The thin strip of knotted buckskin crossed Powers's cheek, splitting the flesh in a welt that stopped just short of his right eye.

The sergeant threw up his hand to his cheek, and the gun dropped again in the dirt.

"Leave it there," I said, "or next time I won't spare your sight."

"Señor Andrew!" called Simona as she rattled back to the scene. Only this time she had Colonel Stevenson with her.

"Sergeant!" ordered the colonel. "Bring your men to attention at once!"

"Colonel, this man . . . ," Powers started in, but it was obvious that his words didn't carry any weight with this commander.

"Forget it, Sergeant. The señora has already told me about the drunken insults. Besides, do you know who this man is? Andrew Jackson Sinnickson has scouted for Colonel Fremont alongside Kit Carson. Sergeant, those three men are on report. And put your own name down as well. Now make your apologies."

There was some grumbling, but no open argument from the three soldiers or their sergeant. A few muttered words passed for apologies, and that seemed to satisfy the colonel.

But when I was coiling up the whip and moved next to Powers, he said quietly, "You may be holding all the cards right now, but there'll be other hands dealt."

CHAPTER 2

Fifteen months later I had all but forgot about Jack Powers and his threat. I had my own cattle spread all right, but things had not exactly worked out according to my calculations.

In April 1848, I was running a herd of about two hundred head, mostly rangy old rust-colored steers. They looked like the hide was stretched over their bones without any meat in between. I had picked up the land on the west side of California's Great Valley by settling an old ranchero's debt to a Yankee moneylender.

I called my place Rancho Libre, or Freedom Ranch, figuring to honor both my American side and the Spanish speakers. Freedom grew well enough in the sage and creosote bush–covered hills, but precious little else did. Fact is, I should have named the spread Rancho Liebre, which sounds almost the same but means Rabbit Ranch. The only critters that thrived and grew to remarkable size were the jackrabbits.

To make matters worse, the hide business slumped. There was still no market for the meat, and after twenty years as dependable as the sunrise, hides were selling for less than two dollars apiece.

The solitude of the place gave me lots of time to think on what my future might hold. For companionship I had only the rabbits and a half-breed boy named Joaquin, whom I won in a card game. I didn't really own him, you understand, but he was only twelve and had nowhere else to go, and anyway, that's a tale for another time.

I also had a dog. At least I think he was *part* dog. Mostly he looked coyote by the set of his muzzle and the prick of his ears. He had a brush wolf's coat and tail, but with some added spots of tan mixed amongst the gray. He was thicker of body and short of limb too. Anyway, however careless of his parentage he might have been, he had adopted me. He trotted up to my campfire one night without so much as a by-your-leave, waited politely for supper, and stayed ever since.

Joaquin and I had built a hut with a canvas roof. It was to keep thieving critters away from our meager supplies. It did give us a place to sleep out of the rain, but April to October we slept out-of-doors.

The winter of my spell at Rancho Libre had been one of too little rain. The feed for the cows was thin, and all summer we had to keep moving them from one little canyon to the next.

We had a big fire blazing at the head of the draw, and after a supper of roasted rabbit, Joaquin had already drifted off to sleep. We took turn-about keeping watch. The few calves we had we could scarce afford to lose to the coyotes or the occasional bear or cougar down from the high country.

I was nodding myself, so I got up to throw another stick of mesquite on the fire. All at once Dog sat up and looked out over the dark valley. Then I heard it too—the clinking of stones struck by shod hooves. It came from the direction of the Tejon, or what they call the Badger Pass.

I shook Joaquin awake, gesturing for him to remain quiet. Boy and Dog faded back into the shadows away from the fire's glare.

My whip was coiled and hanging from my belt. I grabbed my Allen rifle, put it under my arm, and moved silently on moccasined feet down the draw toward the herd.

As yet the cattle had made no stir. I passed quickly to the mouth of the draw and hunkered down to wait. The night was a dark one, with no moon, but the sky was blazing with the light of millions of stars.

Now we had nothing worth stealing and so little to fear from any robber. Still, only men in trouble or in a big hurry travel on moonless nights. This traveler, whoever he was, seemed headed straight for our camp.

A man's night vision is not as good as many of the Lord's creatures have, but his hearing can be a powerful tool if he's trained to use it. My Cherokee father had taught me to tell the shuffling run of the raccoon from the quick patter of the fox. I knew all the sounds the animals make going about their nightly routines.

Shawnee, my paint mare, who was grazing nearby, confirmed my thoughts about the intruder by lifting her head and snorting softly. The solitary rider was coming in cautiously from the east. He had dismounted and was leading his horse, and Shawnee stared at the dark clump of brush that had grown broader in the past minute.

Speaking might draw a bullet if mischief was meant, so I waited to see what was up. Presently there came a chuckle out of the darkness, and a gravelly voice said, "I swear, Andrew, you are as keen as ever, but you still got that piebald pony. Her white patches stand out like lanterns."

"Tor Fowler," I said. "What cause have you got for sneaking up this away?"

"I wasn't for certain it was you," he grumbled. "There's folks in this country now that'll take a friendly howdy and answer back with buckshot."

"Come to the fire," I said.

Tor needed no further urging. He seized on some leftover rabbit like he'd been without food for a week and devoted himself entirely to the business of eating.

Joaquin came back into the light and stared in wide-eyed wonder at this apparition.

Tor Fowler was a mountain man and a wanderer. He still sported the fringed buckskins of one who was more at home with the solitude of the great peaks than the company of men. He had come west as a scout for Fremont. Tor and I had been together in the days of the war with Mexico. At its conclusion, when I saw the chance to settle down and build something, he saw creeping civilization and felt the urge to drift back into the mountains.

When he had filled himself moderately full, Tor sat back and wiped his pointed chin on the sleeve of his jacket. His eyes above the sharp beak of his nose twinkled into mine and gave the lie to the otherwise hardness of his features. "Guess you wonder what brung me?" he said at last.

"I figured you'd tell me when you were ready," I acknowledged. "'Seek to know another's business and you'll always learn more than you care to,' Pastor Metcalfe used to say."

Tor nodded sagely. "True enough, but what I've got to say is like to be everybody's business afore long. Have you heard tell of the gold strike up Coloma way?"

"Gold strike?" I could feel my eyebrows raise clear up to the top of my forehead. "You are about the last man on earth I'd expect to believe in fairy tales."

"Knew you'd say that," he replied, unruffled. "Try this on for size: Do you remember that Sutter fella that kept all them Injuns like slaves to work his wheat fields?"

"Sure. Styled himself captain. Even dressed up a hundred scrawny Nishinam in moth-eaten Russian army uniforms. Called them his soldiers."

"The very same," Tor agreed, with a sidelong glance at me. "Well, all them Injuns have dropped their hoes and their fancy green coats and skedaddled."

"All of them?"

"Ever' one. Sutter's screamin' and nobody pays him any mind. Why, even some Germans he hired to build his mills up and tossed away their hammers and saws to grab picks and shovels."

I considered Tor's words. This wasn't the first time people had expected to find mineral wealth in the Sierras. Way back in Old Spanish days, three hundred years before, California was reputed to be a land so rich that even the tools and weapons were made of gold. 'Course, the same stories told of how Queen Calafia ruled over a kingdom inhabited only by women!

"Don Will Reed told me how, in '41 or '42," I said politely, "some vaquero pulled up a handful of wild onions and found gold dust in amongst the roots. Don Will said it was true, but the little pocket played out and never amounted to much."

A crafty grin stole across Tor's face. With his pointed features it gave him a strong resemblance to a fox. He'd probably have approved of the comparison, but I held it back just the same.

As the boy and I watched, Tor reached inside his buckskin jacket.

Lifting a small doeskin pouch that hung around his neck, he pulled it over his head and hefted its weight. "Come on over here, son," he said to Joaquin. He passed the leather sack to the boy and gestured for him to shake out the contents.

We all scooted up next to the firelight to see. Even Dog crowded in, his ears pricked and his head cocked to one side.

Joaquin pried the knotted strings apart and upended the pouch into Tor's palm. Out dropped not one but a dozen dull, gleaming lumps. The smallest was the size of a pea, while the biggest approached the dimensions of the last joint of Tor's brown, scarred thumb.

Tor passed the lumps to Joaquin. "Dug 'em out of a place no bigger than this," he said, using his wiry arms to show a space the size of a washtub.

"Is it really *oro*, señor? Really gold?" asked Joaquin. The boy's voice trembled a little.

"Tested and proved," Tor vowed. "That big rascal is worth close to thirty dollars all by hisself. Altogether you're holdin' maybe a hundred fifty, two hundred dollars' worth."

"All right, Joaquin, enough gawking," I said sternly. "You and Dog make a circle of the herd and then come back for some shut-eye."

"But, Señor Andrew—," Joaquin started to protest.

"No arguments. Get going."

The boy handed the shiny pebbles back with some reluctance, I thought.

When Joaquin was out of earshot, I asked Tor why he had come so far to bring me this news. "You must have ridden three hundred miles to tell me about your good fortune. Why?"

Tor looked over his shoulder at the gloomy darkness of the hillside before replying. "I'll tell you straight out," he said at last. "These here nuggets does strange things to folks." He searched my face as if reading trail signs. "It won't pay a man to work alone in them wild canyons—but it surely would be worse for him to be amongst partners he couldn't rely on."

I nodded and encouraged him to go on.

"Well, sir, there's nought but four men in this old world I'd trust to partner up with where gold is concerned. Two of them is off somewheres in the High Lonesome, and the other two is you and Will Reed."

Having the approval of a man like Tor Fowler is like being complimented on the keenness of your eyesight by an eagle.

"Thanks," I said, "but are things truly as lawless as I've heard?"

"Not so far," he admitted. "The findin' is still easy but the elbow room only so-so. And greed can't be made to hold still. Before I came south there was already folks from Monterey and Frisco comin' up to stake claims. And I seen two bunches square off over a promisin' hunk of creek bed."

"Anybody killed?"

"Not for want of tryin'. When the score was five to two of folks still standin', the losers moved downstream a ways."

"I've got my ranching to think of," I protested. "I can't just turn my herd loose."

Tor looked amused, but he had the good grace to hide it. I'm certain that the same image of the rangy cows flashed through his mind as was etched in my own. "I'd not expect you to leave your herd," he said, tugging at a shaggy forelock. "I come here first to sound you out afore ridin' on to Santa Barbara to see Will Reed. You are interested, ain'tcha?"

I started to argue, but my heart wasn't in it. Ranching was not exactly turning out like I expected. "Let me have another look at your poke."

A grin crept over Tor Fowler's lean features. "I'll do better than that. I'll leave half of it here with you . . . partner." He rolled up next to the fire and fell asleep.

Joaquin and I took turn-about on guard, and when I came back at gray dawn from my last watch, Tor was already up and gone.

It didn't surprise me any that he had not said good-bye. Mountain men were always wisps of smoke in their ways of coming and going. Not sleeping past dawn nor announcing a departure were two hard-learned lessons of survival that I'll not begrudge a man.

Joaquin seemed to think he might have dreamed the whole thing. I saw him wake and rub his eyes. Then as the recollection struck him, he looked around for Tor. Stretching his hands toward the smoldering fire, he turned one palm upward as he remembered the nuggets. "Señor," he asked me, "was your *amigo*, Señor Fowler, was he really here last night?"

I unbuttoned a flap pocket of my flannel shirt and passed over one of the golden lumps left me by my new partner.

CHAPTER 3

It took Tor Fowler only three days to ride to Santa Barbara and back. When he returned, he was accompanied by a pair of Don Will Reed's vaqueros and a loaded pack mule.

"Hello the camp," Torr hollered, riding up in broad daylight. "Where's that Sinnickson feller who's about to be a rich man?"

He explained that Will, while fascinated with the gold and plainly itching to go for the adventure of it, could not leave home. "Seems that the Señora Francesca is in a delicate condition, and Will don't think it right to leave her."

"And you," I said to the vaqueros. "Did he send you to go in his place?"

"No, Señor Andrew," responded the one named Rodrigo. "Don Will sent us to drive your cattle to his San Marcos range. He says to tell you we will keep them safe against your return."

"Right neighborly of Don Will, too," commented Tor. "Said for us to take right off. Even sent us some supplies." He indicated the mule.

"Seems everything's settled then, with one exception," I said. "Joaquin, I want you to go with the herd and stay with the Reed family until I return."

"On no, señor!" protested Joaquin with alarm. "You and I are compadres—partners, you said—just like you and Señor Fowler are partners. You must not leave me behind!"

"Now, Joaquin," I began, trying to reason with the boy, "this won't be a pleasure trip. Things may get rough. Best you remain—"

"No, Señor Andrew," he said firmly. "If you make me go to the Reed Rancho, I will run away to come and look for you."

I looked to Tor for help, but he just shrugged. "Puts me in mind of me and you, Andrew. Guess he don't leave us no choice but to take him along."

* * *

We traveled north for three days, skirting the western edge of the swampy lands and following the course of the San Joaquin River. The morning of the fourth day found us across the streambed from a tent settlement by the name of Tuleberg. Apt name for a place that only rose above the cattails to the height of a canvas-covered ridgepole. It was near the junction of the San Joaquin and the Calaveras and looked more like a haphazardly laid out army post than a town.

But humans being what they are, everybody tries to invest his efforts, no matter how modest, with a little grandeur. (Like me and my big plans for Rancho Libre, I reckon.) Anyway, this miserable collection of motley gray awnings and shacks was already styling itself a city. There was even a move afoot to rename the place for Commodore Stockton of Bear Flag War fame.

Tor braced a merchant to inquire if anyone had asked Stockton for his permission, but the shopkeeper did not see the humor of it.

We were of a mind to push on to the location of his find on the south fork of the American River, but talk around Tuleberg stopped us.

"Whereabouts you gents figure to make your pile?" inquired a fat man selling two-bit shovels for ten dollars apiece.

"Up Coloma way," said Tor vaguely.

"A pity," commented the chubby hardware salesman with a shake of his head that made his jowls quiver.

"Why? What's wrong with it?" I demanded.

"Nothing. Nothing at all, 'cept it's altogether overrun with folks. Shiploads of whalers, army deserters, scads of foreigners from outlandish places like Peru . . . even kanakas from the cannibal islands. You won't find room enough to swing a cat. No sir, none at all."

"So why tell us? You got a better idea?"

"Just thought you might want to turn toward Calaveras. Some mighty fine big strikes there. Yessir, brand-new."

"So's you can sit downstream here and sell ever'body their supplies? No thank you." Tor said. "We don't need your advice."

"Ease up," I suggested. Then to the merchant I inquired, "This new strike got a name?"

"Angels Camp," was the reply.

After we had passed on out of earshot, I turned to Tor. "What do you really think? Do we go on or turn up the creek here?"

"I just don't like ever'body knowin' my business," he said. "Sutter's land was gettin' awful overrun. Let's go see what Angels Camp has to offer for a couple of old sinners like us."

The trail we followed into Calaveras country had plainly been hacked out of the wilderness not long before. The path was not yet passable to wagons or wheeled carts of any kind. In fact, it was scarcely wide enough for two loaded mules to pass each other. Portions of the way wound through hewn-down clumps of elderberry bushes. The debris of the discarded branches, heavy with fruit, still littered the ground.

Tor pointed out the wasted and rotting piles of dark red berries. "Shameful. Injuns hereabouts make their winter stores outta poundin' acorn meal and bear fat together with elderberry juice. Keeps right well, too."

Ahead of us as we rode, another traveler bound for the mines came into view. He was a smallish man, dressed respectably in a black suit. He was leading a loaded mule, while he himself rode "shank's mare."

The path before us crested a knob of bare rock, then made a sharp turn away from the edge of a sheer drop-off. The streambed lay about eighty feet below, and another eighty feet or so of hillside hung above us.

The lone prospector was struggling with his dark-coated Mexican mule. It had chosen the exact worst place, as mules and humans often do, to turn balky.

"Come on now," the man demanded in a clipped and nasally voice. He dug in his heels and pulled on the lead rope as he backed up the hill.

The mule responded in kind, squatting on its haunches and bracing its forelegs against the stone face of the cliff.

Tor, who was riding in the lead of our threesome, called a halt. As I have said, the trail was too narrow for us to get around the obstruction, so all we could do was keep out of the way of the battle.

We had dismounted and were watching the struggle with some amusement when from behind us I heard the low *hoo, hoo, hoo* of a horned owl. It must have registered with Tor at the same instant as me, because he whipped his Hawken out of its beaded scabbard just as I pivoted my Allen up and cocked both hammers.

You see, as my Cherokee daddy taught me, when a night bird calls in daylight, it's time to wake up! A low rumble and a pattering sound, like a light rain, sounded from the cliff above us. It gained rapidly in volume and intensity as the rumble became a roar.

"Rockslide," I yelled, slapping Shawnee on the rump to get her moving and hollering for Joaquin to get down. With the danger roaring at us from behind, there was nothing to do but hug the ground and pray.

All three of our horses and our pack mule went clattering back down the trail. A boulder the size of my head came bounding down the hillside. It was aiming straight for Joaquin when I grabbed him by the arm and rolled over and over with him to get out of the rock's path.

Not six feet from us the rock struck something and gave an immense leap into the air, like someone who had just sat on a bee. The stone careened overhead in a high arc and flew off into the canyon. After that first flying headache, the hillside seemed alive with bouncing rocks.

A yell erupted from the throat of the stranger. His panicked mule swung around violently and swept him about like a game of crack the whip. It was an act of Providence that saved the man's life. His grip broke free of the lead rope that he'd been tugging on, and the sudden motion flung him aside some distance from the mule.

Not five seconds later, the main force of the avalanche swept right over where he had been standing. The mule gave a high-pitched scream of terror and was carried over the precipice in the blink of an eye.

All this happened in less time than it takes to tell. The roar of the slide had changed to the pattering of odd stones and loose gravel before the body of the unfortunate mule had scarce hit bottom.

Tor and I were already sighting over our rifles in expectation of the attack that would follow this ambush. That rockslide could mean only one thing: someone was up there and had caused it. Who would want to ambush us?

There was a movement near the top of the hill, and Tor and I fired almost in the same heartbeat. It was too far to make out plain, but a swarthy-complected figure in a buckskin shirt cried out, then turned and ran up over the hill and out of sight.

"Stay with Tor!" I yelled to Joaquin, and I took off after our horses and all our belongings. You may wonder how I could charge off that way, since there was no way of knowing how many enemies were waiting for me and without having had a chance to reload. The answer is simple: I was so hopping mad that I didn't stop to think about it! Anyway, I still had the shotgun barrel of the Allen primed and ready. I was not about to let any cowardly murderous thieves succeed in getting away with our possessions if I could prevent it.

I ran along, zigging and zagging down the slope, hoping to take the thieves unawares by appearing from an unexpected direction. I knew Shawnee would not have run far, and I hoped that the other animals would take their cues from her and stop when she did.

The next level spot I came to was a clearing ringed by oaks and elderberry bushes. In the center of the circle of brush were our three horses. They were milling around, stamping and snorting like steam engines. But there was no trace of the pack mule and all our supplies.

I debated with myself over mounting up and riding after the robbers, but the hot anger was off me by then, replaced by more temperate reasoning. I wouldn't gain much by spurring after them alone, not when Tor and I could follow them plain enough after he was mounted again.

About this time, Dog came trotting up with a scrap of buckskin clenched between his teeth. He dropped his trophy at my feet and wagged his tail.

"You did good," I praised him. "Here I was wondering where you'd got off to, and you were on the job all the time."

I picked up the fragment of leather and the lead ropes of the three horses and started back up the trail.

Halfway to the rockslide I met Tor headed down. "You all right?" he asked.

"Only half," I admitted. "They got away with the mule, but Dog here gave them something to remember us by. Where's Joaquin?"

"Left him with Ames. That's the feller who almost took a swan dive with *his* mule. Yankee from the sound of him. Piece of rock grazed him across the head, and he's lucky he ain't kilt. Joaquin's patchin' him up. We can send them along to camp while we get on the trail of those bushwhackers."

The rest of the way back, Tor and I discussed the attack. "Injuns, you figger?" he asked, squinting at the shredded fabric.

"Hard to say. By his coloring, dark like mine, the one who caused the slide might have been Indian, but he could have been Mexican or Spaniard. He lit a shuck too quick for me to get a good look. I never saw any others. Dog left his regards on one, but this piece of buckskin could have come from you just as easy as an Indian."

"Anybody mad enough at you to want to kill you?"

I laughed. "Not so far as I know. How about you?"

Tor gave the matter serious reflection. "Some folks I know ain't gonna go outta their way to shake my hand or buy me a seegar, but I don't recollect anyone after my scalp personal-like."

When we came to the slide, Joaquin was tying off the knot on a strip of shirttail that he had wound around the man's bleeding head. The slightly built figure in black was seated on the ground gritting his teeth. One place on the side of his head was swelled up the size of an apple, and the man's complexion was as gray as the rock dust.

The man stuck out his hand. "I'm obliged to you and this boy," he said in a Yankeefied voice. With evident difficulty he struggled to his feet. "Ee-yup. Best get on with rounding up my—" Ames swayed and would have pitched over on his face if Tor and I had not caught him.

"Guess that settles what we do next," Tor said with a shrug as he tossed the unconscious Mr. Ames across his shoulder. "We'd best take this one and Joaquin on to Angels Camp, and then we'll get to trackin'."

✶CHAPTER 4✶

I think it safe to record that our entry into any town or village back in the States would have occasioned quite a stir. Consider our appearance: a mixed-breed boy and a brown and weathered, buckskin-clad trapper, leading a horse with an unconscious man tied onto the saddle. These were followed by a down-at-the-heels rancher riding on an Indian pony, with a half-grown wolf pup ranging alongside.

And yet, for California in 1848, not only did our assemblage *not* cause any commotion, we did not even provoke any comments! Anyone who had ridden into Angels Camp that autumn afternoon would have recognized the reason at once. Nothing in our dress, manner, or composition would have been the least out of the ordinary. Fact is, while no one paid us any heed, we all found ourselves staring around us quite a bit.

A pretty little valley ringed by low hills lay before us. The nearer slopes were studded with gnarled oaks and gooseberry patches, while the farther slope wore manzanita thickets and tall, shapely pines. The center of our view was a bare plain where two creeks converged, or rather, what would have been a bare plain if it had not been covered with tents and canvas awnings, rude huts, and brush lean-tos.

And the architects of those human habitations—now there was a sight!

A split-plank footbridge crossed the larger channel of the two creeks, and over this rustic roadway passed a parade of people to equal the sideshow of any circus. Three men, lately of some infantry regiment as demonstrated by the remains of their tattered uniforms, were likewise marked as deserters by the lack of any company insignia.

Waiting for the ex-soldiers to pass was a short man whose knees were escaping through the rents in his trousers even as his curly black hair escaped from under the odd bonnet-shaped hat he wore. A plain tan vest was an ill match for his overly large gray-striped frock coat.

Behind this fashionable Californian were two tall men in long serapes that reached to their knees. Flat-crowned, broad-brimmed hats and a haughty and aristocratic manner made me guess that their homeland was the Argentine.

And what did these assorted specimens of God's infinite wit have in common? They were all miners—true examples of the strange breed known as prospectors. Between the six of them there were five shovels, three picks, four tin pans, and a determined air of invincible good fortune. What's more, these six were just the sample on display, so to speak. In the creek bed and on the hillsides all around, there were a hundred more, swinging their picks and swirling the pans.

But we had no time to reflect on these impressions. There was the injured Mr. Ames to be seen to and the not inconsequential matter of our stolen property.

We directed our course toward the most imposing structure visible. This was, I regret to say, nothing more than a long, low tent covered in stained gray sailcloth. Three sides were sheltered by the canvas awning, but the fourth was open to the elements.

When we got closer, we could see that our target was in fact some sort of public building, since a stream of miners was coming and going from the premises.

"Hello the tent," Tor called out.

"Store, if you please, or trading post," retorted the man who responded to Tor's salutation. "Either sounds more dignified than tent."

"That's as it may be," Tor returned, "but I'm seeking a doctor or what passes for one around here, and if I can't find him in this tent, then it don't matter what you call it!"

"Easy, friend," said the portly proprietor through teeth clamped around a short-stemmed pipe. "I didn't see you had wounded. Bring him in. This is as civilized as it gets." Then to the interior of the tent he shouted, "Patrick, clean off that counter—we got an injured man here!"

Now I like to think that I don't surprise easy, and I try my dead-level best not to show consternation even when I feel it, but the identity of that storekeeper's assistant surely did give me pause. You see, it was Patrick Dunn, one of those New York soldier fellows with whom I'd clashed back in Santa Barbara in the spring of 1847.

If he recognized me, he gave no sign of it. At the time, I thought that either he'd been too drunk during the brawl to remember me, or perhaps he'd just decided to let the past lie. Anyway, I figured if he was content to leave it alone, so should I.

Dunn busied himself moving a stack of flannel shirts and a crate of plug tobacco off the rough-hewn plank table.

We stretched Ames out, and the store's owner examined the Yankee's head. Ames was still unconscious, but his color was better. He flinched and moaned some when the wound was unbandaged and cleaned, and it started to bleed again.

During the procedure, the man doing the doctoring introduced himself. "Name's Angel. Henry Angel. This is my store. Doc Den is over at Murphy's Diggings today seeing to a man that came near to cutting his thumb off, but I reckon I can stitch this fellow up. How'd this happen?"

As I filled him in on our experience with the rockslide and the robbery, I watched his face grow grim. "Thievin' Digger Indians," he said. "They just get bolder and bolder. Well, it's got to stop."

I tried to explain that the identity of the attackers was by no means certain and that Tor and I could track them with the aid of Dog, but he seemed not to be listening. "Cannon," he ordered a burly prospector who wore his long black beard tucked into the front of his red-flannel shirt, "round up a half dozen of the boys, and we'll go teach those savages a lesson."

Henry Angel and the other Angels Campers had it set in their minds that the local Miwok Indian tribe was behind the attack of our party. It was the miners' intention to see that retribution was carried out.

"It was them thievin' Digger Injuns, I tell you!" Cannon boomed. "We oughta ride straight to their village and burn 'em out!"

Angel had Patrick Dunn remain behind to watch over his store. Privately, I thought this was setting the fox to guard the henhouse, but I kept my peace. As long as Dunn was acting the part of an upright citizen, there seemed to be no cause to butt in.

We rode out then, Angel and Tor and me in the lead, followed by Cannon and the others. Ames, with his freshly stitched and bandaged scalp, was tucked into a cot. I left Joaquin and Dog with orders to watch over him.

We were within half a mile of the site of the ambush when Tor called for a halt. He directed the miners to follow a trail that veered off down toward the creek.

"What's up?" Angel wanted to know. "I thought you said they jumped you on the main road."

"Did say that," replied Tor tersely. "Reckoned you could go by where the mule belongin' to that Ames feller musta landed. See if you can salvage some of his things, whilst Andrew and me pick up the track on top."

I knew without being told that Tor was trying to keep the miners from attacking the Indian camp. Led by Cannon, the prospectors were of a mind to shoot first and raise questions after. Such an attitude isn't healthy for those on the receiving end. It would be the shank of the afternoon in one more hour. If Tor's device worked, the Angels Campers might spend long enough gathering the scattered supplies that it would then be time to head back.

There were few noteworthy clues on the high ledge above the trail. We found where the swarthy-faced attacker had tied his mount while he prepared the ambush and where he had used a redwood limb to tip over the rock to start the slide. Beyond that we found nothing to identify the race of the man.

"I don't know, Andrew," Tor Fowler said. "Does this strike you as Miwok doings? I've fought plenty of Injuns in my time, but I never saw anything as bald-faced as this."

I agreed with him. "They must have known that an ambush of white men this close to a mining camp would bring destruction on their heads, double-quick. Even if they weren't expecting any of us to survive, who else is there around to blame?"

"That's the point, ain't it?" he mused. "No matter who done it, the Injuns'll catch the blame."

"All the more reason for us to track down the real culprits," I said.

We started to follow the trail that we were certain would lead to the site of Dog's encounter with the robbers. We were no more than a hundred yards along the ridge when the peaceful afternoon was shattered by a sound like a herd of buffalo crashing through the brush of the creek bed. Wild whoops and the explosions of gunfire followed soon after.

"Come on!" Tor shouted, spurring his bay. "Someone's catchin' it!"

Across the rocky surface we flew, sparks bursting from Shawnee's shoes as we clattered slantwise down the slope. I was practically lying along Shawnee's backbone to keep my weight back on her skidding haunches. I had the reins out at arm's length, like steering by the tiller of a sailing ship, but the fact is, I was relying totally on Shawnee's instincts to get us through.

We swung sharply to the left, narrowly avoiding a drop of a hundred feet or more. Shawnee's hooves somehow found a ledge that was no more than a crack in the rock face. In between jolting gasps for breath, I found myself wondering who it was we were risking our necks to rescue, and if they would even appreciate it should we come to grief on their account before reaching the bottom.

A flurry of gunfire up the canyon a ways told us of the ongoing battle. A flock of doves burst out of their roost in the cottonwoods at what was then eye level for Tor and me.

"Hold on, Andrew!" he called over his shoulder as he and the bay plunged ahead.

I could not see past the body of his horse to know what he was warning me about, and perhaps it was just as well. We had run out of hillside, and the last of our headlong charge carried us through a dozen feet of air.

Shawnee took the jump in fine shape, landing in deep sand with scarcely a break in her gallop. Wheeling around like a cavalry squad on parade, Tor and I set off toward the screen of trees and brush that obscured our view of the fight. I shucked my Allen out of the scabbard. Out of the corner of my eye I noted Tor draw his rifle as well. As we got closer, we heard cries of fear and shouts of rage mingled with the gunfire.

Our swoop toward the conflict was cut short by a small dark-haired figure in buckskin and faded flannel that burst from the willows right under my nose. I saw an axe waving in the air, but as I brought my Allen to bear, Shawnee reared and spoiled my aim. The menacing figure jogged aside, making me hurry my sights. I had just drawn a bead again when Tor's cry stopped me. "Don't shoot, Andrew," he yelled. "It's a woman!"

And so it proved. The slight form that scampered into the brush and out of sight had a reed-work basket strapped to her back. Over the rim of the hamper, an infant-sized fist could be seen waving defiantly.

I grinned weakly and waved my thanks at Tor. I wanted to think that even without his warning, my own senses would have prevented a mishap, but then I remembered that Shawnee's unexpected motion had also been needed to keep me from firing. I breathed a prayer of thanks, but the nearness of the tragedy made my stomach churn.

We charged on into the battle, fearful of what we would find, and found that the reality was worse than we feared. An unearthly keening had joined the other noises. It was a high-pitched wail that began at the level of a wolf's howl and went straight to the screech of a red-tailed hawk.

The portion of the creek bottom toward which we rode was an island at a wetter season of year. At the time of which I write, it was a low knoll of cottonwoods and willows surrounded by a rocky plain through which ran a thin trickle of water. The hillock was ringed by Angels Campers with their rifles cocked and steady on a small knot of Indians that had retreated to the clump of trees.

I've lived with Indians and I've fought Indians, but I never before saw anything so one-sided dignified with the word *battle.* A wounded Miwok man sat on the ground, hugging a bullet-shattered forearm and rocking softly with the pain. Another dead man was draped over a boulder. There were three bullet holes in his back. In his back!

The shriek was coming from the throat of a Miwok woman who was huddled over the limp body of a small boy. A young Miwok woman and two children stood looking on, their eyes wide with fright.

At the moment we rode up, Cannon was saying, "What are we waiting for? I say we shoot 'em down and put a stop to their thievin' *and* that caterwaulin', the flighty savages." Without waiting for any agreement on the part of the others, he raised his Hall carbine to his shoulder.

Tor never paused in the headlong rush of his bay horse. Without drawing rein the least bit, his gelding barreled into Cannon's mount. It was a classic *golpe de caballo*, the strike with the horse, that would have done credit to one of our friend Will Reed's vaqueros.

Cannon's arms went straight up and the rifle flew from his hands, the shot exploding into the air. The black-bearded miner followed the carbine in flight, landing heavily on the river-rounded stones with a cry of pain.

A friend of Cannon's made to swing his revolver around to bear on Tor, but I was ready for him. I flicked my whip out and around his wrist, and soon after he joined his partner on the canyon's rocky floor.

"You'd both best lie there awhile," Tor ordered, swinging his rifle around the group.

"And if the rest of you don't want to join them," I added, "you'd better keep real still."

"What is this?" Henry Angel said. "I don't get it. We come out here to catch the snakes that attacked you boys. We nab them red-handed lootin' Ames's supplies, and now you stick up for them. It don't make sense!"

"How do you know that this particular bunch of Indians ambushed us?" I asked.

"Just look!" spouted Cannon from his place on the ground. He abandoned caution in favor of rage. "They got their hands full of mining gear!"

The squaw who was standing dropped a tin pan as if it had turned blazing hot in her grasp. It clattered and banged on the rocks but brought the wailing to a sudden stop. The woman with the dead child continued moaning but softly.

I said, "You understand English? You speak it?"

"I speak," replied the woman who dropped the pan. "We find dead mule and no man around. We no kill."

"Pack of lyin' rats," Cannon announced.

"Friend," Tor said, "I ain't gonna warn you again not to interrupt."

Cannon subsided.

"We no kill," the squaw repeated. "We find only."

"Where were you coming from before you found this?"

The woman gestured downstream. "We pick berries. Fill baskets. Go home."

I pointed toward a reed-carrying basket and motioned for her to upend it. As she obliged, several gallons of dark red berries spilled across the creek bed, blending into the dark red blood of the dead man.

"All right," Angel observed, "but that doesn't prove anything. They could still have caused the rockslide when they saw a way to get something more valuable than berries."

Several of the miners nodded their agreement, especially Cannon.

I ignored this and continued to question the woman. "Did you see anything on your way here? meet anyone?"

She thought for a minute, then said, "Two men. A mule, going toward valley."

"Indian?"

She shook her head. "One Spanish, one white."

"So what?" Angel said. "You don't know that those two, if they really existed, had your animal. Loaded pack mules are all over these hills."

"Think hard," I urged the woman. "Did anything seem wrong with those two men?"

She looked puzzled at the question. Then comprehension widened her eyes. "White man's britches. Seat torn out."

I reached inside my shirt then. Retrieving the scrap of buckskin brought me by Dog, I held it aloft for all to see.

One by one, the miners looked from the leather fragment to the woman holding her dead son. Cannon's friend hastily mounted, and the five turned their horses around and started up the trail toward home, leaving Angel and Cannon with Tor and me and the Miwoks.

Tor gestured with his rifle for Cannon to pick himself up and get on his horse. Tor looked as stern as only a mountain man that was part grizzly bear could look. He stared pointedly at Cannon and Angel, then turned to study the Miwok man who was struggling to stand and the mother gathering the body of her child.

Angel did not miss the suggestion in Tor's look. "We can help you to your camp," he said.

"No!" said the younger woman fiercely, gesturing with her fist at Cannon. "You not touch them!"

We four white men turned our horses, riding away from that place of grief and cruel injustice.

Tor urged his bay between Cannon and Angel. "Seems those 'savages,' as you call them, got a sight more dignity than you," Tor said. "She spit in your eye, didn't she?"

Cannon hawked and spat noisily. "Lousy vermin. Still shoulda kilt 'em. Teach the rest a lesson."

Tor never looked over or gave any sign. He just unloaded a backhanded blow against Cannon's temple with a fist like a smithy's hammer. The bearded man was again swept from his saddle, this time landing on his head. He looked around stupidly as his horse ran off toward the camp. "Thought you'd say that," Tor observed as we rode on.

Tor and I left Henry Angel behind to fetch Cannon's mount. For a long time we did not speak, yet I knew we were of like minds. Calaveras Canyon, which the old Spaniards had called Skulls, had certainly lived up to its grim name. The site of an ancient Indian battle, this place had been littered with human bones left to bleach in the sun. Like Calvary of old, Calaveras had become the scene of a new crucifixion. A man and a child had been murdered, and the white man's law offered no punishment for the crime. To butcher a Miwok Indian for sport or target practice was no worse than shooting a bear. To kill an Indian suspected of thieving was considered a white man's duty!

"'Twas almost Eden when I first come here," Tor muttered at last. "If we live awhile, Andrew, there won't be no more Injuns left for swine like Cannon to kill."

I nodded and followed him as he spurred his mount up the embankment and off the trail into the cover of the woods. Although we did not speak of it aloud, we felt the nearness of evil at our backs.

CHAPTER 5

Back in Angels Camp there were more remarks made about white men sticking up for the despised Digger Injuns than about the fact that two innocent people had been killed and another seriously hurt. If Tor and I were not exactly shunned, nobody was overanxious for our company either.

That suited us just fine. Ames was awake and feeling as well as could be expected for a man who had come within an inch of having his head split open like a ripe melon.

But they don't call Yankees hardheaded for nothing. Ames was up and around after only one day. He said that the inside of his skull was buzzing louder than his family's cloth mill back home. "Reckon you saved my life," he managed to remark to Tor and me. "Ee-yup. I'm mighty grateful."

When Ames heard that our supplies had been stolen in the same attack made on him, he insisted that we share equally in his recovered provisions. We found ourselves outfitted once again, as good as before.

Ames was a trader in dry goods. He had been in the kingdom of Hawaii for several years, operating an outpost of his family's business, when he had heard about the California gold.

With typical Yankee shrewdness, Ames recognized at once that the miners would bring only a limited amount of supplies with them. They would need to replace boots, clothing, and equipment, and they would want it from the nearest source they could find. That source, he had decided, would be him. "You won't find me breaking my back, no sir," he told us. He grinned at Joaquin, Tor, and me. "You boys will be bringing gold straight to me without me digging a lick."

So Ames had come to the diggings alone with only a single mule load of supplies in order to get the lay of the land. He had a ship full of goods waiting in San Francisco for his word to freight them into the hills.

"I'll snoop around here for a few days and look into the competition," Ames told us, meaning Henry Angel's store. "Then we'll see. I might move on up a ways."

The creek banks around Angels Camp were humming with the activity of mining. Tor and Joaquin and I had to travel a day's journey farther upstream to locate a likely stretch of as yet unoccupied creek. We decided to commence prospecting there.

The first order of business was to stake our claim. At this time, the commonly agreed-on rules for the Calaveras region allowed each miner to claim a space ten feet square. We marked the corners of three adjoining squares—one each for Tor and me and a third for Joaquin—by writing our names on scraps of paper nailed to posts along the stream bank. In appearance our claim was then a thirty-foot rectangle that extended ten feet in width up from the water's southern edge.

My claim, which was the farthest upstream, commenced at the middle of a sharp bend in the stream. We had agreed for each man to examine the prospects of his own claim first; then we would concentrate on whichever square showed the most promise.

I filled my first pan with dirt from the bank and carried it to the icy water. Squatting beside the creek, I swirled the water around and around, washing the mud and the lighter gravel over the side. When this had been done until only the heaviest material remained, I tilted the pan toward the sunlight and poked around in it with my forefinger.

"No *chispa*," muttered a disappointed Joaquin, looking over my shoulder. "No spark."

"Don't be too sure," I said. From the iron particles that remained I separated a heavy flake of material. I scratched it with my knife and it did not shatter; between my teeth it felt soft and not gritty. "It's gold, right enough," I announced. "I heard tell that this Calaveras gold was real dark, almost black."

That panful of dirt contained twelve flecks or bits of gold—scarcely enough to cover my fingertip with a button-sized circle of the precious metal, but this was still a good prospect, since the real pocket was not to be expected on the surface.

* * *

It took two days to dig down to bedrock; we saved all the dirt that came out of that hole for later washing. When we hit a layer of quartz, we knew we had reached our limit.

Unlike Tor's earlier experience, there were no nuggets lying in the bottom of the ancient streambed. We found a few pieces the size of kernels of wheat tucked into a crack in the quartz face but nothing to get real excited about.

Resolving to see how the excavated dirt would pan out, we began to work through that chore next. We would then decide whether to continue working these claims or abandon them in favor of moving the search somewhere else.

Our first week of panning the heap of dirt brought us two ounces of the coarse, black flakes, or about thirty dollars' worth at the going rate. Not a fortune by any account but not a bust either. I reminded myself that I owned a herd of steers that I couldn't clear two dollars apiece for, if that, so five dollars for a day's work didn't seem half bad.

We didn't actually divide it up right then, of course. That gold went into the leather pouch that Tor still wore around his neck.

Panning is backbreaking, muscle-tearing, finger-numbing work. Hunkering down on your haunches for eight or ten hours with your feet slipping into a snowmelt stream is no Sunday social. Right off we saw that we needed to build a rocker to help us.

Tor felled a cedar tree and cut a round from it that we slabbed into passable planks. It wasn't that this was so altogether easy as it sounds—rather it was the anticipation that it would improve our gold-finding ability that made the work pass pleasantly.

A rocker looks for all the world like a baby's cradle, which is its other common name. The earth to be washed is loaded into a kind of hopper at the top. When water is poured over it, the gold-bearing dirt sifts through a crack down to a slanted board set with crossbars called riffles to catch the gold. The curved runners on which the thing sets and an upright handle allow the whole device—water, mud, gold, and all—to be rocked from side to side. It is the back-and-forth motion of the water that separates the gold from the soil.

Tor fitted the last of the whittled cedar pegs into the holes cut to secure the handle, then stood back to admire our creation. "Whew, Andrew. It's a good thing this ain't really for no baby. No child would want to be rocked in this contraption! Why, he'd up and die of shame afore he'd let hisself be humiliated thisaway!"

I will admit that it was a touch lopsided. "Let's see how she works," I said. "Even an ugly old buggy perks up when it has gold fittings."

Three men is just the right number to work a rocker. One hauls the pay dirt, one lifts the uncountable number of buckets of water required to run through it, and the third keeps the cradle in motion. Tor and me took turn-about working the rocker and hauling the water. Joaquin loaded in a shovelful of dirt every so often and cleaned the gold dust off the riffles and emptied it into our poke, so his part wasn't too tough.

It isn't that the cradle makes the work so much easier; it's just that you can sift your way through so much more dirt in a day's time. We ended our first month in the diggings with three hundred dollars of gold dust, a working system for proceeding, and an all-fired hankering for something to eat besides bean-and-jerky stew.

"Warm tortillas," Joaquin daydreamed aloud. "*Pollo con arroz,* chicken and rice like Señora Simona fixes at the Reed Rancho. Strawberry jam . . ."

Tor nodded at the recollection. "Mighty tasty, but I'd like to have that chicken fried and served up with a mess of biscuits. What say, Andrew? Do you favor the cooking of lower California or lower Arkansas?"

"I approve of both your choices," I said, my stomach voicing its agreement. "But as for me, give me a piece of beefsteak."

Our imaginary feast was interrupted by an unpleasant, unexpected arrival. A horseman riding at top speed descended the bank of the stream across from us and splashed into the creek.

Dog jumped up, barking fiercely, his ruff raised stiffly above his shoulders.

The rider that clattered noisily into our camp was Patrick Dunn. He rode in with his revolver drawn and leveled in our faces. "Call off that wolf, Sinnickson, or I'll shoot him."

We were nowhere close to our stacked rifles. I let my fingers creep down to the coiled whip hanging from my belt. Out of the corner of my eye, I saw Tor Fowler drop his hand from his knee to the top of his boot where two inches of knife hilt protruded.

At this tense moment, two more riders appeared at the back of our camp. "Not this time, Sinnickson. I told you there'd be other hands dealt. Move your hands up slowly and keep them in plain sight." It was Jack Powers.

Another man that resembled Patrick Dunn was with him. Maybe his brother?

"Get their weapons, Ed," Powers ordered that man, and he dismounted.

"Hold on there!" Tor said. "Who are you, and what's this all about?"

"We're looking for a pack mule that belongs to Patrick here," Powers said. "It was stolen from him."

"Well, just open your eyes, you no-good highbinder," Tor retorted. "Do you see a mule critter in this here camp?"

Powers grudgingly admitted that he did not. "But I know Sinnickson's type. Jew name, Sinnickson?" His ruddy cheeks glowed with a delighted sneer. "You'd figure a Heb for a sneak thief, right, boys?"

Tor's fists clenched, and the line of his jaw tightened. From the look in his eye, I could tell he was fixing to remove the saddle from Powers's horse without having Powers get off first.

"Leave it," I said. "It's not worth getting shot over."

"Smart Jew-boy, huh?" Patrick Dunn laughed.

Ed took my whip and Tor's boot knife, then moved crablike

around our camp to the stacked rifles. He had a .50-caliber hogleg in his hand for protection against dangerous folks like us, but it seemed to me that he kept its muzzle and his attention focused on Dog, who still bristled and was growling low in his throat.

"Well, I guess we can't hang you for mule thieves today," Powers said, leaning heavily on the last word. "But we can't leave without correcting this unlawful claim."

"What's that supposed to mean?" I asked.

Powers rubbed his gun hand through his swept-back, silvery gray hair. "I see you've illegally claimed more of this stream than you're entitled to. How'd you ever think you'd get away with claiming three claims for only two men?"

"We've got three partners. One claim for each partner, just like the mining regs say."

Powers pretended to look around and scan the hillsides while Patrick Dunn laughed loudly. Ed joined in the laughter, but his had a nervous quality.

"Three partners? I only see two broken-down miners and one no-account half-breed boy. Don't you know that Injuns can't hold claims?"

"Joaquin worked his claim, same as us," I said.

Powers shook his head in mock sympathy. "Pity you don't get to town more often. There have been some changes made. I'll wager your claim isn't even registered properly."

"Registered!" Tor exploded. "Our stakes are up, plain as day!"

"So they are," Powers noted. "Ed, Pat, take care of that."

Patrick Dunn whooped and rode around the claim, ripping out our stakes and hurling them into our campfire. He threw a loop of rope around the rocker, then dragged it onto its side. Galloping a ways downstream, the bouncing and bumping cradle held its own till Patrick ran it up against a boulder, and it splintered to pieces.

So much rage and frustration boiled inside me then that the bitter taste of hot bile rose into my mouth. I didn't like feeling like an animal caught in a steel-jawed trap, to be taken unawares and forced to stand by while our camp was destroyed.

My face must have shown the anger, for it was Tor's turn to caution me. "Steady, Andrew," he muttered, "for the sake of the boy."

Patrick Dunn proceeded to retrieve his loop, then dropped it over our tent pole. Another whooping gallop and the canvas was ripped to pieces. Our belongings were scattered, and most ended up sunk in the stream.

Powers nodded his approval, while Ed Dunn looked on and agitatedly fingered his revolver. When Patrick returned, he made as if to toss his noose over Joaquin's head. Caution all gone, I had my shout for Dog and my leap for Ed's gun all planned when Powers called it off.

"Leave him be, Pat," he said. Then to me Powers remarked, "I guess this about evens the score, eh, Sinnickson?"

Ed threw whip, knife, and rifles in the creek, then mounted his horse. The three rode off upstream.

We watched them till they were out of sight, then set to gathering the demolished camp into some kind of order again. All the time I was thinking how Powers was right about this hand he dealt, but after this, the game was still far from over.

CHAPTER 6

We had intended to work the claims until our supplies ran out in a few weeks. The encounter with Jack Powers and what we now knew to be the Dunn brothers changed our plans. Our beans and hardtack were destroyed. Precious cornmeal had been trampled in the mud.

After putting our camp back into some kind of order, we surveyed the wreckage and decided that if we wanted to eat, we had to head for Angels Camp pronto. Fortunately, we had not been robbed. We kept our gold dust in a two-quart canning jar tucked away in the hollow stump of an old oak tree on the bank of the creek. Every evening after dark we had made deposits at our "bank." Now we figured it was time for a withdrawal.

We divided three hundred dollars in gold dust equally between the three of us.

Tor hefted his share with satisfaction. "Beats herdin' cows now, don't it, boys? Let's see . . . at two dollars a hide it 'pears to me I'm carryin' fifty cattle in this here poke. Yessir, it shore do beat anythin' I ever seen b'fore!"

I had to agree with him on that. We had pulled more out of the Calaveras in one month than I could have made from my little herd in two years.

Joaquin, who had worked as hard at the claim as a grown man, never imagined he would possess so much wealth! One hundred dollars in gold would buy him passage to Hawaii on a schooner and a real education in one of the mission schools. Remembering the tales of Mr. Ames about Hawaii, he gazed far to the west, as though he could already see himself at home among the brown-skinned Sandwichers on their island. I resolved to speak with Ames on the matter of Joaquin's schooling at the first opportunity. Schooling was the only way to answer ignorant bullies like Jack Powers and the Dunn brothers. One day, I explained to Joaquin, he might return to California as a man of learning. A judge, perhaps. Or maybe governor of the whole state. He could spit in the eye of any bigot and say his success began along a ten-foot stretch of Calaveras Creek!

The thought of overcoming skunks like Jack Powers fired the boy's imagination and dreams. Eagerly, the boy placed his poke in my care, asking only that he might have one pinch of the stuff to purchase a jar of jam when we returned to Angels Camp.

Having been absent from Angels Camp for a month, however, I had no idea just how much gold dust it would take to buy even a small jar of jam.

The place had sprawled out four times bigger than when we left. Canvas tents, fashioned from the sails of abandoned ships, had sprouted like mushrooms on both sides of the creek. The streets were mud bogs crisscrossed here and there by logs with the bark still on them. Crudely lettered signs hung above the tent flaps, bearing the names of stores and saloons and cafés and even a barbershop. The tinkle of banjo music drifted up to the rise as we looked down in wonder at the transformation.

I rubbed a hand over the coarse black beard that had sprouted below my hawk's-beak nose and eyed the huge oak barrel painted to resemble a fat barber pole. "A shave," I said, remembering the hot towels and lather of a distant life.

"Fried chicken." Tor tugged his long whiskers and cocked an eye at the ragged sign outside a ragged tent advertising home cooking.

"Strawberry jam," cried the newly wealthy Joaquin, licking his lips and pointing straight to the big sign above Ames Dry Goods and Sundries. "Just like the kind Señora Reed makes!"

The waters of the Calaveras were brown and murky from the work and traffic of hundreds of men. The shantytown was hardly more than a pest hole, but to each of us it was a vision of civilization, comfort, and luxury. All of these things were to be bought for a price. As we were soon to discover, even small luxuries were worth their weight in gold!

The dry goods store of Mr. Ames was crammed into a tent created from the weathered canvas of a square-rigged ship. The ship was owned by the Ames Trading Company in Honolulu and had sailed to San Francisco stuffed full of merchandise and Hawaiian workmen. It was Ames's plan to dismantle the vessel and build a proper store from its timbers in San Francisco that winter.

Meanwhile, a second schooner from the islands would keep the San Francisco company well supplied with Yankee broadcloth and all the goods the tribe of miners would desire. The tent in Angels Camp was the forward outpost for what the little Yankee saw as a thriving empire of commerce. Three wagonloads of supplies had arrived the day before we did, and the tent was crammed with crates of merchandise stacked from floor to ridgepole. Miners crammed the space between the boxes, shouting at Ames for the price of blankets or boots or shovels.

Tor scowled in at the mob through the tent flap. "Looks to me like Ames is near to having a riot on his hands. Ain't so shore I'm up to a fresh brawl without a bite to eat first."

Joaquin grimaced as he saw two miners inside wrestling over a shovel. One had drawn a blade halfway from his belt when the two men were forcibly separated by an enormous dark-skinned kanaka, whose bushy black hair brushed the canvas ceiling of the tent. I estimated that the Hawaiian was over six and a half feet tall and as thick as an old oak tree. He made my five-foot-ten frame feel small. His features were coarse, and he scowled like a bouncer in a bawdy house. Such a savage face and enormous stature drove all thought of their quarrel from the minds of the two arguing customers. Both released the shovel and stepped back as if they had just met a grizzly bear face-to-face.

At this moment Ames parted the crowd and appeared like King Solomon to resolve the matter. We remained outside the store and watched the event through the flap.

"Well done, Boki," Ames congratulated the Hawaiian, then raised his hands to the crowd, which now lapsed into respectful silence. "Now listen up," Ames instructed the men. "No arguments in my store or Boki here will crack your skulls and throw you out in the street. I run a respectable, law-abiding dry goods store. No guns, knives, clubs, or fists will be allowed. You want my merchandise, you'll act civilized."

"But that there is the last shovel!" cried a mud-caked miner from the back of the tent. "I been diggin' with my cook pot. When you gonna get more shovels in?"

"I grabbed that there shovel first," cried one of the grizzly combatants. "Then he come along and—" His hand returned to the hilt of his knife, and Boki snatched him by the scruff of his neck. Before we could say howdy, Boki tossed that man out the tent flap. He flew by us and landed spraddle in the mud. It appeared that Boki was the law for the time being.

Men shuffled and sniffed and looked at the toes of their boots. I had seen such looks on the faces of guilty schoolboys caught smoking behind the barn.

"Well, gentlemen?" cried little Ames from beneath the shadow of his giant. "What's it to be? You get in line or Boki gives you the door. There ain't a place between here and Boston has what we got to sell. The line forms there." He pointed at the tent flap and at us. His eyes lingered on us, his pinched face breaking into a grin as the mob broke up and formed a line back out the tent and into the mud of the street.

"Well, now!" he cried. "Well, well, my friends! My friends!" He gathered us in even as his scowling customers shuffled into line. "You're back early by my reckoning. You struck it rich then? Come in to spend a little jack at my humble establishment?"

"We come to spend a little all right," I said in wonder at the scene before me. "Although it 'pears to me that you're the one who's struck it rich."

"A gold mine," he agreed, mussing the hair of Joaquin and thumping Dog on the head. "Anything a man could need right here. Everything a man could want . . . or nearly . . . if he's willing to pay for it." He nudged the toe of my ragged boot. "Three dollars for your road stompers go for forty dollars up here. Ee-yup. You in the market, Andrew?" His eyes glinted with amusement as I blinked at him in astonishment.

"That's near half my poke!" cried Tor, clutching the little bag of gold dust in his coat pocket.

Someone mumbled behind me. "Ten dollars he charges for a fifty-cent shovel."

Then another surly grumble, "One dollar fer one onion. Figure that."

Ames cheerfully replied, "Onions all the way from the Sandwich Islands, lads."

"Mighty expensive sandwiches they make too," Tor muttered.

Ames rubbed his hands together. "Well, lads," he said to us, "what'll it be? Seeing how you saved my life, I'll take you to the head of the line."

I figured that I had just enough to buy a sack of onions if that was what I had in mind. I shook my head, knowing that we would have to recalculate what provisions we could afford to buy.

Joaquin looked hopefully into the face of the storekeeper. "Please, señor. I have been dreaming of Señora Reed's strawberry jam. You have jam, Señor Ames? I have a dollar to spend."

Overhearing the child, someone called, "An ounce of jam is an ounce of gold dust, kid. Ain't you heard the rules for half-breeds around here?"

Ames whirled around. "Who said that? Boki! What low-down skunk thinks he's going to set the prices in my store?"

Boki pointed down at a red-shirted fellow holding a sack of beans. "This one," Boki replied in a surprisingly soft, melodious voice.

"Beans you're buying?" Ames menaced. "Ain't you heard the price of beans for dirty-bearded fellows wearing red shirts has gone up? That'll cost you one pound of dust for every pound of beans. Put up or get out!"

With Boki to back him up, Ames could set his own prices. And if he wished, he could even choose to sell a quart of precious jam to a boy for a pinch of gold dust. This is exactly what Ames decided to do.

As the offended miner tossed down the sack of beans and stalked out, Ames growled, "He's one of Jack Powers's gang. Skunks, all of them. Even if he paid me a pound of gold for a pound of vittles, I'd rather not sell to the likes of him."

And so it was that we discovered that Ames and Angels Camp had become unhappily acquainted with Jack Powers while we had been gone.

"Jack Powers is the very reason we've come into town early," I explained.

"Him and the Dunn brothers wrecked our camp." Tor eyed the retreating gang member. "We ain't et in a while."

At that, Ames left the store in the capable hands of Boki and two other Hawaiians and led the way through the mire to Homecooking Café. Joaquin followed, bearing his jar of strawberry jam.

The proprietor of the Homecooking Café was a rotund, heavy-jowled man, whose bald knob of a head was enclosed by a fringing thicket of bristling gray hair. He had a canvas apron tied high up across his chest, and while we approached the front of his establishment, he was transferring another layer of grease from his hands to the cloth.

Tor whispered to me over my shoulder, "Pay it no mind, Andrew. It don't appear that his cookin' has hurt him none!"

The owner beamed as he greeted us. "Welcome, gents. Mister Ames. Sit down, sit down. I'm John."

We seated ourselves on a variety of what passed for chairs—two empty crates, the top half of a cracker barrel, and an old trunk. Two rough plank tables ran the complete length of the tent and completed the dining arrangements.

"What'll you have?"

"Now yore talkin'," Tor said eagerly. "Fried chicken for me."

The man shook his head. "Sorry, I can't oblige. We ain't got no chickens."

"Biscuits?" asked Joaquin hopefully, waving the jar of jam.

The host of the Homecooking Café thrust out his lower lip and folded his arms across the grease-stained apron. "Nope."

Tor sounded a touch testy when he said, "Wal, now, why don't you just tell us what you do have 'stead of us guessin'."

"Beef or beans," was the response.

We three partners looked at one another while Ames watched us with amusement.

"No beans," I replied for the group. "How's the beef?"

"Excellent choice! Four steaks, coming up." He gave Ames a broad wink and departed toward the back flap of the tent. As he passed through we could see a black cook tending a steaming pot next to an open fire. A dressed beef carcass was hanging just beyond the fire. "Mose," the owner shouted at his cook, "throw four more slabs on the grill!"

"Just like Mama used to make," Tor observed wryly.

Despite the disappointing news about the menu, we were pleased with the prospect of heartier fare than we had eaten in weeks. I took some ribbing on account of my preference being the only choice available, but it was all in fun.

The wait while our dinner was being cooked gave Ames a chance to catch us up on the news of the camp. "Some Mexican fellas from down Sonora way found a seven-pound chunk of gold and quartz. Figures to be worth five hundred dollars, maybe more. How you three doing?"

I was a little chagrined when I answered. "We thought we were doing all right, but after looking at the prices of things—" I stopped so as not to offend Ames, but he only grinned and said that he knew and weren't the prices ridiculous. I went on then, "Anyway, I guess we're making expenses."

"I told you that it was easier finding gold in miners' pockets than in the streams hereabouts," Ames said forthrightly. Then his face darkened. "But I sell honest goods. There's many who deal in second-rate, cheapjack—weevily flour and salt pork that would have gagged George Washington's men at Valley Forge."

"Jack Powers, for instance?" I asked.

"Ah, Powers!" Ames almost spat out the name. "He sits in his tent gambling and scheming like a spider in a web. Make no mistake—his influence runs deep hereabouts. He's made a pile from the crooked card games he's staked and from watered-down who-hit-John in saloons that look to him for protection."

"Is he so hard to read that folks haven't got him figured?" Tor asked. "Seems to me he'd be run outta most places."

Ames shook his head. "There's a class of men in the diggings who work one day and then go to hunting easier ways to fill their wallets. Powers caters to them . . . stakes them to drinks and meals in exchange for their support. He rallies them around causes he favors, like running foreigners off their claims over trumped-up charges so he can take them over and sell them to some greenhorn."

The tent flap gapped open again, and a heaping platter of sizzling beefsteak was propelled into the room by the smiling owner. The trencher on which the seared meat rested was a salvaged barrelhead, but little we minded that. The aroma that accompanied the sight of our meal set our mouths to watering and stomachs to rumbling.

The proprietor set the platter down with a flourish, and the plank table actually groaned under the weight. "That'll be an ounce of dust," he said as we grinned at each other in anticipation, "*each.*" Our grins turned to grimaces of consternation.

Tor's eyes were fixed on the topmost steak, and when he spoke it appeared that he was addressing his words to the chunk of meat. "Fifteen dollars? That's highway robbery."

The owner of the Homecooking Café looked ready to snatch the serving dish back out of jeopardy when Ames spoke up. "It's all right, John. This meal is on me."

Smiles erupted on all our faces, including the host's. "Mighty nice of you, Mister Ames, considering that you already supplied the beef."

"What'd he mean?" Tor asked after the owner had gone to greet some newly arrived customers. "Are you in the cattle business too?"

I was eagerly slicing into my steak. I did not care who had raised the beef or sold it or cooked it. All I wanted to do was eat it. I noticed how dull my hunting knife was behaving and made a mental reservation to see to sharpening it.

"You might say I'm in the cattle business," Ames said. "I sold John a spare team of oxen after my load of provisions got here."

"You don't say," I mumbled around an especially chewy hunk of steak. I saw Tor's jaw muscles working away, and Joaquin seemed to be in particular concentration over his portion.

"Yessir," Ames went on, "at these jewelry prices for meat, I wished I could get my hands on a whole herd."

Tor, Joaquin, and I all stopped midchew and stared at each other. "Do you," I mumbled, having to shift the load of meat to the other side of my cheek, "mean to say an old cow critter like this that was leather clear through his middle sells for fifteen dollars a steak?"

Ames nodded.

Tor worked his quid of gristle around till it was safe to swallow and inquired, "What does that figger out to on the hoof?"

"Well, John paid me a hundred apiece for the team, but real beef stock would fetch more. Why? Do you boys know where you can get your hands on a herd?"

"Right here!" said Joaquin, bouncing up. "Señor Ames, Señor Andrew is a ranchero. He owns a herd *himself*."

"Could it be?" I wondered aloud to Tor. "Could we have had the makings of our fortune right under our noses all along?"

"And Don Will Reed," Tor added. "Don't forget him. He'll be wantin' to throw in with us when he hears about this."

"But is it possible?" I wondered aloud. "Nobody's ever driven a herd up from Southern California before. Not that I ever heard tell of anyway. Could we do it?"

Tor looked me square in the eye. "How much you figure your herd is worth for hides? What's two hundred head times a hundred dollars each figger out to?"

Joaquin whooped and started dancing around the table chanting, "A hundred a head! A hundred a head!"

Tor joined him in an impromptu Virginia reel. The ruckus was so tremendous that John and the cook both hurried inside to see if we were tearing up the place.

CHAPTER 7

I was pacing back and forth in front of the tent flap. My mind was a whirl of calculations: distances from one river crossing to the next, where we could find the best feed along the way, how many vaqueros we would need. A flurry of noise from the street outside the Homecooking Café drew my attention.

Almost involuntarily I stepped through the canvas opening to see what was up. My thoughts were really three hundred miles away, so it took a few moments for what I was seeing to register with me.

Patrick Dunn was riding into town, and he had a prisoner in tow. The description is exact because the man, a tall fellow in South American garb, stumbled on foot at the end of a rope attached to Dunn's saddle. The prisoner's hands were tied together in front of him, and he fought to keep his balance in the slimy mud of the roadway. Patrick's brother, Ed, followed, leading a pack mule.

Apparently the capture had not gone altogether smoothly. Patrick Dunn's left eye was swollen shut, and Ed had what looked like a knife slash across his right forearm.

A circle of babbling and angry-sounding miners accompanied the trio, and when Patrick pulled up in front of a gambling tent, the crowd flowed around the scene like a tide of muddy flannel. As the hubbub grew, more prospectors dropped their tools or their liquor bottles or their cards and joined the audience.

Patrick Dunn got off his horse and called into the gambling establishment for Jack Powers. "Mister Powers, sir. We caught him."

Dunn spoke as respectfully as if he were addressing a judge in a New York courtroom. Here in the Sierras, the judge was self-appointed and his bench was an overturned crate marked *Johnson's Baking Soda.* His honor's muddy boots rested in the churned Calaveras clay, and the heavily bearded spectators in their worn dungarees hardly made for a respectable legal setting.

In contrast, the prisoner at the bar was a tall, haughty-looking man. He was wearing a dark brown woolen poncho, banded across the ends with stripes of blue and yellow. The serape was secured around his middle with a six-inch-wide leather belt.

Below the flat-crowned, stiff-brimmed hat were the features of a man more accustomed to giving orders than of being ordered about. He looked more capable of sitting in judgment on all the rest of the assembly than the other way around. The man's face was bruised and puffy, and a once-straight nose was canted to the side. His cheeks were stained with gore, and his wrists were raw and dripped blood from the hemp cords.

The contrast between the florid-faced Bowery toughs and this man of proud bearing was ludicrous in the extreme, but the circumstances themselves were no laughing matter.

In the diggings, even petty thievery was not tolerated. A first offense, no matter how slight, was punished severely. The theft of money or mining equipment merited fifty lashes or brandings or disfigurement of the ears or nose. Second-time offenders were summarily hanged.

The rules were even tougher for the theft of a horse or pack animal. All a man's possessions and, in fact, his wherewithal to survive in the wilds were transported on the back of some four-footed beast. So death was the standard punishment for being caught once.

I moved closer to hear the proceedings.

"Good work, Pat," Powers praised his lieutenant. "Caught him with the evidence, eh?"

"Yessir, Mister Powers. This greaser was actually leading the mule when we caught up with him. Put up a fight, too, and tried to stab Ed there with a knife."

The tall prisoner addressed Powers in refined Spanish. "If you are the alcalde, señor, you will instruct these ruffians to release me at once! I am Guillermo Navarro, lately of Buenos Aires. My family fled to Chile to escape the tyrant Rosas. I am in California to recoup—"

"Patrick," Powers said with a sneer, "shut that gibberish up, will you?"

"Gladly," Dunn said and cuffed the still-bound Navarro with a backhand across the mouth.

The unexpected blow staggered the prisoner and silenced him, but his eyes blazed with a fierce hatred.

"Just a minute," I said, shouldering my way between two stocky miners. "Does he get a say in this or no?"

Powers looked mighty displeased at the interruption. I believed then—and still do—that he actually understood some of Navarro's words. But with the Spanish speakers cowed into silence, Powers anticipated no opposition to watching the scene play out according to his own script.

Looking me over thoughtfully, Powers remarked, "Choosing to side against your own kind again, are you, Sinnickson? A man could get a bad reputation doing that too often around here."

A rumble in the crowd told me that the story of the attack on the Miwoks had changed some in the retelling.

Powers went on. "Or maybe thieves of all colors *are* more *your* kind, eh, Sinnickson?" He laid a lot of stress on my name when he pronounced it.

"Just hear him out," I said. "This man comes from a wealthy, high-class family in his homeland." To Navarro I said, "Go ahead, señor. I will translate for you."

Navarro inclined his head in a nod of appreciation and resumed his speech. "I came to California to recover my family's lost fortune. When I located a claim and established my camp, I discovered that I needed cash for supplies more than I needed a mule. So I sold the mule to—" Here he stopped and pointed at Patrick Dunn.

I explained to the crowd what had been said so far.

"He sold it to me all right," growled Dunn, "but how did he get the mule back again? Ask him that."

I put this question to Navarro, who shrugged and replied, "When

I awoke yesterday, the mule was grazing again near my camp. He must have broken free and returned to the last place that he regarded as home."

When I translated this, there was a general stir in the crowd. Nothing definite, just a clearing of throats, shuffling feet—that sort of thing.

I judged that a number of the onlookers were inclined to believe Navarro's story. What is more, his calm manner while telling his side spoke well for him. For a man facing death, he looked neither shifty nor cringing. He spoke uprightly, like one with truth on his side.

Powers scowled. It was not in his interests to have his bully boys lose face in front of the miners. To Patrick Dunn, Powers said, "How was the mule secured when you had him last?"

"Tied up tight to a picket line and hobbled."

"And what did you find in the morning?"

"The hobbles were slashed off and the lead rope was cut!"

"Hold on!" I said. "Does anyone else vouch for this?"

"Are you calling me a liar?" Patrick roared. "Taking a stinking greaser's word over mine!"

Here Powers chose to appear judicious, even fair. "It's a good question, Patrick. Can anyone support your story?"

"Sure," Dunn bellowed. "My brother saw it, same as me. Ain't that right, Ed?"

Ed Dunn looked at his boots and mumbled something that no one could hear.

"What was that?" Powers demanded. "Speak up."

Talking quickly as if in a hurry to get it over with, Ed said, "It's the truth." He shot Navarro a momentary look that had emotions I could not read, then went back to staring at his feet. He rubbed his left hand over and over his wounded right arm.

"Hang the greaser!" shouted a voice to my left.

"Stinkin' foreigners makin' off with all our gold and stealin', too!"

"What are we waitin' for? Hang him now!"

"String him up!"

"Wait!" I yelled. "How do you know—?" Then I stopped, since I could not make my voice heard over the crowd. I laid hold of my whip handle. I figured I could clear a space around Navarrro long enough to buy him some time.

A calloused grip caught my wrist and yanked my hand away from the lash. The fiercely bearded face of the man named Cannon thrust into my own. "Not this time, Sinnickson!" he roared. Then something crashed into the back of my head and I dropped like a stone.

How long I lay unconscious in the filth of the Angels Camp street, I don't know. Not long perhaps, for they told me later that what followed took only a minute or two at most.

When I woke up, my head was ringing like two dozen blacksmiths were hammering inside it. I tried to stand, but the best I could manage was to get up on one elbow.

In front of me, not twenty yards away, dangled the lifeless body of Guillermo Navarro. He had been hoisted into eternity at the end of a rope slung over an oak limb. All around, the street was deserted. Even Powers and his vermin had disappeared.

Joaquin came running to me, followed by Tor and, more slowly, Ames and Boki.

"Señor Andrew," Joaquin gasped, "are you all right?"

"Just help me up," I slurred. My next look went to Tor. I wanted to ask him where he had been, why he had not come to help.

He saw and answered my unspoken questions. "I'm awful sorry, Andrew," he said, biting his words off short. "This big feller held me back." He stabbed his thumb at Boki's massive girth. "He grabbed me from behind and sat on me."

I gave Boki a look of anger and reproach, but it was Ames who answered for him. "Don't be blaming Boki, Andrew. I told him to keep Tor back, and I held on to the boy myself. Yessir, and a mighty good thing too. If you three had interfered, they'd have hanged all of you, sure."

✯CHAPTER 8✯

The ground was pocked with places where prospectors had dug in search of gold, then abandoned. Heaps of brown earth and broken rocks made the clearing look as if it were a colony of giant ants instead of a graveyard. Soil barren of gold was the only ground fit for burying the dead miners of the Calaveras goldfields.

Wood planks were too precious to use for building a coffin, so we cut down the body of Guillermo Navarro and wrapped him in a red woolen blanket for burial. He was carried to his makeshift grave on the shoulders of half a dozen of his countrymen. Only another dozen Spanish speakers joined the solemn procession up the hill. Tor and I followed with Joaquin. Ames, who provided the shroud, came after with Boki. There were no other mourners. Those who might have come under different circumstances were too frightened by what they had witnessed to associate themselves with the proud and noble Navarro even at his graveside.

"I assume he was a Catholic gent," said Ames as they laid Navarro's body in the damp hole.

There was no priest for a hundred miles. The sad fact that the dead man would be launched into eternity without a decent burial distressed each of his comrades. They looked sadly from man to man and asked who would say the proper words for their friend. There was no one to speak. None who knew how to pray. There was not a copy of the Good Book among them. Hats in hand, they simply gazed at the body over the rim of the grave.

I understood their language well and explained to Ames and Boki the problem. "Easy enough to cut him down and put him in the ground, but there isn't a one of them who knows what to say. No Scriptures to read from, I reckon."

Tor furrowed his brow. "It ain't fittin' a feller to git hisself hung without reason and then can't git hisself buried proper on the same day. You go on, Andrew. Say somethin', why don't you? You know the words in the Good Book. Go on and say what you know about it."

I had indeed gotten my own schooling fresh out of reading the Good Book. I had not had any primer except the Gospels of Matthew, Mark, Luke, and John. As a child I had hated memorizing Scriptures every day, and I had resented the message those words had taught. But I was grown now. Sadder and wiser from living in a world such as this. Long since I had learned that nothing was certain in life from one moment to the next, and the only thing I could truly count on were those words I had been forced to learn as a child.

Yet I hesitated to speak. After all, Navarro was not my companion. I had never met him before the hour of his death. What could I say?

The question was answered for me. Tor stepped up and nodded to the small assembly. He spoke in the Spanish language. Truth to tell, his Spanish was much more refined than when he spoke in his own tongue. "My friends, we are new to your small circle, but in our hearts we are one with you in this tragic hour. Great injustice has happened here, and how are we to answer to it?"

"We have no priest, señor," cried a short man dressed in a poncho similar to that which Navarro had worn. "For us there is no justice. They killed Guillermo only because they wanted his claim and he would not sell it."

"This is true," enjoined another.

There were nods all around.

The man in the poncho continued. "We are simple men. Guillermo Navarro was a great man among us in our homeland. What can we say to put his soul at peace? If it was one of us in that grave, he would know the words even without a priest. He once studied for the priesthood but married instead. He was a man of God. One who treated others with love and kindness. He is . . . was . . . the father of three young sons. What can we say? Bad men have done this thing to a good man. Where is there justice? Where is God that He would allow such a thing?"

"Well, Andrew?" Tor questioned me. "You know the Book backward and forward. Can you speak to this?"

"It isn't my place," I replied in English.

Tor did not accept my answer. He put a hand on my shoulder, then addressed the others. "Here is one American who tried to stop the lynching of your friend. He is a learned man and perhaps can speak the words of a priest if you permit—"

A chorus of "*Sí! Sí!* Tell us the words, señor!" erupted from the company while I frantically searched my heart for some answer.

After a time, the group fell silent. Wind scraped the treetops and made a hushed whisper. I looked at the red shroud and then at the rugged hills of the Calaveras, and I prayed that the good Lord would speak not only to the men around me but also to my own bitter heart as well.

"This place is called Calvary," I began in Spanish. "Named after a place where long ago the one truly innocent man in all the world was murdered." It was cool, but beads of sweat stood out on my brow.

I switched into English, for my memories of Scripture flowed better that way, while Tor translated my words for the others. "Seems to me that Jesus who died on Calvary knows just what happened here today. Seems He experienced some of the same as Guillermo Navarro here at the hands of a mob. Folks accused Jesus of things He was not guilty of. Hired guns were paid to bring false testimony against Him. He was tied up and beaten. He was paraded through the streets. His friends were afraid to speak for Him . . . afraid of dying themselves. . . ."

At this a sob erupted from the man in the poncho. He cried out the name of his friend and dropped to his knees on the mound of earth beside the grave. "How can you forgive me, my friend? I should have fought! I should have died for you! Oh, I am a coward! A coward!"

There were others among the group who wept silently and reflected on their own fear and failure.

I remembered Peter who had cursed and denied that he even

knew the Lord, and for just a moment I glimpsed the true meaning of the first Calvary. My own words were not enough. Could never be enough.

"Since the Garden of Eden men have been full of death and darkness. We know the kind of lust that justifies murder and the kind of fear that keeps us from standing up for what is right. We who stand here alive are responsible for the death of an innocent man. No. I do not speak of Navarro. I speak of the One at whose feet Guillermo Navarro now bows. I speak of Jesus. The Innocent who died at Calvary because of your sins and my sins shouted across the ages, 'Crucify Him! Hang Him from a tree!'"

Tears flowed from the eyes of the men as Tor repeated this.

"I have failed!" cried Navarro's friend. "What can I do? What?"

"Remember what Jesus said as He died: 'Father, forgive them, for they know not what they do.' He was thinking of this moment when He spoke those words. He was seeing me and you. He was watching the men who hanged Navarro. Jesus' friends took Him down and buried Him. They mourned for three days, but then Jesus rose from the dead. He is still alive!"

I stopped to let those words sink in before I continued. "He says that one day every knee shall bow and every tongue confess that He is Lord. Those who have loved Him, like Guillermo Navarro, will see heaven. Those who have denied Him, who have not asked forgiveness for their sins, will wake up one day in hell. All the gold in Calaveras Canyon will not save them. One day they will be dust like your friend, but their eternal souls will wish that it was they who died this day instead of this innocent man. This I believe.

"The Lord is merciful to those who love Him. His eyes see all things. Pity the men who have done this. Rejoice for Guillermo Navarro, for his place in eternity is forever established. His battle is fought and won and finished on Calvary."

We sang a hymn then and prayed some. Each man knelt and asked forgiveness for his failure and many sins. Each left that barren, desolate place with something new born in his heart. We were forgiven. We somehow had a glimpse of Christ's death for us on faraway Calvary.

There was much in my own heart that was forever altered on that terrible day. I knew I would never forget the grief of being unable to stop an innocent man from being lynched. Something in me cried, "Never again!"

No. As long as I had breath in me, I would not stand and see another Calvary. . . .

CHAPTER 9

The aroma of sage and autumn oak leaves mingled with the scent of sea air. As we rode across the vast Santa Barbara rancho of Will Reed, Shawnee seemed to recognize each steer and heifer of my herd. She nodded at the black, slat-sided, long-horned beasts as if to greet them. Perking her ears and nickering softly, she let me know that she was pleased to be home again, pleased to be in familiar pastures with the prospect of doing what she was born to do.

As for Dog, he seemed to agree with my sharp little mount. There was a spring in his step as we passed by the herd. His mouth was open in a dog smile that made Joaquin laugh with pleasure.

"Look, Señor Andrew!" the boy called. "Dog smiles at Señor Toro." He pointed at the rangy steer as the critter raised its head from the dry grass and eyed Dog suspiciously. "And Señor Toro remembers Dog nipping his heels, I think. He seems not too happy that his shaggy master has come back from the goldfields!"

Tor hooted. "Gold on the hoof, Andrew. Reckon that ol' Toro ain't gonna be none too happy when he figgers out Dog is takin' him north to be et up!"

"We just won't tell 'em till it's too late," I enjoined. I did not say so, but it did feel mighty fine seeing those old familiar hides again. Like my horse, I knew I was not born to spend my life grubbing for gold in an icy cold stream. Herding cattle was something I knew. I had done it when my only prospect was to make two dollars a hide for shoe leather. Now I looked out across the Santa Barbara hills and saw my fortune.

My herd mingled with that of Will Reed's. Since I had purchased them from the Reed Rancho, many of my heifers bore Will's *Leaning R* brand. I had added two notches to the right ear of each, as well as my own *Lazy S* brand. Will had given me a good price on those heifers, and I hoped now to return the favor. Had he heard of the hungry miners of the Calaveras? Had he looked out over his thousands of cattle and imagined the worth of his stock? Such a vast herd could feed every one of the prospectors in the north this year and for many years to come.

Tor tugged his beard thoughtfully as he eyed the grazing beasts of the hillsides. "Andrew," he ventured cautiously, "you ain't got but two hundred cattle. Now that's more'n I got, which makes you a rich man."

"We're partners, Tor. Didn't you come looking for me when you heard about the gold strike?"

"It didn't exactly work out the way I figgered."

"Sure it did. We just found a different sort of gold. We're partners, and there's the end of it."

He nodded slowly. "What are we fixin' to do after we sell this bunch? I mean . . . they're fine fer a start. But I don't fancy bein' a rancher for a month and then goin' out of business."

I had spent the miles considering this very problem and had come up with a plan. "I've got it all figured out, partner," I said as we topped the rise and the white frame home of Will Reed came into view below us.

At first glance the place seemed exactly as it had when we left it. The two-story, New England–style home seemed out of place in the midst of the brown, oak-studded valley. I had heard once that Will had seen a picture of just such a house when he was a young man. After his marriage to Francesca he had ordered every plank, nail, and window from Boston and had them shipped around the Horn. Will Reed was a man who put muscle and action to his dreams. I hoped that he would do the same when he heard my plan.

The rubble of an old adobe cookhouse lay where it had fallen during the quake of '46. Smoke rose from the chimney of the new wood-frame cookhouse, and we caught the scent of bacon on the breeze.

Tor raised his face to the aroma and patted his belly. "Been dreamin' of Simona's bacon and biscuits. I'd of given a bag of gold dust just for a bite of her cookin'!" He urged his mount to a slow canter down the gently sloping lane.

The sun glinted on the red hair of two young men as they strolled out of the barn and looked toward our dust.

"By the color of their hair, that'll be two of Will's boys, I reckon," Tor remarked as I rode at his side. "He's got hisself a whole litter of redheaded young'uns. I ain't met but a few since most is in Hawaii at school. These'uns must be just returned."

At this information, Joaquin's face brightened. He leaned forward in his saddle as though to look more closely at the two Reed brothers.

I lifted my hand in greeting. A tentative wave replied. As we came nearer, I saw that the older brother was perhaps fifteen or sixteen. The younger was little more than Joaquin's age—twelve or thirteen. They could not have finished their term at the mission school in Hawaii. Why then had they come home to California? I felt a vague sense of uneasiness at that thought. Had some family tragedy come upon the peaceful rancho in our absence? Was Will all right? Francesca?

Truth to tell, the rancho seemed too quiet. Normally the barns and corrals were a swarm of activity. Vaqueros came and went with unbroken regularity. The only people in sight this morning were the two brothers, who eyed our approach with evident suspicion.

"Where is everyone?" I wondered aloud.

"It ain't Sunday. Ain't in church," Tor responded, scanning the hills and herds beyond. He pointed toward two vaqueros on the rise bringing in strays. Weeks before, there would have been a dozen hanging around the cookhouse waiting for the dinner bell.

"Somethin's up, Andrew," Tor said. "Mebbe this ain't gonna be as easy as we figgered."

There was an odd, deserted air about the place. Too many cattle. Not enough vaqueros. I remembered the tales we had heard of the sailors deserting their ships and leaving them to rot in San Francisco Bay while entire crews struck out for the goldfields. Could that be happening here as well?

At that instant, the tall, muscular form of Will Reed appeared in the opening of the barn. His eldest son, Peter, joined him. I knew Peter well from the days of the Bear Flag revolt. Nineteen years old now, Peter was as tall as his father and looked as strong as a grizzly. He recognized my piebald horse instantly and shouted my name. "Andrew!"

Will laughed at the sight of us, as though he had known all along that we would be back. We were a grubby-looking bunch. The best bath we had managed was a dip in the Rio Bravo three days before.

"Home from the goldfields so soon?" Will greeted us with an edge of amusement in his voice. "Struck it rich already, have you?"

Interest sparked on the faces of the younger brothers. They eyed us with open curiosity.

"What I want to know, Will Reed—" Tor grinned and glanced at the smoke from the cookhouse chimney—"we ain't missed breakfast, have we?"

* * *

One platter was heaped high with fried eggs; a mountain of bacon was piled on the other. Fresh melons, warm tortillas, butter, and strawberry jam were all washed down with cool buttermilk and coffee with thick cream.

We ate the feast as though we had not eaten anything at all since we left. Simona cocked a disapproving eyebrow at Tor as she placed another plate of eggs in front of him. His mouth was too stuffed to say thanks, and he grunted like a hog at the trough.

Simona scowled at Tor and opened her mouth as if to scold him, but Francesca silenced her with a stern look. "Our guests will be needing more bacon, Simona. See to it, *por favor.*"

I always said that Francesca Reed was a first-class lady. She ignored the fact that we seemed to have forgotten our table manners, but all the while she kept her sons eating proper by just raising an eyebrow at the three of them. Napkins in place, silverware held just so, they said their "please and thank you, ma'am" and "will you pass the butter" like proper gentlefolk, while we stuffed our grizzly faces. Peter, James, and John they were called, and they were just as polite as apostles, too. Will and Francesca kept them from asking questions until we three were working on our second platefuls of food. Joaquin wiped his mouth on his sleeve and blew his nose in his napkin.

"Mother?" John muttered in disgust, as if he did not care to share breakfast with the half-starved, half-breed boy across the table from him.

The thought crossed my mind that I had neglected the boy's upbringing in some ways. I was about to send Joaquin out to eat in the cookhouse when Francesca intervened.

"You have had some great adventures in the goldfields, Joaquin?" she asked kindly.

Her sons leaned forward attentively, seeming to forget Joaquin's ill manners.

The boy talked around his mouthful of eggs and babbled on about the first gold dust he had panned from the Calaveras. "Plenty of gold, Señora Reed. But no eggs. You see? The miners are paying one dollar in gold dust to buy even one small egg. I have eaten three weeks of gold dust this morning," he added happily.

"This is true?" Francesca turned to me.

"Yes, ma'am. One dollar for an egg. And a stringy steak is worth a whole ounce of gold," I explained.

Tor mumbled confirmation.

"Are they all as hungry as you, then?" Will was amused. "I'm not surprised. A man can't eat gold dust, can he?" He nodded at his sons as though he had been telling them this before we brought our tales of hunger and hardship home. "Like I said this morning, boys, every vaquero who lit out of here will be back soon enough. Won't take them long. You'll see. Give them a few weeks scrounging around in the cold water and nothing to eat but hardtack and grizzly bear meat . . . they'll wish they could get their hands on a *Leaning R* steer."

"Aha!" Tor and I interrupted at the same instant.

"The very thing we came to speak to you about, Will!" I cried, mindful that the subject had come first from him.

Will nodded, not yet comprehending my meaning. "I'll wager you've met up with more than one of my men there. Seventy-five of the best vaqueros in the country . . . two thirds of my men . . . just bolted one night and left us shorthanded during branding time. I'll not wish them to return, but when they come crawling back, I'll put them to honest employment again. Feed them and—"

"Feed them!" I cried, perhaps too eagerly. "The very thing!"

It was then that I unfolded my great plan for feeding the hungry miners of the goldfields. They were paying real gold for overcooked cart oxen. What would happen if they laid eyes on the *Leaning R* brand of Will Reed coming up the trail?

Will let me go on through two more cups of coffee before jerking me back to reality. "A thousand head, Andrew? Three hundred miles through the tules and the rivers of the big valley?" He shook his head. "It sounds difficult but possible . . . except for one small detail."

Had I left something out? "What is it?"

"There are no vaqueros left to help you drive the herd." He gave a slight shrug. "My sons have come home from school to help me here on the rancho. There are perhaps two dozen other vaqueros who did not desert. Most have families. They have been on the rancho for several generations. I can't go myself, you see." He gestured toward Francesca, whose baby was due any time. "We cannot spare any more men."

It was Peter who drew himself up and challenged his father's reasoning on this point. "But, Father, if we take one thousand head to the north, that will be one thousand less we have to tend here at the rancho. Could you not spare a few of us for such an enterprise?"

"A few of us?" Will glared down his nose at Peter.

The younger brothers jumped in. "Yes, Father! We can do it! The branding is finished! We managed all of that shorthanded, didn't we?"

I had not spoken of the lawlessness of the gold camps. No word of the murders or lynchings had been mentioned. Nor had the name and evil dominion of Jack Powers been raised.

Somehow, however, Francesca Reed sensed that there was much more yet untold of our story. She raised her chin defiantly to her sons. "Your father needs you here. That is all that I shall say on the matter. You are just children. You cannot go to such a place."

John set up a gruff protest. "Children! Look at him!" He pointed at Joaquin, who suddenly became a hero. "He is younger than I! He has been there and back. He has a gold claim on the Calaveras River.

He has been a partner to Señor Andrew and Señor Tor. Do not call us children, Mother!"

Silence at the table.

Will cleared his throat. "I reckon I was a lot younger than Peter when I set out to come west." He narrowed his eyes in thought. "It was the stuff to make a man of me."

"Will?" Francesca warned, apparently seeing the wheels turning in his mind. "They are not you. Peter is older. Yes. But James and John are . . ."

"Good hands," Will finished. "And I reckon such an adventure might come to a happy conclusion for them were they to ride at the side of Andrew and Tor. And there is great fortune to be made, even if it is only half as much as Andrew tells us." He turned to me. "I get two dollars a hide for my stock. Ten thousand head are grazing on my rancho. I will send one thousand to the north and split the profit with you and Tor. We can spare Peter, James, and John, and I'll find vaqueros to make a dozen hands for the drive. What do you say?"

Will put out his hand as the boys whooped and Francesca looked daggers at all of us. In this way the deal was set. In our jubilation, we could not guess that the misgivings of Francesca Reed held real portent of the danger we were to face in the coming weeks.

CHAPTER 10

Will Reed chose seven of his remaining vaqueros to accompany his sons and us north. They were not selected because of great skill, he explained, but because they were single men. There were no wives or children to leave behind in their journey.

Were they loyal? Men we could count on? To this Will shrugged and replied that these had come to the rancho after nearly every other vaquero had vamoosed at the first rumor of gold. If that was loyalty, then he supposed they were faithful as old dogs.

They were also as mangy looking as old dogs. A scruffier looking lot I had seldom seen. Alzado, who seemed to tell the others what to do, looked mean enough to top a grizzly bear in a Who's Uglier? contest. One look at the long knife stuck in his boot top made me rub my throat and think a while about sleeping real light on the journey.

"You need anything done," Will said confidently, "just ask Alzado."

Five other vaqueros—Rodriguez, Garcia, Ramos, Sanchez, and Ortiz—were a close second in appearance and smell to Alzado. The last man on the crew was named Gomez. He was softer than the rest, dressed somewhat cleaner, and bowed and smiled a lot to Will, his sons, and now to Tor and me as well.

"Pure toady," Tor muttered as Gomez disappeared around the corner of the barn. "Makes me want to wipe my boots off, he does. Give me a tobacco-spittin' grasshopper like Alzado over that smooth, puffed-up toad any day." He shook his head. "Truth to tell, I ain't real sure of any of these fellers, Andrew. I say we take the Reed boys and you and me and Joaquin, and leave these 'uns behind."

I considered the proposal, but a thousand head of cattle meant that we needed more than two grown men and four boys to handle the drive. I reminded Tor of the fact that these seven had remained on the rancho and not jumped ship like their comrades. Tor did not seem comforted by this fact all the same.

It took a week to gather the herd and cut out the young heifers from the steers. Will was not overeager to sell off breeding stock. A wise decision. Keeping his heifers here in the south meant fewer calves in the north. If this was to be a truly profitable enterprise, he said, we had to consider such matters.

All in all, the herd was a much handsomer looking lot than our vaqueros. Those cows smelled a mite better too, but we put our doubts aside and after a long benediction from the mission priest, we headed out of Santa Barbara.

On the advice of Will, we did not head straight north along the King's Highway that linked the string of missions along the coast. That route was crawling with highwaymen, he told us. Thieves and cutthroats who paid homage to Jack Powers were thick along that way. Even if we managed to drive the herd past them, no doubt word would reach Powers that a thousand head of cattle were moving north on the coast. If the bandit king ever put two and two together, Will rightly said, the herd would be stolen and we would be lucky to escape with *our* hides, let alone the cowhides.

For this reason we chose to drive the herd over the mountains and straight up through the marshy San Joaquin Valley. It was a more difficult journey, to be sure, but the country was mostly inhabited by a few remaining bands of Yokut Indians. Gentlefolk, the Yokuts would pose no threat to us. Tor and I had often remarked how many of them had died off from white man's diseases and the malarial mosquitos brought from the North by French trappers. Taking our herd to the goldfields through the Central Valley might make for a more difficult trip, but at least we would not have to fight men as well as the elements. It was our hope that our arrival in the North would be met by great amazement and hungry miners with pockets filled with gold!

* * *

I've never been one to get the wind up easily. I'm not superstitious, nor does the night breeze sighing in the cedars give me the "williwaws," as Tor Fowler would have said. Still, the experience of our first night on the cattle drive did provide ample reason to think that things were not going to be smooth.

One day out of the comforts of Santa Barbara, we were pushing the herd into the narrow defile of Gaviota Pass. The Canyon of the Seagulls had come to the world's attention two years earlier; since it was there that the Californios had laid an ambush for Colonel Fremont. You can bet my thoughts went back to those days, because Tor, Will Reed, and I had each had a hand in preventing the success of the trap.

Anyway, on this occasion, with a thousand head of cattle and a largely unknown group of men, I had little time to dwell on past history. Gaviota was still a wild place, with a primitive, dangerous feel to it. Its rocky canyons and steep, narrow trail were favored by outlaws, renegades, and grizzly bears for the waylaying of unwary travelers.

We rolled the herd up for the night into a blind arroyo. We had not pushed as far as I would have liked, but Tor reminded me that cow critters and men alike both need a little time to settle into a routine. The first passage had to convince both the herd and the vaqueros that it was easier to keep walking forward than to get punished for standing and bellowing to go home.

I posted the first two night herders with instructions to call their relief in two hours. We could have kept more men on watch together, but with the herd all bedded down and placid, there seemed no reason to give up more sleep.

I've heard it said that the toughest watch is the one just before dawn, but in my experience, this is not so. The anticipation of the first glint of gray light along the eastern rim of the world always seemed to sharpen my senses—watching for it, you see.

For me, the hardest part of the dark hours is between 2 and 4 AM. Seems like every sound is magnified and every worry, too. You keep thinking about how far off the daybreak is, and what you most want is to get next to the fire and sleep. There must be something to it, because Pastor Metcalfe always got called out in those hours to attend some poor old soul's shuffle off this mortal coil.

Which is why I assigned myself that shift on purpose. The three Reed brothers took the first watch. Tor took the second. The Reed boys were fast asleep beside the fire when Tor shook me awake at two by the set of the Big Dipper.

"Everything all right?" I asked.

"Sure, nice and quiet. Not even a breeze stirrin'," he said, but with an added comment left hanging in his voice.

"But what?"

"Can't put my finger on it exactly. Peter said there was somethin' in the air durin' his watch. Jest a feelin', he said. Ever'thing near the mouth of the canyon seems settled, but where the arroyo backs up to the rocks I get an urge to look over my shoulder some."

"Indians, you think?"

"Not likely. Not here. 'Sides, they can read Will Reed's brand, same as us. If they wanted a beef, they'd just sashay in and ask for one. No, it's somethin' else."

"Grizzly?"

Tor shrugged and yawned. "I'll leave you to it," he said, rolling up in his bedroll. His vaquero partner had already turned in, and Tor was sawing logs even before I shook Joaquin awake.

I told the boy of Tor's cautioning words. "Do you wish us to ride with you, señor?" he asked. By *us* he meant him and Dog, who had been sleeping across Joaquin's feet.

"No," I said quietly. "You and Dog sit here by the fire. I'll ride the circle once and come back."

The farthest back piece of the canyon pinched off against a rock wall, topped by a high, brushy hillside. It was plastered with chaparral and sage and would have made tough going for a limber squirrel, let alone a man on horseback. For that reason, it felt as secure as a corral fence at the rear of the herd, yet the hairs on my neck prickled.

Shawnee had made no sound to indicate that anything was amiss, but her ears pricked back and forth as if searching for an expected but missing sound.

"Easy," I cautioned her. "Let's just sit and look around a spell." No breeze meant no scents on the coolish night air unless we got up close, so quiet watchfulness was the order of things.

After a time, I was ready to write it off to an uncommon case of the jitters when a steer lying off a ways from the herd caught my attention. Sometimes the lack of movement can be just as telling as a twitch or a wiggle. This animal was lying too flat and too still—dead, without doubt.

I nudged Shawnee closer. She moved reluctantly as the warm smell of fresh blood reached us both at last. Dark, raking marks stood out on the neck and shoulder of the rust-colored hide, and the corkscrewed position of the head told the rest of the story—mountain lion! Big, smart, and fearless, I judged, from the way he had brought down the steer with a single blow and in complete silence. Of even greater interest to me was the cat's present whereabouts.

The Allen shotgun was already in my hand, and Shawnee backed away from the kill without being told to. You see, lions prefer to strike from behind, and neither my paint mare nor I intended to give this one any opportunity.

Shawnee walked us very deliberately around the herd in the direction of the fire. We did not want to compound the loss of the steer by flying through the drove in the middle of the night and causing a panic that might end in a stampede. In point of fact, even after reaching the fireside, I did not shout an alarm. Rather, I motioned Joaquin to join me, then roused Tor.

He had the mountain man's knack of coming instantly awake, and after a few words of explanation he had a grasp of the situation. "Well, Andrew," he said, looking away from the fire into the dark canyon, "could be a young cat. Mayhap you skeered this here cougar away from his kill."

I shook my head. "Shawnee or I would have heard him go, the brush being so thick and all."

"Figger you're right . . . which means the other explanation must fit."

"What, Señor Fowler? What does it mean?" asked Joaquin, his eyes as round as saucers.

"He means that what we've got is an outlaw lion. A young one might be run off from his prey that easy. An older one would usually stay and fight for it, or else he'd have already drug it off in the brush. But this one didn't do either. He just killed for the sport," I explained.

"And h-he . . ." Joaquin kind of stuttered and reached out to hug Dog around the neck.

"Right," I agreed. "He'll be back. If we don't deal with him, he'll kill again . . . maybe tonight, maybe tomorrow night . . . but he'll follow the herd till he gets tired of the game."

I saw a shiver start at the base of Joaquin's spine and work its way up till it came out his shoulders with a final shudder. To his credit all he said was "What do we do about it, Señor Andrew?"

Tor nodded his approval, and I gave the boy a squeeze on his arm. "What *you* need to do," I said, "is stay here with Dog. I don't know if I could keep him from running that cat, and either he'd get hurt or the herd spooked or both."

We woke Alzado, the Yaqui—meaning "warrior"—vaquero. He was a sullen-seeming cuss who grunted more than he spoke—and that but seldom—but he was fearless. Built lean and tough and with all the pride of a people who had never submitted to the Spanish conquest of their homeland, the Yaqui tribe was feared by the others but much admired too. Out of our band of seven vaqueros about whom little was known, Alzado seemed the most steady to take out into the darkness to face a rogue lion.

We each took a torch from the fire, and again we rode slow and easy back to the spot where I had found the steer. But when we got to the place, there was no carcass to be found. Dismounting, we left Alzado holding the horses, while Tor and I scoured the ground.

"Could you have mistook the place, Andrew?" Tor asked. "On a dark night such as this, one clump of brush looks pretty much like another."

"No," I argued, "I'm certain this is it." We raised the firebrands overhead to give us a wider ring of view. "Look here," I said. "There's blood here on the grass." I pointed downward at the stain that looked pitch-black against the shadowy brush.

But Tor was not watching where I directed. "No doubt you're

right," he said, "but in that case he's kilt another one." Fowler's outstretched right arm gestured beyond the glare of the torches some few yards to where another steer's body lay on the grass.

It was all I could do to keep from swearing. Not only was this the first night of the drive, but I had scarce been gone ten minutes since viewing the previous victim. It was with relief then that I saw the downed creature move. "Look, Tor," I said. "You're wrong."

We had already taken a few paces in the direction of the animal. Its horned head lifted and pivoted in our direction, wobbling awkwardly as if drunk. That's when we saw the baleful yellow eyes staring back at us over the neck of the steer. In the flickering glow of our burning branches, we watched as a huge cougar raised the head of the dead steer by the grip of his powerful jaws clamped around its throat.

The cougar sprang upright, dragging the six-hundred-pound cow as if it were nothing. Tor and I both fired, but our shots took effect only on the dead carcass. The mountain lion flung its prey aside and bounded into the chaparral with a defiant roar and a crash. It was gone for now, but we knew it would be back.

CHAPTER 11

There was no further sleeping that night. The vaqueros, roused by our gunfire, rushed about with some confusion.

The Reed brothers, showing the character typical of their parents, were in favor of setting out on the trail of the big cougar at once. Opposing this was the opinion of some others who felt such a plan was *muy malo*, very bad. In fact, Gomez and Rodriguez were ready to call it quits and return to Santa Barbara.

The plan we actually adopted was more cautious than the one but less cowardly than the other. Tor and I formed a picket line of men around the rear of the herd to guard against the mountain lion's return. It was our intention to wait for first light, then track the animal to where it holed up.

There were no more disturbances, even though we watched until gray dawn reduced the number of visible stars to three. It was a very grumpy group of men who stretched out the kinks and gave up the vigil.

I instructed Peter Reed to ride the point and lead the herd out of the arroyo and up the trail. Tor and I would set out to do the tracking. We were accompanied by the Yaqui, Alzado.

During the night watch, the fawning vaquero Gomez had been one to raise his voice in support of abandoning the drive, but he sang a different tune when the sun came up. "Please, Señor Andrew, allow me to accompany you. In my country I am known as a great hunter."

I caught Tor's raised eyebrow and considered that perhaps the man needed an opportunity to redeem himself but could not agree.

We three would track the cougar till noon, then break off the hunt and rejoin the herd. All the rest were needed for the drive. “No,” I said. “You and Joaquin take charge of the remuda.”

I planned to return to the point where the cougar had bounded away into the darkness, intending to follow its trail. Tor and Alzado set off directly toward a rocky pinnacle that looked to be a likely spot for a den.

“Señor Andrew,” Gomez called out, riding after me, “I have something to tell you.” He cast a furtive glance toward the pair of riders ahead and waited until Tor and the Yaqui were out of earshot before continuing.

“Not necessary,” I said, taking his action for embarrassment. “I already know what you are going to say.”

The vaquero swept off his sombrero with its sugar-loaf crown and rubbed his hand across his forehead. “You do?”

“Sure,” I replied. “Don’t give it a thought. I don’t like my sleep interrupted by a thieving cougar or a band of hostiles or a snake in my bedroll, for that matter.”

Gomez stroked his thin, black mustache with a quick nervous gesture. “Señor is making the joke?”

Now it was my turn to be confused. “What are you driving at then, if this isn’t about last night?”

Gomez reined his palomino alongside me. There was a moment’s jostling of horses as Shawnee laid back her ears and with bared teeth warned the gelding from coming too close.

When the stomping settled, Gomez gestured for me to lean over. In a conspiratorial voice he whispered, “It is about the fierce one, the Yaqui.”

“Alzado? What about him?”

“He is not to be trusted, señor.”

“What do you mean?”

“I have seen him before, señor, in the company of *malditos*, bad men and robbers. He is hot-tempered and will kill when the mood is on him.”

“So?” I said, trying to sound less concerned than I really felt. “Has he made threats against me or mine . . . or you, perhaps?”

Gomez looked as if I'd kicked him in his pride . . . as if my words cast suspicion on his motives (which of course they did). "Ah no, señor. I only wished to be of service. But if my words are not welcome, then I will keep my own counsel."

"Just see that you keep a sharp eye out for that mountain lion," I said. I pointed downward to a pug mark the size of a horse's footprint. "He's big and mean too, and he's been a lot more trouble than Alzado."

Gomez drew himself up haughtily and spun the palomino around in the direction of the herd of replacement mounts.

As I looked on, Peter shouted the orders that roused the men and the cattle and set both upon the trail. Then I turned to the task of picking my way along the increasingly steep dry wash as it wound up into the wild.

The sun had climbed high in the sky when I reined Shawnee to a halt and reflected on the lion. His tracks had led me on a meandering path, looping in and out of the low hills. Twice I had come upon the bloody remains of other steers killed and dragged into the brush. Three times I lost his trail entirely, having to go back to the last clear print and then ride widening spirals around until I picked up the marks again.

He seemed to have been going nowhere in particular. The commotion around the camp and the shots fired had not scared him into hightailing for home; that much was certain.

Shawnee and I circled another low hill, then were led to its crest. The barest hint of a crushed place in the weeds showed where the cougar had stretched out to take his ease.

"What was he playing at?" I remarked to Shawnee. I stood in the stirrups and found myself gazing out over the canyon where we had spent the night. The dust of the drive had already disappeared, and it was time to think about riding after my herd.

All at once it struck me. Not only had we not scared this particular lion back into the high country, but we had not even driven him away from his sport. Or at least not far away. While we stood guard, he had spent the remainder of the night prowling around our camp, looking for an unprotected way in. While we had been watching for him, he had circled all of us. The thought was enough to give a man the willies.

Tracking him now seemed pointless. We would have to outguess him and get there first or he would continue to be trouble. I set off into another canyon, toward where I expected to find Tor and the Yaqui.

Shawnee and I were partway up a steep hill when we heard the gunshot. I had just turned my head to check my bearings when the ringing echoes bounced through the canyon. Shawnee took off as if she had been the bullet fired from the gun.

Up a narrow trail we raced, following the barely visible track of an ancient path that curved across the chaparral-covered slope. Around the base of a wind-carved, sandstone spire we charged, and then out of the corner of my eye I caught a glimpse of a figure lurking on a ledge.

The next instant, a knife flashed in front of my face and a forearm like a bar of iron struck me across the neck. Shawnee plunged, unbalanced, rearing and shaking herself, while I parted company with my saddle and lit with a crash in a patch of sage and greasewood.

Instinctively, both my hands closed around the wrist of the attacker's hand that held the knife. Over and over we rolled, fighting for possession of the blade, for what seemed like an eternity, before I ended on top and pressed the point downward toward my assailant's throat.

"Don't, Andrew!" Tor shouted. "Let him up!"

The savage face panting a few inches beneath my own belonged to Alzado. So did the twelve-inch sharpened steel. "He tried to kill me!" I yelled back.

"Not so! Look up on the trail—on the rock just ahead."

I looked. The snarling jaws of the great mountain lion parted in a scream of hatred and pain. He crouched in a crevice right beside where Shawnee's next few strides would have carried us if we had not been swept off the trail by Alzado's leap.

While my head was still spinning and my breath was coming in short jerks, Fowler took careful aim and fired. Even at the moment of his death, the mountain lion jumped straight outward at his pursuers . . . a defiant lunge of bared claws that carried him across twenty feet of space before he hit the ground, dead.

"That cougar was crazy—more so than ever since I wounded him and let him get away," Tor explained. "If Alzado hadn't jumped when he did, I don't know what mighta happened."

"Why didn't you yell or something?" I said.

"No time," Alzado gasped. "Then, no breath." He added, "Señor is *hombre fuerte.*"

A strong man, he had called me, and I knew he was reliving just how close the point of the knife had been to his throat.

"I'm sorry for the mistake," I said, stretching out my hand and pulling him to his feet. "And mighty in your debt, too."

Alzado shrugged. "It was nothing."

"Nothin'!" Tor snorted, raising the dead lion's head and pulling back the lips to expose two-inch-long fangs. "That wounded cougar was duckin' in and out of the brush and the boulders, and Alzado was right behind him on the blood trail with nothin' but that pig-sticker in his hand."

"Where's your gun?" I asked him.

"I have none."

"Well, you do now," I said. I handed him the Allen. The barest hint of a smile wrinkled the corners of his mouth, and then it was back to business as usual. "*Gracias*," he said, and then, "I will skin the lion."

Shawnee and Tor's mount rolled their eyes and trotted a nervous distance away from Alzado's big bay. Even minus his insides, the cougar's rolled-up hide made a large bundle behind the Yaqui's saddle. We three rode in a jovial mood, congratulating ourselves on the success of our effort and discussing the cunning of the adversary. I also noted an occasional admiring glance downward by Alzado as he studied his new rifle. Each time I saw that look, it made me check my boot top where the bone hilt of my newly acquired Yaqui knife protruded.

By the swirling dust on the horizon, we knew that our line had been true and that we had almost reached the drive. It crossed my mind that there would be some new stories to tell around the cook fire this night, and perhaps the morale of all would get a boost.

Behind the mass of dark shapes that was the herd proper was a separate, smaller bunch of animals that made up the remuda. Joaquin was driving the string of horses into a grassy hollow enclosed by willows for a noon rest. I nodded approvingly to myself and directed our course that way.

I was looking again at the rolled-up lion skin and thinking how impressed Joaquin would be. As we rode over the rim of the small bowl, the horse herd appeared right below us. I saw Joaquin's small figure snatch something off the ground and point it toward us. A puff of smoke clouded his face, and something clipped a lock of Tor's hair. A second later the report of the rifle reached us.

I set Shawnee at a gallop and waved my arms while shouting, "Don't shoot! It's us! Joaquin, don't shoot!"

The warning was unnecessary. A cuff from Gomez caught Joaquin upside the head and knocked him sprawling. The vaquero grabbed the boy and shook him fiercely. "Stupid, stupid boy!" he yelled in Joaquin's face. "You almost killed Señor Fowler!"

Gomez had drawn back his fist to strike the boy again when I reined Shawnee to a halt of flashing hooves and flung myself off her back. "That's enough!" I ordered. "Joaquin, why did you shoot at us?"

Tears were streaming down the boy's cheeks, and his throat was too constricted to answer. "Señor Andrew, I . . . he—" He stopped, too choked to say more. Then he turned and ran off.

CHAPTER 12

The next several days slipped by without incident as we moved the herd through the mountains by way of Tejon Pass. The terrain was rough and progress slow. A cold wind blew in our faces, while above us the light of the sun was darkened by the migration of millions of wild geese and ducks. This served as a reminder that winter was just around the corner. We had to deliver the herd in the north before the first snow arrived or face being stranded in the valley for the winter.

Peter, James, and John Reed worked with the skill and grit I had seen demonstrated by the best Californio vaqueros. They made even the hardest work into sport. Each hour was filled with contests in riding and roping. When matching their skill against the other riders, the brothers worked together like three fingers on the same hand. Dozens of times each day I could hear their laughter echo across the herd. They were polite to others of our little band, but there was the strong bond of kinship that naturally excluded anyone else from entering their tight circle.

The other vaqueros treated the Reed brothers with respect due to young princes in line to inherit a great kingdom. Alzado would not think twice about barking commands to Joaquin, yet he pressed his thin lips together and held his peace when Peter, James, or John rode by. Many times I noticed conversations would die away when the Reed brothers, Tor, or I would come within earshot. Often furtive, uncomfortable looks would follow. At first I believed that this attitude was in deference to our authority. Then I began to wonder exactly what the vaqueros were speaking of that they did not wish for us to hear. Joaquin's behavior became silent and almost fearful in the presence of these men.

Perhaps it was the prospect of weeks of this slow and tedious journey that affected the riders, I reasoned. Then the laughter of the Reed brothers would remind me that some among us were enjoying the adventure. Why then did the vaqueros seem so resentful as we topped the rise and began our descent into the great San Joaquin Valley of central California? Why the hard looks boring into the backs of Tor and me? Why the reluctant nod when we gave the order for some common task?

As I looked out over the enormous, cloud-filled valley below me, I could not help but wonder again if Will Reed had chosen these vaqueros wisely. Without families to return to on the rancho, what was to tie these men to the herd and the job before us? More than once I imagined I glimpsed the thought of mutiny in their eyes. Resentment seethed just below the surface and was put aside only when the fierce Alzado rode among them shouting orders.

The chill I felt was more than a change in the weather. And it seemed that I was not the only one to notice.

Cattle picked their way down the rocky slopes. Ten thousand feet above the herd, the din of a million honking geese covered the bawling of cows. I did not hear the approach of Tor's horse until he was beside me.

Tor jerked a thumb skyward and shook his head as though he had water in his ears. He shouted to make himself heard above the roar. "Don't look now, but somethin's up between Alzado and that smilin' sneak Gomez."

I started to look over my shoulder, but Tor stopped me with a shake of his head. "I said don't look," he instructed. "Best pay 'em no mind. But they had some words. Came to blows in the saddle. Alzado knocked Gomez off his horse. There'll be blood spilt over it if I know anythin'."

"Been building toward it," I remarked, gazing out over the top of the clouds as if we were discussing the valley.

"The vaqueros don't seem overfond of Alzado; that's for certain. They're skeert of him. Maybe that ain't all bad. I'm a little skeert of him, too." He grinned sheepishly. "A right unusual feller. I don't trust him. But then I don't trust none of the rest of 'em neither. Mebbe they'll jest fight among themselves and leave us out of it."

"Don't mind that as long as we get the herd where it's going," I agreed.

Tor looked toward Joaquin, who was riding alone on the far side of the herd. "The boy ain't said two words since the other day. Don't look nobody in the eye. Ducks and runs ever'time anybody comes near. What do you make of it, Andrew?"

"He feels foolish, I reckon."

Tor tugged his beard. "I got me a feelin' . . . mebbe somethin' else."

"You tried talking to him?"

"Don't do no good. You'd best keep your eye peeled, Andrew. I got me a real feelin'. Trouble's on the wind. We're headin' into foggy territory, and somethin' don't sit right here with that Alzado and Gomez and the rest of the mob."

"And Joaquin?"

"Keep 'im close, Andrew. My bones is a tellin' me that boy knows somethin' he wished he didn't know. Mebbe it's somethin' to do with us and the herd, and mebbe it ain't. But it bears watchin'."

There was no use pretending I had not noticed the way Joaquin ate by himself and rode alone and spoke no word to anyone. No use pretending I had not noticed his hands trembling when Alzado or Gomez rode by. Tor's warning was only a confirmation of the same uneasiness I had been feeling for days.

CHAPTER 13

The clacking of a thousand pair of long, curved horns resounded from the herd like the clash of sabres in battle. The cattle seemed to sense the broad, swift barrier of the river just ahead of us. They bawled and tossed their heads nervously as we drove them on.

The river was called Rio Bravo by the first Spanish explorers. The north and south forks came together high in the Sierras and roared down from the mountain through a steep, rocky gorge to tumble onto the valley floor. Since those early days, the powerful river had been renamed Kern, as though it were as tame as a small brook. But the roar of its waters had been the last sound in the ears of many men. Even where the river appeared peaceful, the placid flow concealed a treacherous undercurrent rippling beneath the surface.

Maybe the Spaniards called the river Bravo because it took a strong man to ford it. To the west, it became shallow as it emptied into the marshes of the valley floor. But mud bogs and mires of quicksand made it impossible for us to cross there. Indians told of whole herds of elk being trapped and dying in the swamps after following a buck that strayed only a few yards from the trail.

Instead of risking such danger, we skirted the southern rim of the valley, moving on high ground toward the mouth of the river canyon. The torrent exploded from this boulder-strewn funnel and seemed to collect itself in quiet pools before it sighed and moved on.

There was one possible fording place that Tor and I knew of. I had made the passage several times on Shawnee. With the water low, we had driven my small herd across it easily. But rains had swelled the waters since then. The river was a quarter mile wide now and deep enough that it would have to be swum. It was one thing to wade across a shallow flow. This was another matter entirely. Above us to the east, the current was impassable. Below us to the west lay the quicksand. We scratched our heads and looked the situation over. Were we brave enough to face the river?

Alzado spurred his big bay gelding to the edge of the bank. He stared at the far shore for an instant, then, making the sign of the cross, he plunged ahead, whooping as the horse hit the water. Urged on by Alzado's shouts and the sting of a quirt on its butt, the horse cut through the water without looking back. Straight across he swam as Alzado held its mane and yipped like a coyote. Emerging on the opposite side of the flow, the soaking vaquero reined the horse around, stood in his stirrups, and raised his sombrero in victory. He cupped his hand around his mouth and called over to us, "She is nothing, Señor Andrew! Deep, yes. But slow and lazy!"

As if to prove his point, he rode down the bank and spurred his animal into the river to swim back. Brave Alzado had matched the Bravo with apparent ease. He called the treacherous stream "a woman" and in his mocking smile dared us all to follow.

I unsheathed my bullwhip as all others of our troop took positions at the sides and rear of the herd. Dog was called to jump onto the saddle with Joaquin. I turned to the boy, who seemed not as eager as the Reed brothers for this adventure.

"Stay right with me, Joaquin," I commanded. "Do you hear me, boy? No matter what happens, you keep your horse tight behind me."

Joaquin nodded curtly and wrapped his fingers in Dog's leather collar. "We will follow you, Señor Andrew," he replied grimly. "Me and Dog are not afraid."

I knew Joaquin was not much of a swimmer. He was not even much for taking a bath in a water trough, and we were in for quite a baptism here.

The cattle bellowed their protest as we lassoed the horns of the leaders and whipped and whooped them into the river from all sides.

They made a black, bobbing countercurrent, heads raised and horns tangled. The Reed boys brought up the rear. Alzado, Rodriguez, and Garcia took the high side of the current with me and Joaquin. I spotted Tor on the downside with the soft, frightened-looking Gomez close behind him. Sanchez and Ortiz followed.

Icy water soaked my buckskins and filled my boots. Popping my whip behind the ears of the reluctant steers kept their course straight. The first of the animals emerged on the northern shore, bawled, shook themselves, and trotted forward.

Alzado turned and plunged back into the water to keep the central core of the group moving. I started to follow him, but it was at that time I noticed that Tor was in trouble. He had lassoed an enormous animal around the horns. The critter was floundering! Caught up in some undertow, the beast had rolled over and now was tangled in the reata. To my horror, I saw that the reata was also looped around Tor's saddle horn and somehow caught beneath his stirrup leather. He and his strong bay horse were being pulled downstream.

Gomez, who was within a few yards of my friend, did not seem to notice, or if he saw Tor's predicament, he offered no assistance.

I shouted and rode through the herd as the head of Tor's mount screwed around in a separate attempt to struggle free. With no more than a nudge, Shawnee leaped from the embankment and swam toward Tor as though she knew the urgency. For an instant I saw Tor's hand raise. Light glinted on the blade of his knife as he tried to cut his mount loose from the reata.

Suddenly Tor and his horse parted company. The horse righted itself and, after a moment of confusion, swam toward shore. I could plainly see that the cinch on the saddle had broken. Tor bobbed up once, then went under. The wayward steer paddled on, dragging the saddle after him.

"Tor!" I shouted.

Gomez paid no mind to the struggle of my drowning comrade. He urged his mount in a straight line toward dry land, while Tor splashed and gasped and sank from sight a second time. The churning hooves of a thousand beeves swept past him. One blow would be enough to finish him off! Two more steers broke away to tumble downstream just ahead of me.

Where was Tor? I cracked my whip, urging Shawnee onward, although she could swim no faster. The waters were murky brown. I could not see Tor. Had he been sucked beneath the cattle? Was he swept away?

"Gomez!" I cried as the vaquero passed me. "Get back! Tor has fallen."

The Mexican seemed not to hear me.

Seconds dragged by. Too long for a man to be beneath the water without a breath! I called out to heaven for help! Was the life of Tor Fowler to end in such a way?

I spotted a fragment of red flannel just beneath the surface. "Tor!" I yelled, turning Shawnee toward the spark of color that gave me hope.

Twenty feet from me the hand of Tor groped upward. Then his face emerged for one feeble breath before he rolled and sank out of my sight again.

Fearful that Shawnee might strike him with a hoof, I leaped from her back without thinking. My bullwhip still coiled in my hand, I struck out to where I had seen the color. Diving beneath the surface, I reached through the water hoping to grasp him. Nothing! Another quick breath and I went under again. This time my fingers brushed his limp body. I grasped him by the belt and struggled to hold him up. Only now did my own desperate situation come to mind. Here I was, only a fair swimmer, holding an unconscious man in the middle of a river! My lungs ached for air. I surfaced, gasped, half shouted with terror and joy at what I saw.

There was little Joaquin on his horse, only ten feet from us! He had obeyed my command to stick tight on my tail. Now he held Shawnee by the reins and cried out to me. "Your whip, Señor Andrew!"

Catching his intent, I managed to toss out the lash. He caught hold of the tip and looped it around his saddle horn.

I strengthened my hold on Tor and held fast to the whip handle as the boy towed us toward dry land. Only then did he release Shawnee, who cut a path through the water ahead of us.

I did not let go of the bullwhip or Tor until we were dragged twenty yards up the embankment. Cold and shaken, I lay in the sand until a circle of riders came around, and Dog whined and licked my face. Tor coughed and moaned and asked if he was dead.

We had survived, thanks to Joaquin. And no thanks to Gomez.

I stood slowly and looked at the boy. "What were you doing out there, Joaquin? Don't you know you could have been killed?"

"You said I should follow you, Señor Andrew," he replied. There was a renewed confidence in the boy. He had redeemed himself as well as Tor and me that day.

The herd milled aimlessly about on the north shore of the Rio Bravo, but Tor and I were too tired to care. I waved feebly for Joaquin. "Tell Peter to make camp here." I coughed. "This is as far as we go today."

The boy scampered off, relief written on his face.

Tor retched and coughed up some river water. He was hugging a boulder with his face pressed against it. It was a gesture I understood. Things were still swirling some for me as well. "What happened, Andrew?"

"Your cinch busted," I said. "It's a good thing Joaquin took me so at my word or you and I would both have been in trouble, pard."

Dragging himself upright, Tor stood swaying unhappily and frowning.

"What's your all-fired hurry?" I wanted to know.

"Got a problem," he said quietly. "That cinch was new."

While all the men were shaking out their belongings to dry, Tor and I had an inconspicuous meeting with Peter. The eldest Reed brother had caught up with the wayward steer, still dragging Tor's reata and the waterlogged saddle.

Tor looked with disgust at the battered leather. "Tore it up . . . just flat tore it up. But looky here."

He was right. The horsehair girth was still intact, the metal buckle ring shining. Not a single strand had parted.

Tor ran his hand upward to the leather strap that secured the girth to the saddle. "Now look at this."

Peter and I saw where the leather had ripped across when the weight of the steer and the force of tons of water had pulled against the reata. Tor flipped the strap over in his hand. There—on the back and at a place that would have been out of sight under the skirt of the saddle—was the faint but still perceptible mark of a knife.

"This didn't happen of its own self," Tor growled. "Somebody give it a good start, then waited for somethin' to happen."

"But who?" Peter wondered aloud. "Who would have done such a thing?"

"And when was it done?" I added. "There's no way to tell from this."

"What should we do?" was Peter's next question.

"Here's my thinking on it," Tor said. "Some low-down snake has took great pains to see to it that this looked like an accident. Let's just let him go on thinkin' thataway."

I studied the roiling waters that had so nearly cost two lives, then looked again at the knife mark. "You're right," I agreed at last. "Let's play this close and see who tries to up the ante next."

"Shall I tell my brothers or Joaquin?" Peter wanted to know.

"No," I said. "The fewer who know we're onto it, the smaller the chance of giving the game away. We have to keep this just between us three."

It was to prove a fatal mistake.

CHAPTER 14

Sunlight broke through the morning haze and warmed our backs as we rode on. Lizards awoke and slithered out onto boulders and fallen logs to soak up the last bit of sun before winter closed in.

The feel of Indian summer might have warmed my spirits as well, but there was a chill in my soul that had nothing to do with temperature. I found myself studying each man among us, mentally calculating what motive there might be for attempting to murder Tor. Why stage an accident when a knife between the ribs in the dark night would accomplish the same purpose? I doubted each man in turn and then all of them together.

After a time I talked myself into doubting my doubts. Perhaps the cinch had been cut halfway through long before we ever left on the drive. Maybe our vaqueros had nothing to do with it. Wasn't it possible that the leather cinch had been scored by some disgruntled enemy back in Angels Camp? The man who had done the deed was certainly patient if that was the case. He had been counting on the fact that one day there would be just enough strain on the leather that it would snap at a crucial moment and take Tor with it.

"You're payin' more mind to the hired help than the cattle," Tor commented, riding up beside me. His gaze followed mine to Alzado as the Indian shouted and cursed a wayward steer.

"I expect you're right," I agreed. I had not been thinking much about business. "Trying to figure who it is. Or if it's all of them. Or maybe none of them. Maybe this is an old score," I said hopefully.

"Ain't all of 'em." Tor kept his eyes on Alzado and scanned the other vaqueros who rode in pairs and singly around us. "But it's some of 'em."

"How can you know that?"

"'Cause if it was a bunch of 'em what wanted us dead, there wouldn't be much to stop 'em. They'd of stuck us to the ground while we was sleepin' if they had a mind to. No sir, Andrew, it ain't all of 'em. Mebbe most of 'em is in on this, but there's some of 'em who ain't. Elsewise they wouldn't wait to make a move."

Tor drew a finger across his throat to make his point. "If they aim to rustle the cattle and kill us all at once, I reckon they'll wait till we're closer to the goldfields. After all, we're still some use for drivin'. Takes lots of men to move a herd like this. They won't want us all dead till they see the end of the trail."

"You figure they aim to steal the herd?"

"Can't figger no other reason why they'd want to pick us off one by one."

"You ought to feel real proud, Tor." I tried to make light of our predicament. "They tried to kill you first. I guess that means they're most scared of you."

He did not smile but surveyed the mass of swaying critters. "It's a matter of cuttin' the wolves out of the pack, Andrew. We got to be mighty careful about now. Don't want to bring down the good 'uns with the rotten apples, if you take my meanin'."

"I can't tell the good ones from the spoilt ones," I said. "And that's what's got me bothered."

We both looked at Alzado at the same instant. There was something menacing in the manner of the Yaqui. His face was a scowl set in leather and stone. He was feared by the others, hated by Gomez.

I opened my mouth to speak, thought better of it, and then blurted out my thought anyway. "He could have let that lion kill me. Saved himself the trouble. That would have been one less of us to do in."

Tor nodded thoughtfully. "I been figgerin' on that one too, Andrew. Don't make no sense . . . except . . . we was only a day's ride from the Reed Rancho. If you'd been kilt, we would have turned back for sure. Taken the herd right back to the rancho. Nope. If Alzado is the leader of the pack of wolves, he's thinkin' like a wolf too. Draw the prey away from the main herd. See? Here we are a hundred miles from Will Reed and his help. You, me, Peter, and three boys. It won't take much when they figger we ain't a use to 'em no more."

I frowned and narrowed my eyes as Alzado whooped and whipped his mount to a gallop to head off another stray. Tor's reasoning made sense. And there was that warning from Gomez that Alzado kept company with bandidos. But what about Gomez? I trusted the groveling little snake even less than I trusted Alzado. "You said Gomez and Alzado got into it the other day?"

"I don't trust neither of them two," Tor muttered. "They wasn't arguin' about how to throw a loop, I'll wager. More likely they was fightin' over when to throw it and whose neck they was goin' to throw it around, if you follow me." He rubbed his neck in a nervous gesture, as though he had already imagined his neck in a noose.

"You think there are any others besides those two?"

"Them two for sure. Well, I'm almost sure. And for the rest of 'em . . . I don't know. I just figger I ain't gonna be sleepin' none too sound till we get these critters checked into somebody else's corral." Tor shook his head. "A new kind of claim jumper. Here in the valley there ain't no law to stop 'em, neither."

Tor patted the stock of his rifle. "Just this kind of law. And I'm keepin' her loaded and ready, too." Now he smiled reproachfully at me. "'Course you gave your Allen rifle to our friend Alzado, didn't you? Love your enemy, Andrew, but don't give 'im your rifle, I always say."

Tor did not have to remind me of my foolish gesture of gratitude. A dozen times that afternoon I found myself regretting that I had traded my rifle for Alzado's knife. I looked down at the smooth antler handle of the weapon protruding from my boot top and then at the stock of the Allen in its sheath on Alzado's saddle. I could not help but wonder if my old Allen might soon be used against me.

CHAPTER 15

We were camped along a nameless creek that wandered down from the high Sierras. The Reed brothers stood first watch while the rest of us gathered in close to the fire and tried to get some sleep after a supper of bacon and beans.

There was not much conversation. These men were mostly strays. Lonesome critters without home or family, they worked on one rancho and then another, never staying long in any set place.

Sometimes their pasts found common ground. Garcia and Sanchez talked softly about a cantina girl named Rosa from down Sonora way. The two men had never met each other before coming to the Reed Rancho, but both had loved Rosa. Both had gotten drunk in that cantina. Both had been beaten and robbed. Could their beloved Rosa have been a part of the plot? This common betrayal somehow made them brothers. They cast around in their memories to compare what other places they might have in common. Nothing. Only Rosa and the Sonora cantina. It was enough for a long conversation. I fell asleep listening to their soft laughter and the crackle of the fire.

When I awoke, all was silent. The blaze had died to embers, and I judged it to be another hour before my watch began. Another hour to sleep, I thought, snuggling deeper into my blanket. I opened one eye and peered toward the orange coals. If I stayed put, the fire would die before Tor's watch was up, and we'd all sleep cold and have cold breakfast in the morning. There was a small heap of dry sticks outside our circle. I hoped that someone else would wake up and stoke the fire, but no one seemed to notice the chill but me.

I pulled my blanket around me and sat up slowly. My boots were drying next to the fire. I picked up the right one, shook it out, and slipped it over my bare foot. Standing, I started to put on my left boot as well. My fingers grasped the upper leather and my toes were just above the opening when I felt the tanned hide tremble and caught a glimpse of something moving—slithering—inside my boot. I gasped, tossed the thing way from me just as the air resounded a bright buzzing like bacon frying.

"Rattler!" I cried, stumbling back as the creature spilled from my boot and coiled on top of it. I had not retreated far enough. The snake fixed its black, evil eyes on my outstretched leg. It buzzed afresh, and every man in the camp lay stock-still and watching.

From across the fire pit Peter Reed whispered in a hoarse voice, "Don't move, Señor Andrew. No one move."

Don't move? I wanted to holler and run for a mile. Yet less than a yard from my big toe that rattler held me prisoner. I dared not speak and held my breath as I watched Peter's shadowed form reach cautiously for his rifle.

Even as I lay there, I knew for certain that the deadly creature had not gotten into my boot without help from some two-legged snake in the camp. I was not supposed to find it until a set of fangs had pierced my foot. Even if I had shaken it out, it would have landed right next to me.

Peter stood slowly and raised his weapon to his shoulder. If he did not split the head of the thing with the first shot, I was still a dead man. Even wounded it would strike me.

The hammer clicked back. Every sound was a threat to the rattler. It moved its flat, hideous head from side to side as if to see which part of my flesh was best to bite. The buzz of its rattles quickened until the air rang of the warning.

All around me I could see the firelight glinting in the eyes of the silent spectators watching me. Which one of them had planned this little performance? Whoever he was, his intent was more vile than that of the snake that faced me now.

"Peter . . . ," James Reed muttered his brother's name fearfully.

Beads of perspiration stood out on my forehead and trickled into my eyes. In an instant I expected to feel the fire of fangs ripping into me. Drawing a slow breath, I silently prayed that the aim of Peter Reed would be true.

The young man's eyes narrowed as he stared at the back of the swaying dark head of the viper. His muscles tensed, then the air exploded with fire and smoke.

The head of the rattler tore away and flew past my face. Its jaws opened and closed as though to strike even though separated from the writhing body. The headless thing flipped and fell across my legs. I shouted and grasped at it, tossing it into the fire where it still struggled in death amid the embers.

Alzado leaped to his feet and, grabbing a stick, rescued the body of the snake from the heat. He laid it belly-up on a rock, cut off the rattles, and tossed them to me like a prize.

"Twelve-button rattle," Alzado said. There was a hint of a smile on his leathery face. He was plainly amused by what had happened. "Keep it for luck."

I was about to say that I needed all the luck I could get when Peter stepped forward. He swept his rifle around at each smiling vaquero until their smirks disappeared. It was his way of saying that he would blow the head off any human snake if the need arose.

The men shrugged or looked away uncomfortably, as though to say they understood.

Alzado skinned the snake and fried the white meat. I did not eat any, but I tied the twelve-button rattle around my neck by a leather string as a reminder that the real snake among us was still alive.

* * *

"Wake up, Andrew!" Tor shook me awake, and believe me, after the experience with the snake, it did not take much.

"What is it?"

"Rodriguez is gone!"

"Gone? What do you mean, gone?"

"Made off with the palomino horse that Gomez rides. Prob'ly the fastest mount here, savin' Shawnee, of course."

"Are you certain he's not around somewhere?"

"Positive. He was s'posed to be the guard that I relieved for the last watch. When I got out there, he was already gone. Well, I just figgered he slipped into camp a little early or I'd missed him on the other side of the drove, but the others say he didn't come back at all."

I eyed my boots with renewed curiosity and touched the rattle tied around my neck. "Do you think that means he's been the one trying to cross us up?"

Tor considered this notion before he said, "Possible, or maybe that's what we're s'posed to think so as to make us let down our guard. Or mayhap he was a good'un run off by fear of the others. Naw, Andrew, I reckon we don't know much more than we did, 'ceptin' now we're short one hand and one powerful fast horse."

Not for the first time I wondered if we needed some help. "Maybe you should ride on ahead and fetch Ames with some more hands," I suggested. "Maybe Rodriguez works for Powers."

Tor shushed me with a look and jerked his chin to the side. There, casually coiling a lariat, but well within earshot, was the brooding figure of Alzado.

✵CHAPTER 16✵

The light in Peter Reed's green eyes danced in the reflected glitter of the stream called Mariposa. The fall air was full of a drifting cloud of orange and black wings.

"Butterflies," he said. A grin marched across his freckled features. "That's the stream's name. My grandfather told me that the old Spanish explorers had never seen so many butterflies as in the meadows on the banks of this place."

"It is an amazing sight," I agreed. "And for those pious men to leave off using the names of saints when they went to make note of this river says that they were very impressed indeed."

We were long past the near calamity and only a few days' travel from our destination. The spirit of high adventure with which the Reed brothers had begun the drive had reasserted itself.

"Thank you, Señor Andrew," Peter said, "for bringing me. I have often imagined this spot but never knew when I might get to see it."

The stream curved around a little oak-topped knoll. The herd settled in to feed on a rich, grassy meadow, while we made our camp on top of the rise. Thousands of butterflies floated into the grove of trees until they clustered on the trunks like a heavy drapery. Peter and I stood and watched as the sun went down and the men gathered for supper.

The vaqueros sat apart and talked among themselves. Tor kept the Reed boys and Joaquin spellbound with his tall tales of life in the mountains. He told them the story of how he had experienced an especially difficult time saddling an uncooperative mule on one extremely foggy night, only to have daylight reveal that he was riding a grizzly bear. I think Joaquin and John, the youngest Reed, believed him.

Our discussion came round to the boys' future plans. Joaquin was excited to learn that John would be returning to school in the kingdom of Hawaii. After just one month in the island kingdom, John assured Joaquin, he would swim like a dolphin and glide his canoe over the sea like a flying fish.

James, the middle brother, would be entering Harvard to study law. "Father says now that California belongs to the United States, we must have at least one in the family who knows Yankee law, and I'm elected."

I turned to Peter, who was watching his brothers with some amusement and yet, I thought, a touch of sadness. "What are your plans, Peter?"

The young man took a deep breath. Before replying, he brushed a hunk of dark red hair off his forehead. "Father says I am to go to the States with James. He says we need more Yankee business sense." Peter sighed heavily.

"And you ain't happy to be goin'?" Tor asked. "Where'd you rather go?"

"Go?" Peter said. "I don't want to leave at all. I love California. It has everything—the seashore, the high mountains, the herds and the rodeos, the places still waiting to be explored. . . . If I live to be a hundred, I could never see it all. I'll go to please Father, but I'll be back to stay."

Peter stood up and unfolded the heavy leather chapederos on which he had been sitting. He buckled them on, readying himself to take his turn as night herder, when Alzado and Sanchez came in.

The Yaqui arrived just as Peter returned from saddling his curly-coated horse. As they entered the circle of firelight, I noticed that the animal was limping.

"Hold on, Peter," I said. "Chino is favoring his near hind hoof."

A quick examination showed no obvious injury, but it was plain that the horse would see no duty that night.

Peter started to lead Chino back to the remuda in order to select another mount when Alzado stopped him. "Take my horse, Don Peter," the Yaqui offered. "We have only walked a little, and he is still fresh."

"*Gracias*, Alzado. Shall we swap the saddles?"

"*No importante.* You are of a height with me. Just take him, if you wish."

It was a couple hours later that the wind blew up out of the east. The fire had died down and everyone was asleep, except Peter and the other night herder, Gomez. As near as I could later figure, Peter had posted himself on Alzado's bay at the north end of the herd. It was a place where the oaks from the knoll drooped to drink with the willows.

The Santa Ana winds blow up out of the eastern deserts of California. They whistle through the mountain passes and down the western slopes, sometimes blowing dust in mile-high clouds. The east wind always makes people and critters restless. Sailors look to their anchor ropes, and herds stir and mill about. Most times the wind dies after a while, and the unease passes.

The wind stirred all of a sudden. From perfect stillness, the night changed to high streaky clouds racing overhead. Clumps of butterflies were ripped off the tree bark. They bumbled in confusion across the pitch-black meadow, colliding with the noses of startled cows.

For all that, there was no great cause for alarm. The herd had done twenty miles that day. They were tired, well fed, and would not be easily roused. A little quiet talking or singing and they would have quieted right down. I know this is true and have thought it over many times through the years.

It was the gunshot that ended all hope of calling things back. Somewhere around the south end of the drove, a rifle exploded. Besides the shattering noise, the flash was like a lightning strike in its brilliance.

How can I picture the awful dread with which a stampede is regarded? I could compare it to an avalanche, to a runaway steam locomotive, or to an earthquake and a tornado rolled into one, but no description is really adequate.

The vaqueros awoke with a rumble that they felt in their souls even before the bellowing roars had penetrated their sleep-muffled hearing. "*El ganado! El ganado!*" they cried. "The cattle!"

At that moment, the expression no longer called to mind a placid, cud-chewing band of stupid animals. From a drowsy jumble of fitful complaints, the herd was transformed into a single beast with four thousand legs and two thousand tossing horns, but only a single thought—to get far away from that terrible blast as quickly and as directly as possible.

Any plan to reach a horse and head off the charging mass of beef was discarded in the same second that it entered the mind. The only idea of any interest was to save oneself any way at all.

I struggled free of the ground sheet in which I was wrapped and saw Joaquin nearby still wrestling to get out of his bedroll. I picked him up, canvas covering and all, tossed him toward the branch of an oak, and yelled, "Climb!"

By the flickers of the dying embers, I saw Tor do the same with John Reed. My attention changed then to the hundred or so head of cattle that seemed to be headed directly for me. Individual hooves could not be heard, nor the bawling of separate throats. All sound massed together in a noise so fearful that one felt overrun and trampled even before the first wave of steers reached the little knoll.

Dodging the fastest of the wild-eyed critters drove me away from the trees that had branches close to the ground. I found myself beside an immense water oak of perhaps sixty-foot height and twenty of girth. It gave me protection from the initial rush, but like a wave that rolls both up and back the beach, a stampede carries away all imagined places of safety that it touches.

Over my head but higher than I could jump, a large snag of a limb jutted out. I always sleep with my coiled blacksnake whip close to hand, and as on other occasions, this habit saved my life. A flick upward looped the whip around the limb, and I shinnied up as I have never climbed before. The spiked tip of an angrily pitching horn gored the calf of my leg, but then I was up and out of harm's way.

From my perch I looked out over a flood tide of steers that trampled bedrolls, belongings, and even the remains of the fire. Smaller trees shuddered and collapsed under the onslaught, and the larger ones resounded from the repeated collisions until it was all one could do to hang on.

Across the meadow over by the stream, the moonlight reflected off the water. Silhouetted against that patch of silver illumination, I saw Peter Reed on the bay horse. He was urging his mount in twisting and corkscrewing, trying to move with the flow of a new peril as he was carried along the creek, but it seemed that he would win free to the far side of the water. Up the steep bank should be safety.

I saw the bay rear and plunge once and then again. I saw Peter's shadow rocking with the jolts of the bucking ride. Then the shapes merged with the great beast called stampede, and I could not see either the horse or the rider anymore.

When the rush had passed, we climbed down from our perches and out of whatever other crevices that had presented themselves as refuges. In the head count around the remains of our camp, all were accounted for except Peter. By some miracle, there were no serious injuries. The hole poked in my leg was typical. There were cuts and bruises in plenty but no broken bones. Being camped on the little hill had saved us, I guess. It had slowed down the charge enough for each of us to find a place of safety.

John cried and begged for us to go looking for Peter. I whispered to Tor what I had seen, and then we told the boys to stay and pick up what they could salvage of the supplies while the adults searched.

Dog was missing, too. Every minute or so, Joaquin would whistle and call for him, but he was nowhere around.

Just before we set out on foot, I saw Tor having words with Gomez. The vaquero was the only one of us still mounted, all the other horses having been run off by the stampede. I could not hear what was said, but I saw Gomez waving his arms, then pointing at the sky, the vanished herd of cattle, his horse, and lastly his rifle.

When Tor rejoined me, he made no comment but shook his head with grim disgust.

Tor and I concentrated on the area closest to where I had caught my last glimpse of Peter. There was a chance that he had gotten into the lee of a downed log or crawled into a hole. Perhaps he was injured or unconscious but alive somewhere.

Even carrying blazing pine knots as torches, we found nothing until almost dawn. We had walked much farther along the stream than I thought was reasonable, but we did not want to turn back while any hope remained. How could we face the boys without knowing?

It was the bay horse that we came to first. Turned broadside to the force of the stampede, the bay had been carried along the creek like a twig on the crest of a flood. The saddle was missing.

A whine reached our ears from just west of the stream. Tor and I broke into a stumbling run. Around the next bend, half hidden by a clump of elderberries on the bank, we came upon Dog. He acknowledged us with another whine but did not come to greet us. He sat very still, his head cocked to one side. One forepaw rested on the lifeless body of Peter Reed.

Rolled up and tied over Tor's shoulder was the largest remaining fragment of his bedroll. After standing a moment in painful silence, we spread out the tarp and wrapped the young man's form to carry back to camp.

"Come along, Dog," I said.

Dog remained by a mound of earth near where he had found Peter.

"Come on," I insisted. "What's the matter with you?"

Dog whined and began to dig into the mound. By the time I looked to see what he was seeking, he had uncovered what was left of Alzado's saddle. The thin light of the Sierra morning answered my question right off: The cinch leather had been cut partway through, high and out of sight.

CHAPTER 17

Murder had been done to Peter Reed, and murder was in my heart for the man who killed him. I slung the scored leather cinch strap over my shoulder to use as evidence in the trial of Alzado. Yet I had determined already that there would be no court, no judge, no jury in this case. I would kill him myself with the same cold-bloodedness he had shown toward young Peter Reed.

Dog trotted alongside as we carried Peter's body back toward camp. Neither Tor nor I spoke for a long while. My thoughts flew to Francesca and Will Reed. All the gold in California could not buy them back their firstborn son! Nineteen years of love and hopes now lay trampled—wrapped in a tarp and slung between us like an empty sack. Will had trusted us with his sons. Francesca's fears had proved right. Three brothers had left home, and now only two would be returning. The sense of my own failure filled me like bitter gall. Alzado would pay for this grief with his own life, I determined.

Tor had come to the same conclusion. "Alzado," he muttered, "lamed the boy's horse and scored the cinch. Same as he done mine before the river crossin'. Put that there rattler in your boot. Peter shot the wrong snake."

I nodded but did not reply. Words failed me as we topped the rise and looked down on the little knoll where James and John Reed waited for news of their brother. They stood side by side, off a ways from the vaqueros and Joaquin. Their backs were toward us. Looking southward, no doubt their thoughts had also turned toward home—to Francesca and Will. I dreaded the instant they would notice us and see the burden we carried with us.

"Gomez!" spat Tor. "Fit for hangin' right along with Alzado. Dropped his gun, he says. Fired off accidental, he says. Spooked the herd. An accident, he says. Well, I say he was in on it with Alzado. Murder. The boy woulda made it if this cinch hadn't been cut. No jury gonna see it otherwise."

Below us, the men were standing, kneeling, or sitting in a tight circle.

"Whoa up there, Andrew," Tor said, and we stopped for a better look. Lowering the body to the ground, we ducked behind a heap of boulders to reconnoiter what we now felt was an enemy camp. "There's Joaquin." The boy sat alone and forlorn on a fallen log. "The Reed boys . . ." Tor frowned. "I count only five vaqueros."

For a few seconds I studied the forms of the men below us. Hats, the slope of shoulders, shirts, and shapes told us that one vaquero, besides Rodriguez, was missing. . . . "Alzado is gone," I said.

"So's that big chestnut Gomez was riding," Tor added. "Our pigeon has flown the coop."

When his oilcloth coat gaped open, it was easy to spot Gomez's bright yellow shirt from among the others. The center of attention, he was sitting on the ground, cradling a bloodstained arm.

"Alzado," I said as hate boiled up in me. "He's stolen Gomez's horse."

"That'll mean he got away with the only rifle that ain't been trampled. Gone to fetch his gang, unless I miss my guess."

If Gomez was part of the conspiracy, why had he been left behind? The framework of facts left much unexplained. Bullwhip on my belt and knife in my boot, I once again hefted Peter's body, and we started the descent into our shattered camp.

It was Joaquin who first spotted our coming. He raised his arm and shouted.

James and John spun around to look, ran a few steps, then froze in the horror of what they saw. Making the sign of the cross, they sank to their knees.

Leaving the wounded Gomez on the knoll, Sanchez, Garcia, Ramos, and Ortiz ran to meet us. All four vaqueros were babbling at once.

"Alzado the Yaqui!"

"He and Gomez—"

"They argue—"

"Alzado pulls a knife!"

"He stabs poor Gomez—"

"He steals Gomez's horse!"

"Alzado is gone, Señor Andrew!"

Ramos and Ortiz offered to carry Peter, but we did not relinquish the body until we reached the knoll. We placed the boy beneath the shade of an oak tree. Joaquin brought a blanket to cover the blood-soaked shroud as James and John held tightly to each other and staggered to Peter's side.

Gomez shouted at me, "I tell you, Señor Andrew." He bellowed and cradled his wounded arm. "I warned you that Alzado is a very bad man! You did not listen to me! I gave you warning!"

Tor whirled on the whimpering toady. "Shut up, Gomez! You ain't in the clear in this affair, neither!"

Gomez puckered his mouth like a petulant child and looked mournfully at his arm. "You do not see I am wounded? Alzado has stolen my horse—no doubt to ride for bandidos who will kill us all and steal the herd!"

Impatient with these cries, Tor snatched the cinch from my shoulder and strode toward Gomez. Grabbing the vaquero up by his shirtfront, he waved the severed leather under his nose. "What do you know about this?"

"Nothing!" cried Gomez in terror.

The other vaqueros stepped back, exchanging fearful looks.

"Nothing?" Tor shook him like a rag doll. "The leather cut nearly clean through. Just like mine was at the river. And it was your gun started the stampede!"

"An accident! I swear, señor! I dropped my gun! It was an accident! No, señor! It is Alzado who is the bandido! Alzado who has done this evil thing! I have nothing to do with Alzado! You see—" he waved his bloody arm like a flag of surrender—"he tells me to get off my horse. He says he is leaving. I fight him, and he stabs me and steals my horse. I am left here wounded. Nearly killed! Can you not see, señor? I have done nothing wrong. I only tried to warn you."

James Reed looked up from the body of his brother. "It happened the way Gomez is telling it," James managed to say. "No explanation from Alzado. At first I thought he was going to ride after the remuda. But he rode out of here like lightning and didn't come back. Like Gomez told it."

Tor scowled into the terrified face of Gomez and gave him one more shake, sending him sprawling onto the ground. I heard Tor mutter in a menacing voice, "Mebbe it's so and mebbe it ain't, you little worm. Fact is, 'twas your gun what started the stampede. I'll get back to that later."

James looked hard at the cinch, then at the covered remains of Peter. "Ah, Peter," he choked, "what will I say to Mother? What will I tell Father?"

With Alzado gone, fled on Gomez's horse, we were completely without mounts. That thought alone was enough to rekindle the flame of hatred I felt for the treacherous Yaqui. How were we to begin recovering from the disaster of the stampede and Peter's tragic death? Regardless of what else we may have sensed, the answer in practical terms was "on foot."

I dispatched the vaqueros to search for our horses. Things would level out some once we were remounted, but there was no telling how far the animals might have run in the terror of the night.

Gomez started to whine about how his arm was hurting him, but I gave him no slack on that account. I knew the wound to be minor, no matter his complaints, and sent him out with the rest.

What came next was harder still. James and John were still gathered around the canvas containing the body of their brother. Joaquin stood awkwardly by, unable to speak but unwilling to leave his friends. James looked up at my approach.

"The first three horses we recover are yours," I said. "No matter whose they are, they are yours to take Peter home. I'll send one of the vaqueros or Tor along."

Tor nodded.

"Take Peter home," James repeated hollowly. "Yes, we need to do that. He'll be buried next to Grandfather."

"I'm more sorry than I can say, boys. Peter was just telling me yesterday how glad he was to be here, but I wish now we had turned back at the first sign of trouble."

John sniffed. "When I got scared and wanted to go home, Peter told me not to be a baby. He said being a quitter would shame Father. Peter would never have left without finishing the drive."

"Well," I said simply, "we can't always control how things turn out. If it wasn't that I need to see to saving the rest of the herd for your father, I'd throw in the hand now, too."

"No!" James said sharply. "We're not throwing in this hand!"

"Now, James," I began, "nobody expects—"

"No!" he said again, cutting me off. "We are here in Father's place, and I'm the oldest now, so I decide. I say our job is helping with the herd and catching up to Alzado. Father would be disappointed with anything less."

"But, boys, what about Peter? And your parents need to be told."

James shook his head decisively. "What's done can't be changed, so our folks don't have to hear about Peter till they also hear that we did what was needed. Besides, Peter liked this spot. It's a good enough resting place for now."

Tor, James, and I fashioned crude shovels from tree branches. We dug into a sandy space in the south side of the hill that was overhung by an earthen bank. Joaquin and John found two straight sticks, and these they bound together in the form of a cross by using leather strips salvaged from the remnants of busted reins.

We arranged Peter Reed's body in the cutout under the overhang and collected some rocks with which to cover the spot.

When all was ready, James hesitated when his little brother said, "I don't know, James. We don't have a priest. What if this isn't holy ground?"

James looked around at the sky and the giant, patient oaks, then listened for a moment to the scolding call of a blue jay. "This is right. God is here, even if a priest isn't."

Slanting beams of sunlight brightened the hillside as we dug into the bank, collapsing it over the grave. We rolled the granite rocks atop the place, and when it was neat, John and Joaquin set up the cross.

"Now," James said, "where do we begin tracking Alzado?"

CHAPTER 18

James was right. We could not linger around Peter Reed's grave. Already it was time to think of finding the horses and the herd. Attending to business, so to speak.

Folks fresh from the States or other civilized countries often believe that we of the West are short of a normal set of human emotions. We are described as unfeeling by those with more sheltered lives.

Let me record that such a charge is a slanderous lie. Unless a Westerner is a hardened criminal or has abused liquor, he has no lack of feelings. Nor have our sensibilities been blunted. It is necessity that drives us to set aside emotions and press on.

I put the boys to work collecting all the remnants of provisions and tack. Now every morsel of jerked beef and every scrap of bridle was precious.

Tor and I cobbled together pieces of reins and strips of leather cut from trampled saddles. We were making *jaquimas*, bridle pieces, which the gringos call hackamores, that would work without bits by pressure on the horses' noses and jaws.

Around noon the vaqueros returned, having located neither mounts nor steers. They were a footsore lot—walking far in high-heeled, pointed-toed boots was never done for pleasure.

I watched Gomez flop down with his back against an oak. So he could sit without his pistol grip pressing into his gut, he pulled it from his belt and laid it beside him.

Gomez called Joaquin to him. The boy had recovered a stuff sack full of jerky and was distributing the dried meat to the men. The vaquero gestured for the boy to come closer, then spoke something to him. I saw Joaquin's limbs grow stiff and his spine turn rigid, as if he was hearing something that terrified him.

I wanted to go immediately and find out what was up but decided to speak to the boy privately first. I poked idly about in the dirt, as if I were recovering something of use. To my surprise, there in the dust were two small fragments of Bible pages. My copy of the Good Book, which had traveled with me for more years than I could recall, now was torn to shreds and scattered. I stuffed the fragments of paper into my pockets without looking at them.

After Joaquin completed his rounds to all the vaqueros, I joined him near the fire. "What did he say to you?" I asked.

"Who, Señor Andrew?" Joaquin spoke as if he did not take my meaning, but his eyes flickered toward where Gomez lay.

"What are you afraid of, Joaquin? What did he say to you?"

Again his frame stiffened, and he glanced quickly at the vaquero who was toying idly with his pistol. The bandaged knife wound did not seem to be causing Gomez any great distress.

"He said that we must hurry to find the horses. He says that Alzado has most certainly gone for the rest of Jack Powers's gang, and they will be returning to kill us and steal the herd."

I listened to the last sentence as I was already walking away from Joaquin over to Gomez's relaxed form. "Gomez," I called out, "what do you know of Powers? What are you hiding?"

"I? I am not hiding anything, señor," he said innocently. "I have heard it said that Alzado, the cursed savage, belongs to an outlaw band whose leader is the American Powers. If it is true, señor, it will mean much trouble for us."

Settled some by this explanation, I demanded, "But why frighten the boy? Why didn't you tell me directly?"

Gomez shrugged. "It is only hearsay, señor. I was just telling the muchacho of the great need to hurry and locate the horses. Perhaps he is easily frightened because of the stampede."

I reached down and grasped Gomez by the arm. I will admit that

I took hold of the wrist on the wounded side on purpose. With one yank I stood the vaquero upright, spilling his pistol from his lap and his jerky into the dirt.

"You're exactly right about the need to hurry," I said. "Bring your food. You and I will go search together, and you can tell me all you know or have heard."

Gomez could not very well refuse a direct order from the boss, no matter how tired he was. He made a great show of wincing when he touched his injured arm, but he tramped along out of the camp by my side.

I whistled for Dog to join us, and we three set out. I carried one of our improvised bridles and Gomez carried another.

Once unleashed, Gomez's tongue babbled like the stream beside which we hiked. "There is much I know of Alzado, señor, but much more that is spoken of Jack Powers around the cantinas of the City of the Queen of the Angels, Los Angeles. Powers has used his skill at cards to gain enough money to hire some very bad men. It is said that he will soon rule the gold camps, far from any law that could touch him."

I nodded grimly at the remembrance of how Jack Powers had made himself out to be the law. "Go on."

"This Powers has men who rob and kill along El Camino Real. He has those in the cantinas who report of who has much gold, and soon—" Gomez drew his thumb across his neck and made throat-cutting noises.

"And Alzado?" I asked. "Why an Indian vaquero?"

Gomez looked around as if he expected to see the Yaqui lurking behind a tree. "Powers is very clever. He knows he must have fresh horses with which his malditos may flee their crimes. On each rancho of renown, he keeps those who will steal the best mounts."

I looked down at the knife hilt showing above my boot top. To think of the cutthroat Yaqui around Will and Francesca's home made me shudder . . . almost as bad as the thought of how far he had ridden with me being unaware of his nature.

Dog had been ranging along on either side of us as we hiked. At my command he would explore branching side canyons and dive into thickets. He had on this occasion been out of sight long enough, and I whistled for him to return.

Imagine my delight when instead of Dog's recall, my signal was acknowledged by a bugle from Shawnee. Through the manzanita she came, sorrel and white flashing, leading a band of six horses with her. Her tail was flagged, and she was obviously proud of herself.

"So that's what kept you," I said, rubbing her nose. "You stopped to gather your friends."

My paint mare willingly accepted the unfamiliar bridle, while Gomez had somewhat more difficulty with his mount. "Drive these others back to camp," I said as the vaquero finished wrestling with the *jaquima.* "I'll have another look round for the cattle."

But where had Dog gotten off to? With Shawnee beneath me again, even though we were minus a saddle, things felt a lot better. I pointed Shawnee straight up the highest hill I could see close by in order to survey the countryside.

When we reached shale rock, we wound around the cone-shaped peak, spiraling upward till we emerged above the tree line. There below us was spread the terrain of the Sierras, like a map in a geography book. Looking south I could see the little knoll where we had camped and where Peter Reed now lay buried.

My eyes traced the wandering path of the creek to the point where Tor and I had discovered Peter's body and still farther to where I had met up with Shawnee. I probed beyond that point, searching for the shapes of the cattle and for Dog.

The afternoon sun glared on granite and sand, making it difficult to see. I nudged Shawnee forward a few paces, then shaded my eyes. There was a particular side canyon I was interested in because of a familiar coyote shape that crouched in the narrow throat of the arroyo.

"Now, why would he . . . ?" I mused aloud.

A single cloud of no great size drifted obligingly across the sun. As the glare faded, the back wall of the box canyon jumped into high relief. Standing out against the granite walls were the dark forms of hundreds of cattle, milling about within the confines of the little valley and guarded by the patient watchfulness of Dog.

CHAPTER 19

I have heard it said that one of the cruelest tortures wrought upon man is to deprive him of sleep for long periods of time. Tor and I had not allowed our eyes to close for almost forty-eight hours. While the others slept and worked in shifts, we dared not rest. The menacing thought of Jack Powers was always before us. How long did we have before Alzado reached Powers with the news of our approach? How long before Powers and his henchmen rode out to greet us? Although we were forced to depend on the remaining vaqueros, we dared not trust them.

By the light of our second campfire, the sleepless days and hours closed in on us.

"You're done up, Andrew," Tor said in a low voice as he sat beside me on a log.

"That I am." I could not argue. "And so are you, pard." Tor's eyes were ringed with dark circles. "You look like you've been hit in the face with a board."

He managed a faint smile. "You ain't gonna win no beauty prizes, neither."

We both looked over our sleeping comrades with envy. Gomez and Ortiz stood watch over the herd now. Tor was set to join them, while I was to remain watchful here at the camp for two hours and then exchange places with Tor at midnight.

Tor rubbed his hand wearily over his eyes and gave his head a shake as if to clear away the grogginess. He muttered, "We ain't gonna be no use to nobody if we don't get some shut-eye. Why don't you sleep here a couple hours, Andrew? I'll wake you at the end of my watch, and you can take lookout while I sleep. Long as one or the other of us is out with the herd and keepin' guard, it don't make no sense that the other one of us can't rest a bit."

It was not so much the herd we were watching but the vaqueros. We both knew that. We trusted no one, even though we needed their help. Could it hurt if one of us slept for a bit as long as the other was alert?

In my muddled brain Tor's offer made sense. I nodded, but I do not remember speaking to him. Sinking down, I let my head rest against the log. Tor dropped a tattered blanket on me, and I called Dog to come lie beside me. I closed my eyes with the knowledge that four-footed critters like Dog have some God-given sense that lets them be on guard even as they sleep. At the first whiff of danger my shaggy companion would alert me. One hand closed around the handle of my knife. The other rested on the ruff of Dog's neck. I was lost in profound sleep before Tor took his first step out of camp.

The sounds of the night mingled with my dreams. Far away I heard the nighttime bawling of cattle, and I dreamed myself riding among them. . . .

I sat in my saddle. The Allen rifle was ready across my thighs. Shawnee moved effortlessly as I urged her around the perimeter. Then it was daylight, and somehow I was back in Santa Barbara on the Reed Rancho. Will Reed waved at me from where he rode on the far side of the herd.

Peter was next to him on the curly-coated Chino. Sunlight glinted on his dark red hair, and he turned his face full toward me and smiled. How good and true it seemed to be herding the cattle with the boy again!

"Buenos dias, *Peter!" I called and felt myself smile.*

Suddenly the vision changed. I raised my eyes to see a rider approaching behind Peter. Dust rose like smoke from a vast fire behind the galloping bay. I strained to see who it was coming on so fast! A sense of dread filled me as I recognized the shape of Alzado and saw him bring the Allen rifle up to his shoulder and take aim. I tried to shout a warning to Peter. I tried to call out the attacker's name. I reached for the Allen and realized with horror that I had given my rifle to Alzado! The fierce Yaqui now held Peter and me in the sights of my own gun!

"Look behind you!" I heard the cry.

Was it my voice shouting the alarm to Peter? Was I calling for the boy to face the Indian?

I opened my mouth. No sound escaped. In that instant I realized that it was Alzado who was shouting. Not to Peter Reed but to me. Peter dissolved into a bloody, broken mass before my eyes!

"Look behind you, Señor Andrew!" screamed Alzado. "Turn! Turn! Open your eyes!"

I turned at his urging and saw the grinning face of Gomez on the hill behind me. Beside Gomez were the other vaqueros in a line. They parted, and Jack Powers rode out to lead them.

The earth rumbled, and I heard the low growl of Dog. I felt the warning of his snarl beneath my hand.

"Look behind you!" The voices of Peter and Alzado joined as one.

The dream erupted into reality as Dog leaped to his feet barking at the perimeter of the camp. My eyes snapped open.

"Look behind you!" shouted James Reed, tangled in his bedroll.

I scrambled for my Allen, then realized once again what was real and what was vision. Faces came into focus. I heard the hammer of a pistol click and whirled to see the bloody form of Tor Fowler as he was shoved forward to fall at my feet.

From the shadows, the smirk of Gomez caught the firelight. He leveled his pistol at my gut, then waved it at the bared fangs of Dog.

"Do not shoot!" cried Joaquin. "You promised if I did not tell you would not kill—"

Gomez laughed at the boy and at the shocked look in my eyes. "Did I say such a promise?"

Dog barked and made as if to lunge.

"Dog!" I commanded and with a gesture sent the animal back into the gloom of the brush.

Gomez fired once, but I heard the chapparal cracking as Dog retreated. He had not been hit.

Tor lay in the dust and raised his head. "Andrew . . . ," he moaned. "Sorry . . . pard . . . I dozed and they—"

Ortiz kicked him hard in the belly, silencing him.

Gomez sneered more broadly as the other vaqueros joined him, holding each of the boys in their gun sights. Ramos had the look of a man ashamed. Ortiz and Sanchez took pleasure in our helplessness.

Joaquin clasped his hands together and dropped to his knees to beg for our lives. "I did as you told me, Gomez! I did not tell Señor Andrew!"

Ortiz leaned over and slapped the boy hard across the face, sending him sprawling back with a cry of pain.

"Enough!" I shouted.

Gomez replied with a pistol shot aimed between my feet. "You are in no position to say what is enough," he said with amusement. He smoothed his thin mustache and shoved his sombrero back on his head in a self-assured gesture. "You have never been in a position to say what was enough. That privilege has always been mine. Only you did not know it, Señor Andrew." He bowed in a mocking way.

"Alzado?" I asked.

"The fierce Yaqui?" Gomez laughed. "A spineless coward, that one, *mi amigo.* He would not join us. I spoke to him early about our little business arrangement. He refused to be a part of it."

"And so it was you who cut his cinch."

Again the mocking bow and the smile that told everything. "A shame Don Peter got in the way. Ah, well. One less to worry about."

"Murderer!" Young John Reed lunged at Gomez as James tried to hold him back.

With one blow, Sanchez knocked the boy unconscious, and he slumped to the ground.

"You are the leader of these children," Gomez said. "Silence them, or the next one will die." His fingers were white around the pistol grip. "I am growing weary of the game." He was not bluffing.

"Keep still," I issued the order quietly. A sense of my own foolishness filled me. I had been ready to lynch Alzado, who was the only man among seven vaqueros who had done no harm! Now the five who remained held guns to our bellies while Gomez painted the whole picture.

"This one." Gomez waved the gun at Tor, who remained unconscious. "*Sí.* A broken cinch? I have no taste for murder, you see. But a faulty cinch? What is that but carelessness? An accident. I can take no blame that he did not check. Accidents. I drop my gun and the herd stampeded. It was not I who caused Peter Reed to fall." He looked at James as the boy stared at him with unguarded hatred.

It was plain to me that in spite of his claims to not be a murderer, Gomez planned all along to murder us and take the herd. He had used us much in the way we had used him in order to move the herd close to the northern gold camps. Now our usefulness was at an end.

"You Americanos," he continued, "you steal all of California from us." He nodded toward his compatriots, and I knew this speech was meant for them as much as for us prisoners. "You steal the land. You steal the gold. You steal the cattle. No? Now we Californios take back the cattle. Just a few, señor." Gomez's face broke into a vermin's smile. "And then we will have a little of the gold, too. A small herd. Don Will Reed is a great man. He will hardly miss one thousand head; is this not so?"

"He will not care for a thousand head of cattle . . . but if his sons are harmed, I know Don Will Reed will hunt you like a dog and see you hang for this," I replied. Then, glancing at the others, I added, "He will not rest until you are all dangling from an oak tree to rot at the end of a noose."

Such words had the effect I wished. The vaqueros looked fearfully at one another and then at Gomez.

"I had nothing to do with the death of Peter Reed!" cried Ramos.

"We care only for the herd. For the gold," declared Ortiz gruffly. "We have nothing to do with the killing of men."

James cradled the head of his brother. "My father will see you all dead for what happened to Peter!"

"An accident!" Gomez spread his too-soft hands in protest. "I tell you it was no more than that! Meant to get Alzado out of the way!"

James opened his mouth as if to accuse again. I silenced the boy with a sharp look. Here was our only hope.

"*Sí,*" I agreed with Gomez. "Yes. No one can argue that. You meant no harm to poor Peter. An accident. You could not have known. Will Reed is a man of reason. For the lives of his sons and his friends, he would gladly offer you this ransom of one thousand beeves. What is that to him, Gomez? As long as we are set free. Unharmed."

I directed my words to the other vaqueros who seized upon the lesser crime of rustling as though it was nothing compared to murder. What were a few cattle of a rich man, after all? Will Reed would not mind so much, would he? Not so long as James and John and Will Reed's friends were safe.

They began babbling at once to Gomez that they wanted no part in murder. Don Will Reed was a powerful man. He would not forgive harm done to his sons. The bandits united against the unspoken threat of our deaths. Gomez had lost the fight by his own argument that he was not a killer . . . merely a Californio patriot taking back what rightly belonged to other Californios!

I did not bring up the fact that the brigand he worked for was one of the American soldiers who had fought against the Californios with violence that defied description. No need to bring up the origins of Jack Powers now. Our captors somehow believed that they might escape justice by leaving us unharmed! The truth was that every last one of them would be hunted and captured and brought to justice. Inwardly I memorized the features of each face and the sound of each voice as I vowed that I would lead the hunt one day. For the time being, though, our lives were spared.

"I am no assassin, *mi amigo*," Gomez demurred again. He shrugged. "That is not to say I will not shoot out your knees if you resist me now." He motioned with the gun. "Sit down. Take your boots off." I obeyed, and he gestured broadly. "Yes. That's it. All of you. Take your boots off. *Sí.* And the boots of Tor Fowler, if you please, señor?"

Our boots were thrust into a sack and tied to a horse. "Even used boots are worth something in the gold camp, I hear." Gomez laughed. "I shall sell them at a good price, to be sure."

After this he and his gang bound our wrists together tightly—and our ankles—with leather thongs. Then they separated us, tying each of us with our back to our own tree so we could not help one another escape. Tor moaned and opened his eyes as Gomez mounted his horse and raised his arm in a rigid gesture of contempt.

"*Hasta la vista,* Americanos." Gomez laughed. "By the time you get free or are found, we will be rich men and long gone! *Gracias, amigos*! I shall think of you with amusement in days to come!"

Sunlight topped the jagged peaks of the Sierras as dust from the departing herd blended with the violet haze of dawn.

CHAPTER 20

I counted it a miracle that the five of us were still alive. But we were in need of another miracle—and soon. Trussed up like calves at a branding, barefoot, and unarmed, there was no guarantee that we would not die here. I imagined some future traveler stumbling upon these five oak trees and five human skeletons grinning back.

My legs had no feeling below the knees. My fingers had gone numb right off, leaving it impossible for me to attempt to work the knot. No doubt the bandits had tied us with tourniquet-like tightness for this reason. What good would it do for us to have been left alive, only to die of starvation and thirst? Gomez, while claiming he was not a murderer, was killing us slowly by the same methods I had seen among the cruel Mojave Indians of the high desert. Left like this, we were dead men all the same without some help.

Tor became conscious and realized our predicament. I was at the top of the knoll, and he was at the bottom, facing the broad view of the valley. He could not see any of the rest of us. We were all scattered across the slope. "Anybody there?" he called.

A chorus of voices replied.

"Andrew."

"James."

"John."

And then a voice filled with remorse. "Joaquin."

"That's good," Tor's voice rang out. "Nice day ain't it, Andrew?" It was good to hear humor in Tor's voice. At least the thieves had not knocked that out of him.

"I've been sitting here thinking how glad I am it's not too hot," I shouted back.

"You're right on that score. I'm sittin' about a yard from a red anthill. On a hot day they'd be comin' out to take some sun and a piece of my hide, I reckon. Ain't but a few of the little beggars out on a day like this. They ain't got a whiff of me yet, neither."

I had also noticed a large anthill just spitting distance from my bare feet. In the cold morning air, the critters were barely moving. As the day warmed, I knew they would emerge a thousand strong.

A moment later John called out that there was a colony to the right of where he was sitting, and James reported a nest of yellow jackets just above where he was tied. Joaquin said nothing at all until I called to him.

"You got any mean little animals keeping you company, Joaquin?"

A long pause. "I wish I will die and all of you go free," he replied with such misery that I felt grieved for him. Then the explanation gushed from him. "Gomez said he would not kill you if I did not tell what I heard him say about Jack Powers. He promised. That day I shot at you, it was because he pointed up and said, 'Look quick, boy! There is the bandido Powers coming; shoot him quick!' And then I shot because I wanted to kill Powers, and Gomez slapped me. Later he said if I tell you the truth, he will slit your throat in the night. But now we are tied like hogs and left for the ants to eat when the sun gets hot. I pray that I will suffer more. I pray that I will die and you all will get free before the day grows warm and the ants come awake! May God send His angels to set you free!"

I will admit that there are a few things that make me angrier than a grown man who will threaten and bully a helpless animal, a woman, or a young'un. Gomez had not only shot at my dog, he had threatened and bullied a boy I had taken in as my own. How many days and miles had young Joaquin carried the burden of terror that we would be massacred in our sleep if he spoke up about what he knew?

And now, on top of it, Joaquin carried the weight of guilt that was too heavy for his young soul. This was more brutal than the sting of a whip for a child. Most young'uns don't know that there's a big difference between a mistake in judgment and sin.

Tor spoke up a bit too cheerful for our situation. "Well, it ain't no mortal sin that you tried to keep us from gettin' our fool throats slit, boy. I ain't dead yet, and neither are you. I don't aim to be the main course in no red-ant picnic neither. How 'bout you, Andrew?"

"Nope." Then I added, "Don't let it trouble you, Joaquin. I'd of done the same."

This last was true. I remembered clearly how at the age of twelve I had been bullied by a brigand who threatened the lives of those I loved most in the world. If we got free from this mess, I would tell Joaquin of my own experience at his age and how a man had died because of my mistake.

"Gomez won't get away with this," I told Joaquin. "And you know I don't make idle promises."

No matter how brave I sounded, the thought came to me that maybe Gomez *had* gotten away with it and maybe I *was* making idle promises. The sun rose higher, and the little mound of sand came alive with parades of red worker ants, heading off to search for food.

My feet and calves were numb, so I watched with a sort of detached horror as the first insect crawled out from between my big toe and my second toe. A horde followed, climbing the bottom of my foot and swarming through my toes like warriors breaching the top of a fortress wall. Tiny pinpricks of pain penetrated the numbness, and right before my eyes, my feet and ankles became a mass of red welts.

Moments after the first assault, John shouted that the ants near him were moving his way. When James gave a sharp cry of pain, we knew that he had been stung. The knoll, carefully chosen to provide a painful death for us, was coming alive.

I closed my eyes and prayed for some miracle—some avenging angel to fly our way and set us free!

No avenging angel came with flamed sword to slice our bonds. Most times the Lord does not work that way. Miracles come as ordinary messengers. Ours came that day in the form of my half-coyote dog who trotted up the knoll and whined and wagged and licked my face. Behind him followed a stiff, cold breeze, and on the wind floated the first dark tide of rain clouds.

I cannot say what understanding the grinning stock dog had of our predicament, but he licked a row of ants off my right foot and then tugged at the rawhide reata that held my ankles.

"Yes!" I cried. "Good dog!"

My praise disrupted him, and he stood and wagged and wandered up to lick my face. I inwardly upbraided myself, closed my eyes, and ignored him. Some other voice was speaking to his critter mind, and I knew I must not interfere with its instructions.

Another whine came as Dog sat down to consider me. With my hands bound in front on me and the reata encircling me and the tree, I must have been a curious sight in his yellow eyes. He licked my arm again, and as his tongue rubbed over the rope, he paused, bumped against me, and began to gnaw at the braided leather in earnest.

The sky darkened with the troop of storm clouds.

I heard Tor give a whoop of delight. "I felt a drop! By gum, Andrew! A raindrop!"

I dared not reply for fear of breaking the intense concentration of Dog. He was tugging and chewing the leather with the same enjoyment he might have gotten from a T-bone steak.

"Rain!" cried James.

"I felt it on my face!" shouted John. "Look there! The ants!"

No word came from Joaquin as those few light drops were joined by more and still more.

I opened my eyes as the dry leaves rattled in the oak limbs above me. With pleasure I saw drops splash down on the frantic red horde as they scurried back toward the gravel hill like an army in retreat.

My red, swollen feet and ankles were washed clean of my tormentors! Thunder erupted, and lightning flashed behind the mountain.

Dog paused, looked up, and returned to his work as though his only aim in life was to chew through that tough hide rope.

"Andrew?" Tor called to me. "Andrew!" He demanded an answer.

"Shut up!" I shouted.

Dog smiled at me and crunched his teeth, tugging as the leather frayed and weakened.

He seemed to be wondering why I did not help him. Could I not fight against the loop and break free? his look asked me. My arms were bloodless, dead. It would take me a while to move, I knew, even when I was loose from this hold.

I leaned my head back against the rough trunk of my prison and squeezed my eyes tight. I prayed as I had not prayed before in my life. For God's mercy not only to me but to Tor and the boys. The raindrops broke with the thunder into a downpour, clattering through the branches, drenching me and my fur-covered angel. The rawhide dampened. Dog tugged harder, chewed more fervently, pulled back in a tug-of-war until the reata yielded at last with a sharp snap.

With a cry, I toppled over in the mud. My hands and ankles were still bound with leather strips but I was free of the tree. Dog stood over me, nosing me as if to ask why I did not stand.

"Tor!" I shouted after another thunderclap. "Dog has chewed away the reata! I can't move. Got no feeling in my arms or legs."

Another crash of thunder drowned out his exultant reply.

I lay on my side and eyed a small puddle forming as my arms and legs began the excruciating ache of blood rushing to my limbs. And now the fire of the ant bites took hold. I gasped and groaned while Dog patiently licked my wounds and waited.

The heaviness of my limbs dissipated, and I suddenly felt the soothing coldness of the rain and the roughness of Dog's tongue. I moved my legs and scooted toward the mud puddle. Thrusting my hands and wrists into the mire, I began to work the leather. It stretched and swelled with moisture; at last it yielded, and my hands slipped free.

With fumbling fingers I freed the knots of rawhide at my ankles. Then I grasped the trunk of the oak and managed to pull myself erect on unsteady legs. A moment more of agony broke as the full force of sensation flooded back. Then I gratefully raised my eyes heavenward and knew that what was just a sudden squall for another man was my miracle! What might be a hungry dog chewing through leather, to someone else's thinking, was for me the mighty hand of the Lord!

I stumbled to unloose Tor. Then I raced to free Joaquin, who was bound with my black bullwhip. Tor untied James and John, who half crawled, half stumbled toward me.

We all embraced. We cheered Dog and thanked heaven for the rain.

And we helped each other to the mint patch by the creek bed to doctor our ant bites.

CHAPTER 21

Cold water from the stream and the crushed mint leaves soothed the searing sting of our bites. But there was no remedy to cool the burning anger we each felt toward the men who had deceived us and left us to die.

Still, I felt the obligation for the safety of the Reed brothers and for young Joaquin. We were without weapons and on foot. What chance would two men and three boys have against five armed vaqueros with a talent for ruthless cruelty?

The settlement called Tuleberg was several days' hike from where we were stranded. We would take the boys there for safety; then Tor and I could set out alone to track Gomez. I laid out this plan to the boys as we rigged makeshift moccasins out of a discarded cowhide and a torn saddle blanket left behind by the gang.

James Reed raised his chin proudly, and I saw the determination of his father burning in his eyes. "If we go to Tuleberg, we will lose the herd."

"'Pears to me we already lost the herd, boy," Tor said, sucking on a mint leaf and rubbing his legs.

James turned on Tor angrily. "They killed Peter. Stole my father's cattle. Left us to die! By some miracle we are not only alive but well and strong—"

"And angry," added young John. "I could not look Father in the eye again if we let them get away with this!"

"You youngsters don't understand. It seems to me—," Tor began.

He was savagely interrupted by the fury of James. "No! It is you who do not understand! We can beat them!"

"They have our guns." I tried to calm the boy. "Our horses."

"We have more than they would have if they were an army with cannons!" James cried with clenched fists.

Tor and I exchanged doubtful looks. "James—"

"We are stronger than they!" said Joaquin, joining against our better judgment.

"Yes! Stronger!" John leaped to his feet. "They cannot win! Will not win!"

"We are unarmed," Tor argued. "I don't aim to take you boys home to your mama in a sack, and that's final."

James narrowed his eyes and considered Tor. "You are a coward, Tor Fowler!" he said in a level voice.

This was a foolish thing to say to Tor. I have known the mountain man to knock the teeth out of a man for a lot less than those words.

"Whoa up there, James," I said.

Then the boy turned to me. "And you are a coward, Andrew Sinnickson! You spit in the eye of God if we do not go after Gomez and the others!"

"Spit in the eye!" Tor declared, puffing up like a bullfrog. "Why you little whelp pup! I ought to—"

"He is right, Señor Tor." Joaquin jumped into the fray. "Angels bring the rain to save us! Dog, who is a smart dog, but all the same he is still a dog . . . he chews through the rope! We are free. It is a miracle. Any priest will say it is so. Now you want to run away."

"Not run," I fumed. "Get you boys safe, that's all."

"It is our fight as much . . . no . . . more than yours!" James insisted. "It is my brother who lies buried in Mariposa." He fished a rumpled paper from his pocket, unfolded it to reveal a page from my Bible, and held it up. "I found this. I took it for a sign. For a promise."

He began to read the words from the fragment. "'For who is God, save the Lord? And who is a rock, save our God? God is my strength and power . . .'" James looked up. "It's torn there, but see the rest of it." He gave it to me to read.

I studied the ragged slip a moment and then read aloud what

remained. "'He teacheth my hands to war; so that a bow of steel is broken by mine arms. Thou hast also given me the shield of Thy salvation; and Thy gentleness hath made me great. Thou hast enlarged my steps under me; so that my feet did not slip.'" I swallowed hard and then finished the passage. "'I have pursued mine enemies and destroyed them; and turned not again until I had consumed them.'"

It was here that the page was torn away. I passed the fragment to Tor, who reread the words silently as James Reed stared me down like the shepherd boy David must have shamed the men who said no one could beat Goliath.

"Well, then." Tor blinked at me and then stared at James as if he were seeing the boy in a new light. "I'll be . . ."

"They're just men," James replied firmly. "And dark sinners at that. What hope do they have when they're in the wrong? And how can we turn away when we're in the right? I got to tell you. If I strike out from this place alone, I'm going to do it! There it is . . . the word from God Himself. Isn't it? You think it's just an accident I found that? The rain and the dog? Just coincidence? Right is right and wrong is wrong. And there's a God who knows the difference. Father always taught us boys that this was true."

"That's right," agreed John.

"So you go to Tuleberg if you want," James said, putting his arms around the shoulders of Joaquin and John. "We three are striking out to take back what's ours. If we do not, then no honest man in all of California will be safe! We stop it here, or there will be no stopping it!"

It would have been easy enough, I suppose, for Tor and me to wallop the lot of them, tie them up, and drag them to safety, but the truth was that we two grown men were shamed and instructed by what they said. Two unarmed men and three boys taking back eight hundred head of cattle from an armed gang would be some sort of warning to others who might live by murdering and stealing over honest employment . . . if we did indeed succeed in such a desperate gamble. Could I now discount what I had considered a miracle when I was set free? Could I doubt that God was watching over us? helping us when we were helpless yet expecting us to also do our part in the drama?

These were matters far beyond my understanding and my ability to wholly believe. For what we were about to do seemed so impossible, yet with God nothing was impossible. I knew that what James said was true. Right was right and wrong was wrong.

Deep down I believed that the battle of Good and Evil was an ancient war fought in the fields of men's eternal souls. Many times Evil triumphed simply because good men backed down or turned away or gave up in the face of difficult odds. James Reed did not say all these things out loud, but I heard them as clearly as if the boy had preached a sermon. He, like a young shepherd boy named David, was willing to face what I perceived to be a Goliath simply because he believed unshakably that Good must prevail over Evil.

James retrieved the thin leaf of paper from Tor and returned it to his breast pocket. "If I am killed, Señor Andrew—" he leveled his green eyes on me—"take this to my father. Tell him I died believing this. Tell him I fought like a man." He turned his gaze to the hills. "I could never go home and tell him I ran away from the men who killed Peter."

CHAPTER 22

The owl hoot was low and mournful sounding. Its aching tone brought to my mind a hollowed-out old snag of an oak that stood on the bluff above the Cherokee camp where I grew up. There had been a great horned owl who lived in that snag. Its call had been a beacon from far across the prairie.

The difference was this night owl I knew by name. It was Tor Fowler, and the signal meant that he was in position.

That we had caught up to the rustlers in one day and half a night had more to do with good fortune and divine Providence than how fleet-footed we were. Truth to tell, our feet were sore, and only periodic stops to reline our improvised moccasins with moss and crushed mint leaves kept us going.

When I had spotted the herd from the tall pinnacle, I had not only seen the box canyon but had located another feature of interest as well. This second observation I had not shared with anyone until after the theft of the herd.

It seems that the wandering course of the streambed and the track by which the cattle would be moved curved around the range of hills. By hard hiking and climbing, we five were able to cross the narrow range and traverse in three miles what the herd would cover in ten.

That still left us miles behind, but we never slackened our pace. We knew that with only five vaqueros to handle eight hundred head, they would not be moving any too fast.

We were right. By midnight we were close enough to see the glow of their campfire. At three in the morning by the set of the stars, we were almost ready.

The biggest worry in our plan was right at the beginning. We figured they would have two sentried on the lookout. A loud yell or a gunshot fired by either of them would bring the other three boiling out of their camp. Their pistols would be too much for our fists unless we could even the score some first. "The problem," as Tor phrased it as we had hiked and plotted, "is how to separate what would likely be two snakes from their fangs without wakin' up the rest of a nest of vipers."

On the far side of the grassy plain, Tor, James Reed, and Dog were watching the movements of a night herder. Even though I could not see what was happening with Tor, I watched it unfold in my mind's eye. A hand signal from Tor sent Dog across in front of the guard, close enough to be momentarily in sight, but not so close that the vaquero could be sure of what he had seen.

If it worked, the sentry's attention would be focused on the place where a gray spotted shape had appeared and disappeared. Tor would be creeping up behind, readying himself for what came next.

I motioned for John and Joaquin to stop the moment I picked up the outline of the vaquero on horseback on our side of the herd. He was less than thirty yards away. What was more, from the white patches that stood out against the shadow, he had drawn Shawnee from the string as his mount.

I gave a deep owl call of reply that meant we were also ready. Now it was up to our prayers and the resolve to not draw back once it started.

Shawnee's ears had no doubt been pricking back and forth ever since the first owl hoot. As an old Indian fighter herself, she would know what was afoot.

I moved up so as to keep a sleepy black steer between me and the guard. When the animal moved closer, so did I. Just when I was congratulating myself on how well things were going, the wayward critter abruptly turned off the wrong way, leaving me hanging out like a shirt on a clothesline.

I dropped flat on my belly behind a clump of brush. After a

moment, I started to inch my way forward, but a bunch of dead weeds crackled under me. When the vaquero turned his head at the sound, I ducked my face so there could be no reflection off my eyes.

The sweat broke out on my forehead despite the coolness of the night and the damp grass. One shout, one shot, and all would be lost. If we were caught this time, there would be no second chance. Not even an anthill . . . just five dead bodies left for the buzzards.

Another steer ambled by, actually stepping over me as it grazed. As I held my breath, fearful that it would tread right on me, it too broke through the brush with a rattle and a snap.

No gunshot came and no call of alarm. The vaquero must have decided that the steer had made both noises. When I chanced a peek again, he was facing away from me into the dark.

I thought I heard a muffled thud and the sound of hooves from the other side of the drove, but it could not matter now. It was time to get this show on the road.

Slowly and quietly, I stood up. I shook out the coil of my whip. If Shawnee knew I was there, she gave no sign, giving me the only chance I would have. My first cast would have to be perfect.

In the dark it was hard to judge distances. I slipped a little closer . . . then a little closer yet.

Now!

The whip flicked out, but instead of slashing the vaquero's back, it knotted around his throat. It is human nature that when something grabs you by the neck, your hands instinctively fly upward to try to clear the stranglehold away.

That is exactly what the night herder did. As his grip dropped the reins to reach for what was choking him, I gave a yank, and Shawnee spurted forward. Remember, the night herder was riding bareback with just a blanket under him. The guard slid off backward, like a watermelon seed squirting between your fingers.

By the time he hit the ground, I was on top of him. It was Sanchez. He was dazed from the impact and still trying to uncoil the lash from around his gullet. His eyes went wide when he saw me, but the right I threw at his chin from two feet away laid him out cold.

A low *pssst* from me brought John and Joaquin to my side. We stuffed Sanchez's mouth with rags, then trussed him up with my whip. The pistol had been knocked from his belt by the fall, but the boys scoured the clumps of grass until they located it.

Another crackle in the brush made me whirl around, pistol in hand, but it was only Tor with James and Dog. They were leading a line-back dun.

"How'd it go?" I whispered.

"Like a charm!" Tor's hoarse reply was all smiles. "It was Garcia. Dog got his attention, and I gave him the Paiute rush. I took him clean off the horse while it was between one mouthful of grass and the next. He hit the ground without ever havin' a chance to draw or call out. 'Course," he said without remorse, "I think his neck is broke. Anyways, he ain't movin.'"

Tor and I sat our mounts and waited in the chilly darkness. I was grateful that the serape I had taken from Sanchez was both disguising and warming. We were waiting for the stars to swing round. Too early and Gomez would know something was wrong.

When it was time, I grasped Tor by the hand. "I'm glad to have you," I said.

Tor's reply was grimly humorous. "Thunderation, Andrew! I wouldn't miss this show for all the gold in the Calaveras."

We separated then, one to either end of the camp. We left the three boys and Dog to guard Sanchez.

I held the pistol low across my chest under the serape and moved Shawnee into a slow walk, directly toward the campfire. I needed a chance to locate all three men if I could. These bandidos weren't dumb; even if they did not expect to be attacked, they still slept in the shadows and not up close where the firelight would pinpoint their whereabouts.

I saw Gomez first. He was the one closest to the warmth, which to me seemed right in character for him. On the right, underneath the low-hanging branches of a fir tree was another, but whether Ortiz or Ramos, I could not tell.

Gomez stirred and rolled over. I knew that as he came awake he would be thinking, *What time is it?* and *Is it the end of the watch?* I adjusted Sanchez's sombrero lower to shield my face and cocked the hammer of the pistol, still hidden under the serape.

Sitting up and rubbing sleep from his eyes, Gomez heard the sound of Shawnee's hooves and reached for his gun. Catching sight of the familiar serape relaxed him, and he called out, "*Hola,* Sanchez. *Qué hora es?* What is the time?"

Where was the third man? In just a few seconds the ball would begin, and the location of the missing dance partner was important.

"*Qué ocurre?* What is it, Sanchez? Is anything wrong?"

It was time. I could only hope that Tor had been able to pick up the last outlaw's location from his different vantage point.

I drew the pistol and tipped back the sombrero. "Freeze, Gomez!"

His hand started to move toward his weapon; then he stopped. A momentary flash of anger was replaced by a grin as he evidently sized up the situation. "You have made a losing bet, señor. You are here alone and we are three."

"I don't think this wager was so bad," I said calmly. "Listen carefully, Gomez. Raise your hands over your head. Then tell your friends in the brush to do the same."

The familiar smirk was back. "Why would I do that, gringo? Right now you are surrounded."

"Because whatever happens, you are going to die," I replied. "Do you really think I won't blow your head off from this distance? It doesn't matter who shoots first, because you'll be just as dead."

I was near enough to see his throat work as he thought this over. "Ortiz, don't do anything stupid."

Clearly he was hoping that the remaining unseen gunman would circle and get the drop on me. Was he right?

Out of the dark and off to my left came a familiar throaty chuckle. "It's okay, Andrew," Tor's voice called. "I got Ramos. Caught him with his pants down, so to speak."

That's when Ortiz decided to make his play. I caught a movement out of the corner of my eye, and the pistol bucked in my hand as I snapped a shot into the thickest shadow under the fir branches.

I heard Ortiz yell and saw Gomez going for his gun. The muzzle was turning my way, the barrel pivoting up as I whipped my sights back around and fired.

Gomez was overeager. He shot before he aimed, and his bullet went through the broad brim of the sombrero I wore. I don't know where my slug caught him, but he fired only the one time.

I slid off Shawnee and divided my attention between Gomez and the brush, where Ortiz lay. Tor marched Ramos into camp and roughly ordered him to sprawl on his face by the fire. With me covering, Fowler checked the other two and announced that they were both dead.

"Well, pard," he said, "looks like we got us a herd again."

CHAPTER 23

Three more graves beside the trail greeted the dawn below Sierran skies. Sanchez had his hands tied behind his back, and I had my whip coiled and hanging again at my side.

Tor and I had a serious discussion with Ramos. He seemed the least hardened of all the outlaws, and we surely needed help with the herd. In the end we compromised. We gave him his parole in order to gain a sixth drover to our band, but we kept his gun and knife.

The dewdrops sparkled on the milkweed, and the morning brightened into what we hoped would be one of the last few days on the trail.

"Head 'em out, James," I called.

The boys, who had done the work of men and seen trouble and shown courage and resolve beyond their years, set the herd on the move.

We made Sanchez walk. Aside from being a rough kind of justice, it gave us little need to watch him. Besides, he had the most watchful of all possible guards. We set Dog to keep an eye on him, and you can believe that a meaningful growl and the flash of white teeth gave the outlaw plenty of mind to keep up and not stray.

The day passed without incident. We moved the cattle slowly, keeping them bunched so as not to make more work for ourselves. The herd had been pushed into a narrow place between two low ranges of hills. The trail followed the watershed and curved around to the north about half a mile ahead of where I rode the drag spot.

I was thinking that even eating trail dust felt good after all we'd been through and even better since it would soon be done. Ahead the steers were starting to bunch up and mill around. The leaders had stopped for some unknown reason, as though they had run into a wall around the bend.

I kicked Shawnee into her ground-eating canter. I had been woolgathering for so long that I had lost track of Tor and James, who should have been just ahead of me on either side.

It was too early to halt for the night. Through my mind went thoughts of high water across the trail or an encounter with a grizzly, but there was no serious concern in me.

So I was completely unprepared when Shawnee and I loped around the corner and ran smack spraddle into Jack Powers mounted on his buckskin. Flanking him were Ed and Patrick Dunn.

My move to draw Sanchez's pistol was stopped when I saw that Patrick Dunn was holding Joaquin off the ground under one arm. Ed held a rifle on Tor, Ramos, and the Reed brothers, while a grinning Sanchez collected our pistols. Dog had run off again.

I yanked Shawnee to a savage halt, setting her haunches down. "Let him go," I growled at Pat.

It was Powers who answered. "Not so fast, Sinnickson. Tell me, who is holding all the cards this time?"

"I've got ten men with rifles coming up pronto," I bluffed. "If you know what's good for you, you better light out quick and not mess with us."

Powers laughed until his eyes ran a stream of tears past the red bulb of his nose. And what could I do, while Dunn held on to Joaquin?

"Ten men with rifles, you say? That's rich! I say this sorry band of dog meat is everybody. What you've got is a broken-down mountain goat, a traitor, and three cubs that should have been drowned at birth. Sanchez and Ramos are with us. Rodriguez has been watching you since noon—we just didn't want to scatter the herd, so we waited until now to collect you."

Powers was so sure of himself it made my blood boil. From behind a boulder rode Rodriguez, the vaquero who had disappeared after the snake episode long ago. He also had a rifle across the withers of his palomino. "Greetings, señor!" he said with mocking cheerfulness. "How pleasant to see you again. I see Sanchez and Ramos, but where is my good friend Gomez and the others? I thought to meet *them,* but we were not expecting *you.*"

"Gomez is dead," I said coldly. "So are Garcia and Ortiz. You sure you're on the winning side, Rodriguez?"

"Enough of this pointless jabber," Powers interrupted. "Drop your gun and get over with the others. Pat, throw down the kid. That's the lot of them, except the dog."

We six, since they intended to kill Ramos along with us—it must have looked like he had switched sides—were herded into a small group. Facing us were four men with rifles in their hands and greed and murder in their hearts.

"Gold on the hoof," Powers said, marveling at the size of the drove. "All right, let's get on with it."

A rifle shot from the ridgeline behind me split the afternoon stillness. The slug hit the ground right between the front feet of Powers's buckskin. The animal jerked and danced, bumping into the other mounts while the outlaws nervously tried to regain control.

Patrick raised his rifle to meet the unexpected threat and was cautioned by these words, "Stand easy, boys," said a nasally, Yankeefied voice. "That was just to get your attention."

It was Ames. Beside him with a smoking Allen rifle stood Alzado. Hulking nearby was the grizzly bear figure of Boki, and as if this weren't enough, Dog was wagging his tail among two hundred Angels Camp miners.

"There's your beef, boys," Ames said. "Just like I promised."

Whooping and hollering so that I thought the herd might turn and hightail it back to Southern California, the troop of hungry prospectors charged down the hillside, surrounding both us and Powers and his men.

Tor approached Powers and demanded that the outlaw chief get off his horse. Tor proceeded to explain exactly what was going to happen to the bandit when he did so.

Powers shook his head and waved the rifle. "What's the matter, mountain man? Can't you take a joke? Why, all we did was ride out to meet you same as these others. I wanted to make an offer to buy your herd, not knowing it was already spoken for."

"Why you . . ."

I thought for an instant that Tor would do his Paiute trick right there on Powers, but the would-be rustler and murderer spoke quickly. "Easy there, mountain man. If you want to start a war, remember we've still got our rifles. Besides, a whole lot of innocent people might get hurt."

"He's right, Tor," I said reluctantly. "Let him go."

"But he . . . this . . . low-down . . ."

Words failed my friend, and I have to admit that I didn't like it either, but for once, Powers was right. The cheering, celebrating miners scarcely noticed when a sullen file of riders led by Jack Powers exited up the canyon and out of sight.

CHAPTER 24

Never try to tell me that the Almighty does not have a sense of humor. After all the tragedy and triumph of weeks on the drive, you would think that a period of rest and relaxation would follow.

Rest, yes. Relaxation, ha!

Three days after we got to Angels Camp, we had tidied up the details of the sale. All totaled, the cattle brought in some eighty thousand dollars' worth of dust, nuggets, and three-ounce gold slugs called "adobes."

Then I got sick. Not anything life threatening, like cholera, or dramatic, like pneumonia. No, sir, I couldn't even get sympathy. I came down with the mumps.

The doctor gave me a mess of willow-bark tea and a bandage to wrap around my swollen jaws. When I asked him what else to do, he scratched his head and said, "Ache some, I guess. You'll be better in a week or two."

He was right, but the trouble was, the rest of my party couldn't wait. You see, Powers was still a force to be reckoned with, especially with so much gold at stake. So we had gratefully accepted the offer to journey south in the company of the United States infantry.

The lieutenant of that detail, a young man with the imposing name of William Tecumsah Sherman, set the departure date. When it was time to leave, I was still a week or so from being well enough to travel.

Tor, Joaquin, and the Reed brothers had come to tell me good-bye. It was not a tearful farewell. Truth to tell, they mostly stood way back and laughed at my cheeks.

"I'm powerful sorry, Andrew," Tor said. (He didn't look sorry.) "We'll see your share safe to Santa Barbara and meet up with you there in another ten days or so."

"Just you leave me a thousand of my share," I instructed, "and you won't see me for a month. I've a mind to see San Francisco before I head south. You can start the next roundup, and then I'll join you."

So, a few days after that parting, Dog, Shawnee, and I were finally on the trail. I was headed down the same Calaveras path I had ridden up a few months before. It seemed both a short while and long ages since I had seen it last.

The road had been widened and improved some to accommodate Ames's supply wagons and the tracks of some thousand eager miners who had come after us. I could still recognize the original landmarks though, like the creek bottom where the Indians had been attacked and the precipice where Ames had almost been killed.

When my casual inspection took in the top of the cliff where the rockslide had started, I almost dropped my teeth. I thought I saw the glint of light on metal in the same spot as we were ambushed before. Just a quick flash and nothing to follow, but it took me aback enough that I called Dog to me and looked things over in earnest. I even pulled my brand-new Colt repeating rifle from its boot.

Well, after watching awhile and not remarking another sign, I figured it was just the aftereffects of my sickness and nudged Shawnee forward. We were well along the trail when some distance ahead I saw a mounted man blocking the road with rifle in hand.

It was too far to say if it really was Patrick Dunn. But when I halted and looked over my shoulder, I saw a similarly armed rider closing in behind me. This second fellow looked like Pat's brother, Ed.

You know, I hate coincidences. I turned Shawnee to the side, dashed down a short slope, and splashed across the creek. On the other side, I set her up the incline at a dead run. I had just reached a clump of rocks at the summit when a gunshot from the *far* side of the hill told me that I had ridden right into their trap. I pulled in by the rocks, flung myself off Shawnee, and settled in to watch a bit.

I did not have long to wait. A second bullet smashed into a boulder near my head and scattered rock fragments all around. I fired a blast to make him keep his head down for a second and was gratified to hear a yelp of pain. I yanked the saddlebags off Shawnee and slapped her into a run across the grade. Dog and I ducked back under cover.

Three riders crossed the creek below me. It was the two Dunns and a dark-complected, rough-looking character. This last man shouted, "There's his horse!"

Patrick Dunn yelled back, "Let it go! It's Sinnickson we want!"

I snapped off a quick shot and rolled to a new position as the return fire came in. I heard Pat shouting, "Ed! Ed!"

So I'd accounted for Ed Dunn. But how many more were there, and what was their plan? Another shot splintered the tree bark behind me and reminded me just how bad things were.

"Sinnickson!" a bellowing voice raged. "Sinnickson, do you hear me?" Patrick Dunn screamed at me again, "Sinnickson, I'm going to butcher you! You killed Ed, and I'm going to cut out your heart and feed it to you!"

I knew better than to make any reply, since any sound would draw a shot. All I could do now was wait for one of them to make a false move. By keeping still, I was able to wing the dark-complected killer, but then things settled into a stalemate of sorts. I kept wishing that someone from Angels Camp might come to see what the shooting was about, but in those lawless times, I knew this to be a vain hope.

Sundown would finish me. If a ricochet had not struck me first, the cover of darkness would let them move in close enough to fire directly into my hiding place.

"Sinnickson!" It was Jack Powers's voice this time, trying to work on my nerves.

Where had he come from? I wondered.

"Johns here says he's going to skin your dog," Powers threatened. "Says he owes the dog one from last summer!"

So Johns must be the dark-complected one, I thought. I don't know why, but that was the point at which I gave up despair and began to hope again. Somehow, the humorous idea of that Johns fellow holding a grudge against Dog for ripping the seat out of his britches . . . well, it just struck me funny, and I knew everything would work out some way. After all, hadn't God taken care of things thus far?

It wasn't fully dark in the west, but the stars were filling the eastern sky. I figured the rush was coming most anytime, and I needlessly checked the load of my rifle again.

One star directly east of me seemed especially bright. In fact, it appeared much brighter than usual. As I studied it, it appeared to grow larger and larger.

I was so fascinated, I almost forgot to duck when the bullets started flying. Dog and I ducked back successfully again, and I squeezed off a few rounds to let them know I wasn't done yet.

When I glanced eastward again, the star had visibly grown. It was now plainly a fireball in the sky, and it was headed straight for me! There was a fearful roaring noise overhead; then the sky all around blazed with sudden light. A rushing hot wind that accompanied the shooting star blasted through the trees, and the tops of several pines burst into flames. A second later there was a fearsome impact, as if two buffalo the size of mountain peaks had collided head-on.

The whole hillside shook with the force. Boulders bounced around me, one clipping Dog with a glancing blow. Trees toppled like matchsticks, and a jumble of them exploded into a fire that swept the bottom of the hill on the wings of that strange, unnatural wind.

Through the dancing flames I could see my enemies jumping and running toward the creek to escape the conflagration. One of them shook his fist in my direction, but whether the gesture was meant for me or Almighty God, I could not say.

A few minutes later, Dog and I crossed the bare peak and descended the reverse slope. The body of the man I had shot earlier lay where he had fallen, unmindful of the inferno raging on the other side of the hill. I whistled up Shawnee, and we rode out of the River of the Skulls.

EPILOGUE

It was some six months later that I returned to Calaveras country. After the winter snows had melted and the river crossings had become manageable, Tor and I pushed another herd of a thousand head north to the hungry miners.

If the second drive lacked the adventure of the first, it was also minus the tragedy. Will Reed's vaqueros had returned from trying their hand at prospecting, and there was no shortage of reliable help. By the way, Will and Francesca's child arrived—a red-haired boy they named Simon.

The charred remains of a whole hillside made locating the spot of the ambush easy. There was even a pattern to the way the oaks and firs had tumbled that sort of pointed me back to the meteor's impact.

I had a real worshipful feeling as I walked Shawnee slowly over the ground. I went there with the intention of saying a few words of thanks, and this I did.

The crater on the muddy hillside had already started to erode from the runoff of the melting snow. Shawnee was headed back toward Angels Camp road when something caught my eye.

Washed clean of the clay and standing out against the backdrop of a quartz ledge was a black, fist-shaped chunk of rock. I knew it immediately for what it was—a piece of a shooting star.

But it was more. This misshapen lump of iron was a flaming messenger with a fiery sword sent by the hand of God.

I have kept it with me ever since.

DEAR READER

We hope you've enjoyed these legends of the Wild West—tales of adventurous and courageous men and women who faced down danger, overcame impossible odds to triumph over their circumstances with God's help, and discovered the truth about what is most meaningful in life.

As you travel on your life's journey, you too will face numerous challenges that will impact your heart, mind, and soul. We'd love to hear from you! To write us, or for further information about the Legends of the West series (including behind-the-scenes stories and details you won't want to miss), visit:

WWW.THOENEBOOKS.COM
WWW.FAMILYAUDIOLIBRARY.COM

We pray that through these legends you will "discover the Truth through Fiction." For we are convinced that if you seek diligently, you will find the One who holds all the answers to the universe (1 Chronicles 28:9).

BROCK & BODIE THOENE

✯ABOUT THE AUTHORS✯

BROCK AND BODIE THOENE (pronounced *Tay-nee)* live part of the year in the beautiful Sierra Nevada, in which their Legends of the West are set. Together they have written over 45 works of historical fiction. That these best sellers have sold more than 10 million copies and won eight ECPA Gold Medallion Awards affirms what millions of readers have already discovered—the Thoenes are not only master stylists but experts at capturing readers' minds and hearts.

In their timeless classic series about Israel (The Zion Chronicles, The Zion Covenant, and The Zion Legacy), the Thoenes' love for both story and research shines.

With the Legends of the West (gripping tales of adventure and danger in a land without law), The Shiloh Legacy and *Shiloh Autumn* (poignant portrayals of the American Depression), and The Galway Chronicles (dramatic stories of the 1840s famine in Ireland), the Thoenes have made their mark in modern history.

In the A.D. Chronicles, they step seamlessly into the world of Jerusalem and Rome, in the days when Yeshua walked the earth and transformed lives with His touch.

Bodie began her writing career as a teen journalist for her local newspaper. Eventually her byline appeared in prestigious periodicals such as *U.S. News and World Report, The American West,* and

The Saturday Evening Post. She also worked for John Wayne's Batjac Productions (she's best known as author of *The Fall Guy*) and ABC Circle Films as a writer and researcher. John Wayne described her as "a writer with talent that captures the people and the times!" She has degrees in journalism and communications.

Brock has often been described by Bodie as "an essential half of this writing team." With degrees in both history and education, Brock has, in his role as researcher and story-line consultant, added the vital dimension of historical accuracy. Due to such careful research, the Zion Covenant and Zion Chronicles series are recognized by the American Library Association, as well as Zionist libraries around the world, as classic historical novels and are used to teach history in college classrooms.

Brock and Bodie have four grown children—Rachel, Jake, Luke, and Ellie—and six grandchildren. Their sons, Jake and Luke, are carrying on the Thoene family talent as the next generation of writers, and Luke produces the Thoene audiobooks. Brock and Bodie divide their time between London and Nevada.

For more information visit:

WWW.THOENEBOOKS.COM

WWW.FAMILYAUDIOLIBRARY.COM

THOENE FAMILY CLASSICS™

✪ ✪ ✪

THOENE FAMILY CLASSIC HISTORICALS

by Bodie and Brock Thoene

*Gold Medallion Winners**

THE ZION COVENANT

*Vienna Prelude**
Prague Counterpoint
Munich Signature
Jerusalem Interlude
Danzig Passage
*Warsaw Requiem**
London Refrain
Paris Encore
Dunkirk Crescendo

THE ZION CHRONICLES

*The Gates of Zion**
A Daughter of Zion
The Return to Zion
A Light in Zion
*The Key to Zion**

THE SHILOH LEGACY

*In My Father's House**
A Thousand Shall Fall
Say to This Mountain

SHILOH AUTUMN

THE GALWAY CHRONICLES

*Only the River Runs Free**
Of Men and of Angels
*Ashes of Remembrance**
All Rivers to the Sea

THE ZION LEGACY

Jerusalem Vigil
Thunder from Jerusalem
Jerusalem's Heart
Jerusalem Scrolls
Stones of Jerusalem
Jerusalem's Hope

A.D. CHRONICLES

First Light
Second Touch
Third Watch
Fourth Dawn
Fifth Seal
Sixth Covenant
Seventh Day
and more to come!

THOENE FAMILY CLASSICS™

✪ ✪ ✪

THOENE FAMILY CLASSIC AMERICAN LEGENDS

LEGENDS OF THE WEST

by Bodie and Brock Thoene

Legends of the West, Volume One
- *Sequoia Scout*
- *The Year of the Grizzly*
- *Shooting Star*

Legends of the West, Volume Two
- *Gold Rush Prodigal*
- *Delta Passage*
- *Hangtown Lawman*

Legends of the West, Volume Three
- *Hope Valley War*
- *The Legend of Storey County*
- *Cumberland Crossing*

Legends of the West, Volume Four
- *The Man from Shadow Ridge*
- *Cannons of the Comstock*
- *Riders of the Silver Rim*

LEGENDS OF VALOR

by Luke Thoene

Sons of Valor
Brothers of Valor
Fathers of Valor

✪ ✪ ✪

THOENE CLASSIC NONFICTION

by Bodie and Brock Thoene

Writer-to-Writer

THOENE FAMILY CLASSIC SUSPENSE

by Jake Thoene

CHAPTER 16 SERIES

Shaiton's Fire
Firefly Blue
Fuel the Fire

✪ ✪ ✪

THOENE FAMILY CLASSICS FOR KIDS

by Jake and Luke Thoene

BAKER STREET DETECTIVES

The Mystery of the Yellow Hands
The Giant Rat of Sumatra
The Jeweled Peacock of Persia
The Thundering Underground

LAST CHANCE DETECTIVES

Mystery Lights of Navajo Mesa
Legend of the Desert Bigfoot

✪ ✪ ✪

THOENE FAMILY CLASSIC AUDIOBOOKS

Available from
www.thoenebooks.com or
www.familyaudiolibrary.com